NEON LEVIATHAN

T.R. NAPPER

GdM

PRAISE FOR T.R. NAPPER'S WORK

"Achingly beautiful…gritty and vertiginous and close-focus human in the way only the best SF can manage.
—Richard Morgan, author of *Altered Carbon*

"Each one of the stories in this volume is a carefully crafted masterpiece."
—Adrian Tchaikovsky, author of *Children of Time*

"Heartbreaking…it evokes the depth of Chinese history, the successive wars, the poetry that expresses both the love of the landscape and the pain of the soldier leaving home, perhaps never to return." (for *Dark on a Darkling Earth*)
—Lois Tilton, Locus Magazine

"T. R. Napper's cyberpunk story is a standout [in the collection], featuring a download with the tension of a high-speed chase" (for *Twelve Minutes to Vinh Quang*)
—Publisher's Weekly

"The story is by turns blackly funny, speculatively impressive, and bleakly moving." (for *A Strange Loop*)
—Rich Horton, Locus Magazine

"Wonderfully strange" (for *An Advanced Guide to Successful Price-Fixing in Extra-Terrestrial Betting Markets*)
—Sci Fi Review

"Darkly gonzoid" (for *An Advanced Guide to Successful Price-Fixing in Extra-Terrestrial Betting Markets*)

—Lois Tilton, Locus Magazine

"Thrilling and Moving" (for *Ghosts of a Neon God*)

—Rocket Stack Rank

"The whole reads like a fever dream" (for *Great Buddhist Monk Beat Down*)

—Tangent Online

AWARDS

Aurealis Award Winner for Best Short Story (2016) (*Flame Trees*)
Ditmar Nomination for Best Short Story (2016) (*Flame Trees*)
Ditmar Nomination for Best New Talent (2016 & 2017)
Selected – Best Science Fiction of the Year, Volume 2 (2016) (*A Strange Loop*)
Writers of the Future Winner (*12 Minutes*)
Tangent Recommended reading list (several)

Editor: Adrian Collins
Copy Editor: Mike Myers
Cover Art: J. Caleb Design
Cover Design and Interior Layout: STK·Kreations

Hardcover ISBN: 978-0-6486635-9-1
Trade paperback ISBN: 978-0-6486635-8-4
Ebook ISBN: 978-0-6486635-7-7
Worldwide Rights.

Non-exclusive rights: Flame Trees (Asimov's); Opium for Ezra (Interzone); A Strange Loop (Interzone); An Advanced Guide to Successful Price-Fixing in Extraterrestrial Betting Markets (Interzone); Ghosts of a Neon God (Interzone); The Great Buddhist Monk Beat Down (Galaxy's Edge); The Line (Grimdark Magazine); A Shout is a Prayer (Interzone); Twelve Minutes to Vinh Quang (Writers of the Future); Dark on a Darkling Earth (Interzone).

Exclusive rights: The Weight of the Air, The Weight of the Earth; Jack's Fine Dining.

Produced in Australia
First Edition, November 2019

Published by Grimdark Magazine
Unit 1 / 184-186 Military Road
Neutral Bay, NSW 2089
www.grimdarkmagazine.com

CONTENTS

INTRODUCTION
ADRIAN TCHAIKOVSKY

"Everything is memory, save for the thin edge of the present..."

It is easier to write about violence than to write about its aftermath—the grief, the guilt, the long-held trauma. It's easier to write about the shouted argument than the taut silence that follows. It's easier to write about dreamlike unreality than to invest a reader in the mundane and the everyday. And yet the stories in *Neon Leviathan* balance all these competing demands with a deft and masterful hand. Yes, there are fights, futuristic assassins, blood sports, war on a global scale. But the majority of these pieces exist in the held breath between moments of explosion, and especially in the long echo that comes after. Yes, there are moments when the truth slips through the hands of both readers and characters like an eel, and yet the stories remain grounded in genuine loss and humanity, allowing these disjunctions to resonate in a way the merely surreal might not.

Each one of the stories in this volume is a carefully crafted masterpiece that, whilst it presents a narrative of its own, is nonetheless a window onto a larger world, a current of history that flows a winding path from one to another, carrying us with it. The stories are all (bar one) dated, but given out of order in an intentional juxtaposition, so that the future history Napper tells comes to us like a dream, or fragments of memories imperfectly recalled.

Napper cites Philip K Dick as a major inspiration, and that's certainly on full display, with several stories serving as a homage to the master of troubled realities and the fractured sense of self. The heart of the collection, in fact, is that shifting ground where what the characters believe and what the reader has been told are called into question, the key issue of *what makes us who we are* bleeding out across the boundary between human and machine, reality and memory and self-deception. The *Kandel-Yu* device that features in so many of the stories has its own history hidden within the collection, from therapy to entertainment to a tool of brutal repression. Just as with much of Dick's best work, Napper expertly captures the queasy vertigo of having our certainties about ourselves whipped out from under us. If our own recollection is at the mercy of the outside, then what can we possibly trust?

Napper's own personal history feels as though it pervades the collection. An Australian with more than a decade overseas on the sharp end of foreign aid, he's seen a great deal of how human nature can twist under pressure, or under temptation. I suspect his experiences inform much of the stories' tone and detail. They have an acute sense of place, not just a generic cyberpunk future but an Australian and Southeast Asian one that builds on tensions of race, sovereignty, class division and international relations, all currently front and centre in today's news. Rather than simply fetishize the chrome and brand names, Napper makes sure the 'punk' is right there in his cyberpunk future, his stories full of the dispossessed, the rebellious and the displaced. There are crimes, but they're crimes of desperation rather than cool heists. The slums are not just origin points for hacker heroes, but prisons for protagonists who have no way out. Napper talks of refugees who've lost everything to war, only to come to a land that doesn't want them. He shows us crippling addictions, lives lost to gambling and wishful thinking and PTSD. Real people, with families, without prospects; the price of progress, the shadow of wanton authority.

The scale of these moments is almost always personal. Often the cage the characters struggle against is within them, built from the scars of their personal history. Even when they take on a boss, a bully, a corporation, the stakes are pitched to mean life or death to the protagonist, but perhaps only a moment's diversion to the wider world. No grand abstractions here. Napper makes sure we care for the people caught in the wheels, whether it's amidst the prison brutality of *The Line* or the full-on Orwellian nightmare of the superb *The Weight of the Air, the Weight of the World* (from which the header quote is drawn). And yet, add all these motes together and a whole wider history can be glimpsed. It's a bleak and terrible future he's given us, but only because it extrapolates so very plausibly from the present.

And it's not all joyless. There are victories to be had, even in the shadow of the gallows. There are moments of wry humour, although as the collection progresses and the focus on unreliable narration and unreliable memories builds, some of that humour can leave a disturbing echo, the reader abruptly unsure whether what they're laughing at is actually what is going on at all...

FLAME TREES

2092

I drink you with my sight, and I am filled with fire
From the broken bone of the hill, stripped and left for dead,
Like a wrecked skull, leaps out this bush of blood
I drink you with my sight, and I am filled with fire,
Out of the very—

The van swerved to avoid the kangaroo, jolting Chi Cong Nguyen from his reverie. The drive computer straightened the vehicle back out; the high-beams showed the kangaroos bouncing alongside on the highway. Stupid creatures. At night, they thought headlights were the rising sun and bounced toward them with suicidal enthusiasm.

Chi flicked his torch on, turned, and ran it over the back of the van. All looked good—none of the precious cargo had been flung out in the near-miss. He pushed the hair back from his eyes and put a finger to the cochlear implant behind his ear, switching off the music. The song—"Flame Trees"—always distracted him. An old, old Australian song he'd heard down at the club once and right away programmed into his night-shift playlist.

Kieu said Chi had an old soul that shimmered with recognition when it encountered the old. She would smile that brilliant white smile and add: *that, and terrible taste in music.* A smile touched his eyes, just for a moment, as he thought of Kieu. He took the flat, silver key out of his pocket, rubbing it between thumb and forefingers while the van drove on.

Kieu had said that even before the war. Before he had reason to age so quickly, so young.

Chi settled back in the seat. Nothing to do but babysit the deliveries while the van drove on. The cabin smelled of eucalyptus and the worn vinyl of the seats. Outside, the countryside flew by at the periphery of the headlights. So quiet, out there. So peaceful.

There were spirits in this land, they said. An ancient land, where millennia of habitation had saturated every tree and hillock and river with the Dreaming, the mythology of the oldest peoples in the world. But he never dreamed their dreams or heard their songlines, never saw the flicker of their ghosts in the long grasses or the white trees.

Not like in Vietnam.

Chi Lay awake in his narrow bed until the dawn came. His single room apartment was empty, save a tattered brown couch that had been there when he arrived, and a side table and lamp. On the table a cop of poetry by Tran Da Tu, dust covered. On the wall the empty frame of the *Tai* screen; when it was on it showed only the shopping network, gambling programs, and a Chinese global news channel. Chi hadn't watched in in months.

Chi placed his arm over his face, his eyes in the crook of his elbow. He would be speaking to the doctor, therapist, technician—whatever she called herself—in a few hours. She'd ask him questions she had no right to ask. She'd want to take from him things she had no right to take.

Chi entered her office. White walls, comfortable couch, shining clean steel *Kandel-Yu* machine in the far corner. White doctor, shining teeth, trying to exude a comforting presence, standing as he entered. The *Kandel-Yu* had a reclining chair of the type you'd see in a dentist's, and a neon green halo above the headrest that belonged in a science fiction film. The doctor looked like the type you'd see in a university prospectus, as an example of a successful graduate.

"Doctor," he said.

"How many times?" she asked, indicating the couch. "Call me Sian, please."

Chi sat down with back straight and brushed the hair out of his eyes.

She pulled her chair over and sat facing him. "You look tired, Chi. Still not sleeping?"

He shrugged. "I work late."

The doctor nodded but not at what he had said. "Yes, I know. The truck."

He didn't care for her attitude but was used to it. The bourgeois were all the same, in every country.

The doctor unfurled a flexiscreen on her lap, green-flowing

icons playing across its surface. She glanced down at it, then back at Chi. "You've been in Australia nearly seven years now," she said, calm, matter-of-fact. "We've been through this: your English is excellent. Perfect. You were a journalist back in Vietnam. You had poetry published."

He said nothing.

"You could be writing," she said, still showing how patient she was, still trying to exude sincerity. Chi didn't care that much whether it was real or not. It wasn't going to change anything.

"Do you know any professional poets, Doctor?" he asked.

"Sian. No, no I don't, now you mention it."

"I need to eat."

"But Chi—you can't be happy."

"It's not about happy, Doctor."

"What is it then?"

"It's about getting by," he said, his voice soft.

"Getting by," she sighed, and indicated her flexiscreen with an open palm. "Getting by would be enough. But you hit a man, Chi."

Chi felt tired. A weight, too, just below his heart.

The doctor leaned forward. "You can't go on like this. You have post-traumatic stress disorder."

"That is the name you have given it."

"It's not just a name. It's a thing that is eating you alive." She waited for him to reply and when he didn't she said: "You are the perfect client for memory realignment. You are a text-book example of the subject the *Kandel-Yu* machine was invented for—a decent human being trying to put his life back together after a traumatic incident. You'll be able to move on, afterward."

The Y-shaped scar under his eye flared with pain. "Incident?"

"Well, more than a single incident, then? It's hard for me to define the terms when you're so vague about your experiences. But there are things you saw, things that happened to you in the war, before you came here to Australia. We need to pinpoint those so they can be fixed."

"Fixed," he repeated. "Not even knowing what to fix."

"I don't need to, Chi. All I need to know is what these memories are doing to you. This is the summation of the psychiatrist's report." The doctor flicked her fingers across the flexiscreen, pulling up the relevant file. She read: "Chi Cong Nguyen has been hospitalized on six occasions in the past seven years. The periods of hospitalization have lasted between a week and two months. Other than malnourishment and dehydration at the time of admittance, batteries of tests have not been able to find a physical cause for the illness."

She looked up at Chi. His scar itched and his hands curled themselves into fists, but still he said nothing.

She continued: "The subject has not been able to hold down a steady job. We believe he has had periods of homelessness, though he would not admit to this."

The doctor looked up at him again, her face a mask of concern. "You're not happy; you're not even getting by. This treatment"— she indicated the machine with her left hand—"can turn your life around. I've been working with PTSD for several years now. I know what I'm doing."

"Like what?"

She paused. "What do you mean?"

"Like what sort of experiences have you been deleting?"

The doctor didn't seem to like the word *deleting*. But she smiled sympathetically anyway and said: "I've treated refugees like you, of course, from Vietnam. Some Americans—those who witnessed the madness of the Anarchy. I treated a man who was there when Kiribati went under. A whole nation, wiped from the face of the

Earth."

"Shouldn't we remember that?"

The doctor tilted her head at him. "What do you mean?"

"Shouldn't we bear witness to that loss?"

She furrowed her eyebrows. "This patient was going to kill himself. My responsibility is to him, not to human history."

"But memories are not just for the individual. They make up our collective consciousness. They are a common resource that teaches us who we are and how to be."

The doctor raised an eyebrow, surprised. She said: "I think that's the most words you've said to me in one go, Chi. I agree with you,"—though he didn't believe she did at all—"but that's not up to us. If the patient wants to upload their visual recording of the incident into a historical database, then that is their choice."

"But you've seen all these things. Don't you think they're important?"

She smiled again, though it was a little strained this time. "I'm not the sin-eater. My memories of the procedure are also wiped. The patient has a right to privacy, and the peace of mind in knowing that no one has witnessed their private horrors."

"Sin-eater," he repeated, tasting the unfamiliar term for the first time. Chi looked over at the gleaming *Kandel-Yu*. "No. You're not. That is the sin-eater."

She ignored the comment and made an expression of *firmness* on her face. "Chi, I'm going to be frank with you. These sessions are by court order. My job is to get you prepared for memory removal and help you get on with your life."

"It isn't compulsory."

"The procedure—no, it isn't. Not yet. I lay out for you the benefits of memory realignment, all the ways it can change your life for the better. If you still don't want treatment, we can't force you.

But the approval for your memory alignment will come through soon, Chi, and when it does you're going to need to make a decision."

Chi said nothing. There was nothing to say, because there was no decision to make. He unclenched his fists.

C hi was sick after the appointment. The weight below his heart increased, a dense mass that made him gasp with pain. All he could do was crawl into bed and stare at the ceiling. The walls of his apartment flowed from white to orange to dark purple as evening came. The room was silent, save a blowfly bouncing off a window and later, someone sobbing.

He pressed a finger to the implant behind his ear and called Bazza, telling him he couldn't go with the truck that night. Bazza just said *no worries* and gave him a hot tip on the third race at Moonee Valley the next day.

At least the pain didn't last so long this time.

The knot down there eased off and Chi slept for a couple of hours, near dawn, then went to work the following night.

Next Sunday he was at the club again with Bazza. The Thursday after that he sat in the doctor's office and said nothing for an hour. The machine gleamed and the doctor looked disappointed, and then it was all over, the last session done.

A week later an icon blinked on-retina, indicating a c-mail was waiting. It was an automated message from Medicare: YOUR APPLICATION FOR MEMORY REASSIGNMENT HAS BEEN APPROVED. QUOTE THIS NUMBER TO YOUR MEMORY ALIGNMENT FACILITATOR: B-263-54.

Chi deleted it.

When he had first met Barry Stillwater two years before, Chi was sitting at his local club with a cup of coffee and a glass of brandy, looking at the flame tree that sat on the far side of the bowling green. The place was full, so this old man with a shock of grey hair and eyebrows like thick white caterpillars sat down on the spare seat at Chi's table, without asking. He was looking up at a *Tai* screen as he did so.

"What race they up to in Eagle Farm?" he had asked, roughly.

Chi hadn't known what the old man was talking about back then and so just shrugged.

The old man watched the screen for a while before looking at Chi. "G'day," he grunted, and held out his hand. "Barry, call me Bazza."

Chi shook the man's gnarled hand. Bazza had a stronger grip than he had expected. "Chi."

Bazza eyed him. "Chi? I'll never remember that. Let's call you Gazza. That's a good nickname."

Chi shrugged again. One name was as good as another. He'd felt annoyed, at first, that the old man would presume to interrupt his drinking. But Bazza started sitting with him every Sunday and despite himself, Chi found he enjoyed the old man's company.

Most of the time they simply drank and bet on the races, Bazza giving him tips until Chi knew enough to start making his own wagers.

Sometimes, early on, Bazza would take him to watch the rugby league. Once, when a local politician tried to make an announcement before the game, the raucous crowd booed him off the field, whether or not they had voted for him. Chi found himself laughing with the people sitting nearby when the red-faced man in the expensive suit slunk away. Another time a poor guy tried to propose to his girlfriend—the stadium owners had set it up at half time—on the big screen. The crowd chanted for the woman to say *no no no no*, and Chi chanted with them. She said yes, despite the *crowd*, and they cheered her for that.

Chi drank overpriced beer and laughed and sang lewd songs with the crowd.

Those were good days. Some of the better ones.

Chi said to Bazza after one game: "You're all so rebellious, but your government and China . . ." he'd trailed off.

"Mate," Bazza replied, "this is a first-class country run by second-class people. Never forget that."

Bazza didn't go to the footy anymore. Getting too old, he said, and the cold made his bones ache. He was probably right. The old man groaned when he sat down and groaned when he picked up his beer and was slow, real slow, getting up to get his drinks. Chi had offered to do it for him, but Bazza just said *aaaaahhhhh*, making his cranky sound while he waved him away.

Bazza was a veteran as well. He'd fought with the allies in the battle of Taipei, when the U.S. military had been broken once and for all. But he never spoke about it, which was the way it should be. So they talked about horses and gambling and sometimes their childhoods. Just the easy memories, of course. When Bazza found out Chi was looking for work, he gave him a job as a guard in the van he owned.

Chi had given him a gift wrapped in bright red rice paper as a thank you. Bazza refused to accept it until he found out it was whisky, and then demanded they open it right away and share it. It was as close to the thing you'd call friendship as he'd had since he arrived in Australia, and Chi found it was good enough.

Chi entered the club and took his usual seat. The place was half full, the patrons inside either watching the races or playing the slot machines. It smelled of the sour smell of the inveterate gambler.

That, and tempeh parmigiana. Outside, white-clothed old people played games of lawn bowls and do you remember so-and-so. The clinking of the heavy balls as they struck each other on the green could be heard through the glass.

Without asking, the waitress put a cup of coffee and a glass of brandy on his desk. It was the brown-haired American girl with dark eyes. He was the only person she served at the table—everyone else had to stand over at the bar. She smiled at him like she always did; he pushed the hair out of his eyes and sipped his coffee. She sighed and walked away.

Chi pulled a plastic bag of sunflower seeds from his pocket and began cracking them open and popping them in his mouth. He looked at the flame tree on the other side of the bowls field as he did so. A shock of vivid red leaves that contrasted starkly with the green of the pitch and the grey of the houses behind.

They were bigger, here, the flame trees, less subtle than the ones back home. Still, to Chi they brought back memories of the flame trees scattered along Tay Ho. Where he'd walked hand in hand with Kieu, along the water's edge. Before the war, when hope still existed, where it still existed, when all he had to do was time-travel backward in his mind. All he had to do to escape the infinite present was travel back to that time when he recited earnest poems he'd written for her, and she laughed first then kissed him second.

"Stop daydreaming, Gazza. What race is it?"

Bazza groaned with relief as he slumped down in the chair next to Chi, schooner of beer in hand.

Chi glanced up at the screen. "The third at Flemington."

"Nothing going on there," grunted Bazza. He took a long sip of his beer. He looked down at the sunflower husks piled in front of Chi. "Don't get any of those bloody things on my side."

Chi cracked a sunflower and dropped the shell on Bazza's side.

Bazza glared.

He put a second one there, as well.

The old man looked at Chi. "I've eaten bigger bunnies than you."

Chi suppressed a smile and sipped his brandy.

They sat in silence, comfortable, while Bazza watched the races and Chi cracked his sunflower seeds.

But Chi was never allowed to feel comfortable for too long, and after a time felt something hard, a knot of pain right under his heart. He drained his brandy.

"Bazza."

"What?" The old man was annoyed. His finger hovered near the implant behind his ear—he was probably just about to make a bet.

"Do you ever wish . . ." Chi trailed off.

"*Aaaaahhhhh.*" Bazza made his cranky sound. "Don't give me half a story. Out with it."

"Do you ever wish you could go back, before the Battle of Taipei?"

Bazza's caterpillar eyebrows bounced quizzically. "Go back?"

"I mean," Chi said, trying to grasp the words, "go back."

Bazza looked at him for a long ten seconds.

"No," he said, less gruffly than usual.

"No, I don't, mate. You keep going back to the past, one day you're going to get stuck there."

The old man kept his gaze on him, and when Chi said nothing, returned to making his bet.

Later that afternoon the doors to the club slid open and two large men walked in: Caramel Mike and Ha-Ha Gillespie. Mike was a stand-over man, drug-dealer, old-school racist, and connoisseur of caramel lattes. Ha-Ha never spoke, so it was hard to say what he was. Mike had long, lanky brown hair and perpetually angry eyes. Ha-Ha wore T-shirts that emphasized all the growth supplements he took.

One or the other would usually be sitting at a small table near the slot machines, watching the players. Bazza had told him that they were looking for degenerate losers. They'd offer to clear their gambling debts in return for work as drug mules. Often Mike had been the one to lend them money to gamble in the first place.

This time they walked straight up to Chi and Bazza. Ha-Ha was wearing a tight green singlet with the letters VB printed on the front.

"Bazza and Gazza," said Mike. "The two stooges."

"Mike," replied Bazza. "Not known for your wit, mate. A reputation well-earned."

"Old fuck," spat Mike.

Chi sipped his brandy. Bazza's eyebrows bobbled. "What do you want?"

"Money," said Mike, pupils like pinpoints as he stared down at the old man.

Bazza waved the stare away. "I said you'd get it next month."

Chi hid his surprise as he glanced over at Bazza. The old man had been surlier than usual the past couple of weeks. Now Chi knew why.

Mike cracked his knuckles. "You'll give it to me now, you senile old bastard. You can't pay, we'll take your van and its route. That should cover it."

"Piss off. I'm not selling my van."

The big man indicated Chi with his chin. "You can't keep running a charity service for your retarded friends, Barry. You got obligations."

"You're not getting my van," repeated Bazza, but there was as a quaver in his voice.

"*Lai chú mình.*"

Mike looked at Chi, lip curled in a sneer. "Speak English."

"I said: leave Uncle alone."

Mike looked at Ha-Ha, and then back down at Chi. "The fuck? You don't get to talk to me, Chinaman."

"He's Vietnamese, idiot," said Bazza. "He fought the Chinese."

Mike kept staring down at Chi. "Vietnamese? So he's a coward, then, running away from a fight."

"Mike—"

"Shut up, old man. They're all cowards." Mike jabbed a finger at Chi. "They all run away, and they come here, bringing all their fucking problems with them. Take our jobs and sit around on welfare talking their fucking babble-talk." Mike's teeth showed under his sneer. "But they don't take our women. Do they, Ha-Ha?"

Ha-Ha shook his head *no*.

"Nah," leered Mike. "They don't take our women. Because they want real men, our women. They want someone who knows how to fight. Not some skinny yellow coward who came here on a fucking boat."

Chi stood up. Mike's eyes widened.

Everyone at the club had stopped talking, watching while pretending not to watch the altercation. The only sound was the rapid murmurings of the race caller coming from the *Tai* screen, and the repetitive tunes and ringing of the slot machines in the next room.

When Chi stood up the people in the club didn't see the small Vietnamese man anymore, the one who sat with old Barry Stillwater every Sunday to watch the races. The man they saw wasn't as short as they thought, and his shoulders were much bigger. Now they saw the veins stand out on his neck and the white scar on his cheek blazing, like it was hot.

Chi hit Mike and the big man went down. Ha-Ha stepped

in and Chi hit him as well. The man's eyes rolled up and his head cracked against the table as he went and stayed down.

Caramel Mike was groaning on the floor, trying to push himself up. Chi kicked him hard enough for the ribs to break, and for everyone in the room to hear the breaking. Mike cried out and started coughing as he tried to breathe. Chi dragged the thug by the hair over to the doors, ignoring Bazza, the old gambler's face creased with fear as he said something. Chi pulled Mike up the concrete steps to the bowls green. The old people nearby in their pressed whites gasped and moved away.

Chi threw the man onto the ground, picked up a heavy bowls ball, and brought it down on the man's head.

The first blow cracked the eye socket.

The second blow hit the forehead with the sound of a bamboo rod striking soft flesh. The heavy ball came away wet.

The third—

—was slowed by someone hanging on his arm.

He turned angrily, lashing out. The person fell backward, landing awkwardly. An old man, saying something, arm outstretched. Chi stood over him, bowl gripped fiercely, like he was hanging on to a ball of his hate.

One blow was all he'd need to end this doddering old fool. Then he noticed the old man was shaking. Bazza was shaking. The wind blew gently against Chi's face, bringing the sound of a woman crying.

Then the moment passed.

He dropped the ball to the green and walked away.

Chi sat under the shade of the flame tree, by the road. He took out the small silver key and turned it in his hand, leaning against the trunk. The tree was firm against his back, solid, while everything else around was indistinct. The people on the green were white blurs, the houses along the road grey smudges against a blue horizon.

Chi Cong Nguyen understood then that the flame tree was a gateway between this world and the other. Between the past and the present. He understood then that Barry Stillwater was wrong, that the only way to live was in the past. The only way to escape the eternal present was to an unchanging past. So he rested his back against the tree in this world, like he did in that other world, on the shores of Tay Ho, with Kieu sitting across his legs. One time and place in superposition with the other.

He sat there until the police came, and when they did, he didn't resist.

A week later, two burly policemen dragged Chi into the doctor's office. She watched with sadness as they pushed him down into the *Kandel-Yu* machine. There were straps at the legs, arms, and waist that Chi had never noticed before.

Chi was silent as they strapped him in. The police stood by the door until the young doctor insisted they leave. One of the officers looked at her and said: "We'll be right outside the door if you need us."

She sighed and walked over to where he lay. Her face was a mask of concern, and Chi believed it this time.

"Oh Chi," she sighed. She reached down and pushed the hair back from his eyes. "What have you done to yourself?"

"Sian," he said quietly. "You can't take away my memories."

"I don't have a choice, Chi. There are two dozen memory-feed recordings of you beating an unarmed man into a coma. You have to have this procedure. It's the only way, now." She smiled a strained smile at him. "Everything will change, after this. You'll be a new man."

Chi was looking right through her when he started speaking, softly:

"When I heard my village had been bombed, I left basic training and went there immediately. I had no leave pass, and no one would drive me for fear of the consequences, so I stole a bicycle and rode. It took me two days. I arrived, exhausted, after creeping past roadblocks in the darkness.

"It was the Moon. I was in my village, I was sure of it, but I was walking on the surface of the Moon. Puffs of ash with each step, nothing but craters and grey dust as far as I could see. But I could see enough of the melted roads to find the place where the village had built a bunker. A good bunker, too, made of plascrete and reinforced with carbon nanotubes."

The doctor leaned in close, straining to hear his words.

"A nova bomb is an amazing thing. There is nothing like it in nature. Tornadoes follow the blast; tornadoes of fire that roll across the landscape, eating all the air, gorging on it. Everything burns, everything. I dug all night at the spot where the bunker should have been. Dawn came and I had dug out the entrance. I hadn't slept in two days, hadn't eaten; I was dizzy, seeing things.

"I tried the heavy door, and to my surprise it popped open, easily. When it did, it sounded like the earth was drawing in a long, deep breath. I stepped inside. My village was sitting there, in that bunker, untouched. I smiled, a big smile, water in my eyes, and said hello.

"But no one moved. Not an inch. They were statues. Frozen at that one moment in time, one eternal moment.

"Dead.

"Dead, every one, like they'd all passed peacefully in their sleep. The oxygen had been sucked out of the bunker by the nova weapon. My fiancée, Kieu, was sitting on a bench, her head leaning on her mother's shoulder. Her eyes shone as she looked at me. I knelt in front of her and spoke to her for a time, in there, among all the staring, untouched dead. She was so sad to have died. Kieu had dreams, you see, bigger dreams than could fit into so short a life.

"I wanted to stay and talk to her, console her, but the spirits down there were angry and frightened by what had happened to them. And I was a coward. I kissed her and said goodbye.

"But she wouldn't let me leave. Not until I promised. Kieu had been at work when the sirens sounded, you see. Hadn't had time to get her rare, beloved, yellow-beaked songbird. Hadn't understood what had happened above. Couldn't understand. So she gave me the key. You can't keep it locked up, she said, and made me promise to release it. *War is no place for my bird*. I promised.

"I had nothing to cremate them with. So I shovelled the dirt back over the entrance and left them, just like that. I fear that they will always haunt that place, as I did not clean the bodies, had no food to leave them. Kieu, her family, will never rest."

The doctor was shaking her head, eyes wide, mouthing: *oh no, Chi.*

"Later, when I deserted my unit and was trying to make my way to Saigon, I was walking alone in a smashed forest. Trees were snapped, and the stands of bamboo were tinged red, like they were bleeding. There was one finger of dawn on the horizon—I'd walked all night and desperately wanted to sleep, but all night, in that broken place, I'd heard sobbing whispers and howls carried on the wind.

"I thought I saw a bridge in the distance. It was strange, as there were no rivers, no water, save the drying mud under my boots. I was parched, lips cracked, so I hurried over. There was a bridge. But the supports on either side were gone. I didn't understand, didn't understand how it was hanging there, in the air. Then as the sun rose and the centipedes crawled past my feet, I saw the shadows under the bridge were thick shadows. Solid shadows. People, bodies and bodies piled up on top of each other, wedged under the bridge, holding it up in the air. The Chinese had blown a dam up somewhere, miles back."

The doctor shook her head, eyes glistening.

"The flies were everywhere, everywhere. Swarms of big black flies. I swallowed one accidentally. That night, I dreamed of water, bearing me down, crushing me. I woke up and tried to scream, but I was choking. I was choking on water and then throwing it up. I was full of it. The fly must have been on one of the bodies, inside the mouth of one of the victims. Then into my mouth, bringing the spirit of the dead into me. That's why I chose this town inland, away from water. That spirit inside me cannot bear to be near it.

"The road south was tough. Gene-scramblers had destroyed all the food crops. Chinese troops were everywhere, villages and towns razed to the ground. I could travel only at night, in the mountains and the jungle. I ate bark and bamboo root when I could find it. But I couldn't find much. My skin was tight over my ribs and had started to peel away, every step was agony on my joints.

"Late one night, deep in the jungle, I saw a flickering light. Just a small little thing, so small I thought I was imagining it. But I staggered down through the undergrowth until I could hear voices. I was so hungry, I didn't care anymore whether they were Chinese or not, ghosts or not, and went right in.

"It wasn't ghosts. It was a medical camp. There was a young doctor, so young, younger than Kieu even. She was gaunt, but her smile was the most beautiful thing I had seen in months. There was a nurse there as well, and three soldiers on stretchers. It was a miserable camp. Mosquito nets under tarpaulin, the smell of something ripe, rotting, coming from one of the patients, dried blood on the doctor's smock she'd never had time to clean.

"I begged for food. The doctor just shook her head. She said I was healthy, and they needed everything they had left. They didn't know if they would find food again, when relief was coming. If it was coming, ever. She smiled and called me little brother, and told me to be strong.

"I pushed her onto the ground. I could see bamboo food containers and went to them. The nurse told me to stop, but I pointed my rifle at her and she backed away. There was so little food in those containers, so little. I stuffed some of the rice into my mouth, crammed it in, washed it down with dirty water. It seemed like a feast.

"I had gathered the other containers and was turning to leave when the doctor hit me in the face with an iron stake. I was knocked backward, into one of the tent poles, blood running down my face. I came back at her, in anger, and struck her in the temple with the butt of my rifle. She fell down and just lay there on the ground, eyes staring up at the mosquito net.

"The nurse cried and the patients begged me to leave the food. I took it anyway. I took it all. Left them there with nothing, but the body of the doctor."

He was finished. As Chi had spoken, the tightness below his heart had grown, weighing him down into the chair.

He looked up into the doctor's face, fully aware of her for the first time since he had been brought into the room. There were tears in her eyes.

She was shaking her head. "Maybe the doctor didn't die," she said in a thin voice. "Maybe the patients made it."

Chi thought about the young doctor, eyes staring and unblinking. "No," he said. She died. I killed her. And without food, the patients would have died, too."

"Chi," she said, struggling to keep the emotion out of her voice.

"You know what it is to kill medical staff, like that?" he asked, and there was no emotion in his. His voice had as much life in it as those bodies, preserved in the bunker. "A war crime."

"Chi—"

"These sins cannot be eaten. These sins must have witness, must be witnessed. "You are my witness, Sian."

The doctor was quiet for a minute, refusing to meet Chi's gaze. Her hand, which had been laid gently against Chi's forehead, fell to her side. "That woman," she said, the quaver gone now from her voice, "that doctor. Those people."

She reached above his head and pulled down the neon halo. "This must be done."

She disappeared from his sight for a moment, but he could hear her fingers tapping on something. A screen. Pinpointing his memories. Programming the *Kandel-Yu*.

"I must bear witness," he croaked.

The doctor was in his line of sight again. She set her jaw and put a finger to her implant. "Turn off my visual memory recording. Mark this point and record memory print for later removal."

"Sian," he said, louder. "Don't take these things. Don't take Kieu."

The doctor looked down at him. She seemed displaced, like part of her wasn't in the room with him anymore. She put her finger back to her implant. "Correction. Mark my visual feed and natural memory print from the moment Mister Nguyen entered the office, until the time he leaves my office today."

Chi strained at the straps, felt the heat on his face. "No!" he yelled. "No! Kieu Kieu Kieu—"

The process seemed so short it never even had a beginning. Just the doctor staring down at him with dead eyes and then a bright, searing white light.

Chi and Bazza were banned from the club, so they went and found another for returned servicemen. There were a lot to go around. Chi had tried to apologize, but Bazza just held up a hand and said, "Aaaaahhhhh, *don't worry*, these things happen," and never mentioned it again. Mike woke up from the coma, but never pressed charges. Bazza paid him back. That wouldn't be the end of it, of course.

Chi returned to guarding the van.

I drink you with my sight, and I am filled with fire
From the broken bone of the hill, stripped and left for dead,
Like a wrecked skull, leaps out this bush of blood
I drink you with my sight, and I am filled with fire,
Out of the very wound, springs up this scarlet breath,
This fountain of hot joy, this living ghost of death

Chi switched off the song, irritated. He remembered programming the song, but right then couldn't think why. His fingertips twitched, as though seeking something, a phantom. He felt hollowness in his chest, right below his heart. Deadness. He'd been feeling that for a few days now, along with the twitching of his hands. He sighed.

He leaned his head against the headrest, watching the countryside flash by.

Out at the periphery of the headlights bounced kangaroos, desperately trying to keep up with the van. Stupid creatures. At night they thought headlights were the rising sun and ran toward them with suicidal enthusiasm.

He sat in silence.

Silence, complete, in a land that held no ghosts for him.

OPIUM FOR EZRA

2072

The last thing Barry said to me was: 'I want you to keep this jar of opium and give it to Nguyen only when she needs it.'"

Nguyen was just a few feet away, yet the glimmering of her eyes and the orange tip of her cigarette were the only points visible in the dim interior of the tank. "Well?" she asked.

"You don't need it," replied Ezra.

"Why?"

"Well. You're not scratching at black bugs under your skin, screaming and sweating, vomiting and pleading, for starters."

"Give her the dope, dickhead!" A voice, though inside his head, yelled through the internal comms system. Australian, rough, heavily accented. Main gunner, above, separate compartment. Garry. *Call me Gazza.*

"I prefer Commander," said Ezra, dryly.

"You know damn well why she needs it. And it's her smack, *Commander* dickhead."

"*Gunner*," said Ezra.

Garry grumbled, swore, and cut the link.

"He has a point," said Nguyen.

"Which one, driver?"

"Ownership."

"I liked the other one better."

She waited.

"The one where he called me Commander."

It was silent inside the titan, powered down. Just the water cycling round the fusion reactor, and the crackle-burn on Nguyen's cigarette as she drew deep. Her eyes on him, she said nothing.

Ezra turned in his seat: "Comms check"

His on-retina readout lit up. Red glowing script, trickling down the left side of his vision, illusion of being a couple feet away. Thirty-eight messages. Not from command. Not from air support. Thirty-eight from an unknown sender. Ezra squinted, not quite believing. His tank, the titan-class Eromanga, was alone out in the wasteland: the blasted furnace between the approaching Chinese and the retreating everyone else. The Chinese had bombed it first, nova and gene scrambler, scorching the earth. The Alliance had doubled down in their retreat. Seeding the ground with proximity explosives, nano-viruses, sharp sticks. Anything.

Retreating, until the Eromanga took the field. One tank, stopping the advance. A spectre, haunting the Marscape of bleached bone and cratered earth that was now central Vietnam. A zone only titan-class vehicles could withstand for long periods. Fusion power source, could roll forever. Closed shell, closed system, biological-chemical-nuclear-nano impregnable. Top-of-the-line comms, yes. But jamming drones deployed by two armies plus several hundred square kilometres of anything capable of relaying messages blasted to pieces or eaten by nanobots.

So he shouldn't have any messages. The subject line was visible for each: **'Where are you?'** **'Answer your phone'.** **'I'm outside, open your door'.** **'Don't do this to me again, Ezra. Please'.**

"Nice Guy Eddie," he said. "Who are these messages from?"

"I have no information on the sender, Commander," replied the A.I., metronome pace.

"Any information at all?"

"Only distance."

"Distance?"

"I have determined the source, which is moving. It started at ninety kilometres out, and has closed to eighty-eight in the time between opening the comms and this sentence. I have concluded that I was meant to learn this, Commander"

"Meant to?"

"The source did not seek to cloak the information."

"What do the messages say?"

"The content is in the buffer, Commander"

"Oh. Right, sure."

"Inaccessible for security reasons."

"Yes. Sure. I understand."

"You don't understand shit, wanker," said the Australian.

"I would recommend you not open the file, Commander. There is a high probability it is an A.I. attack."

"I know that Eddie," said Ezra. "Give me distance to the source on-retina, clear the messages."

Ezra *should* know all this. He'd been getting forgetful, lately. Long hours at the helm. Cramps, back pain, dizzy spells. Little bit of pain relief, every now and again, additional to the sync-suit. Not too much. Just enough to take the edge off, stay on mission, help focus, pass the hours.

Upper right, his on-retina read: **distance to unknown – 87 Kilometres**

"I think we're being followed," Ezra announced.

"How'd you figure that, genius?"

Ezra ignored the Australian: "Could be anything. *Xiongshou* assassin, enemy titan, A.I. virus looking to take over Nice Guy Eddie, playing games with his sensors. We're going to move on to Vinh Quang, leave it behind. There were reports of a support station for mechanised units near that location."

Garry's voice crackled over the comm: "Months ago. They'd be cactus by now."

"Maybe," said Ezra. "But everything should be cactus by now, and we keep running into remnants."

A grunt.

"Vinh Quang," said Nguyen, "is close to the Chinese line."

"Noted," said Ezra. "There's a reliable water source near there. One of the few. That's why there will be something. Our extractors aren't getting enough for the Tokamak. The Eromanga is overdue for a bath."

Garry said: "Tell me about it. My balls smell like gorgonzola."

Nguyen said: "What are our mission orders, Commander?"

Garry said: "Yeah, I'm fucken sick of this metal fart box. When do we blow up what we need to blow up? Saigon is calling me."

"Classified."

"Fuck classified, dickhead. Nine fucken months in this BO containment device developing gout. Driving around 'Nam on a magical fucken mystery tou—"

"Sync up. Heat up. Heads up," said Ezra, cutting off Garry's mike before he could fire off any more abuse.

Nguyen said: "Roger".

Eddie, who controlled the right lascannon as well as comms and sensors, replied: "Yes Commander."

Ezra's three screens lit up, bathing him in a green backwash. The bridge of the titan now visible. Twelve feet wide, no more, Nguyen to his left and slightly forward, straightening her seat from the recline, bending over data screens. Short hair, perfect skin, small shoulders, thirty but looked fifteen, no-nonsense, all the time. Sheen of sweat, over her face, from the pain she never spoke about. Best not think about that.

Cramped and close, their home for the last nine months, hadn't cracked the hatch for thirty-three days. Ezra was immune to the smell, now. Just enough sedatives to stop the creeping claustrophobia, the paranoid fear that the world outside wasn't real. All a simulation, a game. His sync-suit kept him clean, disposed of his waste, applied current to stimulate atrophying muscles. Expensive, only a handful made, given to the crews of land and aerial titans. But it wasn't designed for this. Not for nine months straight, the longest in Alliance history. Not for a month without getting outside, stretching the legs.

The monitor spat out the vitals:

Main Battle Cannon: 33% ammunition remaining

Demolisher Cannon: 64%

Lascannon, right: 100%

Lascannon, left: destroyed

Twin-linked .50 Calibre: 28%

Front armour 99%

And so on over the rest of the armour, oxygen and water levels, hull integrity, heat sinks, auxiliaries, all the toys they'd been given to play with. Ezra couldn't help but linger on the worst: left lascannon.

Gone. Bayani with it. Should have seen it, should have seen it coming. And the hull weapon. Demolisher cannon, unused for weeks. Barry up and left the tank. Went to get some air, he said, and wandered off into the jungle.

Garry, his best mate, raged, demanded he come back. Gazza and Bazza, Inseparable. Called themselves the boom twins. The others did too, save Ezra.

Barry had replied: "Sorry, got that doctor's appointment mate. And Sharon's wedding's tomorrow night."

Garry said: "The fuck you talking about?"

And that was it. Static for a reply, then dead silence.

The two Australians. Foul mouthed, insubordinate, bitter. Brave, the best gunners in the Alliance; stoic when it came to personal pain, a stream of vitriol on every other matter. And reliable. As reliable as two men should be with no country to return to.

Until Barry walked into the jungle and never came back.

"Driver, take us forward, cruising speed," said Ezra.

Nguyen tamped out the butt of her cigarette on the dull metal dashboard, slipped the silver driver interface over her head, and placed both hands on the joysticks. The fusion reactor wound up, making a noise akin to young girls, screaming. The titan's mass grumbled in response, growing, roared, growing, the scream of the reactor still audible over it all; through the layers of titanium, injected with spideriron, surrounding the reactor.

Ezra slipped on his noise-cancelling earphones, hands shaking a little. He found himself stroking the slender metal hopper attached to the right of his command set. One finger, gently, down its length.

He breathed. Closed his eyes. Snapped out the plastic nozzle near the neck of his sync-suit and sucked down some water instead. Condensation, whatever gathered on the vast surface of the Eromanga. Piss and sweat, recycled, from the inside. One litre, for each crew member, each day. Every day. Two hundred and seventy-four days.

He said: "Give me visuals, Eddie," and closed his eyes. On retina, against the back of his eyelids, a three-sixty of the landscape

Handful of trees, snapped off at the trunk, dead earth, no clouds. Blue sky, forever. Gentle rise and fall of the plains in the valley, mountains looming in the distance. Still patches of green, on those; nature still had a few surprises left. The target there, as well, at the base. The one Eddie had found. *Just give me anything*, he told the A.I. as Nguyen and Garry had slept. *Closer to their line.*

Nice Guy Eddie wasn't certain—it'd been weeks since any useful information from the Alliance had trickled through—but that didn't matter so much. Eddie could always work the numbers and find something, out there, in the wasteland. Regular, in this theatre of war. It'd look to Nguyen and Garry like it was part of a plan, or at the least satiate their needs. For battle, for meaning. Fifteen days without a fight, both were getting on edge, in their own ways. Nguyen's need for pain-killers rising; Garry, well, needing to blow shit up.

The landscape flowed by, the Eromanga rolling at eighty kilometres an hour. The unidentified target began to fall behind, falling off the on-retina dial at one hundred clicks. The rise and fall of the landscape, hypnotic, the rocks the stumps barely registering on the titan as it ground them underneath. Loud ride, sure, but a smooth one.

"Is that *Imagine*?" barked Garry, in Ezra's ear.

Ezra cleared his throat. "Oh. What?"

"You were humming. Again."

"Oh, was I? Yeah. I was listening to—"

"You've been listening to Lennon's *Imagine*? The fuck is wrong with you?"

"Wrong?" Ezra straightened in his seat. "Well, I don't—"

"Arrogant douche. Wants us to imagine no countries, *I wonder if you can*. Like his fucken vision is beyond us peons. Newsflash, dick-cheese: I live in a world with no country, where there's nothing to kill or die for, my fucken nation wiped off the face of the Earth. The only people think nations don't matter are those living in the safety of one. Look how the Jews fared without a nation. That ignorant spanker."

"Garry, I—"

"Telling us to live only for today. Yeah, well, heard of climate change, cocksucker? That's what living only for today leads to. And world peace? Only people living in peace are the dead. Bleached bones, across these plains, only for them no religion, no possessions, no hunger, not anymore. That's what he's talking about. The plains of the dead. Either that or some bourgeois paradise where every need is met. Rich cunts with everything are the only ones who have the time to start pissing on poor people with only religion or country to hold on to."

"Jesus, I'm just humming a tune."

"Worst fucken song that hack ever wrote."

"Lenin wrote music?" asked Nguyen.

"Shit yeah," said Garry.

"Vladimir Lenin?"

"What? Oh. Nah, not the commie, Nguyen. American twat. Mid-twentieth century."

"English, actually," said Ezra.

"Well he moved to the US, didn't he? That song is pure fucken Americana schmaltz."

"Nice Guy Eddie chose it for my sleep routine," said Ezra. "I can't get it out of my head."

"Don't blame Eddie for your gilded fascism, twat."

"*Gunner.*"

"A Day in the Life. *That's* a fucken song."

"Gunner."

"Fucken Yoko."

Ezra glanced over at Nguyen. She was smiling as she drove, listening to Garry.

Ezra let it go, hand slipping back to the slim locker, side of his seat. Popping it, hand on the jar, shakes in his hand stilled in anticipation, carefully bringing it to his lap and turning the lid. Chair pointed away from Nguyen, out of her line of sight. He tried for half a fingernail's worth and slipped it into his mouth, rolled it over his tongue. Delicious. Like flowers, bitter flowers bitter chocolate flowers, relaxing him, even though the drug hadn't hit. Not yet. His brain, opening up, in expectation, the pain in his back and legs, dissipating. When it came, he'd float in the womb, inside a whale, inside—

A ping on-retina. Ezra grumbled. "What?"

"Another message, Commander."

"Message?"

"From the unidentified source following us."

He glanced at the readout on-retina. **Distance: 68 kilometres**

Below it, the subject heading of the message: **We're coming in, Ezra.**

"It's catching up?"

"Yes Commander," said Eddie. "Also: we are coming up on the target."

Overlaid, on-retina, red dots pipping over green cartography. Former village of Vinh Quang, long burned to the ground, by one side or the other.

"Picking up heat signatures, Commander."

"They see us?"

"I do not believe so, Commander."

Ezra gave the command to Nguyen. The child-scream whine of the engine ebbed as the tank rolled to a halt.

Ezra hit the best part of the high. Brain sharp, body buzzing. Aggressiveness wasn't part of the package, though. Wasn't even inclined to move his hands from his lap. He closed his eyes, a long blink wishing for repose, opened them, and said: "Gunner."

"Yeah mate?"

"Six to seven armoured vehicles, ten kilometres away."

"I see 'em."

"We'll have a line of fire eight out. You set the tactical course for this battle."

"Only one fucken course to take, mate."

The link crackled, them boomed. Cymbals CRASHED, guitar lick intro, wailing on it; drummer coming in on it, smashing the rims; someone yelling TWO THREE FOUR, then a woman, throaty, Australian accent: "*Love is no fun, anymore—*"

Over it all Garry said: "Righty-o, cunts. Hit it Nguyen."

The reactor screamed, the engine roared, Ezra smiled and sank back into his seat.

The singer belted: "*I'd never wanna to push you,*" to a catchy, old-school hard-rock beat, while Nguyen, smiling into her driver's sight, pushed the titan. Slammed it through the top of a ridge, shearing it clean off, dirt and debris flying; the Eromanga didn't stutter.

"*—Money's all that matters for the rich in—*"

Ezra had Garry's viewpoint on one of his screens. He watched, detached, small smile on his face, as the target came into view.

Three tanks plus three armoured personnel carriers and a heavy tanker truck. Mechanised platoon with support. Hanger-like structure, reinforced concrete, set behind, up on the ridge. Weathered but intact. Two silver-domed shelters erected near the water, a thin, stagnant river. Twenty or so troops at ease, environment suits, face masks.

"—*never wanna to lose you*—"

The Chinese just had enough time to stop scratching themselves and look at their screaming proximity warnings when Garry put a sabot plasma round into the middle tank. Sleek, Chinese Type-199, shaped like a fat arrowhead. The sabot round punctured the ceramite and layered nano alloys like tissue paper. Nothing happened, six seven eight seconds, and then a light, like the sun. That's all. Small sun, sitting among the broken earth and stilled river, before everything in the tank that could blow up did blow up, and the turret lifted off into the blue sky.

"—*I said I do!*"

Troops nearby burst into flames. Little roman candles, running around, some jumping into the mud-coloured river, some flailing around on the red earth. Other troops, outside their carriers, running back towards open hatches. The remaining two tanks rotating turrets, bringing their guns to bear.

They dipped out of view as the Eromanga charged down a slope, rising again into view not more than six seconds later. In the rear vision, a great cloud of dust ascended. For the Chinese, it must have looked like the earth was rising to meet them, a tidal wave headed by a titan.

"—*never wanna, never wanna*—"

The barrels of the Chinese tanks were locked, each flashing silently through the visual feed. They both hit, smoke and fire smothering the front viewpoints for a few seconds, a violent shudder passing through his seat. And that was all. Two direct hits and the titan roared on, Chinese tanks backing away as the second was hit by a plasma round, another sun, the fuel tank fifty metres back bursting into conflagration, its heat shields finally failing.

"Commander," said Garry, through what sounded like gritted teeth.

"Huh?"

"They're getting away."

"Huh?"

"Fucken shoot them."

Ezra grunted, pushing himself upright in his seat. A wave of nausea came over him, briefly, as he fumbled with the joystick. It cleared, he gripped it firmly, sight syncing in on-retina. Targeting did most of the work for the twin-linked heavy machine guns. But Ezra still had to be looking at the right thing. Magnification up, seven clicks down to a virtual twenty metres; the enemy, desperate, throwing themselves into the back of an already moving personnel carrier.

Ezra pressed the trigger.

"—*I do, I do, I do*—"

The tracers hit three seconds later, following the stream of explosive-tipped shells, dust and dirt around the base of the carrier thrown up, sparks, chips flying from the rear, spotlight shattered, last man to the hatch coming apart like a watermelon. Then a stream of tracer fire into the innards the vehicle, unerring, *snap* fire appeared, followed by smoke billowing from the inside.

"Fuck," said Garry. "The other one."

"Huh," said Ezra, transfixed, as the APC disappeared under the smoke and fire.

"*Commander*," roared Garry.

Ezra jumped in his seat, dragged his hyper-focus from the dead vehicle to a live tank. The last one, struck by a regular round from the main battle cannon, pulverised. No, not that. Movement on the side of his vision—the last personnel carrier, disappearing over a ridge.

"Fuck," said Ezra.

"Exactly," said Garry.

"...*ohhhhhhhhhhh...*"

Then the laser hit. An intense beam of white light, centred on the rear hatch. Ezra's virtual vision polarized, but the outline of the vehicle and the impact point of the laser remained. The target's armour glowed, melted, beam punching through, into the cabin. The carrier, festooned with flame and superheated metal slag, disappeared over the ridge top. Zombie, rolling on to nowhere.

"YEEEEEAAAAHHH," yelled Garry.

Ezra sighed. "Nice shot Eddie."

"Thank you, Commander."

The music continued, blasting, as Nguyen drove the titan down the final slope towards the encampment, easing back over the last kilometre. Precision, by the book, stopping two hundred metres from the enemy position.

The Eromanga vibrated; Ezra leaned forward to the master override, to switch the music off. Pounding at his temples, now the battle was done. He winced against the sound, head spinning as he reached out.

And vomited all over the command station.

When Ezra regained consciousness he found Nguyen standing over him. Unimpressed as always, coupled with something else he couldn't quite—

"He's awake," she said.

Garry said, "Wake up, smack head." The internal comms, piped directly into his ear, made Ezra groan, his head spin.

Ezra waited for it to pass, tried to push himself up with one arm, was met with resistance. He found himself strapped to a narrow metal gurney. Screens bleeped on the wall to his left. On his right, just enough space for Nguyen to stand, and behind her, stainless steel lockers, inside which were medical supplies and food tubes. The medical station/mess hall behind the bridge, in front of the fusion reactor. Ezra and Nguyen used it sometimes as a place to lie down to sleep, when they couldn't stand one more night in their chairs. Nice Guy Eddie gave them weekly check-ups in there: vitamin D shots, or antibiotics, or vaccine updates, as required.

"Please stay down, Commander," said Eddie. "you're suffering from exhaustion—"

"And a drug overdose!" yelled Garry. He followed it with laughter: the bitter kind. Like he was discovering even his contempt for the Commander had undershot the mark.

"And a drug overdose," repeated Eddie.

The words stabbed at Ezra's brain, he shut his eyes against the pain.

"Eating opium is against regulations, Commander."

Ezra cleared his throat, eyes still closed. "We've violated just about every regulation, Eddie. For this mission."

"What mission?" asked Garry.

"And I've adapted my responses as a crew member accordingly," said Eddie, patient, uninflected. "But as medical officer I can adjudge you unfit for duty."

Ezra's lips were cracked. "Water."

Nguyen popped his water straw from the top of his suit and placed it against his lips. He sucked down deeply, coughed a little, and drank more, opening his eyes. A year in the titan and Nguyen didn't show it. Her skin perfect, save the pallor. No stink, unlike the Australian's eye-watering putrescence; for Nguyen just the clove of the cigarettes she smoked, the earthiness of the dope she sometimes mixed with it. Her lips wet, small, perfect. To touch them, to kiss them—

"Big brother," she said, grabbing his hand and pushing it firmly back onto his chest. It had wandered.

He closed his eyes again. To clear the embarrassment. A year of quiet fascination, with his driver. With—

"I don't think that's going—" said a voice, ringing in the confines of the medbay. Garbled, fritzing, through the back-up intercom of the tank system mounted strategically along the walls. Never used unless their implants went down; it had never been used.

Nguyen gasped, involuntarily, and turned, pulling her service pistol from her hip. Superfluous in the Eromanga; still, she was never without it.

"What was that, Eddie?" asked Ezra. His voice a harsh whisper, words slow, but his mind was starting to come back.

"What was what, Commander?"

"Nguyen?"

She turned back to him, face still in shadow, eyes gleaming, waiting.

"I don't know what that was, but—" he glanced at the figure, on-retina, "—the target is three clicks away. Get us up on the ridge, ready."

"Yes, Commander," she said. Sliding her pistol back into its holster. When she made to turn away, he said: "Could you unstrap me?"

She hesitated, hand on the short ladder up. "I needed that opium, big brother."

Ezra sighed, long. "I know."

She touched the top of her thigh. "For my leg."

Ezra averted his eyes. Looked at the steel lockers, at the red and blue medical lights reflected in them. Tried not the think of the injuries she sustained in the attack that killed Bayani. Legs dangling through his internal hatch, chatting to him below, in his cabin in the left sponson. Laughing, the only person she laughed with, talked at length with. Tried not to think of the moment when the other titan attacked. Out of nowhere. Of the blood, her blood everywhere, staining the metal floor, while Nguyen refused to scream, even as parts of her came away.

Ezra had been on duty. Small nap, after twenty hours at the helm. Some pain relief.

Well. Not quite out of nowhere.

Nice Guy Eddie had grown new skin for the burns, printed a temporary prosthetic leg. Nguyen had received the best medical care in the Alliance. For a field hospital. From a medbay not designed for serious injury. An injury she'd be given no time to recover from, rolling out just three days later, more titans bearing down on them. She locked her jaw and did as ordered.

The new leg caused her pain, the burns never healed. Hurt to move, to get out of her driver's seat; staying in her seat put pressure on the damaged skin. Pain all the time and not a word of complaint. Just a request. Just the opium Barry had given to Ezra before the Australian had walked out into the night.

"Yes, unstrap him," said the voice. Unmistakably female, in English, though with a slight accent. "We need to talk."

Ezra and Nguyen looked at each other. His mind was clearing. The problem with opium was the clarity came in the wrong places. Precise, poetic thoughts about a sunset weren't much use in the middle of a firefight.

"There's a combatant out there," he said, his focus coming down on the right point, finally. "A.I., stealth tech, I don't know. I need to be on the bridge for this, driver. Easy to forget the Eromanga is the most decorated tank in this theatre of war. Easy to forget I'm the most decorated Commander, I know. But it is and I am. I need to be at the helm."

Nguyen hesitated.

Eddie said: "I'm sorry sir, but I must declare you unfit for—"

"I don't think so, Eddie," said the voice, cutting off the A.I. "I need to talk to my brother."

Ezra furrowed his brow; Nguyen did the same, and then unstrapped him, hands working quickly, like she was worried she'd change her mind. She limped away without looking back.

It took him too long to get back to the command station. Nausea roiled him all the way—he'd had to rest his forehead against the short ladder from medbay to the bridge. Back in the chair, hands shaking, the voice said: "Look at what this is doing to you, Ezra."

On-retina read: **distance: 900 metres.**

"What can you see, Eddie?"

No answer.

"Eddie?"

"I think the woman silenced him," said Nguyen.

"Must be an A. I.," said Ezra. He typed a series of commands into his control panel. Thankfully someone—Nguyen, no doubt— had wiped it down.

Ezra managed to redirect Eddie to his panel, text communication only: **Nothing detected, Commander. Ultraviolet, infrared, movement detectors, raw visuals.**

"A ghost," grunted Garry over the comm.

"*Xiongshou* assassin," said Nguyen.

"But how can a *Xiongshou* fuck with Eddie? All they do is dance around like a two-bob watch then get you with the pig-sticker."

Ezra didn't understand what Garry was saying, and couldn't be bothered using the translator. "We need to find this thing. Whatever it is."

"I'll run it down," said Nguyen. "Grind it into the earth." Green backwash from the monitors on her face, sheen of sweat: a sickly, fixated, avatar of war.

"You've certainly created obedient characters," said the voice.

Ezra checked the system stats, pored over the data, tried to find something Eddie had missed.

"Everyone is a caricature, though. The crude, unreconstructed Australian. The quiet, stoic Vietnamese. You should be ashamed of the stereotypes."

"Shut up you Chinese slapper!" roared Garry.

The screaming-children sound of the fusion reactor grew louder. Ezra slipped his headphones on, hands shaking, stomach roiling.

"You're part of a game," said the voice. "You're a programmer's idea of an Australian." It said it and it cut right through the headphones, over the noise of the reactor, the bone deep rumble of the titan.

Garry laughed. "Well that programmer sure has great fucken taste."

Nice Guy Eddie said, via the readout: **Excuse me, Commander; gunner, who are you talking to?**

"You bloody deaf?" barked Garry.

Ezra said: "You can't hear that voice, Eddie?"

What voice, Commander?

Ezra jabbed at his control panel, trying to clear up Nice Guy Eddie's sensors.

"You're trying to get advice from a video game, Ezra. One you've been playing for nine days straight, locked up in your apartment."

I hear the voice now, Commander. They are on the tank phone.

"The tank phone?" asked Ezra. Understanding but not believing.

"At the rear of the Eromanga. They have bypassed my proximity detectors. The most likely explanation is high-level Chinese stealth technology, a prototype I have not seen before."

"Gotta be a fucken *Xiongshou*."

"I agree," said Nguyen. "Only they would have the endurance to stalk a titan, out here."

"I'm not an assassin, Ezra. I'm your sister. The only security I had to bypass was your front door, which the building supervisor opened after I begged him and we both smelled what was coming under your door."

Ezra leaned back in his chair. Rubbing his hands. Just to make sure they were real, for a split second, doubting.

"We'd thought you'd died in here." The voice sighed. She certainly sounded genuine. "Instead we found you marinating in your own filth. Hooked up via some disgusting gamer's suit to this damn game."

"I think we need to drive, Nguyen."

She nodded.

"What's your mission, Ezra?" asked the voice.

Ezra stopped rubbing his hands.

Nguyen's hands hovered over the joysticks.

"I know what your mission is, because I can see it here, on the screen in your apartment."

"I—" he faltered. "The opium it-it's affecting my memories, I can't—"

"That's not opium, Ezra. God, ever wondered why you're taking a drug from the nineteenth century? You're on ice-seven, which helps suspend disbelief while in immersive video gaming. It's illegal, because users get lost in it. Like this. Like you."

"Then how come I don't know your name?"

"You don't know my name?" she asked, hurt.

Nguyen had turned in her seat. Watching him, her eyes glittering in the gloom.

"Commander?" asked Garry. Asked. Voice even. No expletives.

"What's our mission?"

Ezra rubbed his forehead. There *was* a mission, once. He knew that there must—

"The screen here," said the voice, "says mission: Legend of Eromanga—open ended. *You* be the Commander that holds back the Chinese hordes: *you* create the legend."

Silence, in the tank, for ten full seconds, until Garry said: "I know what my mission is. Turn this fucken assassin into a blackened, fucken, crater."

"You're not real," said the voice, annoyed.

"And you're not going to be either, in about ten fucken seconds," replied Garry.

"I'm getting tired of this character," said the voice.

"Get the fu—"

His channel went dead.

"Open the hatch Ezra. It's the only way to end the game."

"How are you turning off the characters? Garry and Nice Guy Eddie?"

"Nice Guy Eddie—good lord, you got that name from a Tarantino movie."

He did like Tarantino. His hand dropped to the locker, ran his finger along it. "How are you controlling the comms system, then?"

"God dammit, Ezra. There's a mute button, just here, over the character icon. I pressed the button. I mean—look at this thing. What's this? Plasma fusion reactor—in a tank? Seriously? That's science fiction. And lascannons? You're losing your mind in your fantasies again."

"I don't play video games anymore," said Ezra. Trying to keep the calm in his voice. "I gave them away when I joined the military."

"*This is all you do*," she said. "Living off the inheritance, after mama and baba died. Already been into rehab once for video game addiction. I can't keep doing this, I can't—" the voice broke down.

Nguyen tapped a cigarette out of a pack. Lit it, blew a heavy slow cloud into the bridge. Still waiting for Ezra.

"This is a simulation," said the voice, regaining composure. "Your gaming buddy, Barry, he contacted me and told me what was happening. Scared to tell anyone, at first, because of the drugs you took. God Ezra." She took a deep breath. "How on earth could you imagine you're the most respected tank Commander in the Alliance? Stewing in vomit and sweat. Strung out on drugs."

She had a point. It never made sense to him, when he was in that opium high, how he had got to this point. Some series of events he could never quite remember, leading him to this point.

"Why can't you just switch it off?" he asked, quietly. Knowing the answer.

"Commander," said Nguyen, warning voice.

"Because you've been hooked up for so long, and have gone so deep, if I unplug this thing you could fall into a coma. The hatch is the switch inside the game, for saving progress. You open it, the lights will come back on. But the drugs, Ezra, the drugs are breaking down the barrier between real and fantasy. God, I warned you…"

She started sobbing.

Ezra sighed. So tired. Nine months in this metal crate. So very tired. A real bed to lie down in, a meal that didn't come from a tube. The ache in his legs, returning now, as the opium high started to fade, the pounding headache.

Yeah. Fingernail of opium and a warm, comfortable bed.

Garry swore, typed, barked commands into his control panel. Nothing doing. Couldn't get back into the comms system. He leaned back in his chair, scratched himself. Shoulders aching, back a tangle of knotted and strained muscles; result of hunching over the targeting console, putting high-explosives into the verified cunts of the world.

From his gunner's nest. Four green-glowing command panels, deep and comfortable seat, wicked sound system. Bunk, just behind the seat. Battered lockers, one with a beer droid, smuggled in last night before deployment. Picture of the missus on the locker, Charlotte, smiling, shapely, blond, ace pilot, flew the Gullfire over Taipei. Looking back at him out of the picture, winking. Five years ago, like she knew what was coming. Whirlwind wedding, wild nights in Saigon, apartment in Kyoto.

He smiled back. Touched the photo with his forefinger.

Then he worked the controls again until he pulled up an internal visual of the bridge. Vision, no sound.

"Mother fucker," said Garry, knuckles white as he gripped the edge of the control panel.

Nguyen was struggling to get up from the driver's seat, service pistol in hand, while Ezra worked the Commander's exit hatch. Ezra, fucking Ezra, weird smile on his face, stepping back as the figure dropped down. Sleek black armour, opaque oval helmet.

And that was it. That's all it took, for a *Xiongshou*. The black blade materialised in her hand, driven into Ezra's chest. The Commander, mouth an O of surprise, his hands on the assassin's shoulders. Nguyen, firing, muzzle flashes, the assassin, head jerking back, then using Ezra as a body shield.

Then dropping him.

Then spinning, whirling, sleek black blur Garry's eyes could not follow, until Nguyen, too, was at the end of its blade.

Internal hatch, to the bridge, down by Garry's left foot. He took the thermite grenade, blipped the timer to two seconds. Looked at Charlotte, looking back, and said: "Sorry babe."

Back down at the monitor. Nguyen, skewered, giving the long stare to the ceiling. Assassin, one arm resting on the panel, the other on the cracked visor of her helmet. And Ezra, moron, somehow back in his seat, hands both clasped to his chest, trying to hold his life in.

Garry said: "You fucken idiot, Ezra."

He reached for the hatch.

A STRANGE LOOP

2093

In the end, we self-perceiving, self-inventing, locked-in mirages are little miracles of self-reference.

– Douglas R. Hofstadter, *I Am a Strange Loop*

A huge clown, jaws as wide as Irving was tall, about to swallow him whole... A woman, black hair with the fringe cut too short, green eyeshadow, skin so smooth it looked real-life airbrushed... The woman—what was her name again?—yelling at him, perfect skin creased with contempt... a red fireworks blast, neon, frozen into the sky... fairy floss and sweat and machine grease in his nostrils and a girl, freckled, *staring up at him with tears in her eyes… and those sounds, tinny music on a maddening, endless cycle, and the clown, swallowing him, while the woman yelled and the girl watched with sadness.*

Irving Kupfermann blinked into consciousness. White room with a white duo, man and woman, standing over him. The woman, young, lips glistening in the bright lights, pressed a paper cup into his hand. "Drink this," she said.

Irving drank, first sipping, then gulping as the extent of his thirst hit him.

The man looked familiar. He wore a white lab coat and grasped a flexiscreen in both hands, looking down into its green-glowing ideograms. The doctor—Irving was pretty sure that's what he was—had a full head of silver hair that probably wasn't real, and a movie star chin that most definitely wasn't. The gold of the heavy chain around his wrist: that would be real. The doctor looked forty, but he stank of money. Probably closer to sixty.

Doctor Eduard—the name floated up and popped into Irving's forebrain—spoke to the nurse. "Potentials for synaptic growth and multiplication high, as are an increased release of kinase A proteins. Emotional response very high; memories appear authentic across all measures. Or the patient believes they are real, in any case." He enunciated each word clearly, like he expected his audience to savour every single one.

"Yes doctor," the nurse replied, smiling, as she eased something from the top of Irving's head—he caught a glimpse of a green neon circle. To his left, coming into view as the nurse moved to one side, was a painting of a tobacco pipe. Below it was written: 'this is not a pipe'. Irving furrowed his brow at that.

The doctor looked up at Irving and gave him the perfect imitation of a smile, his pristine white teeth matching the room.

"You always bring us a first-class product, Irving."

Irving grunted and handed the nurse the empty cup.

"Now: do you remember anything of the memory you just sold?"

Irving shook his head. "No. Not really. It's like a dream. It's there at the edge of my mind… fragments. There was a woman; I think she was angry."

Doctor Eduard nodded. "Best that you sold it to us then. The key to happiness, Irving, is a bad memory."

Irving gave a noncommittal shrug.

"Those remaining fragments should fade away, and by the time you get home today, they will have decamped completely from your cerebral cortex. But, remember Irving," said the doctor, finger in the air, "in the unlikely event any of this does come back to you, you must inform us post-haste. It is a violation of mnemonic copyright to remember things you no longer legally own. In such an eventuality we would need you to return here immediately to eliminate the rogue memories."

"Post-haste," said Irving. "Indubitably."

The doctor missed the sarcasm, smiled insincerely, and returned to looking over his flexiscreen.

Irving leaned back into the chair, relieved at the embrace of the soft, real leather against the back of his head. He'd been seated during the procedure, yet still felt exhausted. "How can I know if I'm remembering things I've sold?"

"Ah yes, very good question," said the doctor, returning Irving's gaze with a supercilious expression that clearly indicated that, in fact, it was a very stupid question. "We have a trace program downloaded from the *Kandel-Yu* machine into your memory pin. If it picks up a specific neural pattern in your cerebral cortex—a unique grouping we call a memory-print—you will receive a warning on-retina advising you that you have begun to reconsolidate memories under license to us here at *Thanks for the Memories*. Often this will happen when you are dreaming."

Irving rubbed at his eye. "You tell me this often, doctor?"

"Very."

The nurse suppressed a giggle.

Irving nodded at her. "Is she an actual nurse, or are the staff here hired to laugh at you?"

The doctor raised an eyebrow. The nurse retained her smile as she said: "A post-graduate qualification, three-year internship, and a field of five hundred candidates for this position."

Her response came easy. Irving pushed his unruly hair back from his forehead. "I guess I've said that before, as well."

"Once or twice," said the doctor, with a smirk. "When you're in a particularly bad mood. Something, I suspect, related to the experience you just sold to us."

"Yeah. Yeah, forget it."

"I was hoping you would," replied the doctor.

The nurse's smiled widened.

Irving rolled his eyes.

The doctor pulled a vial from the pocket of his coat. "This is Neothebaine. Pour yourself a stiff drink when you get home, and add this before you imbibe. The memory eradication procedure should be sufficient to disrupt the neural print containing the target memory. But *this*—" the doctor held the vial up, its amber contents catching the light "—will be sure to wipe any remnants clean. You likely will not remember coming here to *Thanks for the Memories*, and you certainly will not remember either the procedure or this conversation."

"No problem," said Irving, and touched the cochlear-glyph implant behind his left ear, fingertip against the small circle of cool steel. "Exo-memory: remind me to drink Doctor Eduard's date-rape drug when I get home."

His exo-memory whispered back to him, its tone as flat as the steel of the implant: "Yes, Mister Kupfermann."

Unperturbed, the doctor typed something into his flexiscreen. "And finally, your compensation has gone through."

A message appeared on-retina, to Irving's eyes only, in soft green glowing type:

A deposit of 70,500 dollars has been recorded in your UberCoin account.

You've done it! You've hit your savings target. Next steps:

Ask your wife, Ondine Drinkwater, out to dinner to an expensive restaurant

At dinner, explain that through your entrepreneurial acumen, you've become highly successful

Making sure to avoid mention of your numerous trips to Thanks for the Memories

As financial security has always been important to Ondine, it is important that you emphasize both your newfound reliability and your considerable wealth

This will convince her to end your trial separation and let you return home to her and your daughter, Eulalie.

Just a glance at the list made him smile. He'd done it. It'd been a long time, it'd been… Well, he wasn't sure how long it had been. None of that mattered now. He was going to be reunited with his wife and daughter.

Irving pushed himself out of the chair and walked out of the room. The doctor was trying to tell him something; he didn't hear a word the man said. He walked through the expansive, marble reception and stepped out of the large double doors at the front of the building. Irving breathed deeply, smile still on his face, squinting under a hot white sun.

It was time for him to come home.

"Irving."

He looked up and there she was: Ondine. Purple eyeshadow, black hair with the fringe cut too short and that soft, glowing skin. She was underdressed in denim pants and a tight leather jacket, but he didn't notice that. She was twenty minutes late, but he didn't think about that, either. All he could think about at that moment was the time, long ago, when he could have leaned over and kissed this beautiful woman, and she would have laughed and let him.

She wasn't laughing now.

"Ondine," he said, smiling despite the expression on her face. He stood up, dropping the gold-trimmed napkin he'd been playing with, and moved around the table to take her chair out.

"I got it Irving, I got it," she said, but he pulled it out anyway.

She treated that with a raised eyebrow and half-smile. "I'm, ah, sorry I'm late." Ondine's voice was rich, throaty. She could be lead singer in a hard rock band. Or the voice-over for a sexy cartoon character.

"Oh, it's nothing, nothing. Wine?"

"No," she said, brusquely. And then, less so: "Not at lunch. I've got to get back to work after this."

"Well," he grimaced, "You couldn't make dinner."

"Be thankful you got lunch," she said, deadpan.

Something twisted in his chest. "Shall we order, then?"

"Maybe. What's this about Irving?" she asked, indicating his clothes with her chin.

He glanced down. The suit was dark-blue, tailor-made, with sharp creases freshly pressed. He wore a white shirt and smoke-blue tie, set with a silver tie-pin that matched the ring on his pinkie finger. He'd shaved his rough beard off, dabbed on some cologne, and tied his unruly curls back in a short ponytail. The restaurant was none other than *The Prince*—the most sought-after dining spot in town. Gold-gilded cutlery, waiters in blood-red jackets, white light glinting through crystal chandeliers, and the soft murmurings of the good and great as they smiled fake smiles at each other and crunched hors d'oeuvres between perfectly symmetrical teeth.

"I'm trying to make an impression," he said.

"You look like an insurance salesman."

"That wasn't the impression I was going for."

"So you're not trying to sell me something?"

"Just a dream."

"Oh Irving," she said. "Spare the schmaltz, buster. It doesn't suit either of us." But she smiled as she said it, and the twisting in Irving's chest loosened a little.

He pointed at her clothes. "Where do you get to work dressed like that? You a roadie now?"

"I work from home, you know that."

"Doing what?"

Her brows furrowed. "Speech therapist, Irving. Same as always; same as I've been doing for the past ten years."

"Yes yes, of course," he lied. "I meant the same sort of speech therapy you used to do."

She narrowed her eyes. "Right. Sure. The same *sort of* speech therapy as I always did."

Irving carefully hid his embarrassment. "And Eulalie—how is she? Still the smartest kid in class?"

Ondine paused, permitting her irritation to ebb. "Yes. Her teacher thinks she'll be able to skip fourth grade. She…" Ondine trailed off, looked down at her purple-painted nails.

"She?"

She sighed and looked back at him. "She misses you."

"I miss her too," he said, and it was the truest thing he'd said in a long time.

Things went well after that. For a little while, anyway.

Ondine agreed that she may as well stay for lunch, as she was there, after all. So they ate. And it was good. He ordered real meat and Ondine said *oh no*, eyes like circles, but he insisted and they shared a minute steak. They agreed neither of them had eaten meat since they honeymooned in Fiji, and then laughed about getting kicked out of the resort. They'd taken magic mushrooms and—in the throes of a sublime mind-and-body-buzz—broken into the kids' play centre and pasted glitter all over their naked bodies. Ondine had then convinced Irving that they were Moroccan glow worms looking for a burrow. A groundskeeper caught them an hour later, digging a hole in a golf course green with their hands.

Irving excused himself to the bathroom after they'd finished the main. He checked the stalls to make sure he was alone, then put a finger to his implant. "Exo-memory: I want on-retina recall dialled to maximum while I have lunch with Ondine Drinkwater. I don't want to forget a single detail about our lives together—not a detail. Understood?"

"Understood, Mister Kupfermann," whispered the implant. "I am required to remind you that you have previously ordered me to keep all memory prompts down to Level One: *only in case of emergency or direct request.* You said, and I quote, 'I don't need that shit haunting me anymore.'"

Irving looked at himself in the mirror. He didn't recognize the guy in there. The shiny blue suit and the pale, sweaty skin and the ponytail and that ridiculous tie-pin he bought for ten grand at a glittering store full of smug service staff. He looked like a douche. Felt like one, too. The only thing that remained familiar was the nose. Big hook nose that Ondine charitably called 'Roman.' Combined with the bags under his eyes he didn't feel very Roman, right then. He looked like a vulture, picking over the carcass of his marriage.

"Bloody hell," he said, to himself. "Way to ruin the mood, arsehole."

"Sorry, Mister Kupfermann?" murmured the implant.

"Nothing, it's nothing."

"Mister Kupfermann?"

"*What?*" he hissed.

"Are you sure you want your exo-memory turned up to maximum?"

He looked away from the mirror. "You heard me. I want to remember everything."

D essert came. She had ice cream; he had coffee, strong and black. Ondine was quiet, biting her bottom lip as she ran her finger slow around the edge of the porcelain bowl. Irving waited for her to say what she wanted to say.

Eventually she did. "So where did all this—" she waved a hand at the room, "—come from?"

"Hope, Ondine, it came from hope," he said, and reached across the table, putting his hand on hers. She didn't take hers away. "Hope can be the irrational desire for a miracle, despite all evidence to the contrary. But that's not the sort of hope I have. Mine is based on the reality of what we had together, Ondine, and the concrete steps I've taken to reclaim my life. I'm successful now, like you always said I could be. I can be someone you depend on. I'm someone *you* can build realistic hopes around. All this is a manifestation of that—not an idle promise, but a promise kept, to myself, that I was worthy enough to get you back."

Ondine was silent for a time, a strange expression on her face. "You been practicing that?"

"No."

His exo-memory typed: **You have been practicing: seven times this morning and eleven times last night. Twelve in front of the mirror, five while walking in a circle around the kitchen table, once while you were on the toilet.**

He rubbed his eye, annoyed at the contradictory blurb in the corner of his vision. "Yes. Okay yes, I've been practicing." He looked at her. "How did I do?"

"You did fine."

"But?"

For the next few weeks, every time he smelled the bitter scent of strong black coffee, his mind would time travel backwards, and he'd see her as she was then. Something alive and real against the forced elegance of the restaurant and the manufactured glamour of its patrons. He would remember every detail: her leather jacket, creased with decades of loving use; her smooth skin a perfection no amount of genetic manipulation could replicate; and the sadness in her eyes as she first realised, and then rejected, his intentions.

"*But*, Irving," she said, "I'm happy you're back on your feet again. Truly happy, I mean that. And if you want to start seeing Eulalie, then I'll agree to that. Slow at first, with me there, at my place. She wants to see her father again and I want you back in her life." Ondine sighed. "But you and I Irving? That's ancient history. We had a good run. A few good years followed by a couple of terrible ones. It's how these things end all the time, every day: in bitterness and regret. There's no hope left for us, just the rubble."

He gripped her hand harder. "But Ondine. You're not listening. This restaurant isn't an accident. This is who I am now. I'm successful,

I'm a winner—I'm all those things you wanted me to be."

She pulled her hand from his. The softness left her voice. "It isn't about money."

"Bullshit," he said, loud enough for heads turn their way. He lowered it again. "*Bullshit*. It's all you ever talked about."

"That's not true."

"It is precisely true. Always money: money for the rent, for holidays, organic food, fancy medicine, better schools, better fucking everything. You want me to play it back for you right now? I still have all those memories."

As he spoke the exo-memory popped up on-retina, taking some of the heat out of his accusations: **I have many examples of Ondine criticizing you for other reasons. Would you like me to list them?**

Ondine didn't get angry. Instead she sighed, pushing her two scoops of fifty-dollar ice cream absently with her spoon. "I'm sure you could play back those fights. I remember all that, too. And you're right, it was wrong of me to put it that way. When you're angry you reach for the cheap shots, and they were cheap shots. But it was never about that."

"Then what was it about?"

She looked up from the bowl, her face tinged with regret. "It was about ambition, Irving. We used to dream and plan together, about our family, our careers. But you fell into this rut and never got out. You gave up on nano-tech, neglected your daughter. Me. God Irving—you spent more time betting on weather patterns and drinking gin with your pals down at the bowls club than you ever did on trying to make a career. You were just going through the motions of life, constantly looking over the horizon, waiting for your ship to come in."

"That's not true."

Ondine Drinkwater is correct. She encouraged you on 103

occasions to pursue your career. You spent 2,428 hours researching and betting on weather patterns, whereas you spent 41 hours applying for jobs in the nano-technology field. An image appeared above the words, of Ondine, concerned expression on her face. If he gave his exo-memory the command the image would become a playback of Ondine, from many years before, encouraging him to pursue his career. He didn't give the command.

The present-day Ondine continued talking, her voice overlapping with the on-retina accusations. "Remember when you won the University Prize for your thesis on nano-technology and desertification? You could have parlayed that into a career—you had some great companies offer you an internship." She shook her head. "But you said you didn't want to work for free. You wanted the big bucks, straight away, so you turned them all down."

He creased his forehead.

Ondine Drinkwater is incorrect about the University Prize. No record of receiving an award for your thesis exists in your exo-memory. Ondine Drinkwater's recollections of job offers are correct. You rejected job offers from four different companies.

"I never won a university prize."

Her eyes narrowed. "What are you talking about, 'never won'?"

Something itched in his mind. He couldn't remember it. Unless…

"You don't remember do you?"

He set his jaw. "I don't remember because it never happened."

Ondine sighed through her nose. "It was one of the best nights we ever had, Irving. We got wasted at the reception at the chancellor's house; we danced and danced while all the guests just stood around staring at us. Then we snuck off and did it in one of the spare rooms. The chancellor's wife found us the next morning, passed out on the bed. You were naked except for a smoking jacket you'd stolen from the chancellor's wardrobe." She shook her head, half-smiling at the memory. "She didn't even blink. Just told us she was happy someone enjoyed the party, and then cooked us omelettes for breakfast."

Irving was silent.

"How can you not remember that, Irving? And what did you mean before when you said you *still had all those memories* of us fighting?"

"I…" He broke eye contact, looked down into the black of his coffee.

She shook her head. "I knew it. I *knew* it. You're selling memories, aren't you? That's what all this—" she dropped her spoon into the ice cream "—bullshit is. This room filled with wankers, that ridiculous suit. It's another get rich quick scheme, isn't it?"

"No. No it's not another scheme."

You have previously discussed—on twenty-eight occasions— getting rich quick through selling memories, Mister Kupfermann. Your bank account currently has over fifteen million dollars, which you have claimed, in conversation with others, has come from memory sales. While your exo-memory has no direct recordings of you selling memory, it does have twenty-three instances of you approaching a memory acquisition business. It is possible you had these sections of your memory wiped during the procedure. I have scanned the two years since you separated from Ondine and can find no other possible source of your current wealth.

"Okay," Irving said, fists clenching against the tabletop, "Okay." He breathed out slowly. "Okay, yeah, I sold some memories. Just to get ahead. Get my life back together." He tried to reach for her again, but she jerked her hand away like he'd just offered her a dead rat. "I did it for us, Ondine, for our family."

"Oh Irving, you and your bullshit. Every scheme was always

for the family." She threw one hand up, exasperated. "I don't get it. Why would you sell something so good? If your goal was getting back together with me, why would you sell one of the best moments we shared?"

He said: "I don't know," but he did know. Even if he couldn't remember the procedures, he understood the pricing structure behind them perfectly. The most emotionally potent memories always fetched the most money—that and their *uniqueness*. Wiping them from one's own memory, so the rich client was the sole proprietor. "I didn't see it as selling memories. I saw it as an investment in a long, happy future of new memories. Once we're back together, I'll never have to sell another."

"More bullshit." She started to get up from her seat. "And I'm done listening to it."

"Wait," he got up from his seat as well. "Eulalie—I do want to see our daughter. That's not bullshit." As the words came out of his mouth he felt the truth of them, and was relieved.

She rubbed her forehead, but he'd found the right nerve. She sat back down, gingerly, on the edge of the seat.

He took a deep breath.

His exo-memory assumed the pause was an invitation for further information. **Eulalie, your daughter, eight years old.** A picture of his daughter's face appeared above the writing. Hazel eyes like his, black hair like her mother's, a cheeky grin all her own. **Eulalie goes to North Fitzroy Montessori Primary School, her favourite colour is purple with blue spots, and she has a pet goldfish called Squeak-and-Bubble.**

"Are you reading something on-retina?" asked Ondine, sharply.

He refocused on her. "No."

"Bullshit. Same old Irving. Even now, in your grand attempt at winning me back, you can't help but put the freewave on. Is there a cricket game on today?"

"I'm not watching the cricket. I'm not watching anything."

"I don't believe you. It was ever thus—zoned out on some stupid live-feed every time I tried to talk to you."

He felt his face going red. Part anger, part embarrassment. "That's not true."

It is mostly true: you watched sports, betting markets, or Chinese Kung Fu films on-retina during 81% of your conversations with Ondine.

His fingernails dug into the palms of his hand.

Ondine looked at him for ten long seconds before she said: "Do you remember Luna Park?"

It was a test. And it was immediately clear it was a test he was going to fail. "Umm."

"*Do you remember Luna Park*, Irving?"

"Yes." He licked his lips. "Of course."

"Don't lie to me."

"I'm not lying—I do remember Luna Park."

No recording of Luna Park exists in your exo-memory.

"Ah—*stop!*"

Her eyes went a stone-cold shade of bitter. "I will *not* stop."

"No no, not you. It's my exo-memory, it—"

"I knew it."

He hit the table. Cutlery danced, heads turned his way again and a middle-aged man in a red jacket suddenly appeared next to the table.

"Is everything all right here, sir?"

"Yes, yes," said Irving. "We're fine."

Ondine said to the maître d': "It's not a problem. I'm leaving," and got up from her seat.

"I think that would be best," replied the maître d'.

Irving reached out his hand to her, begging. "No Ondine, please don't leave."

Ondine looked down at him, eyes glistening. "You need help, Irving. Professional help. You're stuck in an endless loop of self-denial. You need to find a way out."

She walked away.

"Sir," said the head waiter, interposing himself between Irving and the exit as he rose to follow his wife. Irving's lip curled in anger, but before he could barge past, the man spoke, voice an urgent whisper. "Sir, you are making a *scene*."

"Fuck you," Irving hissed. He pushed past, and jogged from the restaurant, red-faced, as everyone stared.

He couldn't see Ondine when he burst out onto the street. Squinting under the bone-white sun, spinning around, trying to glimpse her receding form in the heat shimmer rising from the sidewalk. His eyes watered from the sun. The sun: that's what he tried to tell himself, anyway, until he sold the memory a few weeks later.

Irving stood in the huge clown mouth that formed the entrance of Luna Park, jaws three times as wide as he was tall. Eulalie waited, looking up at him, a cloud of pink fairy floss in her left hand. She was trying to tell him something, but he had a hand up, trying to stop her from speaking while he read the weather reports on-retina. He'd placed a series of bets on temperature and precipitation ranges in south-eastern China, and the official results were just coming in.

"Fuck it!" he yelled.

"Daddy?"

"Fuck fuck fuck."

"But daddy—"

"Not now Eulalie."

"But daddy I want to go—"

"Not now dammit!" he screamed.

Eulalie jumped, dropping the floss to the ground. Tears welled instantly.

Ondine had walked ahead, not realizing that he and Eulalie had stopped. Now she returned just to hear the end of him yelling. She seemed to be in shock for a few seconds, standing there, her smooth skin glowing in the blinking neon backwash of the amusement park.

"Jesus Irving," she said, picking her daughter up.

"Quiet," he hissed, eyes unfocussed as the massacre of his wagers scrolled down on-retina.

"Quiet? No. I'm not…"

He tuned her out, her words background static to failure's sting. He clenched his teeth as the news got worse and worse, and as Ondine's criticisms started to cut through his concentration.

"Enough!" he yelled. "Enough of your nagging. Enough of your complaints."

She put a hand over her daughter's ear. "Not in front of Eulalie."

"Eulalie," he sneered, focusing now on wife and daughter. "I hate that name. Where did you get it? 'Top ten hippest new names for children' in the Huffington Post?"

Ondine's mouth popped open, struggling to get out a reply.

He didn't let her.

"No! Time for me to speak now. Time. For. Me. To. Speak." He jabbed a finger at her with each word. "You never support my business decisions. You never listen to me. All I get from you is scorn and derision. You didn't even let me have a say in our own daughter's name. Eulalie? What sort of ridiculous name is that!?"

The steam started to leave his delivery as he watched the reaction of his wife and daughter. Eulalie, head buried in her mother's shoulder, sobbing. Ondine, her perfect skin creased with contempt.

"You d-don't understand," he stuttered, his rage train coming off its rails.

"I understand Irving."

"Don't look at me like that."

"Lose another bet, I take it?"

"It's not that simple."

"Oh it is Irving, it is exactly that simple," she said, her voice a terrifying calm. "It's the most uncomplicated thing in the world. You're lazy."

"Don't."

"Greedy."

"Don't."

"Resentful."

"Not in front of Eulalie."

"Cruel, isn't it? Almost as bad as telling your own daughter that you hate her name. Well, I've needed to be cruel for a long time, but I've been a coward. Not anymore. I'm going to do what I needed to do a year ago, and I'm doing here, in front of your daughter, so you understand that it is final."

Eulalie had taken her head from her mother's shoulder and was staring up at her as she spoke.

His eyes flicked to his daughter, then back to his wife. "Don't. I'm sorry—"

"Goodbye Irving."

She walked away. Only his daughter looked back. Watching him over her mother's shoulder, eyes filled with tears.

Irving watched them leave, hands hanging limply at his sides. Nowhere else to go, he wandered back into Luna Park. Into the cacophony of tinny music on a maddening, endless cycle, into the smell of fairy floss and sweat and machine grease, and the clown, swallowing him, while—

WARNING WARNING WARNING: these memories are property of the Mobius Group. Report immediately to your nearest Thanks for the Memories franchise for memory realignment.

Bleep bleep bleep bleep

WARNING WARNING WARNING: these memories are property of the Mobius Group. Report immediately to your nearest Thanks for the Memories franchise for memory realignment.

—bleep bleep bleep bleep—

"No." Irving woke himself with the moan. "No." He switched off the alarm and dismissed the message flashing on-retina.

He lay back on the bed, stared at the off-white ceiling. Moonlight and street light ebbed through the slatted window. The hum of the building's hydrogen generator drifted up from below. He took control of his breathing, the rise and fall of his chest slowing.

"No."

The ubiquitous double happiness ideogram split in two as the doors opened for Irving. The room inside was gloomy, thick with incense. A cymbal and discordant pipes of traditional Chinese music played softly from hidden speakers, and overhead red lanterns swung slightly on a breeze Irving couldn't feel. A young Chinese man in a traditional straight-collared suit sat behind a darkwood reception desk.

"Um," said Irving. "My exo-memory told me I had an appointment."

The receptionist stood and bowed. "Mister Kupfermann. Omissioner Zau is waiting for you. Follow me."

Irving tried to bow back, but the young man had already disappeared down the dim, red-tinted corridor. Irving was shown through a dark redwood door carved with stylistic, Eastern dragons with large, wild eyes. The receptionist closed the door behind Irving, leaving him in an even darker room.

It took his eyes a moment to adjust. Within the gloom lay a traditional study with dark, wood-panelled walls, interspersed with red scrolls marked with calligraphy. There were white-and-blue porcelain pots sitting on plinths; leather-bounds books along the back wall; a golden bust of some old Chinese guy with a receding hairline in one corner; and in the middle of it all, an even older Chinese man sitting cross-legged on a woven mat with arms crossed, hands hidden in dark blue silk sleeves.

The old man had a strand of grey hair clinging to his chin. His eyes were closed.

Irving hesitated, wondering for a moment whether he'd caught the old bugger sleeping.

"Kupfermann *xiansheng*," the old man intoned, in a thick Chinese accent. "Please, sit."

Irving jumped a little. On second glance the man's eyes were open. Sparkling slivers in a lined old face, fixed on him.

Irving stutter-stepped forward. "Omissioner Zau?"

The old man bowed.

"I-I don't remember making this appointment."

"But you have a problem," said the Omissioner. It wasn't a question.

"I've—ah—yeah. Yeah, I've got a problem."

"Sit."

Irving sat, cross-legged, three feet from the Omissioner.

"Tea?"

Irving shook his head.

The Omissioner waited, face inscrutable. It took Irving a long half-minute to realise the old man was waiting for him to speak. He cleared his throat, irritated by the incense. "It's a—it's about a memory I've sold to an extraction service."

Still the old man waited.

Irving continued: "It—the memory—is coming back. And I…" He paused. It felt like he was making confession. "I'm worried about others I've sold. I think things may have got a little out of control—I had this life with my wife. I mean *lunch*—lunch with my wife. She mentioned this—this incident in Luna Park, which I couldn't remember at first, but which I've started to dream about."

A hand appeared from within the Omissioner's sleeve. "Your memory pin please, Mister Kupfermann."

Irving's mouth tightened.

The old man waited, gnarled hand extended.

Irving sighed. He put his finger to his cochlear implant and murmured the password. A soft *click* sounded and the memory pin popped out of the steel. He plucked it between thumb and forefinger and handed it to the Omissioner.

Zau unclipped a dark green bracelet from his wrist and unfurled it, revealing a latest-model flexiscreen. One foot square, paper-thin, soft-glowing green. The Omissioner placed the memory pin on it and hid his hands back within his sleeves. The ancient lines of the old man's face were lit up by reflected green as ideograms and graphs flowed across the screen.

After a minute of looking through the data, the man's disposition changed completely. He took his hands from his sleeves, stopped squinting, and pulled a pack of cigarettes from a hidden pocket. "Dear oh dear. So you're a Johnny," he said, in a suddenly broad Australian accent. He lit his cigarette with a chrome lighter and snapped it shut, throwing it on the floor in front of him.

"A what?" asked Irving.

The Omissioner blew a cloud of smoke upwards. "You know—a memory hooker, an auto-amnesiac. Selling off those crystal-clear, seminal life moments to the ruling class—a Johnny."

Irving paused, trying to get past the incongruity of the broad Australian accent coming out of the old Chinese guy's mouth. "What? What is this—what game are you playing here?"

"Whatever do you mean?" the old man replied, with a half-smile that suggested he knew exactly what Irving meant.

Irving pointed an open hand at the room. "This game."

"This," said the Omissioner, letting his gaze roam around the gloom. "This is all part of the *Mysteries of the East* surcharge." When he said *Mysteries of the East* his accent switched, for a moment, from Australian back to Chinese.

"Mysteries of the East?"

"Mysteries of the East, mate. Rich bastards don't come here just for science; they want a mythic flourish from an ancient civilization. So I charge them extra for their ignorance, and give the same service they'd get from any other memory expert."

"But—but everyone says the role of the Omissioner is an ancient Chinese tradition."

"Oh yeah, sure mate. Thousands of years ago China had the Omissioners. Their sole responsibility was to remind the emperor of important traditions or precedents." Zau took a drag on his smoke, blew the smoke upwards. "But many other cultures had something similar. In pre-Islamic Arabia, people known as *Rawis* were attached to poets as official memorizers. For centuries the Jews had the *tannaim*, who memorized oral law. All cultures, more or less, have had memory experts attached to the elite. The advent of the printing press, books, and libraries changed all that: they democratized exo-memory for the masses. For a couple of centuries, anyway. Until the invention of the cochlear-glyph and the subsequent epidemic of memory decline that has made good recall the rarest of commodities. These days, the virtuosos of natural memory like me—" an ironic grin touched Zau's lips "—well mate, I'm the darling of the elite."

Zau pointed at Irving with the end of his cigarette. "But you ain't the elite. You ain't a repeat customer. You're a Johnny. Your wealth has come from selling off your personal history, right?"

"Well—"

"And you're here to ask me to fix the dog's breakfast you've made of the inside of your head, yes?"

"Well, yes, there's this—"

"Then you're here to ask me to fix the unfixable. I see people like you all the time. Bloody idiots, one and all. You got no other source of income, right?"

Irving started to deny it, out of instinct. But he relented and shook his head *no*.

"Then I can't prescribe a way out of this for you. To fix the damage you've done, to reclaim some of the fragments of these lost memories, I'll need time. Months. But even if you could afford me, the memories I'd reconstruct would mostly be copyrighted. So that's no good." He took another drag, glittering eyes fixed on Irving. "You could purchase the memories of others in order to improve your overall brain function, of course. But I'm not a butcher. I don't trade in the prime cuts of the personal histories of the desperate."

Irving decided to focus on the only part of the little speech that could help him. "How would other people's memories help?"

"You don't know?" asked the Omissioner, with a hint of surprise.

"It's—" Irving rubbed at his eye, he knew this, "—on the tip of my tongue."

"You don't remember. Of course you don't. How could you, after all the things those bastards have done to you?" The Omissioner had let his anger show, for a moment, but he stubbed it out with his cigarette in the ashtray in front of him.

Zau took a long breath, and then said: "When you sell a memory to the ruling class, you're not simply selling one of your experiences. I mean, that's part of it—having their subconscious integrate someone else's experience as their own. The human brain is a wonderful thing isn't it? Takes a distinct event from someone else's life and—with a little nudging from technology and a good night's sleep—absorbs it as one of its own.

"But what you're *really selling* is the vitality and emotion of that experience. The power of these memories is such that when you experience them, they increase the strength and number of synaptic connections in your neural pathways. The rich need this, more than anyone, because nearly all of them are constantly editing their histories. For *everything*: relationships, jobs, family, making their lives seem superior to that of regular people. Bloody hell—some of them have a bad day they'll erase it and replace it with a good one. In the end you get a kind of mass delusion among the one percent—half their lives are based on vivid memories they've bought from Johnnies like you. So they become ever more dependent on top-of-the-line exo-memory to fabricate visual recordings and forge a consistent life narrative. In turn, they become less and less reliant on their own brains to encode new memories, and unused, those pathways atrophy."

Zau took a long drag on his smoke and blew out a long slow cloud, watching as it curled its way to the ceiling. "So, there it is, mate. That's why they pay so handsomely for your memories. Not just for the experience, but to repair brain damage."

Irving felt the dread, sitting on his chest, making it hard for him to breathe. "How bad, Zau? How much have I lost?"

The Omissioner pointed at Irving's memory pin sitting on the flexiscreen. "I can't tell you what memories you've lost. Not at a glance, anyway."

"What can you tell me then?"

"How many memories you've sold."

Irving's breath came harder. "Well then, how many?"

"Two hundred and nineteen."

It felt like a punch in the chest. "Fuck me."

"Hmmm."

"That's bad, isn't it?"

"Mate. It's as bad as it gets."

"Can—can I buy memories, like you said, help repair the damage?"

The Omissioner shook his head. "You're remembering for them wholesale, but they're selling it retail. If you've got no income other than selling memories, then you're nothing more than a snake eating its own tail."

"And you?"

"No. I'm not going re-craft your life into some sort of delusion— that's what mercenaries like *Thanks for the Memories* do. That's simply replacing one form of mental illness—dementia —for another— psychosis. My methods are more sophisticated than those butchers. They're also much more expensive."

"Can you do anything for me?" asked Irving, voice strained.

Omissioner Zau seemed oblivious. "Prescribe you Alzheimer's medication. It'll stabilize your condition, maybe even allow for a partial improvement. You'll never be the way you were, but so long as you don't sell anymore memories you should lead a relatively normal life."

"Relatively?"

"Well—like I said—you have low-grade Alzheimer's. You're mildly intellectually impaired."

"What the fuck?"

Zau paused for a moment. "Apologies. I tend to be less polite with people who won't remember my rudeness." The old man held out his cigarettes. "Fag?"

Irving shook his head.

"Drink?"

"Yeah," Irving said, with a sigh. "Yeah, I could use one."

The old man hopped up, far more sprightly than Irving would have guessed, and disappeared through a bead curtain in a dark corner of the room. As he did so, Irving saw that the Omissioner had no cochlear-glyph implant behind his ear. It had been a long time since he'd met someone unplugged.

Zau returned soon after with a bottle of amber liquid and two tumblers. The Omissioner settled down again across from Irving, poured them each three fingers. Irving downed his in a single hit. It burned his throat, but not too much, and relieved a little of the tension in his chest.

"I could go back to work," said Irving. "Nano-tech pays well, if you stick with it. I could make enough to afford even you." He smiled weakly.

Zau poured Irving another whisky. "No."

"No?" What smile Irving had faded.

"Impossible."

"Why?"

The Omissioner finished his whisky, eyes on Irving. "Imagination, that's why. If you went back to work you'd be largely reliant on exo-memory, and exo-memory never made a new discovery or developed a new idea. It doesn't have the rich associations of a natural memory, cannot accrete the layers of knowledge interacting with each other, which give birth to an original idea. Memory is an *act of creativity*—the ability to form connections between disparate memories, build something new with them, and hurl it into the future so it becomes a poem, or a dance, or a nano-tech innovation.

"And you Irving? You've pretty much lost your ability to create future memory. You used to be good at nano-tech? That's gone now. You can't get that back."

Irving stared at the glass in his hand. He gave a sigh that included his shoulders, and said: "Well, I want to keep what I've got left, including the one I have of my daughter." His throat closed a little when he said *daughter*.

"Sorry mate. But you won't be able to do even that. You keep remembering copyrighted memories, you'll get three years in jail and a fine so big you'll be out on the street." Zau waved his cigarette absently in the air. "You could leave the country, if you're that desperate. A few countries still don't have memory copyright. Belize has great beaches."

Irving looked up at him. "Belize?"

"Belize."

"Fuck Belize."

Zau shrugged.

"Fuck Belize right in the arse."

"That's probably overdoing it."

Irving picked his whisky up, and then put it down again, un-sipped. "What are my other options?"

"Options, chief?" Zau said, eyes narrowing. "You're all out of options. You're a fly, struggling in their web. Being aware of this fact is largely irrelevant. They'll get what they want from you, one way or another. You resist, you'll go to jail, and the judgment against you will include enforced reclamation of that stolen property—" Zau placed a finger on his own temple "—sitting there inside your head. And the government ain't as careful extracting memories as the recall companies. It can get messy."

Irving was silent. He let the words sting him, let the sting linger.

"Unless…" Zau trailed off. His eyes bored right into Irving, searching for something.

"Unless?"

The Omissioner took a long drag of his cigarette. "Unless you settle for the only thing you really can get now: revenge."

"Revenge? Against who?"

"Mate. Against the mercenaries that built this edifice of mnemonic servitude to the rich. Against the recall companies."

Irving stroked his long, curved nose. Revenge was such an exhausting pastime. "Maybe. I don't know."

"What else have you got?" asked the Omissioner. "Your family and career are gone."

Irving narrowed his eyes. "What was that about you being rude, again?"

"I'm just being straight with you mate."

Irving was silent as he turned it all over in his mind. Ondine, looking at him, her face creased with contempt and Eulalie, water-blurred eyes, uncomprehending at the creeping neglect of his fatherhood.

Eulalie.

If he could have been a good father, all the other failures wouldn't have mattered. Everything else was bullshit. If only.

And he thought about the recall companies. Yeah—them, most of all. With their spacious, marble receptions and employees with perfect white teeth and franchises popping up in every city, every suburb even. On the back of *his* dreams, *his* experiences, his *essence*, commodified as a plaything for the lucky rich. They were the ones who had done all this, brought him to this, reduced him to this. Tore his family apart, for profit.

Irving fixed his gaze on Zau. "Maybe you're right. Maybe revenge is exactly what I want."

The Omissioner leaned towards him. "Yes. Good. Now, if this

works out, you won't remember doing it."

"Perfect."

"From a certain perspective, yes. I'll fix it so you won't remember this conversation. You also won't remember that *Thanks for the Memories* stole your life, or that you got revenge for all they've done. What point then, Irving? How does this act exist, if you cannot remember it?"

Irving downed the last of his whiskey, cleared his throat. "Let's not get metaphysical here, Omissioner. The tree still falls in the forest. The world still exists outside the boundaries of my skull. And if I make these motherfuckers pay, well they are going to pay."

Zau nodded, eyes twinkling. "Good. You're going to have to go to *Thanks for the Memories*, have the propriety product you are re-remembering wiped, *and* sell them one more legit memory."

Irving shook his head immediately. "No. I'm done with it. They can take back Luna Park, but no more. I've lost too much of myself—you've just got through telling me I'm going to end up a retard."

"Dementia."

"Whatever. I've done enough damage. Time to draw a line under it."

"Just one more mate. It's the only way to do it. This lunch you had recently, where your wife talked about Luna Park, it has to go."

"Why?"

"Because it is part of a mnemonic loop that will keep sending you back in time to Luna Park, and forward in time to me, here. We need to snip it out, cover our tracks."

Irving opened his mouth to say no, but the image came of Ondine, looking at him from across the table, her expression a mixture of sadness and pity. He rubbed at his eyes with his palms. "Yeah. Maybe that is one memory I could do without."

"Good mate, good," said the Omissioner, eyes shining. "Now, they'll be uploading more than a visual recording from your pin and a memory print from your cerebral cortex. They'll be uploading a project I've been working on for a long time. An offensively expensive virus I've commissioned, one that will bypass—"

Irving held up hand. "I don't care what it is, Omissioner, just so long as it works."

"Oh, it will work. When they take your memory, the virus will plug straight into the *Kandel-Yu* machine. It will ensure that every customer after you experiences an immediate decline in the release of certain proteins crucial to long-term memory formation. They will suffer anterograde amnesia—everything that happens after their trip to *Thanks for the Memories* will be lost."

"They'll still have memory pins."

"Yes, yes, they'll still have exo-memory. That's why it's such a cracker—it won't become immediately apparent. Not before hundreds, even thousands have been exposed. Those infected will be increasingly reliant on a computer to tell them what day it is, where they work, whether or not they ate lunch, who their new friends are, the names of their children. They'll keep going back to recall companies, buying more memories, infecting more *Kandel-Yu* machines. We do this right, the whole system of memories trickling up to the rich, of the desperate selling off chunks of their own soul, will be broken."

Irving laughed without humour. "And here I was thinking I'd never achieve anything in this life."

Zau watched Irving through the glass, doing a stunned kind of shuffle, following his vulture nose down the sidewalk.

"Your insider at the recall centre," said Zau. "She chose well."

"Yes," replied Qiang from behind the reception desk. "She knows a hopeless case when she sees one."

"He's better than hopeless." Zau continued to watch Irving walk down the street. "He's the utterly irredeemable still yearning for redemption."

Qiang waited until Irving had disappeared from sight. "Mister Kupfermann said you'd come to an agreement and that he wasn't to be charged for the session."

Zau looked over at him. "Charge him triple."

"Triple?"

"Yeah. He won't remember what it's for, and I've told his exo-memory to hide it from him. Plus," the old man smiled, his eyes sparkling, "it's for a good cause."

The doors to *Thanks for the Memories* wouldn't open. Distracted by the glare of the sun, Irving had missed the red neon sign flashing CLOSED next to the entrance.

"Exo-memory, why is *Thanks for the Memories* closed? What day is it?"

"Thursday," whispered the implant. "A media release by the parent company, released nine days ago, stated that this franchise was not located in a profitable area, and it was consolidating its branches to maximize financial returns for shareholders. However, multiple sources on the freewave have contradicted this, theorizing that the closure is related to several recent high-profile cases of amnesia. Shall I put the most-read article from each perspective up on-retina?"

"No no, I don't care about the details."

Irving pursed his lips. This was a nuisance. Just a couple more sales he would hit the target he'd set himself. Fifteen million and he'd take Ondine out for dinner; reveal his newfound wealth and success. Just a couple more sales were all he needed to win his wife and daughter back.

"Exo-memory."

"Yes, Mister Kupfermann?"

"Give me directions to the nearest *Thanks for the Memories* franchise."

JACK'S FINE DINING

2038

Minh Nguyen stood in the shadows of the tenements, watching the endless ocean, this vast leviathan. Breathless, no air sifting between the towering slums. Bats beat a leathery rhythm across the sky, over the harbour; dusk approaching. Shoulder pressed against the hot brown brick, Minh was unfussed by the heat, sweat slicked, not bothered, except by the large black flies that bit and pestered in this desolate southern land. The bites of the black flies never brought the blood disease, not like home, so he breathed in the stilled thick air, smiled at his fortune, and made his way to the soup kitchen.

Steeple, cross at an awkward angle. Minh had walked down to the church for a service when he'd first arrived. None of that, anymore, said the gruff Australian that ran the kitchen, no interest. Bread, not circuses, he'd said.

Minh walked past the sallow men women children lined outside, patient tired faces, looping around the back of old sandstone scarred with graffiti. Black tags Minh couldn't read, hieroglyphs of empty rebellion.

His stomach sank when he saw Dave and Hassan, huddled together, in the line, sharing a cigarette. Idle, mean men who looked around at the world with eyes narrowed, jaws set. End of the month, they'd be after a mark; someone they thought easy. Lately those narrowed eyes had been falling on Minh.

Dave looked up at the last moment, opened his mouth to talk, but Minh rushed by, head down, and pushed through the creaking wooden back door.

Into the former vestry, now kitchen. Inside, Jack Sullivan was hunched over the stovetop, peering into a huge pot of soup, sweat on his pale, blue-veined temple. Tommy Jandamaara stood at a long high table pressed against the wall, cutting vegetables. Both were tall and lean, like most men in this country. Tommy, net over his wiry salt and pepper hair, had a cigarette stuck to his bottom lip, unlit while he prepped the food.

The space was scrubbed clean, cramped, hot, filled with the scent of fresh bread. Minh's mouth watered, and on cue, Aurora burst through the door to the eating hall.

"Minh!" she smiled at him and the hunger flutter in his belly was forgotten. Jack's daughter, yet her personality seemed not to share a shred of his DNA. Lithe, alive, used her whole body to laugh, the whole of her heart when she served meals. At her insistence, customers would be seated at a table when served, like a proper restaurant. Fifteen, though she seemed older; the young woman unaffected by it all, the neighbourhood, its residents moving through the heat haze like ghosts. The rusting cars in front yards the smashed street lights the distant sirens. She floated through the detritus, smile dazzling, and the world responded. The ghosts came out of their heat daze, and smiled back, said her name. An invocation on the lips, *Aurora*.

Aurora took a tray she'd set aside and placed it on the table. Bowl of aromatic tomato soup and crusty, still-steaming bread. "Eat up, handsome."

Minh glanced over at Jack; the chef looking over now, face weathered, hair close-cropped. His left hand, holding a long steel ladle, was missing the last two fingers, courtesy of the war. Didn't seem to slow him down at all. "You heard the boss," he said, smiling at his daughter, only thing that seemed to give him a spark.

Minh nodded to Aurora. "Thank you, big sister."

"I'm ten years younger than you," she replied, eyebrow raised.

"Oh. This is a sign of respect."

"Ah. Sorry. Well." She looked him up and down. "You look pale. So, eat your lunch *little brother*, it's gonna be a long night."

He nodded and set about the meal with relish.

First time he'd come, Minh'd gone to the kitchen to try to pay, use his Australia Card—a chip implanted in the tip of the little finger—after finally being assigned it days before. Jack grunted, waved him away. Minh insisted. Jack told him not be daft. Minh offered to wash the dishes. Aurora looked amused throughout the exchange and Tommy, standing over the sink, handed him a dirty dish and wet rag and said: "Shit brother, sure." Job didn't pay, of course, but Minh didn't care. Couldn't stand the idle days, empty, in his hot dim claustrophobic apartment.

Minh mopped the last of the soup with the last of the bread as Jack said: "Righty-O. Time to get to work. Open the doors."

Two hours later, shift done, Aurora, Jack and Tommy were seated at one of the scratched faux wood tables. Tommy swearing and smoking, Aurora laughing and talking, Jack sipping brandy out of a small red glass tumbler.

Minh, dishes done, loitered in the doorway, not sure whether to join them or slip out.

"Minh! Are you hiding?" said Aurora, broad smile, signalling him over. "Sit, please," she said, pulling up the chair next to her. He did so, self-conscious, the way one might feel sitting next to a celebrity.

"Dad," she said, looking over at Jack. "I've been thinking about Minh's suggestion."

"Huh?" Jack, red rheumy-eyed, looked up from his drink.

"About turning this place into a proper restaurant."

Jack coughed into his hand. His glass drummed *rat-a-tat-tat* as he placed it down on the table top. "This is a soup kitchen."

"Universal income changes things, dad. I reckon people have the means to pay." She held up both hands, as though trying to stay her father's thoughts. "Still cheap though, cheaper than anything nearby."

"'Card's not enough to live on, not even close. They come here when they're out of credit, Aurora."

"Bullshit," grunted Tommy around his cigarette.

"Language," said Jack.

"He's right, Dad. We're packed all the time. Beginning *and* end of the month. They come here because the meals are better than anything in the neighbourhood."

"Your food is excellent, uncle" said Minh.

"—and if people can't pay," said Aurora, with emphasis, over a brewing objection from her father, "we won't charge them. We can absorb those costs. Look."

Aurora bent to one side, long brown hair falling over her shoulder, pulled her old model notepad from her backpack, and blipped it on. "Here," she said, placing the screen in front of her dad. "I did a business plan."

"You need to focus on keeping your scholarship."

Aurora rolled her eyes. "I'm at the top of my class. Dad. You're a great cook. You could put your famous pies on the menu."

"'ken legendary," said Tommy.

"It's a soup kitchen," said Jack. "It's for the community."

"And this is a community business. All profits go back into this place, we could upgrade the kitchen. If it really succeeds, the money could go into other charity work. Help more people. I bet Father Kennedy would agree."

It seemed sensible to Minh. He'd overheard regulars at the tables praising the food. One of the reasons he'd made the suggestion.

But Jack said: "What we got here ain't broke."

Aurora made a frustrated sound, down the bottom of her throat. "Where's your ambition?"

"Ambition is like a feral cat," said Jack. "Needs to be shot before it gets out of control."

Aurora looked exasperated and Tommy, cigarette bouncing, said: "Your fucken similes are like a feral cat."

"Language," said Jack to Tommy, indicating the presence of his daughter.

"In Vietnam," said Minh, "cats are called 'baby tigers' on the menu."

"Jesus," said Jack. "You eat cats?"

"You don't?" replied Minh. "But everyone here is hungry."

"Listen," said Aurora, hands up, like a policeman halting traffic. "Everyone stop saying cat." The men went silent. Aurora took a deep breath. "Do you know why we have the Australia Cards? The universal basic income?"

"Dunno," said Jack. "Charity, I suppose."

"Yes," said Minh. "Why?"

"Well—you ever notice the biggest supporters of a universal wage aren't charities or churches?"

"Nah," said Tommy. "It's those rich bastards."

"Exactly. Silicon Valley. The banks. You know why? They need customers for the businesses they own, and they own bloody everything. They need our disposable income. But there's no jobs anymore, the automation *they* invented took them all. Forty percent unemployment, half the rest working part-time gigs. So: they lobbied the government to give out free money."

Jack was silent, thinking, looking at his red glass tumbler.

"This," said the young woman, slender white finger on the edge of the notepad, "puts all the money back into the community, recycles the universal income locally. Everyone around here has small gardens, balcony, rooftop, those community greenhouses where the oval used to be."

"We do this in Vietnam," said Minh. "Our government makes us."

"Desperation makes us," said Aurora. "Dad. It'll work."

The three looked at the lean, austere man.

He didn't look back. "*No.*"

Jack didn't yell it, but he didn't say it quiet, either. With enough force to make himself cough into the back of his hand, and with enough finality to silence his daughter and the smile on Tommy's face. The mood dissipated. Silence, except the fan whirring back and forth, lifting the corners of napkins on tables.

Embarrassed at the consequences of his suggestion, Minh excused himself. No one stopped him.

Minh went out the back way, figuring Hassan and Dave, who'd been eyeing him throughout dinner, might have something in mind. He slipped through a jagged rent in a chain-link fence at the rear of the carpark.

They'd anticipated.

Streetlight smashed, the only light in the long alleyway filtered down from high apartments either side. Dave and Hassan waited, leaning against the haggard fence. He stopped, they walked out of the shadows, pride made Minh stand his ground.

Hassan said, all friendly: "You got a cigarette, mate?"

As soon as the man smiled, split-toothed grin, Minh knew the punch was coming. He'd seen the routine time enough, back home. Knew the sound, sickening, like a thick wet slap, when fist struck flesh. Knew the post-facto rationales for violence they gave, in Vietnam: the victim was greedy, or dishonest, or hoarded medication. In Australia, the reasons were simpler: the victim was a cunt, asking for it. For Minh, though, they'd use the other option: foreigner. In a country with a zero-population-growth policy, economic decline, and not enough jobs, being a foreigner was a mortal sin.

Hassan and Dave were bigger than Minh. And they had reputations.

Yet Minh was calm, and when Hassan lashed out with a fist, he was already moving, the blow only clipping the top of his head. This, too, he was accustomed. First few times it happened he'd been stunned, focussed in on the pain, shocked at the violence. The lesson quickly learned: stasis was death. Minh lashed out with his foot, Hassan doubled, lungful of air expelled.

Thing is, Minh had something better than a reputation.

"In Saigon," said Minh, when he'd moved ten feet away, voice clear in the night's silence. "I killed a man."

The men were stayed by the strangeness of the sequence.

"I held him under. In this paddy field. He thrashed a long time. The eyes of this man, I could see underneath the water, just under, looking at me."

Hassan stopped gasping for breath. They listened.

Minh made the space of about an inch between thumb and forefinger. "This much only, between life and death."

The two men were really looking at him now, seeing Minh with a new filter. His shoulders, broad from carrying supplies on them, ten hours on end, for climate tourists, during the season. Off-season, pulling in long nets from the shoreline, hand over hand, weighed down with bitter salt and nothing else.

Hassan and Dave exchange a glance, the former took a step back. "Bullshit. You better watch yer self, China. Fucken *cunt*."

"'s going on?"

Minh whirled.

A shadow broke away from the dark that embraced the parking lot, behind the two men, and approached. Metal glinted in his hand. Tall. Jack.

Dave and Hassan parted, moved around him and away.

Dave said: "This isn't any of your—"

"Keep moving," hissed Jack, and the violence in it made even Minh start.

The men scurried. Went.

"Uncle," said Minh. "I did not know you were here."

"Had a feeling," said Jack.

Minh smiled and lowered his eyes, both from nervousness. Wondering how much the man heard, waiting for him to speak to it. Crickets chirped and Minh felt the breath of the sultry night on the back of his neck.

"Well," Jack said, instead. "See you tomorrow."

Minh nodded, relieved, and the men parted.

A week went by, the two thugs glowered at Minh, spat when he walked by, but said nothing more. Minh hoped they'd believe his story, pick a new target to get their blood up. But he knew, deep down, it wasn't going to be so easy. People talked about *Asians*—as though they all were the same—needing to maintain 'face'. In Minh's eyes, Australians felt the sentiment just as deeply.

Aurora had asked him to come in two hours early. He did, stopping short when he entered the kitchen.

Aurora and Jack were already there. The former hands on hips, the latter red-faced. Something in the air, a frisson dark, lingering. Jack flashed annoyance when Minh walked in, sprinkled flour on the dough he was kneading, and resumed his work.

Minh, distracted, struck something with his foot. A small sack of sweet potatoes. Next to it, a bucket of cherry tomatoes. To that, cassava. And so on, piled across the close wall. "Oh," he said, and when he looked back Aurora was beaming.

"Isn't it great?" asked Aurora.

Minh smiled, uncertain. Eyes flicking between father and daughter.

She indicated the food with a flourish, like a sales woman in a showroom revealing a new model car. "All from the local community, one hundred percent organic and," she glanced at her father, "*non-returnable.*"

It took him a moment, but Jack smiled. A pause, a change in the tilt of his shoulders, then a small smile. "Bloody hell. This bloody daughter of mine. Thank everyone for their donation."

She laughed. "I've been trying to tell you. There's no donation. How can they afford to do that?" She blipped her notepad and showed him the green glowing screen.

"What's this?"

"Bills. From everyone who gave from their own gardens. Local market rates, cheap as. But we pay. Money goes back to them."

Jack sighed, a long sigh of relief. "Good."

"Well Minh?" Aurora glowed in her victory.

"Yes?"

"You going to help your big sister set up the restaurant?"

He nodded. They did. They'd got tablecloths as well, mismatched. Tall glasses and jugs. Flowers in vases. Two musty, large men turned up with a fridge, Minh and Aurora stocked it with drinks.

"Where this all is from?" asked Minh.

"This? *Donated*," whispered Aurora, side of her mouth. "Don't tell dad."

She had Minh hang a blackboard on the far wall. On it she printed, neatly, in chalk:

Locally-sourced Organic Pies

Awakened Tomato Soup duchessed with Maldivian Spices

Artisanal Fresh-baked Sourdough

Himalayan Tea (infused with Californian lemon)

"What's this shit?" said Tommy, when he turned up, pointing at the blackboard.

Aurora giggled. "Just like they have in Newtown."

Tommy scratched his head. "You ever been to Newtown?"

"Like they'd let me in."

"*My land* and they won't let me in."

"I thought you were from Grafton?" asked Jack from the kitchen doorway, wry smile.

"You know what I mean," replied Tommy, roughly.

"Yeah. Nah," said Jack, smile fading. "Sorry mate. Aurora. Keep it straight. Not everyone is literate. You know that."

Aurora reddened. "Oh."

Jack slipped back into the kitchen; Aurora used the back of her hand to wipe the chalk.

Tommy said: "One more thing Aurora."

"Yeah?"

He indicated the room with his chin. "This place looks *fucking amazing.*"

She smiled, wide, and Minh felt himself smiling with her.

"What we gonna call it?" asked Tommy.

"Oh," said Aurora, brow furrowed. "I hadn't thought of that."

"You hadn't? Ha. First time for everything."

Tommy went to the kitchen and soon the doors were opened, Minh and Aurora working the floor, taking orders. Jack cooked all night, mopping the sweat from his face with a white rag. Leaning over the pastry as he worked. Tommy prepared the basic ingredients, complained about not getting a smoko.

Sometime later Minh and Aurora walked into the back and slumped down on chairs.

"What's wrong?" asked Jack, fingers hovering over more pastry.

Aurora was leaning her head on the back of her chair, looking up at the ceiling. "Restaurant's closed, Dad."

"No customers?"

"What?" Aurora, still slumped, looked at her father from the bottom of her eyes.

"Not enough customers?"

Tommy barked a laugh and disappeared out the back, cigarette and lighter in hand.

"What?" asked Jack, again.

"Dad, it's eleven o'clock."

"Is it?"

"We had to stay open an extra hour."

"We did?"

Aurora sat upright in her chair and Minh smiled. Exhausted, satisfied, both. "Everyone came dad. They're used to businesses closing down here, not the other thing." Her eyes shone with pride, directed at her father. "They loved it, said the food was amazing. Said they'd be back."

Like most Australians Minh knew, Jack avoided the compliment. "Well." Jack glanced down at his pastry. "Better prepare for tomorrow's lunch then. Going to be a big day." He looked back at his daughter and the refugee. "Cleaned up and ready out there?"

"Bloody hell dad."

"*Aurora.*"

She laughed and grabbed Minh's hand, pulling him up off the seat. "Let's go handsome."

Minh pushed himself back up onto his aching feet, elation lifting him, and followed her out.

The restaurant prospered. Every night, every lunch, like the first. Aurora wasn't there for lunches, being at school, so Minh worked the floor by himself. The kitchen was upgraded with a shiny steel oven, and months later, batteries for the solar panels. Jack was particularly pleased by the latter, as they'd no longer have to worry about blackouts during the summer. Eventually all four were paid a small salary. Jack really dug in on this count, refusing Aurora's suggestions, followed by demands, for months. Finally, Father Kennedy himself came down and ordered Jack to do so, said if he was running a business, then he should run a business.

When Aurora turned sixteen she couldn't work as often. Had to focus on her schooling. They hired casual workers to cover. A local woman, Mildred, was known for her delicious cakes, so they started buying them from her, added a dessert to the menu.

Minh was happy. Aurora took him to one of the rare public beaches down south. Out of the city, decrepit bus, but worth it, always worth it. She went with him the first few times, but eventually he started going by himself, just to sit there on the pure white sand and watch the ocean. Even Dave and Hassan let him be, the latter apologising with a complicated handshake that seemed taken from one of those American gangster shows.

Yes. Everything was getting better.

Except Jack. As the restaurant prospered, so Jack declined. His coughing got worse. He tried to hide it from Aurora. Minh saw blood once, on Jack's white tea towel. Minh washed it and said nothing. Aurora knew something was very wrong and made him go to the doctor and he did. Said he did, anyway, told them all nothing was wrong. Just the flu, Jack said. He was skinnier every week, the veins on his temples more distinct.

Late one night Minh and Jack were sitting on the back steps drinking lemonade. Tommy and the casuals gone.

"This time we went to the football," said Minh.

Jack smiled. "When the mighty Rabbitohs crushed those pretenders from Melbourne?"

"Yes. This. At the start, your Prime Minister came out to speak."

"Wasn't listening."

"No. No one did. They all booed."

"Ha. Always."

"This people here, seem rebellious."

"We are mate."

"Yes. But why don't you fight?"

"Huh?"

Minh used his eyes to indicate the world beyond the empty carpark. "These conditions." He held the tip of his little finger up, where the chip'd been implanted. "The rules."

"Ah." Jack rubbed his chin. "Yeah. Well. The world, mate, doesn't happen all at once. Not down here. Creeps up on you. Like a feral cat. Minimum wage stalls for a few years, then a few more. Rents go up in one part of the city, so you move to another, then another again. Go down to the corner shop for fish and chips and suddenly there's a new café with uncomfortable seats and blokes with beards selling tofu and beans for fifty bucks a throw. Next the vagrancy restrictions come in and the walls go up, but by then it's academic: you'd long been too poor to go to these places. Suddenly the fight's over before it began, and yer country's gone." He shook his head. "I could be angry. I should be. But I've got a child. It changes things. You'll see. Instead I'm just going to grind it out, long enough to see my daughter finish school and out of this dump."

It was silent out the back, except the white noise of cars on a distant freeway.

Minh sipped his cool drink.

"You really kill that bloke, Minh?" asked Jack.

It took Minh a moment. He put his glass down on the step. "You heard this, with Dave and Hassan?"

"Yeah."

Minh's throat felt thick, but he couldn't stop the words. Just came out, like some part of him was tired of the burden. "There was this man in our neighbourhood. He sold the medicine for blood diseases."

"Blood diseases?"

"Malaria and dengue."

"Ah."

"Everyone had this. I had malaria three times"

Jack listened.

"I lived with my sister on a canal that was once a street. Like all Saigon. Mosquitos live, nest, breed and die, every place. Ninety-nine percent of the inhabitants have had malaria, the UN said. Or dengue. My sister had dengue. This is bad. It can kill you."

Jack listened.

"My sister did not improve. Desperate, I used our savings for medicine."

"Oh."

"It was fake. Pills, ground up. Just powder. Aspirin. In the neighbourhood, several had died. We understood, finally, it was this man, claims to be middle man for drug company. We call people like this wolf."

Jack listened.

"My sister, she—" Minh felt his throat thicken again. "This things I said to Hassan and Dave. It is true."

"Yeah," said Jack. "Yeah, I figured."

"Why do you let me here, then, to work?"

"I was in Afghanistan, mate."

Minh waited.

"2038 and we're still in that god-forsaken place." Jack let out a long breath. "Killing. I'm not going to be judging anyone on that count. Just so long as you didn't bring it with you. Not here, not around Aurora."

He felt Jack's words in his chest, a pain below his heart. "Yes. I swear. I swear it."

"I know mate." Jack put a hand on Minh's shoulder. "I know." He took his hand away to cough, painful rasping, enough to make the veteran's eyes water.

"Jack," said Minh, after the other man had regained his breath.

"Yeah mate."

"Are you dying?"

Jack quieted. He ran a hand through his short hair, a pallid hand, last two fingers missing. "Yeah. Cancer."

"Why do you not go to the hospital?"

"I did."

Minh waited.

Jack sighed. "I did. What I got is rare, not treatable."

"But you have this thing, Medicare."

"Well. As Aurora likes to say: some healthcare is more universal than others. The drugs aren't on the scheme. My spare money goes to schooling."

"She has a scholarship."

"There's extras mate. Costs a fortune. Uniforms, books, all that. It doesn't matter. Aurora could quit school and it wouldn't matter. The treatment costs hundreds of thousands. More. It's eighteen months 'til she graduates, Minh. That's all I want." Tears filmed the dying man's eyes. "All I want, anymore, is to see that beautiful girl of mine through. My last tour."

Minh said nothing.

Jack rubbed his eyes. "Tommy's not interested, so I better show you how to make the pies, I guess. You still going to the beach, Minh?"

Minh paused over the first part of the sentence, replied to the second: "Yes."

Jack's wrists were resting on his knees. A gentle breeze blew across the parking lot, whispering to them.

"The sea is like a leviathan, Minh. You understand what I'm saying?"

Minh turned to the other man, surprised. "Yes. Yes I do understand this, Uncle."

"The sea is vast and eternal. It has no malice, but it does have raw, unimaginable power. It is indifferent to human suffering. When it kills with its embrace, it doesn't matter if you're good, or wicked.

It treats both the same."

"Yes."

"Like God."

"I—" Minh hesitated. "I do not believe in God this way."

Jack sighed. "Yeah. Well. We'll see."

Three months later Minh Nguyen stood next to Tommy Jandamaara at the funeral home. Aurora sat near the far wall, face broken with grief, relatives Minh had not seen before hovering nearby. Like the young woman's sorrow was a bubble they could not penetrate. Not with words or with their bodies. There were soldiers in the room, full uniform, subdued, murmuring to each other.

Minh didn't know what to do, what the customs were, so he stayed near Tommy, both silent.

It was open casket; Minh stood with Tommy in the line, for viewing. Jack Sullivan looked handsome, laid out there, in the polished wooden box. His uniform hid how thin he had become, his sunken chest. The undertakers, working their art, had removed the death pallor from his face, evident in those last weeks at the kitchen. Gone now, now a man, a man not so old at all, lying there, at peace.

"What are those medals?" whispered Minh. Jack seemed to have a lot of them pinned to his breast.

Tommy said nothing and Minh decided to leave the man alone, grieve in his own way.

Until Tommy spoke, rasping. "Gallantry."

"Oh."

"Saved my life."

Minh turned his head, surprised.

Tommy indicated the uniformed men over his shoulder with

a tilt of the head. "He saved the whole section."

"I did not know," said Minh. "Your uniform."

Tommy was in a grey suit. Cuffs too short, frayed at the collar. "Uniform." He repeated. "Need a country to wear a uniform."

He said something more, under his breath, and Minh realised he was talking to Jack. Quiet, though the words were in a language Minh could not understand.

Tommy walked away. Minh hesitated. People were waiting, behind. He bowed his head and prayed: "*You have fought the good fight, Uncle, you have finished the course, you have kept the faith.*"

Minh shuffled on, went to get a drink of water, when a terrible sob drew his attention. He turned and Aurora was doubled over and something animal came from her throat *guh guh ah-ah-ah*. Everyone stared and a woman, older, passing resemblance to Jack, put a hand on the girl's back.

Aurora cried, her voice broken: "*Daddy!*" and Minh turned away, unable. Unable. He walked from the room, ashamed of himself, the hard bare grief of the young girl echoing behind, and out into the white hot breathless noonday sun. Out past the line of people, faces set, snaking out from the funeral home, and on uncertain feet he walked across the biting hot concrete, not knowing where he was headed.

Later, he found himself on the back steps of the church. No air shifted over the creaking asphalt carpark.

Minh ran a shaking hand through his hair and saw the pale face of his sister. Lying on her bed, eyes open, unblinking, not noticing the flies anymore. Minh stood in that hot close space, so still, not wanting to talk. For his words would move time. These hard words with ugly shapes, words reserved for grief and for sorrow, those words that would break this spell and neighbours friends family would know and make this real. They would move time forward and the funeral would come and it would be true.

But it was true. It was real. His silent tears fell on the hot stone steps. He sat like that, hands limp on his knees, for he knew not how long. Stayed there, so still, until he heard voices and gentle feet in the church and time moved again.

He rose.

Minh watched from the gap in the kitchen door. Tommy now sat with the men in uniform, and these soldiers who looked up at Aurora as she served them were in love with her and in despair. She floated by, Aurora, reborn from her grief not a few hours before, and the ripple of her presence bade laughter and words, the mourners telling stories about Jack as they ate their food and sobbed only a little. Minh stayed in the kitchen and worked the dough like Jack had shown him. The voices drifted in from the room next door and were a comfort and outside, the ocean moved its eternal rhythms. It made its rhythms and so did Minh, moving his shoulders as he worked the dough, part of it all, part of this grand and indifferent life.

AN ADVANCED GUIDE TO SUCCESSFUL PRICE-FIXING IN EXTRA-TERRESTRIAL BETTING MARKETS

2050

The key to walking up and down the stairs was both to randomise, and to play by the rules. The rules said you could not step on every stair, and wherever possible, not step on stairs with obvious stains: knots for wooden stairs, chewing gum for concrete, that sort of thing. So the rules, as such, were not too onerous. Randomising was basically to ensure that the aliens placing bets on which stairs I would step on would have a viable betting market. Some days I'd be creative—miss three steps, walk on one, miss another three. Those times I just knew there was some lucky alien punter up there grinning while they cashed in their long-shot ticket. Most of the time though I'd be rushing, or indifferent, or just exhausted and zombie-shuffling down them, bothering only to skip the last step. Those days I'd simply be guaranteeing minimal, steady returns for your conservative alien gambler. That's what I did this morning, missing only the last step as I slouched off the middle set of stairs, into the kitchen.

Vega smiled distractedly as I entered. She said: "Long night?"

"Haven't been to bed."

She looked up from her toast properly then, and did that disappointed-tilt-of-her-head thing she did. I got it often. "Altair."

"Vega."

Her breadknife, coated in vegemite, hovered above the toast like the Breadknife of Damocles. I wondered how the toast felt about this dramatic tension. She said: "Well?"

I sat down with a groan on the other side of the kitchen bench. I'd been on my butt all night, but I sat down with an authentic groan anyway. I asked, with deliberate obtuseness: "Well what?"

She gave me another head tilt. "Was it worth it?"

I grunted. "Coffee."

"Results, Altair.

I grunted again. "I was down three million."

"Shit."

"Then I tried a series of bets on the Hong Kong trots I'd been planning for a few months."

"And?"

"I went down eight."

"Altair," she said, and she lowered her hands to rest on the edge of the bench. The governor granted a reprieve to the toast, and instead made me the focus of her judgement.

"Then I went a little mad, and bet big on boxed trifectas at the Aqueduct in New York."

"I don't know what that means, but it sounds stupid."

"It was profoundly stupid."

"Isn't that computer of yours meant to be making these bets?"

"It is, but I was busy being profoundly stupid."

She looked me over with a laser-like stare that somehow combined x-ray vision, too. If eyes could burn like a laser *and* see right through you at the same time, that'd be Vega's superpower.

Then the laser canons dropped to their original target and the toast met its fate: vegemite was duly smeared. She took a bite between rows of perfectly even, small white teeth. Her face was very pretty, sure, but that was merely a cunning mask to lure arrogant energy executives into the titanium-trapped cerebrum possessed by the smartest environmental defender this side of the equator. Titanium mind, laser eyes, it's like I'm married to a super hero. She'd look pretty fine in a skin-tight spandex costume, as well.

Vega raised an eyebrow. "Well, you're sitting there smelling of stale sweat. That pungent, nervous sweat you ooze when your horses aren't winning, that once upon a time you used to sweat when we first started dating. But you've also got that smug look in your eye and you're asking me for coffee, so I guess all those stupid bets paid off and you dug yourself out of a hole." She took another bite, then said: "Either that or you're imagining me as a supervillain again."

I laughed. "Come on, let me a least give you the slow reveal."

"I'm running too late," she said, slurping down the rest of her coffee, "for war stories from the battlelines of the race courses."

She entered the miasma of my odour, unconcerned, and kissed me on the lips. I kissed her back, wondering how I ended up with the smartest woman in the Spire. I also wondered how my breath smelled after twelve hours of coffee, peanuts, and feverish incantations to the capricious gods of gambling.

Vega paused on the stairs on the way out and looked back at me. Fortunately she had no consciousness of alien betting markets and therefore did not need to abide by the rules of stair-walking. She pointed her half-eaten toast at me. "You haven't left this apartment in weeks. You're taking me out to dinner tonight, buddy. So you're going to need to sleep, shower, and gargle whatever needs to be gargled to remove that stench of the underworld drifting out of your mouth."

"You prefer spearmint or peppermint?" I asked, smiling.

"I'm not sure that's going to be potent enough."

"Hundred proof rum?"

"Paint thinner might do the trick."

We smiled at each other and then she turned and mounted the stairs.

I heard the door slam upstairs as I moved across the black and white tiles of the kitchen, moving as the Knight moves in chess—stepping only two squares ahead and one to the side. The tiles were large, so there was little risk of stepping on the cracks between. There was no established betting market for my tile walking—I did it more as a ward against generalised ill fortune. A conservative, yet logical approach.

I said: "Kitchen, give me a double espresso."

A flat, uninflected voice replied, "Yes sir."

Ten seconds later a small, steaming cup of coffee popped out of the sleek black tabletop. I picked it up and walked from the kitchen over the floor-to-ceiling lounge-room windows, ensuring, of course, that the overall number of steps to the windows could be divided by three. I worked it so it took twenty-one paces.

I sipped my coffee and looked out at the wasteland. The blasted Marscape of the Australian desert, a thousand kilometres of broken red rocks and earth, suffering under the merciless burn of the sun's long lament. Soon, though, this apocalyptic vista would be terraformed by another form of sand, this one living: silica nanotech. My preternaturally talented wife was playing a lead role in that miracle—the transformation of sand into energy; from the red, baking earth into a frozen silver ocean. It would be the largest solar array in the world and the key to Australian energy independence.

So as I stood there, two hundred stories up in the Spire—a glittering needle pointed at the heavens, every inch coated in nano-silver particles, transforming the surface into a towering solar panel sufficient unto itself to power the city-sized population that lived within its sparkling walls—I stood, there on that monument to the ingenuity of humankind, and contemplated the third race at Moonee Valley. There was a horse called Gliese I had my eye on, racing three days hence. I figured I'd better get upstairs and run it through the system, see what it thought.

Someone cleared their throat. I started and turned, the small cup slipping from my hand cracking on the hard, fauxwood floor.

A heavyset guy I'd never seen before was sitting on the couch, smoking. Feet up on the coffee table, wearing a rumpled grey suit, his grey fedora alongside his feet. He looked like he hadn't shaved in a day and the air smelled of burnt copper. His face was puffy and white and his eyes were just that little bit too close together, dark and glittering, like two black pebbles sitting in a big ball of uncooked pizza dough.

He nodded—like breaking into someone's house, sitting on their couch, and smoking a cigarette was the most normal thing and the world—and said: "Spaceman, how you doing?"

I froze. Well, I was already frozen, but even more so—I was carbonite. Spaceman was a stupid nickname I'd earned in high school. I know what burnt copper smells likes, as an aside, from the time the rocket ship I made for science class melted on the launch pad. The fuel mix I'd concocted consumed the rocket in an inferno of white-and-green fire and explosive curses from the science teacher. As it turns out, maths, and not chemistry, was my forte. So I got the name Spaceman, though it'd been twenty years since I'd been called it.

This biographical detail, however, was somewhat trivial right now compared to the matter at hand: the random stranger in my lounge room. I unfroze and stepped backwards, sidling my way to the kitchen whilst the intruder watched me, amused. I didn't count the steps back, so they may not have been divisible by three. Even worse, the number of steps could have ended on a prime number. I was that distracted.

I pulled out the largest carving knife we had from the rack and said, way calmer than expected: "House: call security. Tell them there's an intruder inside."

I waited. No reply. The intruder smiled, content to slowly blow out a thick cloud of smoke and watch it rise, languorously, to the ceiling.

"House." I repeated.

Nothing.

"House?"

"I've turned off your security system, Spaceman" said the man, "You're wasting your time."

"What? How?"

"With my mind of course."

The point of the knife, which I had lowered slowly in my confusion, now rose again to pinpoint the intruder. "Sure," I said, and then looked up at the ceiling. "House?"

The intruder rolled his little black eyes.

I took a deep breath. "Buddy, you need to leave."

"Oh, I will, I will—no problem. As soon as I get what I'm owed."

I furrowed my brow. I made a lot of bets—or the system I built did anyway—thousands even, every day, but as a point of pride I never took a loan and never welched on a bet. Not since meeting

Vega, anyway.

I said: "I have no idea what you are talking about."

He sighed, exhaling smoke through his nostrils as he did so. "I hate this part."

"What part?"

"The *convincing* part. All you big-time gamblers, making huge bets with aliens on how many cracks you can avoid stepping on, or how many prime numbers you'll see in a twenty-four hour cycle, or on which steps you'll step on, or whatever. All these big bets, yet when we come down to collect you act all surprised, all innocent as to your obligations."

He'd lost me. "Huh?"

He took his feet off the coffee table and leaned forward, speaking slowly. "Are you saying you don't randomise your steps while walking up and down the stairs in order to set markets for extra-terrestrial betting pools?"

"I do," I said, "but..."

"But?"

"But that's all inside my head."

He shook his head, flicking his cigarette butt onto the floor. "Nothing is ever just inside your head. You people just can't seem to get that."

We looked at each other in silence. The intruder lit another cigarette; I wondered whether I was dreaming. Or worse—whether it was starting again.

The intruder cleared his throat and said: "Firstly, stop calling me the intruder. You can call me Bruce."

The knife was well and truly dangling in one hand now, forgotten. I whispered: "You can read my mind?"

"Spaceman, you've been psychically setting markets for my book for the last twelve months; obviously I can read your mind."

There wasn't really much I could say to that. He was right, after all. So I suspended disbelief, if just for the moment. "Bruce," I said, "you're an alien called Bruce."

"I just picked a common name for Australians. Aren't you all called Bruce?"

I shook my head. "I've never heard anyone called that." I moved over to the kitchen bench and sat down with my back to it, eyes on the intruder. The alien. Bruce. "You don't talk like an alien."

Bruce shrugged. "Of course not, if I spoke my true language, your testicles would rupture and your brain ooze slowly out of your nose."

I grabbed my testicles. "Really?"

He laughed. "Of course not. You just wouldn't be able to hear it."

"What's the second thing?"

"Huh?"

"You said, 'Firstly, stop calling me intruder.' What's the next thing?"

"Oh right," he said, nodding to himself. "The second thing is you're not going crazy. That's the problem with human beings, you have phenomenological minds. You can't experience the universe beyond anything other than the narrow space between your ears, which always makes this to-and-fro I have with you people tedious in the extreme. It also usually leaves us where we started: with you convinced that I'm a hallucination and me with no verifiable means of proving otherwise."

"Huh. So your mind isn't in a physical body? Like a telepathic space spirit or something?"

"Or something," he said, dryly. "I'm just an extension, you might say, of a far larger being."

"Like an arm?"

"I'm not quite that important."

"A toenail?" I asked, smiling.

He looked me over, unsmiling. "I guess you'd call me the fist." He took a drag on the cigarette. "This is where things get unpleasant."

Before I knew what was happening, the knife was moving, and my right hand was moving it. I watched wide-eyed as I put my left arm out, exposing the inside of the arm. Slowly, steadily, and without the slightest pause, I put the blade of the carving knife against the soft white skin on the inside of my forearm. I gritted my teeth, a drop of sweat rolled down my brow, but I couldn't do anything but watch as the knife sliced the inside of my arm, a long, deep cut. I tried to scream but my jaw seemed frozen in place. Blood welled in the wound and trickled down, dripping onto the floor.

The ethereal iron grip on my body disappeared and I fell from the stool, landing on the hard fauxwood with a grunt, the knife skittering across the floor. Blood drained between my fingers as I tried to put pressure on the wound and then Bruce was right there, white bandage in hand, binding the gash in my arm. He steered me over to the sofa and sat me down, making reassuring noises. Then he seated himself opposite, put his feet up on the coffee table, and lit another cigarette.

I sat staring at him, open mouthed. I'd never been stabbed before, and certainly never mind-control-by-an-alien-collecting-imaginary-bets-stabbed. You can understand my consternation.

After a time it became clear he was waiting for me to say something. So I did, with a stutter-step. "I… I… I can pay you. I'm very wealthy."

"That's more like it. But I'm afraid your currency is inappropriate," he said affably, like the whole cutting-me-with-a-blade thing was already forgotten. "It's conceptual—the idea of value, represented in spots of data in your archaic computing systems. We did away with conceptual currency millennia ago; it's too volatile, too unpredictable and has a tendency to self-replicate in tune to the vivid imaginations of the grasping spivs that command your financial systems. It's *primitive* to say the least."

He took another drag on his cigarette, exhaled the smoke through his nose. "Our currency is intangible, practical units of energy. They are all real, immensely valuable in their own right. They are currency, but they are also the fuel we use to fold space, the energy that powers our worlds, and the sustenance our beings subsist on. We treat our money with respect."

"Respect," I repeated. I was annoyed, I don't mind saying, and the annoyance was doing battle with my fear. "By creating betting markets based on the imaginary bets of punters from a world of *primitive* spivs?"

Bruce the Alien raised finger and eyebrows simultaneously. "But that is the thing, Spaceman—your vivid imaginations are one of the very few things we cannot predict accurately. The human mind: an irreducible mix of reason and un-reason, logic and rage and sexually-charged aggression. And inconsistent—take *your* neural-atypical brain type, Spaceman—you're a freak among freaks. Human beings have such spectacular, wild irrationality. You people have a one in fifty chance of dying every time you send someone to your Mars colony, but you still have people lining up to travel to that dead red rock; you expose yourself to solar radiation in order to darken your skin, even though forty per cent of Australians develop skin cancer as a result; you have a one in four-hundred-and-seventy chance of dying by infectious disease, yet spend all your medical research on penile erection and three-dimensional printing for new faces and breasts; and speaking of which, one in forty-five heart attacks occur during vigorous sex, yet you people just won't stop banging each other. In this silver building of yours right now there are nineteen couples having intercourse, twelve vigorously, one involving a swing set and loud music by some group called AC/DC. You are truly one of the strangest, most risk-prone species in the galaxy. It's a wonder you've lasted this long."

I put my hand under my wounded arm, relieving some of the pressure on it, unsure of how to react. This day defied a straight-forward emotional response.

"You sit around watching people have sex?" I asked.

Bruce's eyes narrowed. "I study you people, the way you spend innumerable hours studying horse data to input into your betting algorithm."

"Right. I don't ever recall studying a feed of those horses shagging."

"It's all part of understanding the market."

I nodded in the way you nod when you think someone is full of shit: slowly, with eyes wide open in sarcastic agreement. "Right. Research. Sure." I leaned back into the soft leather of the sofa. "You seem awfully risk averse for a species so interested in gambling."

"No one dies gambling, Spaceman. None of our race dies at all, really, though some of us choose to fade away. Gambling using the telepathic betting markets of lower life forms is one of the very few ways we can experience the rush of risk and randomness. It is very popular."

He opened his palms. "No, gambling ain't dangerous at all," he said, and everything in his disposition changed—a seamless transition from affable to threatening. "Not to my race, anyway."

"What does that mean?"

"People in your situation, who make the decision to create betting markets with us, well, you have around a two in three chance of dying."

I shifted on the seat. "What? How?"

"The way all gamblers die, Spaceman. First I break the knees, and when that doesn't work, the neck. I've been doing this a long time, so listen when I tell you that if you do die, your refusal to believe will kill you about half the time. Not being able to pay kills you the other half."

"Okay, okay," I said, making calming air-pats with my good hand. "How much do I owe you?"

"Three energy units."

"Oh. Is that all?"

"Three energy units are roughly equivalent to about two billion dollars, in your currency."

I was silent. My arm hurt. I needed a coffee. A shower. And two billion dollars. "How long do I have?"

"A week."

"You're kidding."

"No. Now, I've got to go. Visits like this cost considerable energy, which I will be adding to your bill. You need to walk up and down the stairs five hundred times today. Completely randomise your steps. We're going to hit the market hard and fast. Your recent predictability in stair-walking has left me out of pocket and my customers placing an increasing number of bets on your most frequent stepping patterns. This will blindside them completely."

"Five hundred?" There were three stories and six sets of stairs to my apartment, all connected. I was relatively lean, but that was from forgetting to eat meals while studying horse-racing data rather than exercise. We had a gym on the bottom floor, though I think the weights were still in their plastic wrapping. I said: "I'm not sure I can do that."

Bruce's black-pebble eyes glittered. "You'll do it, Spaceman. Because if you don't, I'm not going to go after you, not at first anyway. I'm going after Vega."

I felt my face heat up. I stood and yelled, "Don't you dare—" But he was already gone, leaving behind only the smell of cigarettes and burnt copper.

Late afternoon. Drenched in sweat. Wearing the same clothes from the night before. I'd made two hundred and eighty-three trips up and down the stairs. My left ankle ached from where I twisted it trying to leap six stairs at once and the blood was showing through the white bandage on my arm. I lay on the couch, taking a break.

"Altair? What the hell?"

I jumped up. I'd been dozing, apparently. I wiped the drool from the corner of my mouth and looked around.

Vega was standing near the kitchen bench, hands on hips. "What is going on? You haven't even changed from this morning." Her voice held a mix of irritation and disappointment. The latter was always hard for me to hear.

"I'm sorry," I said, voice bruised by exhaustion.

She sniffed the air, then spoke, rapid-fire. "It smells like gym socks in here. You look terrible. And whose cigarette butts are those are on the floor?"

I hesitated. There really wasn't any chance I'd tell her about the alien invader. I said: "Mine. I was stressed so I tried smoking. It was inexplicably dumb."

She took a deep breath. "Why are you so stressed?"

"I, ah, I ran into some trouble. I think there's a flaw in the algorithm for the neural network. All my bets turned sour today. I've taken it off-line while I search for the problem."

Vega nodded, though not at what I was saying. "I take it this means you can't leave the apartment?" she asked.

I only had the energy to nod once.

Her expression was flat. "What's the rush?"

"Huh?"

She paced around the floor, eyes on me, stopping in front of the windows. "Why not take your time fixing the algorithm? There's no reason it has to be fixed today, is there?"

I searched my mind for an excuse, but I was just too tired to think of a supplementary lie.

Her expression softened. "Altair?"

"Vega."

"You off your medication again?"

I shook my head. "I've been off it for weeks and I've been fine. I don't need to be medicated."

"You've been off it for weeks," she repeated. The look she gave said it all: disappointment, sadness, and a healthy dose of *well obviously you need to be medicated.*

Vega sighed and sat down on the couch next to me. She pointed at my bandage with her eyes. "What happened?"

"Oh," I looked down at the arm. "Just tired, slipped trying to make a sandwich. You know."

"Big sandwich?"

I smiled a weak smile.

She put her hand on my leg. "Babe. Your gambling sessions are getting longer and longer, and you're doing more and more of the bets yourself, rather letting your betting machine do them. You're not sleeping or eating, and you're refusing to leave the house. You've probably been talking to yourself for half the day, right?"

There was concern in her eyes. Mine started to gleam. I said: "Yeah." She was right. Bruce seemed so distant now—surreal and unbelievable. I shook my head, grimacing at the thought of the day I'd just endured. "You're right."

She sighed. "We're not going through this again Altair. You're better than this. So this is what we are going to do: we're going to have a good meal, here. Then you're going to take a sleeping pill. In the morning you'll be a new man. We'll go out tomorrow morning, take a nice long walk, and maybe try breakfast at one of those new cafes on the hundredth floor."

She was right, again. She was always right. I nodded.

I showered, washing away the grime and fear. Ravenous, I ate a huge bowl of risotto. Exhausted, I took a pill and fell asleep, Vega's hand in mine.

Vega didn't wake up in the morning.

I didn't notice at first. I woke up, feeling wonderfully rested. Vega's short dark hair was covering her eyes and she seemed deep asleep, head buried in her pillow. I went to the kitchen, got myself a double espresso, walked twenty-one steps to the window and looked out at the Marscape. Then I went upstairs, making sure not to step on every stair, and looked over my new algorithm weightings for weather patterns over the Hong Kong races.

Immersed in the maths, I didn't realise until ten o'clock that Vega hadn't awoken. She was never late for work.

I went back downstairs and found her exactly as I had left her, head buried in the pillow. My chest tightened. "Vega?"

No response.

I walked around to her side of the bed, put a hand on her shoulder and said, louder this time: "Vega?"

She didn't stir.

I shook her, saying her name louder and louder. Her body was limp and cold under my hand. I put the tips of my fingers to her neck. At first I couldn't feel a thing but there, fluttering, weak, was a pulse.

I yelled at the house to get a medical team to the apartment. They turned up five minutes later and I was frantic, yabbering at them as we went down the stairs and getting in their way as they took Vega's vitals.

The female paramedic unfurled a flexiscreen on the edge of the bed and studied the green glowing icons scrolling down the screen. I asked her what was wrong.

She looked up at her partner and then me. "I don't know, it looks..." She trailed off.

"It looks like what?"

"Like a coma."

"She was fine last night," I said, anger creeping into my voice, "just fine. How is that possible?"

Her professional patina reasserted itself. "I don't know, sir. We're going to take her to the emergency room now."

"Yes, yes. Good."

"Does she take drugs?" she asked, as they shifted her on to a silver gurney that seemed to float in the air at the end of the bed.

I shook my head. "No. No never."

"She on any medications?"

"None. Nothing."

"Positive?"

"*Positive.* Now stop asking stupid questions and get her to the hospital."

Her gaze was flat in response. "Right away, sir."

I followed them as they guided the stretcher up the stairs. As I stepped onto the landing near the front door, I caught something at the periphery of my vision. I turned and there, down a short hallway from the entryway, was Bruce. He was standing out in the open in my office, mouth smiling, eyes cold. The paramedics didn't seem to notice him.

The woman looked at me. "Coming, sir?"

I glanced back at Bruce. He shook his head slowly, still smiling.

I rubbed my forehead and put my hand on Vega's chest. Her face was pale, covered in a thin sheen of sweat. The paramedics had stuck a small round device on her forehead, little green lights blinked on and off around its circumference. Tears welled in my eyes. I cleared my throat and said: "In a minute, in a minute."

The paramedics looked at each other. The woman said to me: "We'll put her in the emergency ward on the second floor."

They didn't wait any longer. The door closed. I stood, clenching and unclenching my fists. In my mind I repeated, like a mantra: *black box black box black box black box.* I ducked into the laundry that sat between the front door and my office *(black box black box black box black box)* then walked back to where Bruce was waiting *(black box black box black box black box)*, looking perplexed. I walked right up to him *(black box black box black box black box)* and shoved the screwdriver I was hiding behind my back into his stomach.

Bruce grunted, eyes wide with surprise, and staggered back.

I said: "I remember pretty much everything I've ever read, *Bruce.* It's one of the quirks of my atypical brain."

He was trying to pull the screwdriver out of his stomach, his white shirt a spreading stain of fresh blood.

I continued. "Four years ago I read a story about mind control. A speculative piece, but in a scientific journal."

Bruce plonked down on the hard floor in the centre of the room.

"It discussed new experiments—military experiments actually— on thought patterns and mind control. The thing they proved was this: it's really, really easy to disrupt thought patterns. You just need to repeat the same phrase, over and over and over."

Bruce was looking down at his stomach, his blood-slicked hands unable to gain purchase on the screwdriver's handle.

I circled him slowly. "This is the problem you face when you mess with a crazy person, Bruce: they're crazy. I have this problem, you see, makes it difficult for me to feel empathy. And that's just with human beings. Imagine how I feel about an alien gangster debt collector." I stopped in front of him, looking down. "Who *hurts my wife*."

His fumbling faded. The pool of blood Bruce sat in was large now, expanding. He looked up at me one last time, made to say something, then collapsed back on the floor. His glazed eyes pointed up at the ceiling.

I stayed there, standing over the body.

They didn't call me Spaceman because I immolated the rocket. I had that name before the rocket incident ever happened. They called me Spaceman because I was weird. Borderline Asperger's, they said. I either never spoke at all in class, or spoke endlessly in answer to a particular question until the other kids started laughing and the teacher sent me from the room. I couldn't look people in the eye, catch a ball, or understand the humour in fart jokes.

One day a kid was teasing me, the same as he did every other day. I was much younger, smaller than the other kids—so picking on me, calling me a retard, sticking me in the dumpster, was particularly easy. I just endured it. But this one day I snapped and beat him bloody. I was expelled. And that was that.

The incident was yet another reason why I never understood the world. A bully can ply his trade for years, breaking down his peers psychologically and physically; turning the years of adolescence into a long, drawn out form of torture that some kids take a lifetime to get over. But you break that bully's jaw with a cricket bat, and *you're* the bad guy.

People and their arbitrary rules remained a mystery to me. But maths—this was effable. It was the only thing that gave me solace, and I retreated into it whenever I could. Numbers were pure and clean and ordered, and if you worked long enough, they'd divulge their secrets to you.

I wasn't just good at maths, either: I was a prodigy.

My father used to tell—well, anyone who'd listen—about the time when I was two years old, at family Christmas, explaining arithmetic to my older cousin, who was six. I'd learned it watching Sesame Street.

At nine years old I was the second youngest participant in the history of the International Mathematical Olympiad. At fifteen I received my Master's in Pure Mathematics at Sydney University and at twenty I received my PhD at the University of the People's Californian Republic. At twenty-two I was appointed full professor at the Mathematical Sciences Institute in Australia and at twenty-three I received the Young Australian of the Year Award for my breakthroughs in harmonic analysis and analytic number theory.

"And at twenty-four you discovered horse racing."

I jumped, literally. Behind me, standing in the doorway was Bruce, smiling a rotten-dough smile at me. I glanced back: his other body was still there.

Bruce put a cigarette in his mouth and lit it. He inhaled deep, exhaled through his nose and held the smoke up between index and middle finger. "Got to say. Best thing about being here is these nicotine sticks. Tasty."

He walked around the room, looking over my office. It was sparsely decorated: three large Tai screens for watching the races and an elegant silver neural cap sitting on a small black stand, enabling me to watch the same races inside my head, if I wanted. A battered brown leather couch I could nap on while the betting system was working something over and the system itself: a shiny black box with its sole, blinking red light.

Bruce glanced over all this as he spoke. "At twenty-four you discovered horse racing— that beautiful contest, the perfect mathematical problem. So many variables, so many unknowns: the condition of the track, the weather, the horse's breeding and psychology; the pace of the race; the jockey—their temperament, family situation, what they had for breakfast; the trainer; the level of corruption at each track; and on and on and on. So many variables, so many unknowns, but still a problem that you believed you could divine an answer for. Like you were going to solve the horse racing equivalent of Fermat's Last Theorem."

He stopped at the black betting box, looked down at it. "You could have spent a lifetime at the track, if you'd been allowed. Drinking free tea from an urn, hitching up the only pair of pants you owned, betting your last twenty dollars on a roughie in the last race of the day."

Bruce turned and looked at me. "The best days of your life, right?"

I nodded slowly. "Until I met Vega."

"Until you met Vega years later, no longer homeless, doing pretty well for yourself— wealthy, even. But still a degenerate, still down at the track, day in, day out. All alone, abandoned by your family. But she convinced you to build your system, said you were 'an analogue man in a nano-tech world.' She was right, wasn't she?"

"Why do you know so much about me?"

"Simple. You're my prize stallion, Spaceman. I know everything about you. I study you the same way as you study your horses."

Bruce walked over to his other body, lying on the ground. He nodded at it admiringly. "This is what I'm talking about. Glorious irrationality: like you can take on an advanced alien civilisation with a screw driver. We just never know what you people are going to do next."

"But that blood," I pointed, hand shaking, at the crimson pool on the floor. "It's real. I killed you."

"You can't kill me. I'm a projection. I'm not even here."

"But you're smoking a real cigarette. You can pick things up and move them around. You wrapped my arm in a bandage."

Bruce smiled, shaking his head. "You people really are primitive."

He moved over to me and put his hand on my shoulder. I looked down at it, numb. He said: "Now, Spaceman, we need to make some money. Because I don't know if your wife is going to make it through another day."

Three hours later I was trudging up the stairs, legs shaking with exhaustion. The hospital had been trying to contact me since the paramedics had left. I'd told them to tell me if Vega's condition changed. The woman at the other end of the line said I had to fill out some forms about my wife's medical history. I'd cut the connection.

I slumped down on the top step, arms on knees, my shirt clinging to the sweat on my back. I rested my head against the bars of the railing, looking down the block spiral of stairs descending to the hard floor down below. I bit down on the sob rising in my chest and closed my eyes, pressing my forehead hard against the bars like I was trying to punish my sadness.

After a time the feeling passed. I opened my eyes again, staring downwards. Each flight of stairs was set into one of four walls as it descended, forming a square when looked at from above. The setup was slightly angled, such that the balustrade at the top floor sat directly over the bottom step on the last flight, three floors below.

I sat up straight. I knew what to do. I stomped around my office, yelling for Bruce to come down. A minute later he was there, leaning against the doorframe, fedora shading his eyes, filling the room with the scent of burnt copper.

"Yes, Spaceman?"

I walked up to him, breathing quickly with exhaustion and excitement. "You run the book for the stairs, right?"

"Right."

"So what happens when I choose a combination that hasn't been picked?"

"It won't happen. Every option is covered."

"Let's pretend it did. The prize pool goes to the house?"

Bruce shrugged. "Sure."

"Is the pool bigger than my debts?"

"Easily."

I told him my plan. He pushed the fedora up high on his forehead with one finger, and looked me in the eye. "Are you sure?"

"I'm sure."

He smiled that cold smile, black-pebble eyes glittering, and put his hand on my shoulder. "I knew you'd come through, Spaceman."

I looked down over the balustrade. I'm not scared of heights as such; it is not a particular phobia of mine. But still, everyone is afraid of heights. I read somewhere that human beings have only two fears they are born with as part of their natural condition: fire and falling. I consoled myself that the stairwell wasn't ablaze and swung my legs over the railing, butt cheeks on the balustrade.

I said: "House: call the hospital, have them send paramedics."

"Yes sir. What is the nature of the medical emergency?"

"I've had a serious fall."

"Yes sir."

I didn't hesitate. I jumped, aiming to hit any, or all, of the last three steps. Hit them I did.

It would have been nice if this faded to black. Skip to hospital scene. And it did, eventually. But not before I lay on the fauxwood floor, mouth open in silent scream as I looked at the bones sticking out of my legs. Trying and failing to staunch the blood spurting out of the wounds, numb hands wet with blood. Not before I threw up from the pain, making gagging noises like a sick animal. But yeah, after all that, it faded to black.

White walls, white sheets, and Vega's smile, smiling down at me. She sat on the edge of the bed, holding my hand.

"Altair."

I squeezed her hand back. My mouth was dry, my head clearer than you'd expect, given the situation. "Vega."

"You're awake."

"So are you."

"Hm. I woke up, fully recovered, just in time to hear you'd been taken to emergency." She tilted her head at me. "I wondered what it was going to take to get you out of the apartment."

I smiled. "Maybe next time I'll settle for a dinner date. Less messy."

She smiled back, but the concern in her eyes was clear. "Yeah. I think we're going to have to talk about that."

We were silent for a few moments. Whatever drugs they'd given me were sublime; I could feel nothing form the waist down. I said: "Did they figure out what was wrong with you?"

She raised an eyebrow. "They're idiots."

I shifted, pulling myself up higher on my pillow. "What did they say?"

"They said I overdosed on sleeping pills."

I felt tightness in my chest. "What?"

"It's bullshit, I know."

I rubbed my head. I'd poured her the glass of water she'd drunk just before going to bed that night. I scratched at the thin scar the carving knife had made on the inside of my arm.

Vega was saying something.

I whispered. "What?"

She put a cool hand on my forehead. "You with me? I said: what happened?"

I cleared my throat. "Sorry, what happened with what?"

She raised an eyebrow. "Falling off the stairs."

I took a deep breath and took her hand in mine. "Oh. Nothing. Just, um, clumsy, I guess."

"Clumsy," she repeated.

I lay there in distracted silence, trying to find the line of logic in the stream of events.

"I thought maybe you'd been drinking, celebrating your big win."

"Huh?"

She tilted her head at me. "They told me the drugs you're on wouldn't affect your mental clarity. More bullshit, by the look of it." She put her other hand on my chest, making sure she had all my attention. "I got a notification from the bank last night. Our apartment has been paid off, in full."

I lay there in silence, mind racing, while Vega looked at me, expectant. I gave her a weak smile and she smiled back, strong. The lie that followed was as limp as my smile. "Maybe I did have couple of drinks. I was, ah, going to surprise you."

The truth, as always, was mine to bear alone.

Vega was about to say something when a nurse entered the room without knocking. Blue smock, harried expression, the man nodded at Vega and said to me: "Let's talk about your medication."

Vega stroked my hair and kissed me on the forehead, then excused herself so she could go get a coffee.

The nurse put down a small plastic tray that had little square boxes set into it, each with one red pill, blue pill and green-and-white pill. He indicated them with his hand. "We got a few things here to get your body and mind right."

"My mind?"

He sighed, nodding at the doorway Vega had just exited through. "Talk to your wife. It's just starting you up on your old medication again, that's all. There's also some nano-meds in here to speed up blood production and help your bones knit. You'll be out of here in a day or two." He put a small plastic cup of water next to the tray, and then plucked up a yellow-and-white pill sitting separate from the others. "Take this now, then three of each of these pills for the next six days. In a week you'll need to come back to the hospital for reassessment."

I stared at the tray. There were six rows, three pills in each row, plus the one in the nurse's hand. Nineteen pills.

"Sir?"

I looked up. "Sure, yes, I understand. Thank you."

He raised an eyebrow. "Now don't miss any. You're going to need all of them for your recovery."

"No problem," I said, waving him away

The nurse shrugged and departed, looking down at his glowing flexiscreen and presumably, his next patient.

After he left I looked back at the rows of pills. Nineteen. Obviously I wasn't going to get better taking a *prime number* of pills. If nothing else, this was clear. I took three of the pills and shoved them under the mattress. Sixteen remained. I could work with sixteen. I swallowed the yellow-and-white pill and settled back into my pillow.

I smiled as I thought about Vega, safe, and returning with her to our apartment, together. I thought about standing at the windows, drinking my coffee, and watching my wife's passion transform the very earth on which the city stood.

But more than anything I thought about the third race at Moonee Valley.

GHOSTS OF A NEON GOD
2090

Cigarette dangling from his lips, Jack Nguyen jimmied the panel at the back of the glimmer bike. Col Charles stood in the shadows at the head of the alley on lookout, softly whistling an aria. The bike was a wide-bellied easy rider belonging to one of the wide-bellied, handlebar-moustached Rebels bikers playing pool in the dive bar backed by the alley.

Sweat rolled down Jack's temple as he took a long drag on his cigarette, orange point the only light visible in the dark. His cheap infra-goggles good enough to show the outlines of the shimmer-smooth control panel; that, and the crude scar cut into the back of his hand: 4007.

The security on the bike was above average, but unimaginative.

A hundred panels, just like this, in the labyrinthine alleys, the multi-level underground carparks, in the back lots and back streets of this city.

Jack popped it, pulled the drive card, fried the GPS node, and slipped it into his pocket. Any petty crim who wanted their spinal cord intact was smart enough to leave Rebels' glimmers alone. True. But it was also true that Col and Jack valued a full stomach over a spinal column, right at that moment. And anyway, Jack was young enough to feel eternal. Col was a nihilist, which was the same thing, more or less.

Jack pinged Col through their neural link; Col left his post, ghosted back down the alley. They walked side by side down in the darkness, quickly, through left and right turns back towards the tram lines. Sweat mingling with the tension on their necks, stomachs bunching into knots as they got to each corner, waiting for a steel-toothed outlaw to take to them with a baseball bat.

Invincible, sure, but the Rebels were still the Rebels.

One turn from the tram stop, under the neon glow of an EE-Z-CREDIT sign, they heard the footsteps. Jack pulled the double-edged blade strapped to the small of his back, Col his snub-nosed revolver.

A shadow flitted round the corner, footfalls pounding; Jack pulled back his blade, too late, body colliding with his. He lost balance, ankle twisting wrong, head cracking the edge of a dumpster, blade skittering on the concrete.

When he got to his knees, Col was pointing his gun at a Chinese woman while she spoke rapid-fire in Mandarin, palms open in surrender, also on her knees.

Jack's neural implant translated the words, two seconds after they left her mouth.

"[…soon. Money, I can give you money if you help me. I work

for *bleeeep*. I came here to–to meet a man from *The Age*. Reveal the truth about the next-generation *bleeeep bleep*.]"

Col's face was side-lit by neon, his half ear and scarred cheekbone visible. He licked his lips, uncharacteristically lost for words, glanced back towards the street, people bustling past in the light. No-one saw the trio ten feet in, or at least they all pretended not to.

"Who's after you?" Col asked.

She replied: "[*bleeeep bleep*.]"

Col said: "Hmm. Bleep. Sounds serious."

She looked confused. She also looked, well, she looked beautiful. Even in the dim alley, Jack couldn't help but notice her short, shimmer-healthy black hair. The woman had the kind of skin you kept after twenty-five years of good nutrition, little sun, and no cigarettes. She held her shoulders straight, regal somehow, even as she was on her knees, even as she faced off two thugs in a dark back alley on a steaming city night.

Her face side on, slightly upturned nose, long neck, lips wet. Beauty of a kind Jack wasn't used to seeing in the flesh. Marred only a little by the fear that tightened her jaw.

Col continued: "If it's serious enough for my translator to censor the words, then you have a problem no amount of lucre is able to fix, especially by two petty crooks." Col was haloed by the neon glare, so Jack couldn't see his expression. But he caught the intent in his words easy enough. "We got no time for the conspiracies of the Red Aristocracy, or their scions. But I have time for those shoes—" he pointed at them with the nose of the revolver "—Fujian original, I'd wager—good for two ounces of weed, box of untracked bullets, couple of real meat burgers in Fitzroy."

"Shit," said Jack.

"Exactly," said Col.

Jack looked at the woman. "Give him your shoes, lady."

Wide-eyed she looked between the two. Skin live air-brushed, perfect eyes wet with terror. Jack felt a knot in his stomach, at those eyes. He swallowed, tried to maintain the bravado.

She said: "[You *must* help me. You must do *what is right*, and restore harmony. The fate of your country rests on this.]" She held out her hands to Jack. Knowing, somehow, he was the weak link.

"We don't have a country," said Col, "and restoring harmony—well—that's a bit above our station. Now," he pointed the handgun at her head, "yer fucken shoes."

She took her shoes off—jerkily, a robot in need of an oil change—and got unsteadily to her feet. She dropped the shoes, eyes already elsewhere, then stutter-stepped into a run, into the darkness.

Col raised his eyebrows at Jack, smiling, and scooped up the shoes.

Jack, still on one knee, looked for his blade. His lip bled. Probably bit it when he collided with the woman. He wiped the sweat from under his eyes, fingertips shaking, just a little. "My knife," he said.

Col waved the shoes at him. "I'll get you a better one. Let's get out of here".

Jack took one look back down where the woman had run. Already gone, without a trace. He sighed, involuntarily, and followed Col.

They waited at the tram stop, watching the traffic go by. Glimmer bikes and hydrocars and autobuses, frenetic and frightened in the steaming, sizzling, Melbourne night air. Fifty years past relevance. Even fifty years ago it was the peripheral: to Asia, the

Oceans, the Earth. Now it may as well not even existed.

They hopped the tram at the end of the line and walked. Past midnight, shirts soaked with sweat, on aching legs into the construction zone, an unfinished second CBD for the city. A half-dozen blocks from home they popped their memory cores from their neural implants, easing them out between finger and thumbnail. It sucked not having the freewave on-retina every time they came back, but better than being tracked down by the authorities. Col said their minds needed time to breathe anyway. That the constant interface with the freewave made them more malleable for the megacorps, stunted their individuality.

Jack didn't know about all that. He just wanted to watch the cricket, and a few yuan gave him a PoV grandstand seat right behind the bowler's arm at the Members' End.

Through half-completed office blocks, past complete, but empty, restaurant strips. Through shadows cast by the future. Col whistled Vivaldi, *Winter*, pitch perfect. Light came from the pale moon, from the neon company signs on the towering yellow cranes, high above; from twenty gallon drums, where groups of sallow-faced transients stared into the flames and made no conversation.

The young men eased themselves through a hole in a chain-link fence, over the dusty ground, and through an external exit they'd hacked. Forty-eight bare plascrete flights. First part of their security system. Cardio wasn't big among the malnourished homeless or the street thugs. Second part was a security swipe Jack had coded to their thumbs. The third part Jack hoped they'd never have to use.

Puffing, they walked through the huge office space, bare hard floors, wiring dangling from the walls. Col paused, looked around the dark, cavernous space, seeing things Jack would never see. "These labyrinthine and endless rooms, doors, and stairways, they lead nowhere Jack."

Jack paused, then pointed at the engraving next to the door. "Nah mate, this leads to the kitchen, see?"

He walked into the next room, smiling, as Col tried to elaborate.

Jack flicked the lights. The room was in the centre of the structure, windowless. Surveillance drones shouldn't be able to pick up the light. If they were rigged with thermo-optics they were kind of fucked, but the only citizens who could afford the high-end stuff didn't live in these parts.

The meeting room was long, white walled, even carpeted. The kitchenette in the next room, like the lights, functioned after Jack had connected up the wiring to the glimmer tiles and glimmer glass that coated the building in solar particles. Cooling, too, when they wanted it. Best accommodation either had had in years.

Jack dumped the drive card and goggles on the long plasteel meeting table that dominated the room. It was strewn with instant noodle packs, stripped copper, a baggie of black market tobacco and a flexiscreen he still hadn't managed to hack. He grabbed his comic from the table edge, went through the kitchenette—salvaged toaster, three-day old bread, gas camping stove on narrow benchtop—and into the bathrooms.

Jack ran his fingertips reverently over the dark cover of the comic. A man with a briefcase, casting blue shadows on a wall. Shadows filled with the faces of people. Faded, just the name *100 Bullets* legible on the front cover. Stolen from some wealthy bastard's Tesla Europa. A real book, comic book anyway, just sitting there on the passenger's seat.

He sat on the toilet, found his place, absorbed. When he'd finished he used the bucket to flush. Hauling water forty-eight floors a definite downside to the accommodations.

When he got back out Col was at the long table, drinking a bottle of water, eyes closed as he savoured it. Cooled, right from the unit in the kitchenette. The light picked out Col's scar, dirty purple, running straight from a point near his nose round to his missing half ear. Druggo, ice-six trance, came at them with a samurai sword when they were trying to score down in St Kilda.

The woman's shoes were on the table, black and shiny. Col's battered .38, cylinder popped and empty, rested alongside.

"That true about being able to get some bullets?" asked Jack.

"They're real leather. A box of bullets, GPS dot removed. Sure."

"Any left?" asked Jack, pointing with his chin.

Col reached inside his jacket, pulled out a foil-covered package. A very small one. He placed it on the table in front of him, carefully unfolded the foil. "Yeah. For tonight, anyway." He pulled some papers from the same pocket and started rolling, spider fingers dancing, conjuring two perfect joints.

"That woman," said Jack.

"Yeah?"

"What was she going on about?"

"Trouble."

"She seemed pretty intense."

"Rich people always get intense when something doesn't go their way."

"Col."

Col looked up from his joint. "Jack. She was pretty, I get it. A damsel in distress. But she, and her problems, are out of our league. Out of our fucking galaxy, mate."

"Yeah," Jack said, a non-answer.

"We've had a long, hard day of petty crime, comrade." He held up the joints. "We need to unwind."

"Yeah," said Jack, a real answer.

Two floors up to the roof. Jack hadn't figured a way to disconnect the smoke alarms in the building, so they'd had to pop the access panel to the roof. Easier to break into one of these places than smoke in one. They sat on the half-metre ledge, legs dangling over infinity. The neon city shimmered out to the horizon, unstable, somehow, under Jack's eye.

"This," Jack held up the joint, and pointed it at the scene, "and that view. Makes this city seem like—like something else."

"Yeah?" asked Col. Interested.

"Yeah. Like it's not all real, you know?" Jack's eyes were glazed. "Like it's part illusion. Like it's…" He trailed off.

"The information isn't in the drug. It's in you."

"Yeah?"

"Yeah. Opens the doors of your perception. *Your* perception."

"Nah mate," said Jack. "Pretty sure it's the joint."

"Your information is right, Jack. This city runs over with ghosts and neon gods."

Jack nodded, not understanding, and passed him the joint. It looked like Col wanted to make a speech; harder for him to do it supping on a J. Col inhaled, orange tip burning against the darkness, while Jack took that small space to absorb the quiet.

"Gotta move out soon," said Col. "The government rolled over on their latest claim, so Chinese money's coming back in."

"Huh?"

"Chinese claim over North Vietnam."

"Oh. Where'd you get all this information?"

"The news, dickhead, like everyone else."

"Oh."

"Thought you'd know about that."

Jack straightened. "Why?"

Col shrugged. "Yeah. Sorry mate."

Jack looked at the yellow crane, the number 789 emblazoned in red neon on its cab, towering over a giant hole in the ground in the next lot. Fingers of ochre rebar spread their tendrils from the walls of the pit under construction lights. The lights had come on a week back, stayed on. "Yeah," said Jack. "The cranes been moving again. I heard Three Toes Sally lived up in one of those for a while. Wind kept her awake."

"There's no solitude, anymore," said Col, looking out over the city, swapping without explanation to the conversation he wanted.

This is what Col did, instead of uni. Ruminated from the top of abandoned buildings. He should have been doing it on campus. Smarter than most of those rich cunts. Talked just like them, too, especially when he was getting high. "There's no contemplation, no quiet choices," Col continued. "No place to be alone, even in our own heads. We are a product of the freewave. The *single most* important product. Every moment we use it we contribute to the knowledge of the mega-corps. Monetizing our data, freely, willingly giving them the information they need to perfect their control."

"Sure no contemplation with you talking all the fucking time."

"The freewave is central now to what we do as a species. Indispensable."

Jack inhaled.

"Ever wonder if we actually exist?" asked Col.

"Shit. Mate. Seriously. Have another toke."

Col accepted the doobie, did as asked. Then continued:

"When our decision-making is nurtured by corporate algorithm, when so many of our experiences are *their* simulations of experience, when we've outsourced our memories to be stored and filed away, by them. When our every moment is sampled, deconstructed, and built back into Trojans—advertising, architecture, news reports—that reformat our lives. How can we exist, then, when we're someone else's dream? They create these cities, Jack, and cities are huge external memory devices. But the memories are not ours, always those of others."

He waited, like Jack was meant to say something. So Jack said: "Yeah."

Col continued: "They create the spaces within which we live our lives, moulding us to fit into the places they define—public or private, park or car park. We are created and re-created by our spaces. It's a constant feedback loop. Space shapes behaviour—what you can do in it, what you can't. It's identity. Here, we can exist, in a space not fully imaged, but once their minds return to this place, we will be gone."

"Right."

"We can only exist in the places they've forgotten. Our external world was colonised centuries ago, given over to the oligarchs. Our internal spaces are being colonised, as well. Our desires, choices, even our memories, poured into the moulds they inscribe."

"So it's their fault we broke into this building?" asked Jack. "Don't think the judge will see it that way."

"Small acts of resistance. Heterogeneity in the face of crushing corporate assimilation."

"Wow. Sounds noble, mate. And complicated. Hetero-what-the-fuck. Shit. Though I got to say: that Chinese woman looked like a large act of resistance, to me."

Col was silent.

"But we nobly stole her shoes instead."

Col just blinked and looked out at the city.

"Fucken revolutionaries, mate."

Col stayed silent, like always when Jack bit back. Preferring the arguments in his own head, the ones he always won.

Jack inhaled deep on the joint to reduce his anger. He let a long cloud trickle from the side of his mouth. "I got an idea where we should go."

"Yeah?"

"Yeah."

"Well?"

Jack wet his lips. "Out of the city. Sleep under the stars."

"Be at one with nature?"

"Well."

"Mosquitos. Forty-degree heat at five in the morning. Working as indentured labour for some fat-bellied yokel who lets the prettier workers sleep up in his house. That's not our place, Jack. The sunlight would burn us away; we'd disappear. This," said Col, nodding at the view. "This is our universe. You can't escape the universe; you just endure it."

Jack scratched at the scar, the 4007 that'd been carved onto the back of his hand. Held down and cut there. It itched, sometimes, in the night air. "I feel like I'll rot, if I stay here."

"Well, that's the universe. Entropy."

"Ah fuck it," said Jack, backhanding Col on the shoulder. "How the fuck can I get high with you around? I'm going to bed."

Col half-smiled, but his mind was already somewhere else.

Jack inhaled a bowl of instant noodles and pulled himself into his sleeping bag. Army surplus. Best investment he'd made in his twenty-two years.

He stared at the ceiling. In that space after consciousness, but before the dreams come, his mind turned over the image of that young Chinese woman. Desperate, sincere in her desperation.

Mid-morning, stomachs empty, three blocks from home when the police caught them. Cop car in a near-empty street, parked in the shade of a skyscraper's shell, one officer with his arms crossed, another holding a pulse rifle. Mirrored sunglasses, both.

The first uncrossed his arms. "Jack. Col. Don't even think about running." He took off his shades.

"Officer Bella," said Col, "this isn't your beat."

Mid-thirties, dark eyes, lean. They'd encountered him a few times, past couple of years, Jack knew him now. One of those cops who looked like they'd eat your liver, should circumstances allow.

Waves of heat rose from the road, white sun right into their eyes. They eased over to the other side of the road, where a canvas hanging from old scaffolding gave them shade.

Bella stopped two steps from the cruiser, the other cop remained stock-still. The second was big, square jawed, emotionless. Looked like he belonged in one of those fascist recruiting c-casts the cops had been running lately: *the blue line between order and chaos, the difference is a few good men.*

"I heard you two found yourselves some trouble," said Bella. The sun glinted off the shiny black peak of his hat.

Jack's stomach found a second knot. He couldn't resist the urge to glance back, at the mouth of an alley. Thin, cop car wouldn't fit, no way. Dark, led to a jungle of rusting scaffolding, chain-link fences futilely protecting piles of fine white dirt turning brown, half-imagined new buildings, and mounds of the uncleared rubble of the old.

Bella stepped three more to the middle of the road. Shadow behind him, shadows in front, his oiled boots gleaming. His eyes narrowed against the sun. "Been treating our honoured guests with disrespect."

Jack licked his lips. Not the Rebels, then. He drew his intent away from the alley, back to the cop. The woman, Bella knew the woman. But—

"Don't know what you're talking about," said Col.

"Where were you, last night, little before midnight?"

"Hmm," Col scratched his chin, feigning an attempt to recollect. "Vinnies soup kitchen down on Albion. Pumpkin, as I recall."

"Got any witnesses?"

Col shrugged, nonchalantly. "How many do you want?"

Bella's face was stone. He stepped into the shadow on Jack and Col's side of the street, his partner shifted the pulse rifle in his arms.

"This is serious. Colin Charles, and you, Jackson Nguyen—" he pinned each with his eyes as he said the names "—have found a kind of trouble way beyond breaking into cars and squatting on building sites. You're going to need to come with us to the station for questioning."

"Of course, officer," said Col.

Bella nodded, once, in satisfaction.

"One thing first, though."

"What?"

"Who's that in the back of the car there?"

Jack looked over at the white-and-blue. Sure enough, through the tinted window, the outline of a third person, sitting in the back seat. A black, unmoving outline, watching them.

Bella swallowed. "A detective."

"Name?" asked Col, still feigning everything.

"Not your concern, now—"

"Why so nervous, officer?" asked Col.

Bella took three steps and punched Col in the stomach. So quick all Jack had time to do was stare, open-mouthed, at Col curled into a ball at the feet of the officer. The second cop pointed his pulse rifle at Jack's head.

Bella made a show of loosening the handgun at his hip, resting his hand on the grip. "Listen, you little cunts. You're coming for a ride, and you're going to keep your fucking mouths shut. I don't reckon either of you can afford a dentist. Now—" he reached for his handcuffs.

Jack would rationalise what he did next as one of those out-of-body experiences ice addicts and religious fundamentalists always carped on about. Watching, detached, external, at himself, borderline slow motion.

Bella pulling the stud on the hard leather pouch for the cuffs.

Jack moving so Bella was between him and the second cop, reaching out, hand grasping the grip.

Bella, surprised, frozen for two seconds too long as Jack popped the cop's pistol from its holster.

Calm as Buddha himself, Jack pointing the gun at Bella's head and saying *Move and you're dead, pig.*

The second cop yelling, the back door of the cop car popping open, Jack raising his voice and saying it again so everyone heard, everyone believed.

The second cop backing away, not quite knowing what to do with the gleaming pulse rifle.

Jack aiming, pulling the trigger, barrel aimed at a point near the second cop's leg. The gun said *click.*

Someone else said: "Let me have that, mate." A friend's voice, speaking through pain. A hand.

Col's hand. It pried the pistol from Jack's.

In his other Col had the stub-nosed revolver resting against Bella's temple. No hesitation, he thumbed the safety on the police-issue and fired three shots at the car.

Jack yelled, ghost returning to body, ears ringing, breathing hard.

Noise, air expelling from the rear tyre of the police car. Bella on the ground two metres away, hands over ears, eyes wild in his head. Second cop gone, third shape no longer there in the back seat.

Col leaned in, his whisper fierce: run, *run*.

They ran. Into the labyrinth.

Neural pins out, baseball caps pulled over their eyes, they walked in a part of town they weren't used to: a rich part. Col had insisted; his fence for the shoes lived nearby, above an organic wine bar. Police-issue pistol long gone, thrown away as they ran from the scene. GPS trackers in its bullets, in every component, the hottest and the worst thing a crook could hold on to.

Col had sold the woman's shoes, part money, part trade for some second-hand clothes rich people'd pay ten-times the price if you called them *vintage* instead of *second-hand*. Faded jeans, white shirts, red sneakers, weird-smelling denim jackets. The fence, sharp-featured, eyes-darting, one hand resting on top of the other, halo of black-grey hair, called them ironic. Said no-one would recognise them.

Jack didn't know how irony worked as a disguise, but it worked. They walked down Chapel Street. Past massively muscled men, arms and necks writhing with tattoos, drinking elder flower tea from tiny glass cups. Talking skin care and resorts.

Women, blonde, Jack couldn't tell them apart. High heels, muscled calves, power jackets, briefcase, angry.

Chinese, too, students, children of the Red Aristocracy, bearing Dolce and Gabbana or Fujian original purses like totems, like shields.

Jack and Col walked among them, heads down. Facial recognition cameras on every street, the duo wore the large sunglasses that were fortuitously in fashion with men. Walking funny, Col had made Jack put a rock in the heel of his shoe. Some surveillance tech could pick up a unique gait. Police could use the on-retina feeds of regular citizens as well, to find suspects. If they had a warrant, if it was serious enough.

They'd shot at cops. Pretty serious.

They avoided eye contact.

Their mouths watered. At the real coffee, the real meat, large-lipped women, soft-skinned men who'd crumple in a fight. They walked through longing to eat, drink, fight and fuck. But they didn't have enough money for that, not in this part of town.

Jack paused among the tables of an outdoor café. A group of white-teethed patrons had just left, half-eaten salads, fries, tempeh on their plates. He glanced around. No waiters present. He'd taken two steps before Col's hand found his upper arm, pulled him away, dragged him between shopfronts to an alley.

"Don't be fucken stupid," said Col.

"I'm hungry."

"Same here. But we can't draw attention."

"There's money left over. Let's buy something."

Col shook his head. "Not here. Too expensive. We need the cash."

"We need to go get our stuff."

"No."

"Yes."

"We go back," said Col, "we die. I can feel it Jack. Death is waiting there, for us."

"Fuck that druggo talk," said Jack, angry, stomach gnawing, mouth parched. The alley smelled of garbage, fermenting in the heat. "We got to run, we need our food, our sleeping bags. We need to make money: my tools are there. That flexiscreen—we'll get a thousand bucks for that. They don't know where we're staying, Col—how could they. We walk there, no trams, no transit ID. Early morning, we get our shit, and split. Hang out down the uni, look for some kids leaving by car, need to split the recharge bill for the ride. Fuck—" Jack pulled at his shirt "—we look like fucking students now."

"I can't leave."

"We got no choice, mate."

"It won't let me leave, Jack. The city will punish me if I try."

"*Mother fucker*," said Jack, voice raised. They both glanced back towards the alley mouth. No-one was there, no-one noticed. Jack lowered it: "What? Fucken voodoo? Then where? Then how?"

"Poorer suburb, trailer park maybe."

"With what money?"

"From the shoes, with what we can steal. We can manage."

"Yeah," said Jack. "Maybe. But for that we'll need to sell what we got back at the building site."

"Listen—"

"No. I'm done listening to your space cadet bullshit. You want to hide among the bogans? Fine. I get it. They're our people. But we won't hold a trailer two weeks without decent cash and a way to make more. No more spirit-talk, fuck-knuckle, *we get our shit.*"

Col was silent. Not used to Jack stringing so many words together, nor to him having a strong opinion on much at all. He stepped away, leaned against the wall, eyes somewhere over Jack's shoulder. His lips moved, speaking to himself.

A door set into the alley, iron, ten feet down, opened. A man stepped out holding a black guitar case in hand, and a spare tire—including gleaming rims—in the other.

Jack sighed and stepped back, letting the man walk between him and Col. Jack pulled a cigarette from his pocket and leaned against the opposite wall of the alley. Lit the smoke, inhaled deep, taking pleasure in the pain of the smoke as it bit his lungs.

Col said, eventually, softly: "That Chinese woman. She pulled us into her world."

The Chinese woman. Begging, beautiful, vulnerable, untouchable. If Jack could just get her name—

Jack was about to reply when a red message appeared on-retina: *warning—you are not allowed to smoke within fifty metres of a restaurant, café, bar or betting agency within the City limits.* **Fine: Five thousand dollars.**

A pause, and then the words:

The City cannot read your neural pin. Please remain where you are until a parks and gardens representative can arrive in person and issue your fine.

"Fuck," said Jack. He chucked his cigarette, turned, and ran down the alley with Col.

Yao Li followed the spore, superimposed on-retina. Pulled from police files, the DNA signatures of Colin Charles and Jackson Nguyen were easy to follow. Not many traversed the streets of the restricted construction zone, and these two kids were degenerates and petty bandits: neither had the skills nor the tech nor the money to hide themselves.

Yao Li had felt a tic of irritation when given the assignment. But that tic stayed far beneath the surface. Nothing, but nothing, came anywhere near the unbroken pond of his surface.

Instead, he simply nodded after the upstart executive had given the order. Thirty years old and already treating Yao Li with disdain. Dispensing with formalities, not even offering tea when he had entered the office. Sixty stories up, plush red carpet, painting of Confucius in a heavy gold frame on one wall, views out over the city. The executive had given him the task, bluntly, staring at him through superfluous steel-rimmed spectacles. Two boys, knew too much, loose ends. Yao Li bowed and left.

Four years in this city at the end of the world. At the periphery of anything that mattered. For taking out the wrong man in Macau, one of their own, a Baosteel senior executive. As punishment they'd sent him, their best, to a city that could fall off the face of the Earth unnoticed and unmourned by the rest of humanity.

Yao Li had not killed the wrong man. He'd killed precisely the right one. A middle-aged and ambitious former military officer, ended by a young and ambitious princeling from the Red Aristocracy. A business rival dispensed with, an undignified act caused by an uneven temperament. But Yao Li was loyal to the family of the princeling. So he had done as ordered. His reward was not being shot by firing squad, but rather exile.

Just a few months, they'd told him.

Now four years. Li would have preferred the firing squad.

Yao Li bypassed the lock to the building in eight seconds, ghosted up the forty-eight stories in under six minutes. At the top, breathing even, not a bead of sweat.

Head to toe black shadow black, unseen as he drifted through a large open office space, teeming with DNA. Sound: snoring, gentle, next room. Li's carbon alloy hand, sleek, matte black, easing the needle pistol from the holster at the small of his back. Each needle had neurotoxins enough to kill a large man twice over.

The chest of the boy rose and fell, rose and fell. Lying, fully clothed, red sneakers on his feet, mouth parted, vivid purple scar across his cheek. Stillness. Water, dripping from a tap in the next room. Wind caressed the building.

Yao Li, black on black, noiseless, watching.

He raised the pistol and fired two shots: neck and ear. The boy's eyes popped open, mouth gasped for breath. The boy turned his head towards Yao Li.

Yao Li blinked, surprised he had been able to move at all. Loss of all muscle control, instantaneous, then death, were the only aftereffects. The eyes came to rest on Yao Li, sheathed in the dark, still the eyes sought and saw the assassin. Stared right into him, eyes glazing, then glazed, then looking at nothing at all.

Yao Li looked away from those eyes, inscribed a ward in the air with his human hand. His shadow parted from wall shadow. To the stairs, soundless. His ears had picked out and isolated sounds two floors above. Shoes scuffing on plascrete, the click of a cigarette lighter, long inhalation of breath.

Glided up, out onto the roof. Yao Li paused, listened to the Milky Way as it flowed across the sky. Bright up top, stars shimmering, boy sitting on the edge of the building, looking out at the city. Smoking a cigarette, book on the ledge, next to him.

Yao Li pulled the black leather-gripped handle from his belt. He clicked the recessed button near the hilt, the blade materialised. Black, gleaming, nano-sharpened edge, curved. He stopped forward, blade of his Dao sword pointed at the back of the sitting boy. Fast, he decided, between the ribs, into the heart, painless. Dead before the awareness of that fact reached his brain.

Yao Li glided, the boy blew a cloud of smoke into the air, the wind sang through steel construction cables. Three metres away, moving, Li pulled back the blade.

A second person came at him from the right, peripheral, completely silent. Yao Li hissed and turned, defensive pose. He had detected nothing—no sound or movement, but still he'd come, a figure swathed in shadow like Li, its pale white face floating above darkness. No-one, in more than a decade, had got the drop on Yao Li.

Nothing, nothing was there. Yao Li spun, heart beating fast, and spun again, but still nothing. Just rough plascrete, unfinished wind turbines, and the first drops of rain.

Someone said *fuck*.

Yao Li turned again, Jackson Nguyen was looking at him, eyes wide, a revolver in his hand.

Jack Nguyen stared at the killer. Barely visible all in black. But under the stars the blade it held shone. Its eyes shone as well, with an intent that was absolutely clear.

In Jack's hand the revolver. The one Col had bought a box of untracked bullets for earlier that day, from the fence.

He didn't think. He just squeezed the trigger.

The killer grunted and moved, a blur, right at Jack.

Jack stepped back, firing again, wild, tripped, fell backwards. He grasped for an edge, for anything, but found only air. A long second of empty space, wind rushing past his ears, until he crashed into something hard. He groaned, blood on his lip, looked up on instinct. Only blackness above, but he was sure the killer was there, watching, aiming.

Jack had fallen ten feet to their third security measure. A construction platform, one metre wide, three long, cabled from top to bottom of the skyscraper. One of a number of temporary, open-air elevators attached to the side of the building.

Jack slammed the control panel with his palm, the floor gave way underneath him. Only ever meant for escape, Jack had programmed it to drop, stone cold, with gravity, before a graduated slowdown over the last two floors.

He gasped, the air lifting his clothes and hair, the only sounds the screeching of cables and the bellowing of the wind. Hoping, praying he'd rigged it right, that it would work.

It worked. More or less.

Screaming the last few metres, sparks flying, Jack gripped the railing like it was the hand of god. His torso whiplashed, the lift stop-starting the last few feet. Instinct. Flopping over the rail into the dirt. Rain getting heavier, big fat drops. Revolver long-gone, flung into the abyss.

Stumbling and falling, palms scraped, back on his feet. Jack staggered out to the street, rain beating harder, first wet in months. Dry earth drinking it in, steel and asphalt and plascrete roaring in pleasure as the rain beat down beat down.

Jack stopped on the road, trying to get his bearings, wiping water from his face with his forearm. Someone whispered, close, mouth right at his ear: *he's coming*. Jack spun and spun again, hands up, ready to punch and tear. Nothing. He blinked. Empty streets, road slick with water, blue neon beer signs. *Run* whispered the voice, fierce, familiar. Jack took two steps onto the road, spinning, stumbling. *RUN*, it yelled.

He ran.

Right down the centre of the street. Fear propelling him, in the open, no thought to turn or hide. Heart pounding in his chest, scream tearing against the back of his throat, some sublime terror rising within, a subterranean instinct, knowing, knowing, death was stalking.

Big Kev Campbell drove down Rutland, fast. Late to work, again, taking a short cut through the construction zone. One more warning away from the sack. The company wanted to replace them all with auto-driven trucks, but the union had won a rare victory, guaranteeing jobs until the driver voluntarily left or was fired. So the company, the sons-of-bitches, took any infraction they could find to knife the working man. Get them off the books, replaced by an automaton designed by some silver-spoon fucktard from Zhongguancun. Driverless vehicles were one-hundred percent safe, these cunts said. Bullshit. More like no holidays, no sick leave, no fucking pay claims, ever.

He made a hard left. Horses all a wash. His sure thing ended up with a nice view of the field. Few beers, consolation, no harm in that. But a few minutes, a couple of beers, and these cunts didn't care—all they wanted was him gone.

Rain hammering the windshield, wipers on full, truck humming, warm in the cab. A couple of long blinks, shake of the head. Tired. Long day in the sun at the races.

Kev spun the wheel again, took the hill at pace down Harrow. Streets wet and deserted, the wind whipping the rain. He eased up on the accelerator as he sailed into the next, turning the wheel into the right—

—at a man, standing in the road, an apparition. Young man, body in shadow, pale face, white face, vivid purple scar, staring right into the headlights—

—Kev swore and yanked the wheel away, straightening, brake pedal smashed to the floor, *FUUUUUUUUCK*

Yao Li ran, free flowing, despite the hole in his lung. In spite of it. On-retina, his combat medical system reported clottocyte nanos had amped up the coagulation, stopped the bleeding. Pumped pain killers enough to ease the piercing agony in his chest, upped the adrenalin. It made him feel uncomfortably close to euphoric. A gunshot high, he'd heard it called.

He hurdled a fluoro-orange construction barricade, winced as he landed, but continued his rhythmic, practiced stride. First time Li had been shot and the shame of it burned harder than the bullet. By the hand of a petty brigand. His exile was perhaps deserved, after all.

Heightened senses picked up the footsteps ahead, the rumble of a truck, DNA spore all over the road. A vagrant and a bandit, yet Yao Li had exposed himself, had allowed…

He set his jaw. Yao Li would take this boy's head. Clean the skull. Place it in his vault.

The white static of the rain was filtered out by his hearing, allowed him to pinpoint the *splash splash splash* of the target running. A few percent of infrared into his vision, and the outline of the boy was clear, a hundred metres up the road. Yao Li ate up the distance between them easily, stride strong, ignoring the rain that battered his face, the tightness in his side.

The needle pistol in his hand again, arm out, horizontal, perfectly steady.

Headlights lit up the road ahead of him. The truck was turning down his street. Yao Li, focussed on his prey, ignored the vehicle as it bent into a turn. The boy's back a wide, easy target.

The truck, angling away from him, swerved suddenly.

The scream of brakes, infra-filter blinding Li as the high beams lit him up. His foot slipped, teeth gritted, he leapt.

Jack turned at the blast of the horn.

The image imprinted: the killer, black silhouette in the beams of the truck, forward-flipping high out of its path, high and free of impact.

Almost. Until ankle clipped.

The body spun in the air, a stick broken and thrown. The recycling truck fishtailed, its driver forcing an impossible angle on the steering wheel, the rear back corner swinging around and swatting the spinning shadow a second time, propelling it across the wet road, over the gutter, flip-flop rag doll, propped against the wall.

The recycling truck slammed through a construction barricade, crushed a low brick wall, shuddered to a halt. The driver's cab door flew open; a middle-aged man with lank hair, large stomach jumped out, eyes wide staring at a spot on the street. He swore.

Jack walked back through the rain, breathing heavy, road surface glistening in the street lights. Neural pinged Col. Silence.

The driver saw Jack approach. "Did you see the other man?" he asked. "The one I missed?" He looked around, frantic. A man with a tenuous grip on a mortgage, a family, a life, that slender thread taut, about to snap.

Jack walked right past him. Wiping the rain from his eyes with the back of his sleeve, he stepped up to the shadow creature. It was a small, surprisingly small. A Chinese male. Only five feet tall. Body broken, eyes calm, fixed on Jack, still alive, utterly devoid of emotion.

Jack bent down, picked up a metallic-blue needle pistol from the ground. The killer groaned, his body shifted, but that was all. Legs shattered, bleeding out onto the slick plascrete, sticking out at obscene angles, arm lolling, palms open. Jack straightened, turned the weapon over in his hands.

Over his shoulder, he heard the *plop plop plop* as the driver turned and ran into the rain.

Jack said: "I reckon this'd be untracked and undocumented. No doubt about it."

The small man in black said nothing.

The pistol shone in Jack's hand. He looked for and found the safety, clicked it, and pointed the gun at the man's head.

"Why?" he asked.

The man seemed to smile at that, the corner of his mouth

twitching upwards.

"I guess you're the type of man who'd never talk," said Jack, quietly.

The man didn't talk.

"It's that woman, isn't it? You all think there's some grand conspiracy. That she gave us something important maybe. Told us something. We just stole her shoes: did you know that?"

That twitch-smile at the corner of the assassin's mouth again. But still, he said nothing.

"You're gonna die, mate. So may as well give it up, what was this all about?"

The Chinese man opened his mouth, his lips glistened with blood. In Mandarin, he said: "[All of life is a dream walking. Death is going home.]"

"Yeah," said Jack as the translation came through. "Yeah I figured. More fucken voodoo. No straight lines in this city."

Jack sighed. He'd never know. He'd never come close to knowing. Instead, he said: "Tell me this, then—did you kill Col?"

The killer nodded, no hesitation.

Jack nodded back and shot a needle into the man's face. Then a second. Then a third. The killer lost all muscle control, face twisting in on itself, mouth popping eyeball popping, something guttural came from the man's throat. Then he was gone.

Jack looked down at the body. Slowly, he went to one knee. Then both. His hands flopped down onto his thighs. His body shook, starting from the chest. A pain buried deep there, shaking his whole frame as it came loose.

"Motherfucker," croaked Jack, through tears.

He'd known before the man had replied. Known Col was dead. Jackson Nguyen looked out at the neon, shining up from the darkling earth. At the city of ghosts, both dead and living. Col with them now, always with them. Ghosts to history, ghosts to the present, moving through the shadows of the world. The universe.

He felt the city reach out and embrace him with its vast indifference.

Sally Redacre walked from her last lecture, elated. Semester done. Subjects passed. Parents and their six-hundred grand tuition fee placated. Out into the carpark. She paused and looked for the guy—Jack something—who had answered her uninet message about the car share.

She was a little surprised to see the guy waiting over near her ride. She didn't recall telling him what she drove.

Early twenties, denim on denim, cigarette in his hand. Asian, Chinese maybe. Too thin, but handsome. Trying to hide it under a Melbourne Storm cap, pulled down over his eyes. But his eyes were soft, his jaw strong.

"You can't smoke in the car," she said, annoyed, surprised. She'd never met anyone who smoked.

He dropped the cigarette, crushed it under his red sneaker.

She raised an eyebrow at that, but also noticed the rolled up sleeping bag and backpack at his feet. Graphic novel sitting on top. That reassured her, somehow. After an awkward silence she said: "Well, um, Jack. I got your credit transfer, thanks."

Jack scratched the back of his hand. Sally couldn't help but notice a rough tattoo of the number 4007 there. Deliberately distressed-looking, she supposed, in line with the latest fashion.

"What a lovely tattoo," she said, still attempting conversation. "Does that number have some special meaning to you?"

He pulled his sleeve so it re-covered the tat and said, in a broad Australian accent: "Yeah. It's the amount I once owed to bookies down in Geelong. They put it there as a reminder."

She took the deadpan delivery as dry humour and laughed. "Well, I suppose we should be going. You have family in Adelaide?"

"Not yet."

She took this as more humour, smiling. "Ha. Well, let's get going then."

"Yeah," he agreed, hand on top of the car, looking back at the city. He seemed to be listening to something and for a moment, floating on the breeze, Sally thought she heard someone whistling classical music.

"Yeah," he said again. "It's time I left."

THE GREAT BUDDHIST MONK
BEAT DOWN

I walked down the steps. I didn't like matter transporters.

I was halfway to the lobby door when the concierge said: "Mister Kandel, a moment." The concierge was a gleaming automaton with a head carved from walnut.

I walked back to the reception desk. The robot's suit smelled like wet carpet.

"Yes?" I asked.

"You've lost your memories. We'd like to help."

"Who's we?"

"We baked you a slice of apple pie."

The concierge put a plate holding an acute triangle of apple pie on the counter, steaming. "Thanks," I said. I picked up the plate and left.

I ate the pie as I walked down the street. It was cold out, flurries of snow starting down, so the hot pie was most welcome. I was licking the pastry crumbs off the plate as I arrived at the pharmacy.

I gave the plate to a store boy as I entered; he remarked how well I'd done in eating it all. I wasn't really taking notice of him, though. Neurons had started flashing:

– (image) green halo, hovering above my head – / – (voice): desuetude, decline of neural pathways. Everything we've always wanted – / – (image) the bright blue-glowing logo of Baosteel – / (image) man in an expensive suit holding a purple pill between thumb and forefinger –

I looked around the pharmacy blinking, white and clean with rows of medicine, all neatly labelled.

"You've come for your medication," said the pharmacist.

"But I've just eaten this pie," I said, by way of explanation.

"I see," he replied. "Who gave you the pie?"

"So I'm not sure I'll be needing my medication."

The pharmacist pulled a photon-repeater from under the counter and levelled it at me. A little red light blinked on the side. The barrel stared at me, unblinking.

"Buddy," said the pharmacist. He wore thin, silver-rimmed glasses. He was a mild-mannered man with precise white hair. He held the gun as though it were some innocuous thing. Like a clipboard. "You always need your medication. Without your pills you'll be unable to continue your work." I felt I knew this pharmacist very well, but right then I couldn't remember his name. I couldn't remember my work right at that moment either, though some part of me agreed that it was indeed very important.

I thought about running away.

"Don't even think about running away," said the pharmacist.

I turned and hit the door with my shoulder. The façade of the shop shattered as I dived out into the snow, hot white heat behind, freezing white in front. Glass showered the street, flame too. I rolled onto my back and patted myself down for wounds. Nothing. Not a scratch. In the gutter, I raised myself to my knees. Out in the street, pedestrians bustled up and down the sidewalk, heads bent against the thickening snow, oblivious.

Inside the brightly lit store, the boy and the pharmacist looked at me. Anger from the pharmacist, wry amusement from the boy. They didn't move. Just stood there, like statues.

I dusted off snow and glass and then continued down the street, thinking about pie.

The street was full of robots. More than I had seen in a long time. I wondered if it was robot pride day or some such thing. But they didn't seem to be singing songs or holding placards. Just walking down the street, oblivious. Some sheep. Some tigers. Some human-like. Chromium and wood-panelled heads bent against the cold, like everyone else.

I bought a ticket at the box office. I was late, so the usher had to shine a torch down the aisle, showing me to my seat. The movie was about a drunken poet eating someone's brain. I laughed a lot. It was just me in the cinema, though halfway through a brass monkey came in and sat at the other end of my aisle. I couldn't help but notice every other scene it'd move a couple of seats closer. Finally, during a particularly funny moment where the poet beat up the Buddhist monk for requesting alms, the monkey took the seat right next to me. It smelled like soap, the back of its brass hands were covered in fine black fur.

"You know," it said, "you're in the wrong business." The monkey's voice was extremely high-pitched. It grunted a bit before and after it spoke. Still, it seemed to take itself quite seriously.

"I feel like some whiskey."

The monkey sighed. *Oo-oo ah-ah, sigh.* "I suspect that's because you think you're in a cinema, and someone in the movie is drinking whiskey. You're very suggestible, in the state you're in. Is someone drinking whiskey?"

On screen the guy was drinking whiskey straight from the bottle, off-stage, just before a poetry reading.

"That so?" I said. "Well the scene before this, the poet peed on another guy's eyeball when the second guy tried to look at him through a peephole in the cubicle. I hope you're not thinking of following me to the toilet."

"What?" *Oo-oo ah-ah.* "What on earth are you watching?"

I pointed at the screen by way of explanation.

"I'm not in your reality," said the brass monkey. "That's the problem."

"Do you have any pie?" I asked.

"I'm glad you asked." The monkey opened its chest cavity and pulled a slice of cherry pie from it. "This will help."

I ate the pie while the monkey watched. There was a softness to its green glass eyes I found quite strange.

"Good?" it asked.

"Tasty," I replied, around a mouthful.

"Do you know what year it is?"

"Do I get more pie if I answer correctly?"

"The year, Kindred." And as the name left her lips I realised it was mine.

"Well," I said. "It's 3096."

"No Kindred, no. It's—"

There was a commotion up at the doors to the cinema—people yelling, feet stomping, flashing blue lights. The brass monkey grabbed my hand. "Come with me," it said, and its voice seemed more human female now than monkey.

"I'd quite like to watch the movie."

The lights came on. The movie froze on an image of the poet lying in a garden bed, two cops standing over him, hands on hips. I looked around, the monkey was gone. Men came walking down the aisle. One of them looked a bit like the pharmacist, though he'd lost the silver-rimmed spectacles and now was wearing a suit.

"How the hell did you get *here?*" he asked. His voice had an American accent, refined. The men with him all looked Chinese. They kept craning their necks to look around the cinema.

I held up my ticket stub. "The usual way."

"Oh," he said. He smiled and it was rather a convincing one. "About your medication." He put a hand into his pocket and pulled out a small purple pill. "You missed your last dosage. You're a very sick man, partner."

I connected this memory with the other—the flash-bulb memory of a man offering me this same pill in some other place. A sterile place with white walls and leather straps hanging from a bedframe.

I'd been feeling pretty placid the whole day, even after he shot at me with a photon-repeater. But as he offered me the pill, a fear crept its way down my chest, finding a place to nest at the pit of my stomach. I licked my lips and glanced toward the green exit sign, down near the silver screen.

"Now don't do anything hasty. You're being manipulated. They are trying to implant false memories in your mind, to distract you from your important investigation." He took another step, pill in the palm of his hand.

I yelled: "Flying nova kick!" And flew through the air, my foot colliding with the pharmacist's head. He exploded in a cloud of red and sparkle and I landed in a combat pose. The Chinese guards took one look at the glittering remains of their boss and ran.

I strutted down the street. The snow was getting heavier. I was smiling, thinking about whiskey and another slice of pie when a Buddhist monk came out of the white flurry in his orange robes.

I yelled: "Crouching tiger punch!" and hit him in the face.

My aim was off, my blow striking him at the top of his forehead. The monk yelped and staggered off, holding his head.

I winced and swore. The two bottom knuckles were bloody. I held my fist to my chest, slipping on the sidewalk as I tried to hurry away from the swaying monk.

The snowstorm built. I couldn't even see the cars parked along the road. I wasn't cold, though—just the opposite. Sweat rolled down my forehead, my neck. I blinked the sweat out of my eyes and pushed my way into the next door that presented. A fortuitous choice: a cool and dimly lit slice of my imagination. The bar had a neon blue Pabst Beer sign above the bar, red-leather booths, and a nostalgic haze of cigarette smoke.

I took a stool at the wood-topped bar, sighing as I did. The place was lightly sprinkled with humans in fedoras, drinking beers and murmuring sad stories.

The bartender rolled up.

"Glass of ice and a double of Lagavulin Sixteen," I said

"Separate?"

"Separate. And a good cigar, if you have one."

"Of course," said the bartender.

A body sat on the stool next to me. I hadn't heard it approach. It said: "Did you enjoy your pie, sir?"

I turned to look at the newcomer. It was the walnut-headed concierge, wearing loose tracksuit pants and top. Its dark eyes shone as it looked at me, and it still smelled like wet carpet.

"Just come from the gym?" I asked.

"I'm on the run, Kandel. They're after me."

"Better have a drink then," I said, and signalled the barman.

He rolled over, placed a glass in front of each of us. He pointed his finger and whiskey came out the tip, filling up each in turn.

The concierge seemed about to say something. "Actually, I do need a drink," he said instead, picking up his drink and taking a long slug.

As he placed the glass back down he said: "Do you know who I am, Kandel?"

"I didn't know robots drank whiskey."

"I'm not a—" the robot sighed. "I think you need more pie."

"Hmm," I agreed.

"We couldn't get any more into you."

"A packet of chips will do then."

"This is serious. They're out to get you. Wipe your memory, brainwash you, have you do their bidding."

I pulled a napkin from the bar, poured the ice into it, then folded it and rested it on the top of my knuckles. "You're sounding paranoid there, Mister Concierge."

The robot finished its drink. Its sleek, chromium hand shook as it put down its glass. "Tell me something, Kandel, what were you doing yesterday?"

"Well," I said. "Well I—" I picked up the cigar the bartender had clipped and placed next to the drink. I wet the end with my lips. It lit itself. I savoured the taste, sighing out a thick cloud. "I haven't been sleeping too well. The days—well they've been blurring into each other lately."

"Okay then. What's your occupation?"

"I—I."

"The name of your wife? Your daughter?"

"My—My daughter?"

"You see." The robot leaned forward. Its breath was stale. "You don't even know who you are. Didn't even know your name, until Eulalie said it to you."

That fear I'd felt earlier, with the monkey. It was returning again. My lips felt dry. I wet them with some whiskey. The truth was I couldn't remember any day, at all. There was the sense of events, of a life lived, but every time I tried to look at it directly, my gaze elided. Slid out from under my concentration. I didn't even know who Eulalie was, though it felt like a name I should remember.

"Why do you even care?"

The robot put its hand on my upper arm. "We're old friends, Kandel, we went to Shanghai Jiao Tong University together." I couldn't help but notice that the robot's words didn't quite match its lips. Like badly dubbed live speaking.

"Right," I said. I pulled my arm away from him, worked on my cigar instead. The automaton watched as I had the bartender refill my glass. "So what's the solution?" I asked.

"You come with me," it replied, equal parts desperation and excitement. "There's a place. It's safe. We have all the pie you can eat. No one can touch us there. We can get you back, there. Back into our reality, back to the real world."

"Hmm. And how do I know you're not with them?"

The robot straightened in its chair. "With *them*?"

"Yes. Them. The pharmacist. He keeps trying to give me my medication."

"Kandel, my friend. I'm trying to save you."

"Maybe I should hop in a matter transporter, set the destination for random. Live quietly near a gin bar. Take up golf."

"You can't run from this. None of us can." The robot's tone had drifted into pleading.

"There's one just over there."

"One what?"

I pointed. The matter-transporter booth sat against one wall, clad in mahogany and polished steel.

"You're better off taking the train, believe me."

I sighed a cloud of cigar smoke. "Why?"

"Because matter-transporters don't exist. That door you're pointing at looks like it leads to a janitor's closet."

"Right."

"It's 2100, Kandel."

"Okay."

"I know you think it's—"

"3096."

"But here, in the present, the Glimmer Train connects all of Asia. You can get anywhere, from here."

"Sure."

The robot paused. "Do you know where here is, Kandel?"

I finished my drink. I was starting to get a little buzz. "I think I'll go for a walk." I hopped off the stool.

The concierge jumped off his and grabbed my arm again. "Don't leave. Don't go through that door. Come with me—there's another way out of this place they don't know about."

I looked around the dank and small San Franciscan bar. Wood front door, green exit sign for the back. "They'll probably figure it out."

"No, Kandel. Please."

I pulled my arm from his. "Look, the pie was great. But I have this urge to drink. A lot. Alone. Well, until I find myself a broad. A nice big round one, lonely, you know the type. Get a little loose, have little fun."

"A broad? I don't know what you're talking about. You're a happily married man, Kandel. You don't even like alcohol."

"God, I sound like a bore."

"You're the finest neuroscientist of your generation."

"Yeah, but do I know how to Watusi?"

The robot continued, insistent. "You discovered a way to reverse the generalised reduction in Kinase A proteins. You found it—a cure for the systemic decline in synaptic growth in the human brain. You're a hero, Kandel, you changed the world. Or were going to, anyway. Until Baosteel got wind of your discovery. They drugged you, wiped your memories and replaced them with ones suited to their interests. You've been helping them perfect a new exo-memory system. It's control, Kandel, control of everything." The robot grabbed my sleeve one last time. "The corporations—mind control, control of history, the future. Only you can save us, Kandel. *Don't go through that door.*"

I walked out the door.

The concierge stumbled out after me. The snowstorm had died down a little, though it was still hot outside. A man wearing wrap-around sunglasses bumped into the concierge, spilling his coffee down the robot's front.

The concierge gasped, gleaming hand grasping the coffee stain. It half turned, sparks popping, and collapsed onto the pavement.

The outlines of the concierge blurred. Sparks were drops of blood, then sparks again, the walnut head was actually walnut hair, dyed, on a middle-aged Chinese man wearing grey sweat pants. Then back to the automaton, twitching. I looked up. The object in the man's hand looked like a gun, then a Styrofoam coffee cup.

The snowstorm increased in intensity. A blizzard. I steadied myself on the wall, white all around, barely able to see my feet. I used the wall to guide me away from the concierge and the sunglasses.

That went on for a few minutes until the blizzard started to fade and I could see my hand in front of my face again. A blue-and-red neon Budweiser sign caught my attention. I lurched toward it, breathing heavy in the heat, and found myself at the counter of a hole-in-the-wall bottle shop.

A woman with a red eye patch said: "Well? Want do you want?"

"Tsing Tao Rice Whiskey."

She gave me bottle of Smirnoff du Czar in a brown paper bag. I thanked her and threw a few red dollar bills on the counter.

The snow had cleared enough to reveal a large, lush green park further down the road. I pulled the cork on the vodka and sucked some down as I made my way over. The shaking in my hands abated. It was a pleasant park. Two small lakes, stone bridges, coconut palms. I shrugged off my coat and sat down with a sigh on a green metal bench.

The strength of the snowstorm ebbed and flowed, white static occasionally blocking my view. People walked past, avoiding eye contact with me. Wind rustled the branches of a tree nearby. A huge green-and-ochre lizard idled across the paved walkway, not three meters from me, and disappeared into lush foliage.

One-third through the bottle the brass monkey appeared. Walked straight up, gleaming in the sunlight. It was a little taller than I remembered, and had the gait of a human. It sat next to me without asking.

Hmm. Jasmine. It was the finest damn monkey I'd ever smelled.

"It's a defensive mechanism, Kindred," she said. Her voice had changed. It was sultry now. Like a lounge singer with pack-a-day habit.

The vodka was making me sweat. I managed a confused grunt.

"You're retreating from reality and layering it with one of those detective novels you're always reading."

"Oh."

"Don't pretend you don't understand me, Kindred," she said, voice tight.

I took a swig of the bottle. "Well. If that's true," I said, booze heat on my chest, "then the femme fatale in this story is a metal monkey. Now, you'd think I'd give myself a more alluring projection."

"They want to take you back to Shanghai. Plug you back into their program. They've developed the next-generation Baosteel Infinity pin. Or *you've* developed one, anyway. They'll—they'll change everything."

"Though if you are the femme fatale," I said, "it means you're leading me into a trap."

"We have a facility in Bhutan. The government is isolated, sympathetic. There's de-facto protection from India. We'll be safe there."

"Shi-iiit. Sure sounds like a trap."

Her voice softened when she said: "I'm your wife."

"Wow. They did things differently back in 2100."

"No I—I'm not a monkey."

"That's a relief. I could be the greatest neuroscientist in the world—but you fuck one brass monkey."

"*Kindred*," she said, softness gone. "You don't swear. You're not yourself."

I sucked on my bourbon, then burped. It smelled like apple pie. "Yeah, yeah lady. I'm the most boring man in the world. Gotcha."

"You're starting to sound drunk."

"Tell me something, monkey."

"My name is Eulalie, Kindred."

"Tell me something, Ukulele."

The monkey sighed. "Yes?"

"Who was the Buddhist monk I punched? In your reality?"

"You punched a monk? Why?"

"I don't know. I thought it was symbolic or something. I keep seeing them around, suspicious bastards. Orange robes. Beady little eyes."

"You're in Bangkok."

"Oh."

"There's monks on the street all the time."

I sucked down some more bourbon. "Probably a good pad thai around here. You hungry?"

"You *are* drunk."

"Cause I'm *really* fucking hungry."

The snowstorm was all but gone. The pharmacist walked up to us, dressed now in a finely cut suit, a white homburg on his head. The brass monkey jumped from the bench and interposed herself between us.

The mild-mannered man said, over her head: "Come home, old friend. Come take your medication."

"Go fuck a donut," I slurred.

"The real world is San Francisco, partner. The real world is you, an alcohol and ice-nine addict, in rehabilitation."

I grunted.

"You, a successful private detective, need to return to your practice. Re-open that case—the one that tipped you over the edge. The Baosteel corruption case."

"Cool," I said.

"Liar," said the monkey.

"Who is the monkey then?"

He didn't even blink. "The monkey is part of their program. I mean, buddy: a world-renowned neuroscientist who doesn't drink or smoke. Faithful to his wife. Kidnapped by a Chinese memory-pin manufacturer in order to perfect the final version of their next product—does this sound like a real person to you? Does this grand conspiracy have even the faintest sniff of the truth?"

A drop of sweat rolled down the man's cheek. His Adam's apple bobbled while he waited for my answer.

"Why did you try to shoot me earlier?"

"I didn't," he said, without hesitation. "Your rehabilitation program includes memory readjustment therapy. A malicious entity has infiltrated this system and is trying to force a psychotic break from reality. Prevent you going back to work. They're trying to stop us."

"You're here, in this reality now, aren't you?" I asked.

The monkey interrupted: "They brought you to Bangkok to meet other experts in the field. We're in Lumphini Park in the centre of the city. He can't touch us, not out in the open like this."

The pharmacist ignored the monkey. "I'm here, old friend. I've always been here. I'm your partner at the agency. I was there three years ago, when you went into rehab for the first time."

I waved a bottle at the park. "Where am I?"

"The Dante Sanatorium. We're here, just two friends, four white walls, and one purple pill. Take it, and this psychotic episode will end. You don't need to save the world, Kindred. You just need to save yourself." He reached into his jacket pocket and brought out the pill.

I stood. "Fuck it. Time to get out of here."

He smiled.

I hit him in the face with the bottle. The impact jarred my arm; the pharmacist crumpled.

Chinese men wearing sunglasses appeared. From behind trees, from the shadows of a nearby stone bridge. There was one even squatting behind a metal bin just three metres away.

The brass monkey grabbed my hand. *"This way."*

The men with sunglasses ran after us.

The brass monkey put a finger to its ear. "Come on, *come on.* Give us some cover."

As we ran across the open grass, the snow started up again. Harder and harder. I tripped over my own feet, elbow hitting the ground. But the monkey was there, pulling me, yanking me along.

I heard a pop and slam and there I was, in the blissfully cool interior of a car.

The brass monkey was sitting opposite, legs crossed. It had flowing dark hair I hadn't noticed before. We were in a limo, apparently. She indicated the seat next to me with her hand. A steaming slice of cherry pie was on it. I took a bite. Delicious.

"How did you know he was lying to you?" she asked. The robot monkey was fading now. In its place was an attractive Chinese woman wearing jeans and a T-shirt. She wore several large brass bracelets on each wrist.

I finished chewing while I thought it over. Pastry crumbs dusted my lap. Not full Chinese actually, she was Eurasian. Pale, smooth skin, a small smile, lips that would make a bishop blush.

"Well," I said. "I understood everything the concierge was saying. About neural decay, about the Kinase A protein, all that. Everything, right there at the front of my brain. A strange knowledge for a detective."

"Hmm. Pretty good deduction, for a neuroscientist."

"Just logic," I sighed.

"So why so glum?"

"Oh I'm not glum."

"Kindred."

"I'm fine. Eulalie."

"You wanted to be a private detective, didn't you?"

"Well."

"And that stuff about large-bottomed women—I was watching that, you know."

I felt myself go red.

"Whatever you have swimming around in your subconscious," she said, leaning forward in her seat, "is best left to the novels, mister."

I smiled, still a little red, and looked at the window. At the steaming streets of Bangkok. The glimmer scooters and the yellow auto-buses and the lady-boys standing on street corners laughing, and orange-robed monks walking slowly through a mad, chaotic city.

Eulalie Yu watched Kindred Kandel as he finished his pie. Inside the top pocket of her jeans was a silver blister. Empty now, each green pill broken in two, contents mixed into the pastry.

Bhutan.

People would believe anything.

THE LINE
2099

This is going to hurt."

George held the goateed man in an arm-lock, face down on the canvas. The man managed to turn his head to one side and gasp: "No."

George bent down, easing the strain on the arm for a moment. Sweat rolled down his brow, from the tip of his nose onto the man's back. He whispered, "Yes."

"BREAKER... BREAKER... BREAKER..."

The waves of the chant broke across his concentration. The floodlights centered on the cage burned his eyes. But beyond, in the twilight of the stadium, he could see it was packed, as usual. Most had come straight from work, wearing the red and fluorescent yellow coveralls of the operators, or the blue and yellow of the mine technicians. There were a smattering of brown faces in the crowd, but that mob usually stayed away from fight night. Understandable. Emotions always got a little high by the end.

In the front row were the dark-suited executives, on their feet with the rest of the crowd, punching their fists in the air. A glassteel partition separated their comfortable faux leather seats from the plastic provided to the rest of the crowd. The redhead—Langer— was there of course, in his regular front-row spot, his white shirt soaked through with sweat. He pointed his rust-red akubra at George's opponent, bringing it up and down, like he was trying to break the man's arm himself.

George shook his head against the noise, against the heat of the room. The air conditioners were on full blast, but five thousand sweating, jostling bodies made the atmosphere dense, inescapable.

George looked down at this opponent.

Fight Night couldn't end with a submission. One fighter had to be unconscious, incapacitated, or dead. George ended most fights by breaking his opponent's arm. The Corporation gave a medical exemption for injuries received on Fight Night, fixed the fighter free of charge. Even used nanotech to knit the bones, have them back at work in a couple of days. A break was the easy way out. Merciful even.

Except for this moment.

George levered the arm until he felt the snap vibrate through his hands, sharp and final. He let the limb drop. The goateed man writhed on the canvas, clutching at his elbow.

George stood to his full height, his lean muscles coated with sweat. He looked around at the crowd, faces all in shadow.

"BREAKER… BREAKER… BREAKER…"

The tumult grew; they chanted his name over and again. George didn't acknowledge them. He walked to the side of the cage.

His corner man passed him a towel and water bottle over the top. "Too easy."

George drank deeply then handed the bottle back. "Yes."

He mopped his face with the towel and waited for the announcer to make it official. Then he walked over to the steel gate. It clicked open. He ducked his head as he stepped out. Two fighters, stripped to the waist, waited to enter for the next bout. George moved quickly up the stairs between the stands, away from the cage. The crowd reached out to him, patted him on the back, called out his name. He let the sound wash over him, the hands he brushed aside.

The Cochlear Glyph implant behind his left ear—silent during the bout—started broadcasting as soon as he left the cage. As he glanced up at the giant scoreboard above the stands, the c-glyph whispered the odds for the next fight. When he looked away the feed switched to the murmurs of the commentators discussing the match. The only time the implant was silent was in the ring. How he looked forward to those rare minutes, when the itching in his mind finally ceased.

George made his way to the change room and sat heavily on a hard-plastic bench. He held out his arm while his corner man undid the bindings on his fist.

"Know what that fight was, George?"

"I wouldn't really call it a fight."

Burgess smiled. He had a round face. Pleasant, some would say, if not for the tell-tale redness of his neck and bloodshot eyes. "Not many would." He threw the first wrap away and begun work on the second. "That victory made you the most successful cage fighter in the free zones."

"Is that so?"

"They've been talking about it through the Interwave all week," Burgess tapped his finger behind his left ear, against his own c-glyph implant. "Haven't you been watching? You certainly can't help listening to it."

"I've learned to tune it out."

His corner man laughed. "No wonder you're still sane." He paused, pulling a small capsule out of his shirt pocket. "Different strokes."

George pointed his chin at the pill. "That shit will rot your brain."

"Probably." Burgess shrugged. "But what difference does it make here?"

"All the difference in the world."

Burgess raised his eyebrows. "Really? I'm not the one spending all my spare time getting kicked in the head."

George smiled. "I'll kick you in the head free of charge. You'll get the same result as that shit—" he pointed at the powder "—and save yourself some money."

Burgess returned the smile. "And you wonder why you don't have any friends."

"I never wonder. Friends are a liability."

"So is having broken the arm of half the people you work with."

George grunted. "Ha. True enough, true enough."

His corner-man cracked the capsule between his teeth, closing his eyes for a few moments. When he opened them again he seemed to find it hard to focus. "This can't last forever George."

"What?"

Burgess scratched the side of his face slowly, pointed vaguely at the room. "This."

George looked at his fist, flexing it. "Yeah. I know Burgess. I know."

George sat alone at one of the long tables in the mess hall. A score of rows were in the hall. Each could seat more than a hundred. The morning diners moved around him quickly, ate quickly, departed quickly. No-one wanted to be late. In the distance were the cyclical tunes and bells of the slot machines.

George took a bite of corn bread and scooped some beans. He grunted. Not much flavor in either. The entertainment screen built into the breakfast counter murmured at him through his implant. He ignored it. The endless stories of imminent war bored him. He didn't want to look at the betting markets either: the line on live female births next year in Sichuan Province, or the line on soya tonnage harvested in Hunan for June. Nor was he interested in placing a few credits on the temperature range down in Perth on the next Wednesday, or the odds of rain falling in the Free Economic Zone any time in the next six months. Weather investments weren't his thing. None of the markets were for that matter. All except for one. Fight Night.

George tapped the scratched touchscreen, flicking past the markets and newsfeeds until he found the icon for solitaire. George was halfway through his second game when three ascending tones sounded in his ear. The voice of the c-glyph, flat and uninflected, followed: "Probationary Citizen George Duulngari. You are required at an executive meeting in the gaming hall in three minutes."

George glanced down at the time-stamp on the counter screen. "If I do that I'll be late for my shift."

"Your shift has been cancelled, courtesy of Vice President Langer."

George raised an eyebrow. "The redhead himself? I'm honored."

"An understandable reaction."

George returned to tapping his finger on the solitaire game, sipping at a cup filled with a thin, bitter liquid they insisted on calling coffee.

After a minute: "Mister Duulngari. Why are you not proceeding to your meeting?"

George indicated the entertainment screen with his hand. "Just savoring my day off."

The c-glyph Artificial Intelligence couldn't see him gesture, of course, just force of habit. He'd never got used to having conversations with voices inside his head since arriving in the zones.

"For every minute you are late to a meeting with an executive, you will be given a productivity penalty," said the voice, with the rhythm of a metronome.

"Cheers. You're very efficient."

"Efficiency is productivity's midwife," quoted the voice.

"So is the whip."

The usual response from the AI when perplexed by a statement was to act as if it hadn't heard it—pretty human in that regard as well. "You are now one minute late for your meeting. A productivity penalty has been applied to this quarter's pay."

George sighed and stood, wiping his mouth on his sleeve.

The sound of the slots was deafening as he entered the large archway at the rear of the cafeteria. Five thousand machines spewed sound and fury into the dark, cavernous hall. To one side of the door, an image of Langer shimmered into life. He was half a head shorter than George, and nearly a full body wider. He wore his usual tailored black suit and rust-red akubra. His trousers were a couple of inches too high, the grin on his face a little too wide.

"Breaker, so glad you could join me."

George walked over. "Are you a projection of the actual Langer, or are you one of his day copies?"

The simulation of the man shrugged. "Not relevant. If you're speaking to me, you're speaking to Langer. We carry the same authority."

"So you're a day copy."

The too-wide grin was shortening. "The Vice President receives a download directly from his day copies every twenty-four hours, summarizing all our decisions. In the five years he has been in his position, he is yet to change or even question one of those decisions."

George looked him up and down. "They certainly feed you well in the executive."

Langer's eyes flashed. "You want to play it that way," he said, "that suits me fine. I'm here to discuss business, not enjoy the stellar conversational skills of a cage fighter." He pointed at one of the aisle between the slots. "Let's walk."

The Vice President moved into the gloom. George hesitated for a moment before falling into step.

"You're the most successful fighter in the history of the free zones, Breaker." He said, though his tone didn't make it sound like a compliment.

George said nothing.

"You've become something of a legend here in free zone three. But this success has its consequences. The odds for your fights have left you almost unbackable these days. Pretty soon no-one left will bet on you."

"I will."

Langer nodded, but not in agreement. "Sure. I've seen your record, same as everyone. You've made good money on yourself, especially at the start. But these days you face diminishing returns." He stopped, lifted his akubra up with one hand and wiped a gleam of sweat on his forehead with a white handkerchief.

He pointed at George with a closed fist. "How'd you like to

make some real money?"

George winced and started moving again down the aisle. Rows upon rows of faces, brown and white, sat at the machines with eyes glazed. Or closed. The players held one thumb out, pressed on a glowing red pad on the front of the slot, making the reels spin and spin again. George felt a tugging on his implant as he passed each machine, each one reaching out, asking him to play: the familiar ache returning for a moment.

Here in the hall, if he closed his eyes the nanos attached to his optic nerves would activate. A perfect, three dimensional image of each machine would appear in the darkness behind his eyelids. A few lines of script would provide the current jackpot on the machine, the comps accrued from playing. A woman, chosen by complex algorithm to appeal to George's tastes, would sit smiling in front of the glittering, hypnotic pattern of the wheels. The vision of the room would be crystal clear, clean and bright, with smiling patrons and carpet that didn't stick to the soles of the shoe. No wonder so many played with their eyes closed.

George waved a hand at the banks of machines. "This was all I did when I first arrived, got into it real quick. But that's the way the Corporation set it all up, right? It's just this or the dope."

Langer placed his handkerchief back in the top pocket of his jacket. "We're in the middle of the desert. People need to be entertained."

George stared straight ahead as he walked. "I'd work twelve hours, come back and play for four more, then collapse into my bunk. I'd wake up in the morning and my implant would be urging me to play. I'd see the slots behind my eyelids, floating, waiting. But I didn't need any encouragement: I'd always get an hour in before work. I could never stop thinking about it when I wasn't playing and I never wanted to stop when I'd started. It got to the point where winning or losing didn't matter anymore. Even though, of course, I was losing everything. In the first two years here I never slept with a woman, got in a fight, or popped an ice-nine."

Langer shrugged, glancing over the machines as they passed. "This isn't a nanny state. People's personal choices are their own."

George stopped and looked at the man. "Then it got really bad. I went at it for three days straight, lost for three days straight. Missing work. I couldn't distinguish between playing the slots and dreaming about them. What was real, what was imagined. So exhausted I had some sort of seizure, thrashing around on the floor until they sedated me and put me in the infirmary. I remember how the Corporation gave me a few days off to 'recuperate'. You know where your mob sent me?" George clenched his fists, his knuckles cracking.

Langer's eyes had glazed over. "I don't know where we send the addicts and the weak. And I really don't care."

"You piece of shit!" George threw the punch he had wanted to throw for six years, his fist driving into Langer's face. His hand, of course, passed clean through, hitting the face of the slot behind. The machine rocked, a crack appearing across the screen.

Though a simulation, Langer jumped back a step, mouth parted in surprise. George stepped close, his voice low. "You gave me a free hotel room. At a casino in the rec-quad: a fucking casino." He pointed a bloodied fist at Langer. "You want me to throw the fight?"

The surprise had already slipped Langer's face. His eyes went hard, like water over smooth stone. "In the third minute of the second round."

"Why? Hope Corporation owns every slot machine in the free zone, half your workers go broke on them before their contracts are up, and then you own them, too. You are the book for Fight Night. So you're winning every time I win anyway. You don't need the money. Even a big score on this fight is trivial, for the Corporation."

"Nothing is trivial, here."

"What does that mean? Why this fight?"

Langer looked him over, eyes shining in the reflected glow of the machines. It really was a very good day copy. "I might be a Vice President, Breaker, but in the end I'm just a company man. I'm a company man because I always put the Corporation first. It'd be smart to show everyone that you can too."

"Yeah, it would," said George, looking down at his hand. One of his knuckles was split and bleeding.

There are a hundred types of pain in the world; it's impossible to avoid them all. As far as George could figure, the only choice you had about it was which one you'd embrace. He looked up. "Here's your answer. Fuck you."

Langer shook his head, eyes gleaming under the shadow of the akubra. "Just wait until I find out about this. You've made a very big mistake."

"Wouldn't be my first." George turned and walked away.

When they pulled the bag from his head the light blinded him. He coughed, barely able to breathe in the heat and thin red dust. His body ached from where they had beaten him with their force batons. After they had dragged him from his bunk, late at night, and set upon him.

Behind him stood a half-dozen security personnel, black sentinels silhouetted against the maddening heat. A second figure stood directly next to George. As his eyes adjusted to the light he saw it was Burgess. One side of the corner man's round face was swollen, his bottom lip split. He smiled weakly. "You might be right about that 'liability' thing."

Less than a metre in front of them, the edge of the yawning chasm of the Great Yandi Pit: one kilometer deep, maybe five wide. The wind whipped at their clothes, pulling at them, beckoning them toward the abyss. A black Humvee rested nearby on the crushed red rock. The door slid open. Inside sat the vice president, in the flesh. He held the akubra in his hands. He seemed to be adjusting the brim.

"I'm asking you twice: lose your next fight George."

George's voice came out in a croak. "Not going to happen."

Langer looked up, nodded at the guards. One stepped forward and brought his force rod down on the back of Burgess' head.

George turned. "No."

Burgess pitched forward. He was looking at George with bloodshot eyes when they struck him. He seemed surprised. His mouth was open, trying to speak.

George looked after him as he disappeared into the depths of the pit. His chest heaved. It felt like he was choking. "Motherfucker."

"Why yes. Yes I am," said Langer.

George tried to speak, but let out a sob. He fell to his knees.

The red head watched him from the cool and shadow of the vehicle. "Really George? That's all it takes? One dead drug addict? Maybe you're not the man I thought you were."

George coughed, cleared his throat. The ground was warm under his knees, the sun stinging the back of his neck. "You're the one sitting behind ten men. Come over here, little man. Come over here and I'll show you who I am."

Langer smiled. "That's more like it. You'll need to bring some of that to the ring for your next fight. But not too much." He turned and swung his legs over the side of the seat, so he was facing George, "We have a problem, Breaker. It's the audience. The punters, the…" he gestured with his left hand, "the people.

They love you. And fear you. These are powerful things, powerful emotions. The problem as I see it is this: you didn't earn these things by yourself—far from it. You're a freeloader. You've manipulated our system. The one we invented, built, and paid for. An operation like this, like Hope Corporation, isn't an accident. It's a work of art. You see, what you're doing, by using the system to your own advantage, is taking us for a ride. And there are no free rides here in Hope Corporation. The user pays."

The vice president ran one finger along the brim of the akubra. "This law is immutable. The user always pays."

George watched him in silence.

"So you'll throw this fight," he pointed at the pit with his hat, "or you'll follow your friend. And if we do have to put you in, well… everyone will think you're just another jumper who couldn't take the heat, the desert, and the time. Another brown stain baking at the bottom of the Yandi, soon forgotten. We win either way."

The redhead placed the akubra on his brow carefully. 'So— what's your answer?'

George closed his eyes for a half a minute. When he opened them, he looked at the place where Burgess had been standing.

He slowly got to his feet. "I'll take the fight."

He'd drunk hard after Yandi. Missed work, knowing they wouldn't care. Wouldn't dock his pay. Wouldn't say a thing. And he played again. Yeah, he played. Six years of living clean, saving his pay, betting on himself on Fight Night. A small fortune.

In three weeks it was all gone. The last of his liabilities sunk into the slots.

So when he stood, finally, in front of the tumult, he felt light as air.

"BREAKER... BREAKER... BREAKER..."

The crowd was as big, as loud as it had ever been.

A fighter with a heavy jaw looked at him through slitted eyes. He moved forward slowly across the canvas, watching George from behind two large fists.

George stood, arms by his sides, watching the man. He smiled a small smile.

The man paused, lowered his fists slightly. "What? What are you grinning at?"

"This is going to hurt."

A SHOUT IS A PRAYER
FOR THE WAITING CENTURIES

2071

I'll give you a roll of barbwire
A vine for this modern epoch
Climbing all over our souls
That's our love, take it, don't ask

A ny food?" asked Phuong.

"No food," replied the woman.

"Rice, old rice, bamboo shoots. Anything."

"No food."

"I have a child; we haven't eaten in two days."

"We all have children. Here, take some water."

Phuong reached out in the darkness, a smooth, cool wooden ladle caressed her hand. She fumbled for the bucket, filled the scoop with water, and held it out for her daughter, who grabbed it and slurped noisily. Phuong felt for Trung and passed the scoop to him. He rested his hand on her shoulder as he drank. Her skin tingled at his touch, familiar, yet always new. Then she took her turn, cracked lips and swollen tongue welcoming the cool stream of water.

Her eyes adjusted to the dark as they drank; further along someone had a battery-powered lamp, its thin glow enough to paint the outline of those hiding in the rough-ceilinged room underground. Women and children, not many men. Not many of those left. Not many young women of fighting age, either.

The woman who'd passed her the water had an AK-47 slung over her shoulder. The sheen of the polished metal gleamed in outline.

"How long has the bombing lasted, older sister?" asked Phuong.

"Hard to count," said the woman. Her face was impassive, drawn. "Two days, maybe three. The freewave's jammed, nanos unusable. Time's different, down here."

Thunder rumbled in the distance, long, growing.

"They are coming," whispered the woman. "Get down."

They did. Huddled together, pressed against the dirt floor, covering the child with their bodies. Phuong hugged her daughter, who was so good, so quiet. Three years old, and never complained, never cried. Trung, his lean arms around his wife. Holding them both.

The storm came.

None of them could take their eyes off the meat. Sizzling, marinating, tantalizing, just lying there within reach, in rows on silver frying pans. The head chef, tall white hat askew, loitered nearby like a bull mastiff over a fresh bone, growling at any of the staff who came too close. Behind the chef, behind the others, all around, were invisible cameras with eyes cool and unblinking, watching the rows of real meat, ensuring the integrity of each rare, tender morsel.

George Duulngari let his eyes linger, like everyone else, as he passed through the kitchen. He straightened the white jacket they'd given him as he walked, too tight across the shoulders, too much room around the waist. He moved through the bustle, the swarm of waiters and waitresses and assistant chefs and despotic minor managers bustling around the gleaming cleansteel kitchens. They made room for him, back here, all of them.

Back here they knew who he used to be; out there they didn't give a damn. George took a deep breath, face carefully blank, and walked out into the ballroom. From the heat and hustle of the kitchens to the leisurely orbiting souls in the cool, crisp air of the grand ballroom. It was brighter, out here, everything was brighter. The gowns and the suits and the glowing, flawless skin and most of all, the teeth. The straight, even rows of designer teeth. Each a symmetrical stanza, a polished white tribute to the wealth and standing of its owner

Somewhere, classical music played while the guests circled each other with the empty smiles and polite nods that only the truly rich could perfect. Their conversations like stones briefly skipping across the surface of their own narcissism, across some tantalizing reveal of the wonder of their own identity, before they departed to a new group to skim their stones across. To a new group with ready vacant smiles, each waiting politely for their turn to speak about themselves.

George picked up a tray and plotted a careful course through.

It held Australian sparkling wine and Belgian beer and Californian cider, together worth a week's pay, maybe two.

George eased his way through fragments of conversation, offering the drinks to those who caught his eye.

"…that colour is divine—vermillion?"

"…my concern is nanotech diversity; we've got to wait days…"

George paused as a woman with superfluous eyeglasses signalled to him. She was talking to a man attempting a regal bearing. She said to the man:

"…then the waitress served *me* the Bluefin sashimi and my *husband* the Wagyu beef. That, professor, is the sort of everyday prejudice that sadly still exists." She paused to pluck a glass of champagne from the tray and continued talking. She didn't look at George. He slipped away, unnoticed, a ghost haunting the lives of the living.

"…for environmental reasons, converting the home theatre to a…"

"…thinking of having a new face printed for my birthday…"

"…have you seen the new…"

"…a Vinyasa retreat in the foothills of Ubud…"

(Swirls wine glass) "…comes on *wide* to the palate, now doesn't it…"

"Waiter. You there. *Waiter.*"

George slowed, the automation of his drink delivery disturbed. He looked around to see a woman and a man, both tall and attractive in the most standard and forgettable of ways, looking at him. The man smiled, George couldn't help but stare at his teeth. They shimmered in the lights of the ballroom, hovering in space like the Cheshire cat's. The woman had a matching, disingenuous smile and a red dot on her forehead, between her eyes. The latest token of this mob's faddish spiritualism, he figured.

The man was saying something.

"Sorry?" asked George.

"I said," sighed the man, apparently irritated at having to repeat himself. "I'd like a double of single malt and some French champagne for my partner."

George held out the tray so she could take a flute of the sparkling.

The man's eyes narrowed. "*French* champagne, not the insipid Australian version. And a double of *single malt* whisky, and make damn sure it is an *Islay*, the best that this place has." His wife suppressed a laugh (obviously, the way people do when they want you to see them pretending to be polite) when her man said *insipid Australian version.*

George thought about a straight right to the bridge of the man's nose, the spurt of blood, the roar of the crowd.

Instead he nodded. "Right away."

And so the night continued, with the rich exercising their prodigious appetite for expensive alcohol and food, and the remainders servicing those appetites. There was a lull sometime after nine and George sat down on one of the plastic crates near the kitchen's exit, prying off his shoes with a relieved internalized groan. The shoes he'd borrowed from his neighbour were too narrow for his feet, the soles worn and thin.

He leaned back, head against the warm polycrete wall, and closed his eyes. A commotion a half-minute later made him open them again.

A waitress was walking between benches, tray of plates in hand, a half-dozen wait staff crowding behind her. When she dumped the tray near the sinks, the crowd increased. George slipped his shoes back on and walked over, pushing through the mob.

Sitting on one of the plates was rump steak, half eaten. It filled the air with the scent of its iron-rich opulence. The young waitress, with pretty eyes and crooked teeth she'd try to hide by never smiling, turned to the chef, nearby.

"We can eat it, right?" she asked.

He nodded. "The contracts are lax here. They don't cover garbage."

"Who gets it?" She asked, and it was clear she wanted it to be her. Everyone standing there wanted it.

The chef looked around at the staff. "I don't care. Just as long as you don't stand around staring at it all fucking night. I want the wait staff out of my kitchen, now." He turned without waiting for a reply and moved along the bench to where a line of rich chocolate-and-truffle deserts were being created by keenly focused young chefs.

"It's mine," said George. He didn't have a loud voice; in fact Nhung always accused him of mumbling. But everyone heard him.

The girl with the crooked teeth made a thin line with her mouth and turned her eyes to the floor. The others backed away.

As George grabbed the plate someone said: "Now just a minute there."

George turned and looked down at one of the managers. Bill or Bryan or something, young, had a habit of giving out superfluous instructions to people who knew their work a lot better than he did.

The young manager's smooth face started to redden. "I mean, you can't just take it." He didn't say it strong, didn't attach himself to the words. Just surrendered the sentence to the air.

George looked him in the eye. The man looked away. George turned without a word, plate in hand, and pushed his way through the back door, twenty pairs of eyes glaring at his back.

The still, dry heat of the night hit him as he exited. Quiet, outside. Just the low whine of a hydrogen generator and in the distance, a barking dog. Overhead he imagined he could hear the

Milky Way as it flowed, and the call of the Larrpan looking for passengers to take to Baralku. George moved along the wall to a plastic chair that had been placed under a circle of pale white from a lone overhead bulb.

He held the plate up, nostrils flaring as he inhaled the scent of the half-eaten meat. He placed the plate carefully on his knees and used knife and fork to slice off a neat triangle of steak. Pink in the centre, brown on the outside, slathered in some sauce so rich he would have drunk a cup of it, if he could. He bit down, eyes closing in pleasure as the juices lapped over his tongue, bathed his gums. As he chewed his stomach jumped in anticipation. He groaned.

Laughter—or more tittering, you'd call it, dragged his attention away. A woman and a man stood a few metres away, watching him from the shadows. The woman wore an elegant gown that exposed soft, white shoulders that gleamed under the stars. The tips of their cigarettes glowed orange in the night.

They stepped forward, closer to the circle of light. The man looked at him with contempt, the quiet curl of disdain in lip and eye. The woman—her expression was worse, much worse: pity. Like she'd just found an abandoned puppy by the side of the road.

The disdainful one said to his friend, as though George weren't even there: "They let them eat our leftovers here. Disgusting."

"Oh Xavier," said the other. Then she looked at George, nodding sympathetically as she asked: "Hungry?"

George chewed the meat and swallowed. It wanted to stick in his throat on the way down. He couldn't taste the flavours anymore.

The woman stepped closer again, into the circle of light. "It's not fair that you eat our scraps." She held out her little finger, showing the three laser-inked dots on the tip. "Let me give you a credit transfer. Go and buy yourself some fresh groceries—something *healthy*."

George stood, plate in hand. He was a head taller than her. Whatever she saw in his face, she didn't like, the film of fear running down over her eyes. She backed up out of the light, towards her friend.

"Maybe we should go, Xavier."

He agreed. They threw down their cigarettes and left, walking fast.

George stared down at the cigarettes, orange points burning out on the polycrete. Then the plate of half-eaten food, still in his hand. He clenched and unclenched his jaw, felt the string of shame on his cheeks, in his stomach. He threw the food in a nearby bin and went back to work.

I'll give you a car bomb
A car bomb exploding on a crowded street
On a crowded street exploding flesh and bones
That's our festival, don't you understand

I'll give you a savage war

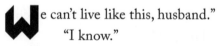e can't live like this, husband."

"I know."

"Our daughter will die, if this goes on."

"I know."

Sweat coated their skin, dripped from the tips of their noses, rested salty on their lips. How her daughter slept, Phuong could not understand. But she did, as they sheltered under the bamboo floorboards. As the swarms of mosquitos plagued them and thunder, man-made, roared in the distance. As the scent of sweat and dirt, and the smell of something else that overlaid it all, ripe and dead, eddied in the space under the house. As the hunger plagued them, only tree bark to eat and still, dirty water to drink, the gnawing in their stomachs unceasing. Her daughter slept despite it all, thin arms above her head, little fat lips slightly parted, she slept.

"Then…" she trailed off. Not wanting to know the answer.

"South, we'll keep going south," said Trung, his voice soft and empty. "We'll keep to the Ho Chi Minh trail. There's nothing else."

"The war is everywhere. Even there. Especially there."

"I know a man."

"What man?"

"We fought together. He has a boat."

She sat in silence.

"Is that the only way?" Phuong asked.

"Yes."

"We have nothing to pay him with."

"I can pay him."

"What with?"

"I can pay."

"What with," she repeated, quietly, her fear of his answer rising.

Trung didn't give her one. He took his old army pistol from his canvas satchel and began to clean it. Just his eyes and the pistol shone in the dimness under the floorboards. The dull, eternal metal of the gun and the bright fleeting light of his eyes.

Phuong hugged her knees and watched her daughter sleep.

George woke to opera. Drifting down caverns and tunnels, through the open front door, some old aria in a dead European language, echoing, resonating, enchanting. Old Mister Nguyen loved his opera, and everyone else down here learned to love it to, after a while. You could close the front door to the circulating air and the early morning music, if you really wished, but no one did.

It was cool underground. Still and silent, at night. George had never slept well, but he slept like the dead down below. The temperature was constant, whether it was twenty-five degrees Celsius outside, or over fifty. Port Hedland was mostly over fifty these days. He lay in bed, savouring the first few seconds of the day when you forget who you are, those few seconds before your feet hit the floor, before the hard reality of the world comes crashing in.

He swung from the bed, feet touching the cool stone floor. The walls, too, were sandstone, patterned swirls of maroon and rose left by the tunnelling machines. Easy, calming to the eye in the soft, clean light of the underworld.

He walked out to the living area.

"Yo Adrian," said George.

"Rocky," replied Nhung, smiling at him.

Nhung, her black hair tied up, was wearing her white dental assistant uniform, the dress ending around the knees. Her full lips were wet from the tea she was drinking and her eyes tired from another sleepless night with their daughter. Three years old and Kylie still needed her mother to share her bed with her before she went to sleep. Eyes tired, but warm; eyes that were a shield against others and a window for George and George alone.

George walked over to his daughter, sitting up on the high chair, drinking from a plastic cup. He kissed her on the top of the head. "Trouble, how are you?"

His daughter looked at him, put down her cup, and cocked her finger like a pistol. She blew a raspberry.

George smiled. "What was that?"

"A fart gun," said Kylie, in her squeaky little voice.

She pointed it at him again and blew another raspberry.

George grabbed his nose. "Gakh." He swayed, eyes rolling up in his head. Kylie giggled as he staggered from the small kitchen, to the open lounge, and collapsed onto the sofa. "Blurrrrgh." He played dead.

Kylie laughed.

Then he rose slowly from the sofa with arms outstretched, and let out a zombie groan.

"Are you a monster?" asked Kylie, eyes wide.

George responded with a groan and lurched towards his daughter.

She giggled and shot him again with her fart gun. George fell over and flopped around on the ground.

Nhung smiled. "Okay, enough farting, you two." She put a bowl of soy porridge in front of Kylie. "Now, eat your breakfast."

Kylie wrinkled her noise. "Yuck."

"It's good for you."

"It's stupid for me. But you can have it." Kylie tried to give her mother the bowl.

Nhung put it back in front of her. "*An di.*"

Kylie pouted. She picked up her tiny spoon and started poking the porridge with it.

George walked back to the kitchen and poured himself some coffee. He sat at the small table with a sigh and sipped. Black, bitter, thin: he didn't know it any other way.

Nhung sat opposite. Their knees touched under the table.

"How was work?" she asked.

He shrugged.

"That bad?"

He sighed and sipped his coffee.

"That bad," she said, no longer a question.

"How much do teeth cost?"

Nhung held her tea cup in both hands. "What do you mean? What sort of teeth?"

"Rich prick teeth."

"*George*," she said, eyebrows raised.

"What's a prick?" asked Kylie, distracted from her porridge shuffling.

"A naughty word, Kylie. Naughty daddy."

"Naughty daddy," repeated Kylie, grinning at him.

"Naughty daddy," he agreed. "Now eat your breakfast."

Kylie made another face and resumed poking the food with her spoon.

"Anyway," said George. "Teeth?"

"You don't want to know."

"Come on."

She sighed. "The basic treatment: straightened, whitened and nano-hardened teeth—that costs a million."

George started to swear, then caught himself. Instead he repeated, "A million." He grimaced, as though tasting something far more bitter than his coffee.

"It lasts a hundred years, once it's done. No decay, no fillings, no cleaning—not ever." Nhung sipped her tea. She laughed without humour and said: "But that's just the basic model. You can implant a connection that stimulates the pleasure centre of the brain. So you could have implants inside your teeth—fully programmable—that give you an endorphin kick, a cerebral orgasm when they sense you eating chocolate, for example."

George shook his head.

"My boss told me about a job he did for a rich client—an executive from the freezones. His teeth were programmed to fire neurons in the part of his brain associated with hearing. When this guy ate a particular dish—some sort of steak, I think—he'd hear a symphony."

"What do you mean?"

"I mean, he ate music."

They were silent. George looked at the scratched, fauxwood tabletop, the flavourless food in front of his daughter, the white scars across his knuckles. "I guess that's what happens when you give people too much money."

"Lot of wealthy people at the function last night, I take it?" asked Nhung.

"What do you reckon."

"Anyone famous?"

"I don't know. Those people all look the same to me."

"White people?"

"Rich people."

She smiled. "Tell me about it. I can't see past those perfectly symmetrical teeth."

"Yeah," George said, nodding in agreement. "Same. I can't help staring. Sometimes the skin. That glows, too. But usually just the teeth. It's like I'm hypnotized."

He pressed his tongue against the gap in his own teeth. George was lucky. His genes had given him a row of mostly straight, strong teeth. A bit yellowed from his days of smoking black market tobacco, missing two halfway down one side of his mouth ('bicuspids' Nhung called them) from a fight down in Dampier when he'd lost his mouthguard halfway through the first round. But good teeth, overall.

Nhung's teeth were perfect: white, small, straight. They had to be, of course—couldn't have a dental assistant with a row of baked bean teeth. She was meticulous with them. Brushing three times a day, flossing, buying an overpriced solution to wash her gums.

They were both lucky, as far as teeth went. Most of the people underground struggled with bad teeth and gum disease. Made it harder to find work. Service industry didn't like hiring people with bad teeth. Upset the customers, they said. And if you got a rotten tooth and had to have it pulled, you were gone. The debt would crush you.

Nhung sighed, got up from her seat and went over to the small fridge. She pulled out a bowl and placed it in front of Kylie, taking away the uneaten porridge.

Kylie squealed with pleasure as she looked into the bowl.

George raised an eyebrow. "Blueberries?"

"Mister Morrison owed me for going over his teeth a few weeks back."

"Nice."

To her daughter—who already was shoving fistfuls of blueberries into her mouth—Nhung said: "Take the bowl down to your play area. I want to talk to daddy."

Kylie jumped down from her chair without a word and ran off smiling a blueberry smile, bowl in her hands.

"Mother will be over in thirty minutes," she said.

George made a pistol out of his fingers, put the barrel against his temple, and blew the wet sound of flatulence.

"Just be thankful she's not living here."

"She's never going to live with us."

"In Vietnam—"

"We're not in Vietnam."

Nhung started playing with her teacup, distracted.

"I'm sorry babe. It's a small place and your mother and I just don't get along. "

"She likes you fine. It's not that, anyway."

"Then what?"

She looked up at him. "They're upping the rent again."

"*Mother fuckers.*"

"Yeah," she said. "Mother fuckers."

They sat in silence.

She kept turning her teacup in her hands, eyes down.

"There's more?" George asked. "Okay, say what you want to say."

She looked up at him with something approaching regret. "You could get a government subsidy."

His eyes went cold. "No."

"You're entitled to it."

"No," he said, firmly.

"George."

"Nhung. How am I indigenous? I'm one-quarter black, and most people look at me and think I'm white. I never lived with my mob, I don't know the language and my tribe's elders are all long dead. So tell me—how am I indigenous?"

"Does it matter?"

He didn't bother answering that and she didn't try repeating the question.

George let out a long breath and put his hand on hers. "Maybe I could qualify for some more money. But it's imaginary money—it's all quarantined. Some bureaucrat arsehole in an office somewhere deciding where every cent goes. I never see it. They even choose the food I eat, in order to encourage a balanced diet. Like I'm a child." He touched the cool metal of the cochlear implant behind his left ear. "I take that money, the bastards will switch my geo-locater on permanently; they'll scrutinize everything I do. These people Nhung… I just can't."

"It would give us some room. Some room to breathe, George."

"Not with that money. It would suffocate me, living that way."

She gripped his hand and sighed. "I know George, I know. I'm sorry."

"Maybe I can get the union started again."

"The union?" She gave a short laugh. "Ha. What century are you from? You start a union and the only thing you'll achieve is an extended stay in a political prison."

"We fall behind in the rent we'll end up in a debtor's prison. I'm not sure I can tell the difference between the two." He paused, looking down at their hands. "I could…" he trailed off.

"Don't say it George, don't say it."

He looked up at her. "I could fight again."

She withdrew her hands from his. "I'd rather you went to jail than fight again."

"Nhung."

"No." She stood, her voice raised. She glanced over at Kylie and lowered her voice, whispering fiercely. "Never again. Never again watching a live feed of you fighting some custom-built killer while five thousand people scream for your blood. Alone in this house, six months pregnant, worrying my daughter's father was going to end up a vegetable or a cripple or *dead*." Her eyes glistened, but her mouth was firm, her voice strong. "This family is staying together. No hospital beds, no prisons, no pointless self-sacrifice. You hear me, George Duulngari?"

She stared him down. He looked away. "Yeah," he said. "Yeah."

I'll give you twenty endless years
Twenty years seven thousand nights of artillery
Seven thousand nights of artillery lulling you to sleep
Are you sleeping yet or are you still awake

The spiders burst from the dirt floor of the cavern. Each with a single eye glowing a fierce red in the centre of its back, and the terrifying *tikka takka tikka takka* of their metal legs as they rubbed against each other. The cavern was dimly lit with sensi-stones, absorbing the heat in the air and turning it into a dull, orange light. Thirty refugees, packed all in against each other; thirty of them, trying their best to ignore the smell and the heat and the cries of toddlers.

Until the spiders burst from the floor. Then the screams started, first in fear, then in pain.

Trung grabbed Phuong's arm, she picked up their daughter. They didn't hesitate. They knew what the fist-sized spiders brought: agonizing death, slow and inevitable. One bite that caused a spreading necrosis of the flesh that no nano-med, no matter how powerful, could halt. The Chinese called them the Number 17 Counter-Insurgency Device. The Vietnamese living underground had another name: *Nu Hon Trung Quoc*, the Chinese Kiss.

Someone unbolted the door at the end of the cavern and families were pushing through, bowed over to avoid hitting their heads on the roof. Trung shoved people out of the way and dragged Phuong through the narrow doorway.

Beyond, a narrow, low tunnel. They ducked and ran, crablike, along the confined space. Trung barged into the back of an old man, knocking him to the ground. Phuong tried to step around him but was being shoved from behind, her sandaled foot landing squarely on the old man's thin back. He let out a grunt of air as she pushed him into the dirt, and another as the next person stomped on him as well.

Phuong didn't look back. She clutched her daughter and ran, chest heaving, breath hot in her throat, as Trung pulled her by the arm and the person behind jammed elbows into her back. She staggered, Trung dragged her upright. Darkness and screams, desperate, pleading, screams, echoing down the tunnel. And if the screams paused for a few moments, the *tikka takka tikka takka* unrelenting, right behind them.

Keep running, keep running. Her daughter didn't cry, just buried her head into Phuong's shoulder and gripped her little arms around her shoulders. Trung looked back. Fear stained his face.

They plunged onwards into the darkness of the tunnel. There was no air, down here, in these catacombs they'd built. Claustrophobic, in these dead spaces they called freedom. Phuong gasped for breath, her arms ached from holding her daughter. They ran towards a thin sliver of light ahead, elbows scraping against the walls, heads banging into the ceiling. All the while, behind them the screams and the *tikka takka tikka takka*.

They tumbled into another chamber, dimly lit by sensi-stones. Three others were there, young women, chests heaving. Trung pointed his pistol back into the darkness of the tunnel and fired, two, three four times. The *boom boom boom boom* in the confined space ear-splitting, enough to make her daughter finally cry out.

Trung slammed the door closed, throwing a bolt across it.

Phuong put down her daughter and gasped, trying to regain her breath. "There are people. Coming. You. Can't close. The door."

Trung said nothing. Instead, chest heaving, he emptied the shell casings from his pistol, brass ringing against the floor, and reloaded it. Sweat stuck Phuong's shirt to her back, her daughter whimpered, clinging on to her leg. The women in the room ignored them, moving towards another exit in the opposite wall.

"We can't close the door—people will be trying to escape."

He looked up, a sheen of sweat on his thin face. "Those spiders are attracted to warm bodies," he said, quietly. "They bite only once, then burn out their control core. So they can't be reused by insurgents."

"What are you saying?"

He clicked the cylinder for the revolver in place. "We need to keep moving. They'll dig through the earth around this door."

"What are you saying, Trung? Were you shooting at the spiders?"

Trung held her gaze. "No."

He moved to his daughter, picked her up with his free arm, and followed the women out the other door.

Phuong wiped the sweat from her eyes with the back of her hand. It was shaking. Those that shared the Trail with them—the old and the very young mainly—were back there. She reached out, laid her fingertips on the small door for a few moments, the rough grain of the iron rubbing her fingertips.

She breathed out and followed her family.

George long-poured Paddy the Greek three fingers of gin. Paddy nodded his head at the end of the pour, picked up the tumbler, and closed his eyes as he sipped his drink. His hand trembled.

George went back to cleaning tall glasses with a white cloth and staring into the flashing neon signs above the slot machines. The cyclical tunes of the slots, once an interminable distraction as he tried to take orders or simply stand for a few fleeting moments and quietly think, were now habituated into background noise. A few months working day shifts at the Blue Galah and he barely noticed them anymore.

Before noon, so the place was quiet. Just Paddy up at the bar in his regular spot, taking his third gin of the morning, and the zombies at the slots, eyes glazed as the wheels turned and turned again. Promising, but never delivering, the golden ticket to a new life. It didn't matter that they never really paid off: the patrons weren't there for the money. There were there to die the slow death of their addiction. Until the shame and the debt buried them in the dead red earth.

George was drawn from his reverie as the doors swung open and the blinding light of the morning sun split the gloom. As soon as the two men stepped off the bottom step, George knew there'd be trouble. He could always smell a fight coming, and these two reeked.

They sauntered in wearing Xiong original suits and white-topped patent leather shoes. One of the guys was big and big everywhere. The shoulders, the arms, the thighs, the fists. He had a set of steel teeth, glinting under the neon of the slots, and a magnum-sized chin. The smaller guy was the boss, obviously. He wore black leather gloves and an air of insouciance and entitlement only the very rich can really replicate. He seemed vaguely familiar.

George straightened.

The boss man smiled at George and said something. George didn't hear it; he found himself distracted by the dazzle of the man's teeth. They seemed to glow with a blue hue in the dank underground of the bar. They sparkled, too, though covered in diamond shavings.

"Sorry mate?" asked George.

The man said, with a simulated patience and continuing smile: "I said, your best whisky my good man." He sat down on a stool in front of George, passing his fedora to his man to hold. His man sat with his back to George, watching the barflies and the slot addicts, doing his best imitation of what a bodyguard should do in a dingy bar.

Up close, the boss man's eyes were bloodshot and he reeked of cigarettes and booze. Down from the spires no doubt, slumming it in the dugouts, looking for the raw edge of existence long since rubbed out over on the right side of the tracks.

George threw his white rag over his shoulder, grabbed a bottle from the shelf and poured two fingers of whisky into a clean tumbler. He placed the glass and the whisky in front of the man.

Blue Teeth looked at the bottle. "*This* is your best whisky?"

"It's what you came here for."

The man's faux smile wavered for a moment, before returning. "Why, I think you may be right."

The man drank the whisky in one hit, grimacing in the aftermath. He pulled a pack of Double Happiness cigarettes from the inside pocket of his jacket and tapped one halfway out with a gloved finger, then removed it with his lips. His bodyguard lit the cigarette with a silver lighter.

"Any *action* in this part of town?" asked the boss.

George shrugged, and moved back down the bar to continue wiping the glasses.

The man moved three stools down, so he was sitting in front of George again. That put him a seat away from Paddy the Greek.

"There must be some local hangout. Some little-known establishment you people frequent." He took a drag on his smoke, eyes on George. They may have been bloodshot, but something sharp sparkled in there. The man continued. "Dog fights or human fights, card games, women, opium dens, blacklegged memory pins."

George shook his head.

"No?"

"We got slot machines and cheap gin, same as every other place."

The man with blue teeth turned to Paddy the Greek and said: "What about you, champ?"

Paddy the Greek rose from his stool without a word, drink in hand, and disappeared into the dusk between the slots. For an alcoholic Paddy had great instincts.

The man poured himself another drink. "I've got to say, I'm a little disappointed. This place lacks *vitality*."

"It's eleven on a Thursday morning."

The man stared at George's hands, resting in the bar. "I've

seen you before." He closed his eyes for ten long seconds. George stomach twisted. The man would be searching his memory pin, pulling up old images, watching them against the back of his eyelids. Hard to see a way out of this one. Blue Teeth opened his eyes again. "Ah yes, George Duulngari. I watched a fight of yours, six years ago."

George said nothing, started wiping down the bar counter.

"Made a bit of money on you—a nice return on investment."

George kept wiping.

Blue Teeth took another drag on his cigarette, blowing the smoke upwards in a thick cloud. "I'm always on the lookout for good fighters."

George knew who the man was now. Dan Hancock: second cousin to one of the CEOs out in the freezones. Practically royalty. "I don't fight anymore."

Hancock indicated the bar with his wave of his cigarette. "No. You work in some anonymous dive in the wrong end of town."

"It's an honest living."

"Compared to fighting? Not really."

"No. Compared to running fighters down to freezone three."

"Ah. So you do recognize me," Dan Hancock said. He nodded at George. "You're a hard man to read, I like that."

"You're easy. I like that."

"Really," Hancock said, and stamped out his cigarette in a nearby ashtray. "What am I thinking now?"

"You're thinking of a way to provoke me into fighting your man here." George said, indicating the bodyguard with his chin. "Test out my skills. If I win, you're going to make me an offer you think I can't refuse."

Dan Hancock raised his eyebrows. He pulled the cigarette pack out of his pocket, drew another one with his lips, eyebrows still raised. "Maybe too smart though. I like that less."

When fighting a bigger opponent, as a general rule, you'll lose. No matter what the movies say, fighting is largely a matter of physics. A difference in size can only be made up for with luck, or a far superior skill level. George was not a small man by any means, six foot tall, lean and muscular, broad shoulders, he'd fought middleweight in his time. The problem was Hancock's man was a heavyweight, upgraded. Hancock's man would inevitably have the standard combat add-ons: toughened bones, adrenalin spur, endorphin modulation, possibly nano-infused carbon joints in the shoulders, hips, knees. If this man with the lantern jaw had any idea, he should be able to crush George and easily.

But hired goons rarely had any idea. Hancock's man had turned in his chair to face George. He grinned, his steel teeth gleaming red in the backwash of neon from a Double Happiness sign over the bar.

"Oh—you're alive," George said. "I thought you were a hat stand." Then he turned to Hancock. "This meat coat hanger the best you got?"

The goon snarled and grabbed George by the collar, pulling him forward. George slammed the flat of his hand into the man's throat. The goon's eyes widened, his face went red and he staggered backwards, big hands at his neck.

Throat. Knees. Eyes.

The three most vulnerable areas. The biggest man in the world couldn't keep fighting with one of those taken out.

George leaped the bar in one, smooth movement, landing lightly. The man put his fists out to block, but George kicked low with his right leg, smashing the side of the man's knee. The man wobbled, grimacing, his steel teeth flashing in the gloom. George kicked the knee again, hard. The man drew his leg up, grimacing in pain. Less than George had hoped—he'd hoped his opponent would be writhing on the stained polycrete floor by now.

They circled each other. Six feet away sat an old woman with stringy grey hair, forgotten schooner of beer in one hand, the other pressed against the large button on the slot machine. She didn't even notice them.

The man moved towards George, who manoeuvred himself away, until his back was pressed against one of the slots.

George was lucky. The man was an idiot.

The goon threw a punch hard enough to take George's head clean off. George ducked it easily, the man's hand smashed through the glassteel screen of the slot machine. The goon grunted as he pulled the bloodied mess of his fist from the slot, groaned as George punched him in the balls and went silent as he took the full force of a round kick to the temple. He fell awkwardly, head cracking hollowly on the hard floor.

George rounded on Hancock.

The boss man nodded, eyebrows up, as if to say *impressive*. He pulled another cigarette from the pack with his lips, speaking round it as he said: "This trip down below hasn't been a waste, after all. You're going to make a fine addition to my stable, George."

George's chest heaved as he brought his breathing under control. "There's two different ways for me to say no to you, Hancock. You're about to get the hard way."

"Come now. This can be lucrative for us both. No need to get ugly."

"Ugly is all it ever is," George said, squaring his shoulders. "I've worked for men like you all my life. Soft-handed, entitled, looking right through people like me, invisible, right up to the moment you want something from us."

Hancock smiled. "George, you're too sensitive. This is a business proposition, that's all. *Mutually beneficial*."

George took a step towards him, fists clenched.

Hancock held up a hand. His grin was gone. "Listen: this is how it is going to be. We don't make a deal here, I'll go to the police and tell them you beat up my man here, unprovoked." He put a finger to the cochlear implant behind his left ear. "My memory stream will be tweaked just enough so it looks like you started the fight. Man like you would get three years for something like that." He pointed at the shattered face of the slot. "Double that for damage to private property."

George growled. "Going to be hard to look at that memory pin with it torn out of your skull."

Hancock laughed. "Can you really be that ignorant?" George's hands curled into fists as the man sneered at him and said: "My memories aren't just stored here, in my head. They're duplicated, backed up elsewhere."

George eyed the man, breathed in and out steadily. Then, for the first time since leaving home that morning, he smiled. "That's a relief."

Doubt interfered with Hancock's sneer. "How so?"

"You've backed me into a corner."

"And that's a relief?"

"Yes. Liberating. To be all out of choices. I can't see any way out of it. I can't see a single path that doesn't end with me fighting for you in freezone three."

The self-assurance returned to Hancock's face. "I said you were smart."

"Nah mate. Not so smart at all."

Hancock had a moment to register surprise as George's fist collided with his mouth, but only a moment. He sprawled against the bar, head snapping back as George followed up with a left, right, left, all to the man's mouth. Trying to bash out those blue gleaming, eternal teeth.

I'm still here, sweetie, so many love tokens
Metal handcuffs to wear, sacks of sand for pillows
Punji sticks to scratch your back, fire hoses to wash your face
How do we know which gift to send each other
And for how long until we get sated

I can fight. This is my country."

Trung reached out and held her arm, fingers on the bare skin close to her shoulder. "Yes, you can fight. Better than me. You are as brave as Dang Thuy Tram. You will need to be, to get our daughter away from here, where it is safe."

"Who knows if it is safe?"

He nodded at the landscape, the outlines of the world revealed as the burnished orange line of the sun slouched over the horizon. At the ground pock-marked with craters, and the lines of thin men and women, clasping battered AK-47s, preparing to hop into faded green military transports. At the hundreds of once-white refugee tents, flapping in the morning ocean breeze. The morning breeze, a relief against the heat, wet and suffocating, that drowned them all; the heat that caused old men and women to collapse on the Ho Chi Minh Trail and dead bodies to swell like balloons. At the horizon, where pyres of smoke stained the sky and where the bare earth, riven with gene scramblers, yielded not one grain of rice.

"This is no place for our beautiful girl," he said, gently. Their daughter stood between them, holding the hands of her parents, a small genetic fusion of their being, linking them forever.

"There has to be another way," said Phuong. Her eyes welled with tears.

"That's the price. I help Older Brother Tuan run people out of the south for a year to pay for your tickets, then six months more for mine."

"He's your friend. He should not do this."

"He's my friend, which is why I will help him. My price is half what he charges others. We have both acted properly."

Phuong was silent.

She breathed out. "Then walk with your daughter until we are to leave."

Trung nodded and picked his daughter up. He was about to walk away when Phuong said: "But you'll follow us? You promise?"

"I promise. Nothing can keep us apart." He replied. But there was a sadness in his eyes as he said the words, a sadness that twisted in Phuong's chest.

Trung turned and walked out slowly along the shore to show his daughter all the boats clustered there. Smooth polycarbon or wood or pitted iron hulls gleaming as the morning rays struck them. Gleaming in the morning gloom, gleaming with possibility, while the land behind remained in shadow. The breeze brought Nhung's laughter back up the hill, happy in her father's arms.

Phuong waited until they were further along the shore before slumping down on the rough earth. She plunged her fingers into the dirt, watching Trung hold his daughter. Watching them bathed in the morning light.

She covered her eyes.

Nhung looked up in surprise as George burst into the room. She was standing in the kitchen, frying some noodles on the pan. George rushed to where Kylie played on the thin carpet with her trains, her little brow creased in concentration. He picked her up and hugged her against his chest, his face pressed into her unruly mop of dark hair.

Kylie squirmed and giggled. "Are you a monster?"

George kept hugging her.

Kylie squirmed around so she could look at Nhung. "Mummy! Daddy monster is getting me."

"George—is that blood on your hands?" asked Nhung.

"Mommy! Is Daddy a monster?"

Nhung stared at the scene, fearing what it meant. Knowing. She put down the noodles and walked over to them both. "No," she said and put her arms around them both. "No."

A pause, then, "Why is Daddy crying?"

Nhung said nothing. George's shoulders shook.

"Mummy? Why is Daddy crying?"

Nhung grabbed George's chin, raised it from his daughter's hair so he was looking at her. Something was broken, in there, behind his blurred eyes.

"They made me," he said. "They're coming."

She looked at him in silence for a few moments. "How bad?"

"Bad."

"Where will they take you?"

"The freezones. Ten years, at least, on a debtor's contract. They'll make me fight again."

She put her hand on his wet cheek, silent for a long half minute. "Then fight."

They held each other and George whispered to his daughter. Kylie stopped wriggling after a while and instead gripped her father tighter, little arms clasped around his neck. He whispered to Nhung also, forehead pressed against hers. She closed her eyes and said *you too* and *I know* and *always*.

A few minutes later the internal security communications

system crackled into life and a disembodied voice echoed through all the apartments in the dugout. "Resident George Duulngari, we have a warrant for your arrest. Present yourself up top immediately, or we will enter and take you by force."

George whispered to Nhung to close the door behind him, and then, loudly into the room he said: "I'm coming out."

It didn't matter. They fired tear gas down into the corridors. George pulled up the bottom of his shirt, covering his mouth. His eyes stung and lungs burned as he left the apartment and walked through the clouds of yellow gas, as he ascended the stairs and walked out into the baking hot, still afternoon. All around were black-masked security personnel, waiting.

There he was. Just a silhouette, to them, against the gas. Just a silhouette, rising from the earth. Not a man. A silhouette.

George broke the leg of the first man that came at him. The second he struck under the chin guard of the helmet, in the throat. The third he drove into the fourth that came at him, causing the force rod of the third to discharge into the chest of the fourth.

The others, they stood back then. Hesitant, looking at each other, waiting for someone else to go in first. George laughed. The silhouette, he laughed at them all.

They shot him with pulse rifles, crackling blue lines intersecting with George's head and chest. Arcs of electricity playing over his body, his teeth. George fell to the ground in spasm, thrashing against the current coursing through his system. As he lost consciousness, his throat choked with electricity, still he laughed.

Lastly, I'll give you a tear gas grenade
A tear gland for this modern epoch
A type of tear neither sad nor happy

Drenching my face as I wait.

Tran Da Tu, Saigon, 1964

Phuong gave her daughter the letter. Nhung looked into her mother's face. Lined and weathered, though all emotion had been baked out by the unrelenting sun of her new country, it gave nothing away as she stood watching her daughter.

Nhung opened the envelope. It read:

> *Some rich prick dropped these. Get a place down in Freo. See you in ten.*
> *Always.*
> *Always.*
> *George.*

Something rattled in the envelope. Nhung tipped the contents onto her hand. Four teeth rolled out onto her palm. Shimmering blue, perfect, each seemed to glow with its own inner light.

Nhung made fists with her hands, scrunching the letter in one hand, the teeth in the other, pressing them into her palm. She looked down at her daughter, playing with her trains again. Nearby the overturned sofa, slashed open, its stuffing pulled out. Her tomato plants had been torn from their pots, the contents of every cupboard in the kitchen emptied onto the floor.

The police had turned her apartment upside down after the case had been completed, looking for anything that could be sold off to pay for their debts. They'd taken the second-hand holo-unit, an ivory flute Nhung had been given when she was very young, even George's trophies. They cleaned out and closed down their bank accounts, as well. But it wasn't much.

George had known what would happen. That's why he had

gone to her mother with the envelope.

Kylie played in the middle of it all, oblivious.

Nhung's eyes glistened, but she did not cry. She never cried. Her mother had taught her that.

Phuong put her hand on her daughter's arm. "You will survive this," she said, in Vietnamese.

"What do you care?" said Nhung, replying in Vietnamese, emotion straining her voice. "You didn't like George. You barely talked to him all the years we were together. *You wouldn't even look at him.*"

Nhung turned from her mother, gave her her back.

Phuong mumbled something behind her.

Nhung sighed. "What?"

Phuong cleared her throat. "I said: that's not true. Oh daughter, that is so far from the truth."

Nhung turned back slowly to her mother. "What do you mean?"

Her mother never talked much, never said much more than a sentence—except if it was about food—but now the words poured out, quickly. "You won't remember your father. But he was the same as George, in so many ways. The same flawed courage. A manhood that stared inwards. And a love for you, my daughter, larger than the sun."

Phuong took a step forward and grasped her daughter's hands. She blinked slowly, and the shadow of sorrow passed over her face. "Too many memories. It hurt to see you two, and feel the weight of that memory."

Nhung was too drained to question. She just held her mother's hands for a time, before turning to Kylie. "We've got to go now, darling. Pack up your trains."

Kylie ran her train over the floor, smiling. "Where we going?"

"Our new home."

"Is Daddy coming?"

"Yes," she said, the word catching in her throat. "No. Not yet. But he will. He's going to come home. I promise"

Kylie looked up. "Promise?"

"I promise. Nothing will keep us apart."

TWELVE MINUTES TO VINH QUANG

2089

The restaurant smelled of anchovies and cigarettes. Lynn hated both, but still, it reminded her of home. Comforting and familiar. The anchovies in the sauce wouldn't be real of course, and the tobacco almost certainly illegal.

It was three in the afternoon, but the room was still pretty much full. Patrons sipped glasses of tea, shrouded in the smoke and dusk, mumbling to each other in low-pitched conversation. Blinds were down against the windows, the only light emanating from shaded red lanterns hanging from the ceiling, casting the faces around her in crimson twilight.

The only light, that is, bar a government advertisement on the far wall. The picture of a decaying wooden boat on the high seas, the inhabitants of which were anonymous splotches of yellow staring over a thin railing. The holotype glow of the deep blue ocean was overwhelmed by the intensity of the red block letters stamped over the picture:

ILLEGAL

Everyday, middle-of-the-road fascism: it just had no imagination.

A small bell above the door tinkled as it opened, spearing an unwelcome slat of white sunlight into the room. Heat, too, gusting in to swirl the smoke and swing the lanterns. A shadow filled the doorframe, pausing perhaps to adjust its eyes to the gloom within. Maybe just pausing for effect.

An ancient Vietnamese woman behind the back counter came to life, pointing a gnarled finger at the new customer. "*Má Mày. Dóng Cửa Lai đi.*" ["Close that door. Your Mother!"]

The silhouette shut the door, emerging from the light into a broad-shouldered man wearing an immaculate tailored suit, deep-blue necktie, and an air of contempt for the room he'd just stepped into. He removed the black homburg from his head and ran a hand over his gleaming, jet-black hair, combed straight back. As he did so, Lynn glimpsed a tattoo snaking up under his sleeve.

The man walked to the back counter. Lynn turned to watch as he did, adjusting her silver nose ring with thumb and forefinger. He spoke in hushed tones with the old woman, glanced back at Lynn, then turned and started speaking again rapidly. The grandmother waved him away before disappearing through a beaded doorway to the kitchen beyond.

He walked back to her table, hat in hand, face set. "Mister Vu?"

"Vu Thi Lynn." She paused. "And that's a *Miz*, Mister Nguyen."

He made a show of looking her over. Her hair in particular came in for close inspection, dyed, as it was, the hue of a fresh-pressed silver bar and molded into a spiked Mohawk. She sported a tiny black leather jacket and a pair of thin eyebrows that could fire withering disdain at fifty paces.

His shoulders were hunched, like a boxer's. "Is this a joke?"

"What are you having difficulty processing, Mister Nguyen? That I'm young, a woman, or," she waved at hand at his suit, "that I don't walk around with the word 'gangster' tattooed on my damn forehead?"

His eyes narrowed, lips pressed together. Then the flicker of anger was gone. "Perhaps you don't know who I am."

"All I know is you're late."

Mister Nguyen placed his hat on the table and played with the large gold ring on his index finger, looking down at her with a studied grimness.

Lynn stifled a sigh at the posturing. "Look, we have business to attend to, and I was led to believe you were a businessman." She indicated the seat opposite her. "Let's get to work."

He nodded, as though to himself, scanning the room as he took his seat. Appeals to *business* usually worked with these people, imagining, as they did, that they were part of some traditional brand of professional criminality stretching back through time to the Binh Xuyen of Saigon or the Painters and Dockers Union of Melbourne.

"We doing this here?"

She nodded. "I've never been here before. There are a hundred places like this in Cabramatta. Neither of us need return here again."

He looked around the room once more and took a palmscreen out of his pocket. He mumbled into it, pressed his thumb against a pad on the front, and then pulled a thin tube from the top. It unrolled into a translucent, wafer-thin flexiscreen. Soft green icons glowed across its surface. He looked at her. "So, what's the rush?"

"No questions, Mister Nguyen."

He clenched his jaw. He knew he couldn't argue with this statement of professionalism either. "The transaction will take thirty minutes to complete."

"Thirty minutes?"

Nguyen drew a cigar from the inner pocket of his jacket, and set about clipping the end with a steel cigar cutter. "The government tracks every freewave signal going into Vietnam. Our transaction can't be direct." He put the cigar in his mouth, took his time lighting it with a heavy gold lighter. He snapped it shut and puffed out a thick cloud of smoke. "We relay through a few different countries first before ending up at a front factory in Laos, right near the Vietnamese border. My contact there gets word across the border to a small town on the other side: Vinh Quang." He pointed down at the flexi-screen with the end of his cigar. "The money for the equipment—that's easy, will only take a few minutes. Unofficially, the Australians don't give a shit about private funds going to buy weapons for the Viet Minh. The money for people is tougher to get through clean. You know—the whole refugee thing."

Lynn nodded. She glanced over at the government ad on the wall, red letters glowing fierce and eternal. Yeah. She knew.

Money, of course, was always an exception. Five million dollars and you and your family would be granted a 'business residency' in Australia. The government funneled the arrivals into Cabramatta and the nearby suburbs, very quietly, so the general public wouldn't get too heated up about it.

The rest who arrived by boat were thrown into internment camps for a few months before being returned to Vietnam, where inevitably they ended up in Chinese prisoner-of-war camps.

Nguyen placed the cigar cutter and lighter on the scratched

tabletop. "You insisted on being here when the money went through. It takes thirty minutes."

"You know the saying," she said, "trust everyone, but cut the cards."

He shrugged. "Sure. I need to keep the line open, verify who I am, confirm we're not a part of some Chinese sting operation. If we miss a call, I fail to enter a pass code, they burn the link."

She nodded.

He puffed on his cigar like a man who believed he was in charge. "You said you wanted to move twenty million. Minus, of course, fifteen percent for my fee."

"You told me the fee was ten percent."

"That was before you criticized my clothes."

"You look like a cross between a pimp and a wet echidna. I think I went easy on you."

His eyes went hard. He glanced at her hair, opened his mouth to retort, then shook his head. "I did some asking around. Everyone has heard about you. High profile means a higher risk."

"You didn't even know whether I was a man or a woman before today."

"The authorities could be observing you."

"They're not."

He inhaled deeply on the cigar, blew the smoke directly into her face. She closed her eyes for a moment, felt her hand clench into a fist.

Nguyen was oblivious. "Your regular guy got done for tax evasion. I have the contacts. And you're in a hurry." He opened his hands and smiled. "The fee is fifteen percent."

Lynn glanced around the room. A couple of faces were turned in her direction. She shook her head, a small shake—one that could be mistaken for Lynn trying to get the smoke out of her eyes.

She looked back at him. "I want a business residency for two families. That's ten million. The rest goes to weapons."

"I assume these families are on an Australian government watch list. They'll need new identities?"

She raised an eyebrow in the universal signal for *obviously*.

"You know these people?" he asked.

"No."

"Then why are you getting them out?"

"You appear to be asking questions again. Now, what did I say about that?"

He brought his hand down hard on the plastic tabletop, causing the condiments on the table to chatter. He took a deep breath. "No respect."

Lynn sipped her tea, watching him over the lip of the glass.

He took a long drag on his cigar and returned the stare. Then he blinked away whatever he wanted to say and began manipulating the glowing symbols on the flexiscreen, whispering into it from time to time.

Unobserved, Lynn allowed herself a small smile.

Through the nanos attached to her optic nerves, the c-glyph could broadcast data and images that only she could see. Some people would have multiple freewave screens open all hours of the day. Watching the betting markets or reality television or point-of-view pornography. As a general rule, if you were in conversation with someone and their eyes glazed over, or even closed, they were finding some facile freewave feed more interesting than your company.

Lynn tended to keep her visuals uncluttered. At the moment all she had loaded up was the timestamp in glowing green numerals that appeared, to her brain, about a foot away in the top left corner of her vision.

15:33

She marked the time. Thirty minutes to Vinh Quang.

They waited. She turned and signaled the grandmother, ordered a late lunch. A soft chime sounded a few minutes later. Nguyen closed his eyes and put a finger to the c-glyph behind his left ear, listening as it whispered directly into his eardrum. He murmured a response, paused, and then mumbled again.

He opened his eyes a few seconds later. "The money for the equipment is through."

She nodded, touched her own c-glyph, fingers against the small circle of cool steel. "Anh Dung?" She listened to the reply, nodded once.

"Everything check out?" Nguyen asked.

"Don't worry, you'll know if it doesn't."

Nguyen slurped his tea and settled into his chair, content to watch the slow burn of his cigar. The minutes stretched out. Nguyen didn't try to engage her in conversation; the first transaction had gone through smoothly: things were going well.

Until the bell above the door tinkled again.

Two men entered. As the blinding light returned to the dusk of the room, she could see that they weren't from around here. White men with cheap fedoras, crumpled suits, and the empty gaze of detached professionalism. Government men. They scanned the room, their eyes stopping when they found Lynn.

She held her breath, moved her hand to her belt buckle.

They walked right up to the table, removing their hats as they approached. "Mister Nguyen Van Cam?" Lynn's hand stopped, hovering above the lip of her jeans, she breathed out slowly.

Mister Nguyen looked up. "Who wants to know?"

"I'm Agent Taylor, Immigration Enforcement Agency." He

flipped out a badge featuring an Australian crest, emu and kangaroo glinting chrome in the red haze. He pointed to the man next to him. "This is Agent Baker."

Nguyen was silent, his cigar trailing an idle string of smoke to the ceiling.

The time glowed softly at the edge of her vision.

15:51

Twelve minutes.

Nguyen was struggling to conjugate a response when the grandmother appeared between the two agents. The top of her head didn't even reach their shoulders. She looked down at Lynn when she spoke. "*Hai thằng chó đẻ này làm gì ở đây vậy?*" ["What are these two sons-of-bitches doing here?"]

Lynn's spoken Vietnamese was close to fluent, but she kept her translator on when she was working. Though less frequent, this part of town also echoed with Laotian, Burmese, and a hundred Chinese dialects. Smart to be tuned in to those wavelengths.

So the c-glyph whispered the old woman's sentence into her ear, coming through in English a couple of seconds later. It made it look like the grandmother was speaking in a badly dubbed old movie.

"They won't be here long. Can you get them tea?" Lynn asked.

"*Bác bỏ thuốc độc vô luôn được nha?*" ["Shall I poison it?"]

Lynn smiled a small smile. "No. Just tea." The men were moving their hands to their c-glyphs. Apparently they'd entered the restaurant without their translators turned on.

Lynn indicated a couple of seats nearby. "Gentlemen, why don't you sit down? Drink some tea with us."

One of the agents answered. "No thank you, Miss. We are here to take Mister Nguyen in for questioning."

"Now?"

"Now."

Lynn leaned back in her chair, used her eyes to indicate the room they were standing in. "Here's the thing. You're deep in the heart of Cabramatta. Not the safest place in the world for an immigration enforcement agent."

They looked around the restaurant. Perhaps noticing for the first time the quiet that had descended on it. All eyes in the room focused on them, the atmosphere turning like a corpse in the noonday sun.

"Gentlemen," she said.

They looked back at her.

"Just smile, grab a seat, and conduct your business politely. You'll be out of here in a few minutes, no trouble."

The agents exchanged glances. One nodded. They dragged chairs with faded red seat cushions over to the table, smiling strained smiles as they sat down.

Nguyen cleared his throat, a sheen of sweat on his forehead. "What's the charge?"

The official looked across at him with dead eyes. "People smuggling."

"Do you have a warrant?" asked Lynn.

He turned back to her. "Are you his lawyer?"

"No." She indicated Nguyen with an open palm. "He's my pimp. Can't you tell?"

Agent Taylor didn't seem keen on smiling. "People smuggling is a very serious offense."

Lynn nodded. "Yes, I've seen the advertisements. Very, very serious—imagine trying to help Vietnamese civilians flee cluster bombing and nerve warfare? China would be livid. And we couldn't have that."

The agents suddenly seemed a lot more interested in her. Taylor looked her over and then held out his hand to Agent Baker, who removed a palmscreen from his pocket and passed it to his partner. It looked a bit larger than a regular model, maybe four inches across by six long. The retina scanner he flipped up from the end must have been specially fitted. Lynn cursed inwardly.

"Would you mind if I did an identity check, Miss?"

She pointed. "What is that?"

"The retina scanner?"

"That model. That's official immigration issue isn't it? An expensive unit, I believe."

"Miss. The scan please." The agent had one of those voices trained to convey authority. Imbued with one extra notch each of volume, aggression, and confidence.

"I'm afraid I can't agree to that."

His gaze rose from the adjustments he was making to the scanner. "It's the law. We're making an arrest. You appear to be an associate of Mister Nguyen."

"I'm Australian. You have no jurisdiction over me."

"Sorry Miss, but we don't know that until we test it."

"That seems a conveniently circular argument."

"If you've done nothing wrong, then you have nothing to worry about."

Lynn raised an eyebrow. "Ah, the mantra of secret police and peeping Toms everywhere."

The agent's professional patina didn't drop. Not surprising, a person in his position would be subject to a wide range of creative abuse on a daily basis. "Like I said—it's the law."

"I read an article about this once. If you run my retina prints, I'll be listed as present during one of your arrests."

He responded with a shrug that indicated that while she was

right, he didn't really care.

"And I'll be flagged as a person of interest for immigration."

"I didn't design the system, Miss."

"Of course not. An empty suit couldn't design a system so diabolical; your only function is to implement it."

Still no response. Not a flicker. She sighed and pulled out an unmarked silver cigarette case from her jacket pocket. "Do you gentlemen smoke?"

Agent Baker let out a humorless laugh. "You think we can afford to smoke on a government salary?" He glanced around the room, at Nguyen. "In fact, I doubt anyone here can afford to smoke. Legally, anyway." He looked back at Lynn. "Do you have a license for those?"

Her fingers lingered in the open case. "I thought you were in immigration, Agent Baker, not drug enforcement. Haven't you gentlemen got enough on your plate for today?"

The man pointed at his partner. "He's Baker, I'm Taylor."

"You people all look the same to me."

He raised his eyebrows. "White people?"

"Bureaucrats."

The one on the right planted his elbow on the table, holding the palmscreen up at about her head height. The other agent turned to watch the room, hand slipping under his jacket. The patrons, seeing a hated ID check underway, watched him right back. Lynn snapped shut her case, *sans* cigarette, and placed it on the table.

15:56

"Here, hold it steady." She placed both hands on the palmscreen and held her eye up to the scanner. A small, black metal circle with a red laser dot in the center. She looked into the beam. The red glare caused her to blink.

"Try not to blink, Miss. It just needs five seconds."

She put her eye in the beam again, counted to three, then blinked rapidly. A chime in a minor key emanated from the palmscreen.

The agent sighed. "Miss." Firmer this time. "Just place your eye over the beam. Don't blink. It's over in a few seconds."

She failed another three times, eliciting more sighs and even a curse. She smiled sweetly. The smile didn't feel at all natural on her face, but their displeasure was satisfying nonetheless. On the sixth attempt, she allowed it to work.

16:00

He looked at the results of the scan. "Miss Vu. I see you have full citizenship."

"I'm aware."

"But your parents do not. They are Vietnamese–Australian."

She sat in silence. Let the threat hang there for a few moments while she studied it. "What the fuck does that mean?"

"Nothing." He snapped down the scanner, put the palmscreen in his coat pocket. His flat stare lingered on her. "I'm just saying they fall under our jurisdiction."

Under the table, she slowly slid her pistol from the small holster under her belt buckle. She moved it to her lap, hidden in the shadows, easing the safety off with her thumb. "My parents have nothing to do with this."

Again, those dead eyes. "If they've done nothing wrong, they have nothing to worry about."

The grandmother reappeared, placed a pot and two glasses on

the table. She glanced down as she did so. From the angle she was standing, the old woman could see the pistol Lynn clutched in her hand. She leant down, whispered close to Lynn's ear. "*Bỏ thuốc độc dễ hơn.*" ["Poison would have been easier."]

Lynn gave her a small smile in reply.

Agent Baker took one sip of his tea before turning to Nguyen. "Time to go." He pointed down at the flexiscreen sitting on the table. "That yours?"

Nguyen puffed on his cigar. Like Lynn, he seemed to be figuring the best answer to that particular question.

"Mister Nguyen, is that your flexiscreen?"

Nguyen began to speak, but Lynn cut him off. "Yes. Yes it's his."

The agent started to rise from his seat. "You better bring it with you."

16:03

A soft chime emanated from the screen. The four faces at the table turned to look at it. No one spoke. A few seconds passed and the chime sounded again, the ideograms on the flexiscreen increasing in brightness, insisting on attention.

"Mister Nguyen," she said. He didn't respond. He just sat staring at the screen. Her voice was firmer the second time. "Mister Nguyen."

He started and looked up at her.

"Why don't you answer your call while the agents here show me that warrant."

He looked from her, to the screen, over to the agents, then back to her again. He wiped the sweat from his brow with the back of his hand. "Sure." He put a finger to his c-glyph and closed his eyes.

"Gentlemen." Lynn held out her hand. "The warrant." She felt surprisingly calm given she was responsible for a crime occurring three feet away that could get her thirty years in prison. She focused on her breathing.

Inhale.

Exhale.

Inhale.

Agent Baker glanced over at Nguyen, who was now mumbling responses to someone only he could see. The agent sighed and reached into his coat pocket, pulled out the palmscreen, and pressed his thumb to it. "Verify: Agent Baker, immigration enforcement. Display warrant for Nguyen Van Cam, suspected people smuggler."

He waited. Nothing happened. He pressed his thumb to the screen again. Still nothing. It was dead. No sound, no light, no signal. He handed it to his partner. The other man looked at the dead screen, then up at Lynn. "What's going on here?"

She slowly slid the pistol back in the holster, eyes on the two men. "You tell me."

The agent held the screen up. "All official communications are contained in this, including the warrant. It's a closed system. It was working fine a few minutes ago. Now it's dead."

She leaned back in her chair. "Well, I'd say you boys are shit out of luck."

"This doesn't change anything."

"I disagree. It changes everything." Lynn signaled for the grandmother to come over to the table. She did so immediately. "This is private property. Unless you're conducting government-sanctioned business, you should leave." She turned to the old woman, addressing her in the formal Vietnamese mode, "Right, elder aunty?"

The grandmother looked at the two men, her eyes sparkling. She found a phrase for them in English. "Piss off."

The agents rose from their seats. One reached under his jacket. The other looked around at the customers, at the faces staring back at him from within the red haze, coiled with silent anger. The agent placed a hand on his partner's shoulder. "Let's wait outside. Warrant and back-up will be here in fifteen minutes."

The other man nodded, still staring straight at Lynn. He let his hand drop, looked over at Nguyen. "Don't even think about leaving." Then he spun and walked out, his partner right behind.

Lynn turned to the old woman. "We need some privacy."

The old woman set about ushering the customers out the front door. No one needed much encouragement. It wasn't worth witnessing what was going to happen next.

Soon all that remained was the smoke and the scent of anchovies. That, and two of her men. They walked over from where they had been sitting, one stood behind Mister Nguyen, one next to Lynn. They were big men.

Nguyen glanced up at them, then back at Lynn. "We should leave, now." He started to rise from his seat, but a heavy hand fell on his shoulder and pushed him back down.

Lynn shook her head. "Not yet, Mister Nguyen, not yet." She indicated the door with her eyes. "Your men in the car outside have been sent away."

"What?"

She sighed and folded her hands on the tabletop. "You led two immigration agents to our first meeting."

"I didn't know they were following me."

"You led two immigrations agents into our first fucking meeting." She didn't raise her voice, but the steel was in it this time.

Nguyen said nothing, just bowed his head and looked at the burnt-out cigar between his fingers.

Lynn pointed at the cigarette case. "Fortunately I keep a dot scrambler on hand for times such as this. The one I stuck on the agent's palmscreen will wipe any record of my retina scan, and freeze the unit until a tech can sit down and unwind the scrambled code. And this," she pointed to her nose ring, "is a refraction loop. You know what this does?"

He shook his head.

"To the naked eye I looked normal. But when you take the memory pin from your c-glyph and play back this scene, the area around my face is distorted. The light bent and warped. They'll still have my voice print, but I can live with that."

She placed the cigarette case in her pocket.

"So I'm in the clear," she said. "You know the laws on human memory. If it doesn't come from a memory pin playback, it is inadmissible as evidence. What with the frail psychology of natural memory and all that. Those agents won't remember what I look like anyway. Not if I change my hair." She reached up, touching the spikes with her palms. "Pity. I quite like this style."

She sighed. "There is, unfortunately, one loose strand. I didn't activate the refraction loop until after you'd walked in. Those agents," she waved at the door, "could subpoena your memory pin."

He stared at her for a few seconds, processing what she was saying. "I'll destroy it. I'll give it to you even. Right now."

She shook her head. "It is more than that. You're sloppy, and that makes you a liability. You know the names of the families I just paid for, and—"

"—I'll wipe all my records. You can have every—"

"—Enough." Her eyes flashed. "Enough. You endangered my parents. This isn't business, this is personal." She paused, watching the man squirm under the heavy hands pressed down on his shoulders. "That's the secret, by the way, Mister Nguyen. This business we have chosen—it's always personal."

"What are you saying?" He struggled to rise. The man next to Lynn stepped forward and drove a fist into Nguyen's face, rocking the gangster's head backward. Nguyen sat there for half a minute, one hand clutching the table, the other over his eye. When he pulled his hand away blood trickled down his cheek, the eyebrow split and already swelling.

Lynn indicated the man who had struck him. "This is Mister Giang. How is your family doing, Mister Giang?"

A voice, deep and clear, answered. "Well, Miz Vu."

She kept her eyes on Nguyen. "They been out here some time now haven't they?"

"Nearly three years."

She nodded. She pointed at the man behind Nguyen's left shoulder. "This is Mister Lac. His family arrived only six months ago. Have they settled in well, Mister Lac?"

"Very well, Miz Vu."

"Did your younger sister get into university?"

"Yes. She will be a teacher." A note of pride in the voice.

"Good. If there are any problems with tuition, you let me know."

It was hard to tell in the shadows, but Mister Lac appeared to nod in reply.

Nguyen watched her now out of one eye, fear blossoming behind it.

"Mister Giang?"

"Yes, Miz Vu."

"Could you take Mister Nguyen out to the back room and put a bullet through his head?"

Giang moved to where Nguyen sat and grabbed him by the upper arm. He and Lac hefted him out of his seat. Nguyen stuttered. "Wait, What? You can't kill me." Spittle fresh on his lips, his good eye wet. "Do you know who I am?"

Lynn stood. "Yes I do. You're a mercenary," she said. "And I meet people like you every day of the week."

She nodded at Giang. He punched Nguyen in the stomach, doubling him over as the air expelled from his lungs, his cigar butt dropping to the floor.

That was the last she saw of him—bent over, unable to speak, being dragged from the room.

She turned to Mister Lac. "Get my parents. Right now. Take them to a safe house. If they argue—*when* my mother argues with you—just tell her that their daughter will explain everything in a couple of days."

Lac nodded and left.

The grandmother walked in as he was leaving, handed over a warm bamboo box. "*Cơm của con nè. Bác đoán là con muốn take away.*" ["Your lunch, child. I guessed you wanted take away."]

The scent of rice, sharp chili sauce and aromatic mushrooms rose from the container. Lynn smiled a small smile. "Smells delicious, older Aunt. *Cám ơn bác.*"

Grandmother nodded. "*Con bảo trọng. Con đi há.*" ["You take care. You go."]

"You too. *Con đi đây.*"

Lynn straightened, fixing the ends of her hair with an open palm. She faced the front door. Twilight to heat, crimson to blinding white. Lynn hated the world out there.

She reached for the door handle.

THE WEIGHT OF THE AIR,
THE WEIGHT OF THE WORLD
2090–2091

"*The struggle of man against power is the struggle of memory against forgetting.*"
Milan Kundera, *The Book of Laughter and Forgetting*

Monday June 5th, 2090 // Seaweed Green – Papaya Orange

Karla Tessier-Denk stood in the prodigious marble foyer, relishing the cool air that washed over her. She'd had to walk at least a hundred metres from the bus stop in unfiltered sunlight, and was perspiring heavily. The other employees strode past, straight-backed, expensive suits, purposively, sweatless.

A red-dot pulsed on-retina, upper left of her vision, and turned into the words: **Identity Confirmed**. A voice said, via her neural implant: *Welcome to the Cultural Adjustment Bureau, Miz Tessier-Denk, and congratulations on your new position with the State. This way please.*

The **Identity Confirmed** faded, replaced by a green-glowing map. Overlaid, a red arrow and the words **You Are Here**. A red line extended from where she was standing, over the green cartography. She got her bearings and followed it to a cleansteel bank of nine elevators, up to the thirty-third floor, the knot in her chest tightening as the numbers rose. All she had to do was set a personal a record for *not fucking up*, and she'd be able to see her—

The doors opened, revealing an open-plan office filled with erect, well-dressed bureaucrats working with resolute purpose. She followed the directions to a cubicle with two work stations. The empty one was appointed with a *tai* screen, two rolled-up flexiscreens, and an ergonomic chair that looked comfortable enough to fall asleep in.

The other station held a young woman. Eurasian. Perfect eyebrows, one of them creeping upwards, unimpressed. Erect posture, white blouse, hands folded in her lap. Karla took a couple of long blinks, simultaneously pleased to have such an attractive cubicle-mate, and intimidated by her aura of severe professionalism. Karla became acutely aware of the sour smell of sweat she was emanating, the dryness of her throat. She sneezed.

The Eurasian waited.

Karla extended her hand and said: "Karla Tessier-Denk, the new—well, I'm not quite sure of my position title, but ah, pleased to meet you."

The woman looked at the extended hand. Karla realised it was the one she'd sneezed into, apologised, wiping her hand on her pants, immediately wished she hadn't done that either, gave up trying to talk anymore and sat down on her chair so at the least the redness in her face was hidden from the woman.

"Eulalie Chen," the woman said. "Your supervisor."

Karla turned. "Oh. My? Oh. Pleased to meet you." A loss at how to continue she said: "*nihao.*"

Eulalie's face, already smooth, turned to stone. "I'm not Chinese."

Karla blushed. Again. Inwardly screaming at herself. *Stop. Fucking. Up.* Outwardly, she said: "Oh. Sorry. I'm just—just trying—"

"I know what you're trying to do."

"Please. If you could not flag—I mean. If…"

Matter-of-factly, Eulalie said. "I can see you're a green. I'm sure the insult was not intentional."

Karla sighed and leaned back in her very comfortable chair. Two coloured blips hovered above Eulalie Chen's head, on-retina, marked her as double green. Seaweed-green community standing and jade-green political. Long time since she'd met a jade. Glancing around the office floor, it looked like most were double greens, or yellow-green at worst.

"Orange on political though," Eulalie said. "Unusual."

"Oh. That." Karla swallowed, and switched to the talking points she always used when asked. "It all happened a long time ago. Bit of a firebrand at university—product of a mis-spent youth" (cue rueful smile). "You know, Miz Chen, I don't even recognise that person anymore. No problems in the fifteen years since. Not one. But you know how static political ratings can be. *Justifiably,* of course."

"Hmm," said Eulalie, in a way that gave no indication of

whether she believed. Then it was her turn for talking points: "I will not be giving you a formal briefing about your work here at the Cultural Adjustment Bureau, as that is classified. All you need to know is that your tasks will be varied. You will need to be intellectually nimble and culturally nuanced. The work will ebb and flow as societal forces dictate and as your abilities are clarified by those monitoring your performance." She directed her eyes at Karla's work station. "So sync up. Get across your brief for this week."

"Yes," Karla agreed. "I'll get right to it. Thanks. I won't… Thanks." She smiled unconvincingly and turned back to her work, relieved the conversation was over.

Almost as an afterthought, Eulalie said: "Unlike the rest of the State, we have a six-day work week here at the Bureau. Friday is our shift's day off. The section usually goes for drinks Thursday night. You should join me."

Karla swivelled back to her and said: "oh," and it came out a little more excited than she had intended. Like she'd just found a mint on her pillow. *Oh.*

"To discuss your work practices," said Chen, eyebrows flinging disdain across the cubicle. "You and I will be required to share cultural adjustment orders from time to time, should the need arise. If we are tasked with a June Fourth Incident, you'll need to be prepared."

Karla nodded, too quickly, for too long. She didn't know what a June Fourth Incident was, but she was terrified of Eulalie rescinding her offer of drinks and so just said *yes, of course.* Eulalie Chen turned back to her work without another word and stayed that way for the rest of the day.

Tuesday 6th – Thursday 8th June, 2090 // Seaweed Green - Papaya Orange

Karla's tasking turned out to be simple. Not quite as artistic as she'd hoped; not really what she'd imagined at all for the Bureau. But a pleasant introduction. Her job for the week was to write reviews for new, state-approved movies. The Cultural Adjustment Bureau was the last government agency to vet new movies, and the first to respond after release.

There was a wave of comic book films coming out, like always, so Karla sat back on her chair, closed her eyes, and watched them all against the back of her eyelids. Not quite the same as the immersive cinema experience, but enough to make her smile and think: *this is my day job?*

As per the guidelines, her reviews were effusive.

On Tuesday afternoon, Eulalie swivelled and said, without preamble: "Find something to critique in every movie."

Karla blinked at her, taking a few seconds to turn the on-retina movie off and track her sentence. For a split second she had a shirtless Shang-Chi superimposed over her vision as she looked at Eulalie. Standing there, on her desk.

"Sorry?"

"Your reviews. They are fine. You write well enough. But you need to remember these are published under the auspices of a respected geek culture wavesite. The reviews have to seem real. Find a little something in each movie—vigilantes given any sort of sympathy, for example—and critique it. This keeps the studios on their toes. It also gives citizens something to argue about, make it feel like they are participating in a meaningful discussion. Just make sure the movie gets a minimum of four stars out of five." She said it all with an authority Karla didn't think twice about brooking.

And so she did as instructed. An ill-conceived product placement; an insufficiently uplifting ending; and a rather laboured argument about a fight scene in which the two combatants were from different ethnic groups, and which therefore promoted disharmony. Still, all three reviews were published unchanged, sparking a satisfying level of discussion in the comments.

For Karla's last review of the week she excoriated the new Green Turtle movie for an overly sympathetic portrayal of the villain, Batman. She called Batman the 'Darth Vader of the comic book universe'. The latest incarnation was pretty damn dark. Karla was never much into comics, but the work of the past week had got her up to speed. Batman had started drinking the blood of his victims, apparently. Like, removing the heart from the chest cavity and chomping down on it: the CEOs of his corporate competition, bureaucrats from the tax office, hookers he took back to his mansion. But there were also a couple of scenes of Batman being pensive and conflicted in conversations with his butler, Allie. Karla found it all a bit incongruous.

Karla leaned back in her chair and thought it over. End of the week and she was feeling a little daring. So she added: *If filmmakers insist on making Batman more complex, they need to go back to the villain's comic book roots as a billionaire industrialist. Herein lies potential. A place to mine if they want to bring this character over from the dark side.* She nodded to herself, chuckling a little.

Karla took a sip of coffee and read over the article several times, tweaking, perfecting, agonising over commas. She took a deep breath and sent it through to Eulalie.

She eased herself back into her comfortable seat and waited for her supervisor's comments, pretending to reread the Bureau's guidelines on Reviews and Cultural Commentary.

Eulalie continued working, murmuring commands into her

cochlear implant. As did the others in the office, the low susurrus of voices in the office the only sound. No chitchat. Not one person humming to themselves, or laughing at some virtual correspondence, or swearing at a disappointment. Nothing. Just the steady, purposeful work of the most respected agency in the State.

She kept waiting.

At seven, Eulalie packed up and left without a word. Karla tried to catch her eye, but she ignored it.

Deflated, Karla synced a final update, grabbed her battered black briefcase and departed, out through the expansive foyer and into the cloying post-dusk heat. Sweating at the bus stop, shaking her head periodically, staring at a spot on the road.

A message pinged on-retina from an unknown number. She opened it:

It's Eulalie. We're meeting at the Drunken Angel at 7.30. See you there.

Karla smiled.

Karla entered the crowded bar, at first assuming she'd got the wrong place. Not classy. Not refined. Not exclusive. The Drunken Angel was a loud, grimy joint jumping with an eclectic mix of clientele. Construction workers with hi-vis vests, long-haired thickset men and women wearing heavy metal t-shirts, and a smattering of office workers, ties loosened, pints of beer in hand.

She went through the front bar into a dank, long back room filled with booths and loud music. Up at the black-topped bar, Eulalie sat with someone. Karla sucked in her stomach, ran a hand through her hair. She'd been a sprinter, back at university. Had a top-notch physique. Amazing thighs. Called herself a *renaissance woman*. Ironically, but, you know, kinda believing it on the inside.

Long time ago. Fifteen years of cheap wine, savoury snacks, and unused gym memberships had been unhelpful.

Eulalie whacked her friend on the arm and pointed at Karla as she approached. "Here she is, Miz *Nihao*." Eulalie shook her head, smiling. "Dickhead."

Karla stopped, stunned, not quite sure how respond and Eulalie found that funnier still. Her friend smiled wryly and got up from his bar stool. South Asian. Great hair. Worked on the same floor at the Bureau. "Kevin," he said. "Good to meet you Karla. I've been keeping this warm."

"Oh," Karla started.

Smiling Kevin left before Karla could ask him to stay, moving over to one of the booths. She noticed it was filled with some familiar faces from the Bureau. Karla took her stool, Eulalie asked her what she wanted. She replied: *red wine, something quaffable.*

Once Karla had glass in hand and Eulalie had a fresh beer, the woman asked: "So what answer did you give on the test?"

Karla sipped her wine. "Um. Which question?"

"Which question?"

"Oh." Karla said. "The last one. I recommended changing the weekend to Monday—Tuesday."

Eulalie paused, eyes narrowed. Then laughed. She laughed and when she did it was with without restraint, her head back, mouth open wide. "Wow. No wonder you got the job. Beautiful, just beautiful."

Karla took a moment to adjust to this new person she was talking to. Alive, sensual, using her whole body to laugh or drink or to ask a question. She wet her lips with wine. "What did you answer?"

Eulalie shrugged. "Military parade. It's the standard answer. Most new applicants think they're fucking geniuses when they give it. Yep, military parade, invent something horrible the Japanese did sometime in the past. Or take something they did do and tweak it a little, change the dates and locations as required. It'll ring true in the minds of most citizens. Kill off any proposed protests dead, that's for sure. Who's going to turn up bemoaning some hippy bullshit in the public square on the day our men and women gave their lives fighting the eternal enemy, right?"

"Right." Karla nodded. "Smart."

Eulalie shook hers. "Standard. Swapping out the weekend, that"— she pointed with her beer— "is fucking smart," and downed the rest of it.

Eulalie caught the eye of the heavily bearded barman and signalled another. They clearly knew each other. To Karla she said: "Don't give me that look. I'm not allowed to swear?"

"It's not that, it's just—" she gave an uncomfortable laugh. "I'm just getting used to the work Eulalie and the pub Eulalie."

The woman made a face. "Oh come on. Who the fuck is the same at work as at home? Look, the Bureau has every right to be up our arses. Conversations and feed activity, the point our eyes are looking at on-screen, bowel movements, everything." She opened her left hand, gesturing with her beer in the right. "All justified of course, given the sensitivity of our work."

"Of course," Karla replied, but her warning radar went off. Made sure she didn't add, or subtract, to anything being said.

"So don't stress."

"Says the double green."

"Ha." Eulalie quirked a corner-mouth smile. "Fair call. *Bad girl.*"

Karla smiled despite herself, quite liking the name.

Eulalie continued: "I'll do all the swearing and inappropriate remarks, deal?"

"Deal," Karla replied, and they clinked glasses.

"So what do you want to ask?"

"Huh?"

"Come on, you arrived with a burning question there, right behind the eyes. Out with it."

"Um."

Eulalie made the *come on come on* motion with her hand.

"The Batman article?"

"Ah," Eulalie rolled her eyes, "work. Um, yeah. Good *Star Wars* references. The boss will like it."

"So um…"

"Oh," she said, eyebrow raised. "Did you want a pat on the head?"

"Well, no, I—"

Eulalie pouted, reaching for Karla's stomach. "Did you want a tummy tickle for being a good boy?"

She batted away her hand. "Ah fuck off."

Eulalie laughed. "That's the spirit." She paused to sip her beer and said: "There's two of me, Karla; don't ever forget that."

"Okay."

"So," Eulalie said. "Got a girlfriend. Boyfriend. Fuck chickens. What's your story?"

"Straight to that, boss?"

"Isn't it always about that?"

"Ha. Yeah." Karla gave her wine a rueful smile, real this time. "I'm divorced. From a woman. Young son, four, nearly five. She has custody. He's coming over tomorrow actually, first time I've had him unsupervised in nearly two years. The new position at the Bureau— well, gave me an immediate upgrade on my visitation rights."

Eulalie said: "Ah. I see. Well I'm glad to hear it," and Karla believed her.

"So I can't stay for too long tonight. My wife's lawyer is allowed to review my expenditure log. They see me out drinking heavily the night before, well," she moved her shoulders, "you know."

"When's he coming over?"

"Oh. Not until three. After school. Then five full hours. I'm kinda nervous, actually."

"In that case," Eulalie said, and turned to the barman, ordered and received another wine and another beer.

Karla furrowed her brow; Eulalie made an innocent face. "It's on me," she said. "Just stay for a couple more so I can get you a little tipsy, subject you to some low-level sexual harassment."

Karla laughed, shaking her head at this woman. She also found herself sucking in her stomach.

The night was fun. Wrong. Correct that. It was a great night. She and Eulalie talked for hours. Karla got bold with drink, started doing impersonations of stupid shit she'd done in the past, cracked jokes on the borderline of a shame penalty. Eulalie laughed at them all uninhibited, bought the drinks, touched Karla on the arm when she spoke. Later, they parted with a hug and an awkward kiss that missed the cheek, but didn't quite hit the mouth, either. Eulalie Chen laughed, eyes sparkling, and walked away with exaggerated swagger.

When Karla got home she was buzzing.

She heated up a large bowl of leftover rice and tempeh, mind playing over make-out scenarios with Eulalie, and sat down with a large glass of water to watch her *tai* screen. The first channel had a historical drama about the life of Chairman Mao. The Chairman Mao actor looked at the crumpled cigarette between his fingertips, and said: *"If there aren't any businessmen, I can't even buy cigarettes, let alone talk about market prosperity—we need to invite them back."*

Karla grunted and said to the apartment: "Good lord. Jeeves— get me a home shopping channel. Fucking vacuum cleaners, or something."

"Excellent choice, ma'am," replied the apartment with a rich, toffy English accent. Karla had given it the name and personality. She'd thought, well, if she was going to have a butler. Jeeves continued: "Do you have a preference for the Suck-o-Matic or the S-U-X 3000?"

"Less dry wit, more vacuum cleaners."

"Of course, Ma'am."

Jeeves put on the infomercial for the S-U-X 3000 and that's how Karla fell asleep—mouth open, empty glass resting in her crotch, leggy blonde pitching excitedly as the vacuum drone picked up a bowling ball and put it back in the cupboard.

But in her mind's demimonde, just as sleep was falling, her brain went *tic-tic*, saying: *Eulalie's too good to be true. Too good to be true.*

Friday June 9th, 2090 // Seaweed Green - Papaya Orange

Karla groaned her way out of bed, went to the kitchen, drank a large glass of water with two aspirin. She took advantage of her higher water ration and had a long, hot shower.

Out in the living room, towel around her breasts, she stopped and shook her head. "Shit."

Karla still couldn't quite believe the upgrade she'd been given upon joining the Bureau. From a one-room-plus-study-nook-and-aging-kitchenette located out in the outer suburbs; from thin walls with a domestic-dispute/fuck-and-make-up couple on one side, and a shuffling old man who spent a good thirty minutes every morning clearing his throat on the other. From the faint scent of mould, ever-present.

To this.

Two-bedroom, ensuite and bathroom, brand-new chrome-and-blue-highlighted kitchen. Couch as big as her old apartment; an AI system—Jeeves—that made breakfast, pithy comments about current affairs, and tasteful suggestions for Karla's wardrobe; and no sounds of neighbours emphatically copulating. Not a peep. She ran a hand through her short wet hair and looked out through the floor-to-ceiling windows. And then there was the view.

The metropolis, spread out to the horizon under a luminous blue sky. Twenty million souls and Karla could see most of them from up here. The wealthy in their skyscraper-spires of the city centre, surfaces coated in glimmering solar particles. A step out to the townhouses, piled on top of each other, steel cheek by brick jowl, fitted out with only the best appliances and AIs, perfect for the aspirational middle manager. Then the apartments of the type Karla now lived in, forming a perfect ring around the wealthier denizens on the inside, like a keep. Beyond the ring to the kind of hovel that Karla used to live: among the neon-lit bars and street walkers and abandoned churches and temples, and glimmer trains that always ran on time. Further again to the accretion of towns that formed around the edges, barnacles on the ship of progress. The drug dealers and the veterans and low-skilled workers, clinging to the world by their nails, lest they sink into the crushing dark depths. Beyond that—well, she'd never travelled beyond the city limits and saw no reason to. The whole universe was this city; this city the universe, replicated all over the world.

Karla put on a clean shirt with a picture of a tank; Kindred had chosen it for her thirty-sixth birthday, just past. Then she sat, leg bumping up and down, tight black ball of anxiety right below her heart. Before today she'd only an hour, once a fortnight, under the baleful glare of her ex-wife's nanny at the local indoor park. Her boy, her beautiful boy's development like flip-cards, rapidly moving snapshots where her son would be that little bit taller, have new words in his vocabulary, new expressions and obsessions whose basis Karla would never have time to divine. She wondered if she'd be able—

A ping on-retina and Jeeves whispered discretely, via her implant: *Excuse me Ma'am, but Ambrosia Whitewater and Kindred Whitewater are waiting at the door. Shall I let them enter?*

Karla said: "Yes yes, of course." She took a deep breath, smiled a relaxed smile and walked to the entrance.

Ambrosia waited in the doorway, arms crossed, expression on her face best described as *displeased*. Lawyer, hair tied back, calves looked like they were carved from wood. Gym membership, tennis lessons, exclusive private school, cocktails with the girls, father a merchant banker; she liked pop psychology, had strong opinions on female representation in the Marvel franchise. Back to work two days after their son had been born; Filipino nanny moved into the guest bedroom.

Kindred hid behind his other mother's legs.

Karla said: "Hi Ambrosia."

With Kindred squashed in behind her, Ambrosia took two steps in, raised an eyebrow, looked around the apartment and said: "Well. Better late than never."

Karla winced inwardly.

Kindred poked his head around the curve of Ambrosia's behind.

"Who's that?" asked Karla, hands on hips.

Kindred rushed out: "It's me, silly mummy." Handsome, eyes serious, brown curls Karla wished her ex-wife would let grow out. Superman shirt, Spiderman shorts, Green Lantern socks.

"Which superhero are you?" asked Karla.

Kindred raised his arms above his head, fists clenched, and yelled: "I'm one hundred Kindred!" with a flailing of karate chops that ended with a strange crab-dance.

Ambrosia rolled her eyes, gave Kindred a perfunctory kiss on the head, turned and left without another word.

When the door shut Karla picked him up, and swung him round and around. Hugging her son's chest to hers, his little legs swinging out behind.

"Weeeeeeeeee, weeeeeeeeeeeeeee!" yelled Kindred.

When Karla put him down Kindred yelled: "*More more!*"

So Karla swung him more, until she was gasping for breath and had to collapse onto the couch.

Kindred clambered onto her, little knees and hands jabbing her groin and breasts. "More Mummy, more!"

"I could," said Karla, between breaths. "But then I might forget about your present."

"Present?" asked Kindred, with much gravitas. "Did you know I like presents, Mummy?"

"I had an idea."

"Where, where?"

"There." Karla pointed. Next to the kitchen bench was a very large box of Lego: Batman in the Bat Cave.

Kindred gave a long, low-pitched yell that managed to sound strangled by all the glee in it: "Whoaaaaaaaaaaaaaaaaaaaaaaaaaaaaaaa aaaaaaaaaaaaaaaaaaaa." He ran over to the box, touched it, ran back and jumped on her stomach. "I love you Mummy!"

Karla felt her heart swell, tears mist in her eyes. "I love you, Son."

Kindred ran back over to the box, hugged it, and said: "I love you, Lego Bat Cave."

Karla's heart immediately deflated, but she roared with laughter anyway. Kindred looked over. "What's so funny, Mummy?"

"Nothing, nothing," said Karla, blinking away the tears, still laughing. "Let's get to work. We've got a big job ahead of us."

Kindred nodded, serious. "Roger, Mummy."

Fortunately there were no dead whores or bloodied hearts in the Bat Cave. Just a bat-attack plane, prison cells for his enemies Wonder Woman and Green Turtle, a large armoury of machine guns, and Batman at his desk, brooding over banks of *tai* screens.

At one point Kindred looked up and asked: "What's an edible complex?"

"Edible complex?"

"Yeah, edible complex."

"Where did you get that from?"

"Mummy One. She said Mummy Two has an edible complex."

"She never even met my father," said Karla, to herself.

"What does that mean?"

Karla popped her eyes wide, stared.

"Mummy!" he said, beaming, knowing what was coming.

"*Grrrrrr.*"

"Mummy!"

"It means," growled Karla, "that I'm hungry!"

"Mummy!"

Karla jumped on her flailing son, pulled up his shirt, and blew raspberries on his stomach. Kindred squealed, laughing, trying to get away.

It took them all evening, five hours. Karla finding the pieces, pointing at the instructions, and Kindred figuring it out, snapping them in place. God the kid was smart. Four years old, sweating with concentration, looking at diagrams even Karla found hard to parse, and pinpointing the precise spot for the specific bit, every time. Karla said *good boy* and Kindred beamed and said *thanks Mummy*, moving closer, sitting on her lap while he worked.

Karla felt that ache, right below her heart.

When the time came to leave, Ambrosia stood in the doorway, foot tapping, arms crossed. Kindred put his arms around Karla's shoulders and hugged her tight. "I love you Mummy. Let's never *ever ever ever* take the Bat Cave apart."

Karla laughed and said: "Of course. It will always be here, for you to play with. Always."

Kindred said "Thanks Mummy!" and hugged her again, leaving only reluctantly when Ambrosia promised ice cream when he got home.

The door shut. Karla slumped down on the couch. Stared at the Bat Cave. And burst into tears.

Body shaking. Shaking with laughter. With relief. With two years of sadness and anger and self-loathing. With joy. With that exquisite, perfect pain sitting just below her heart. With more she couldn't identify, with a tension she hadn't quite known she'd had, pouring it all out.

Later that evening Karla logged into her Ego feed.

The title screen materialised: **Ego – for the Glory of You**, and then faded slowly to reveal her profile.

Karla's page was inoffensive, a minimum of detail bar the automatically generated colour ratings, occupation, marital status, academic record, and credit score. It was as dull as they came. She'd been too terrified to say or write anything on her site—if her community standing left the green zone she'd be fucked.

But but but. A post about starting work at the Cultural Adjustment Bureau was untouchable. She dictated:

Finished my first week at the Cultural Adjustment Bureau,

then spent the whole day with my son. Best time I've had in years!
She read it over, wasn't quite sure of the tone, so changed it to:
Most rewarding few days I've had in a long time. She added an on-retina snap she'd taken of Kindred standing next to the completed set. Her son was beaming, looking ecstatically down at the Cave.

And there it was. Karla had conflated seeing her son with the new position at the Bureau. Now the two were connected. No viewer could flag it as a community or political violation, without fear that they themselves might be flagged.

The likes and smiley faces and happy dances pinged on the post almost immediately.

Karla logged out and leaned back on the sofa. "Cunts."

Saturday July 15th, 2090 // Seaweed Green - Papaya Orange

A month later Karla worked her first June Fourth Incident. She had a range of duties in the interim, none too challenging. A few days gushing on car forums about a new car model, the Tesla Europa; a week or so calling a prescribed list of public intellectuals paedophiles, and flagging them for shame penalties for every statement they made; and a bizarre ten hours straight tracking down anyone talking about 'yellow rubber ducks' on the freewave and calling them traitors. She had no idea what the last one was about, no idea at all. Eulalie simply said: "You'll be given a fake identity; say anything you want—you won't be given a shame penalty."

Karla was halfway through writing an article about the benefits of activated almonds when Eulalie tapped her on the shoulder and said: "It's happening."

Eulalie seemed nervous, gripping her hands tightly together.

Karla followed her to an expansive meeting room, took a seat next to her. About thirty officers sat down each side of the long dark table; Karla recognised many of them—Kevin from the Drunken Angel was sitting opposite.

A man, large in body and in presence, entered the room via a recessed door. He looked around fifty-five. Grey vest, no coat, white business shirt with a stiff collar. An impressive coif of full-bodied, wavy hair. Stick a fork in that hair, and it'd stay there. Stubby fingers that drummed a tattoo on the table edge as he sat and looked up and down the seated staff with black glittering eyes. Eyes that didn't miss a fucking thing.

On-retina, a name popped up: **Whittaker Babbitt Jnr. Director, Cultural Fast Response.**

Oh, Karla thought—*that's* the name of my division. Eulalie had told her it was classified.

No on-retina colour rating floated above the director's head. Karla blinked a couple of times, trying to figure out where it was. Took her a full half-minute to realise *he had none.* With the exception of children (who got community scores at seven, and political ratings at fourteen), Karla had never met anyone without their colours on display.

Without preamble, Babbitt said: "Listen: protest marches are planned for the weekend of July twenty-second. One week from now. These political agitators claim insufficient compensation and consultation preceding the construction of a hydroelectric dam on the Canary River. They say several houses were demolished without proper authorisation, and that at least twenty residents—who had refused to leave—were injured. These deviant-roaders further assert that this unfortunate accident was due to corruption. The owner of the company building the dam is coincidentally a nephew of the Minister for Renewable Energy." Babbitt looked them over with black, depthless eyes. Karla swallowed as they passed over her. Babbitt continued: "Listen: these are the claims. False claims, utterly false. It is important that the public understands this potential incident in the correct manner, and that the cultural ramifications are consistent with social harmony and economic progress. Actions?"

Several people put their hands up.

Babbitt said: "We require ideas other than that of a military march. We need to give that well of inspiration a respite, allow it to replenish."

All put their hands back down.

Eulalie nudged Karla with her foot. She tried to ignore it, but Eulalie did it again, harder, and Karla raised her hand. Just seemed to levitate upwards, all by itself. Babbitt looked at her, waiting. Karla's voice croaked as she tried to speak. She cleared her throat and tried again: "We could move the weekend, sir. Swap it with Monday—Tuesday. Tell the universities, government, and major business to proceed on that basis."

Several around the table gave her strange looks; several more couldn't even bring themselves to look at her.

Babbitt sat in silence, watching. Karla licked her lips, preparing to unleash an angry kick back at Eulalie, when Babbitt said: "Yes. Karla Tessier-Denk, Third Secretary, Fast Response. I liked that idea when you provided it on your entrance exam."

Karla smiled.

Babbitt continued: "But I only half like it now."

Karla stopped smiling.

Babbitt looked around the table. "Innovative, promising: the kind of thinking we need at the Bureau to renovate the manner of our responses, and stay ahead of cultural anxieties. But it is an administrative action, not a cultural one. So I agree this change should be made, but say this: the Bureau needs to complement it with something more."

Silence, for a full minute, before Eulalie raised her hand. When Karla turned to look at her she noticed Eulalie's free hand, under the lip of the table, gripping and un-gripping the material of her pants.

But when she asked: "The injured are in the local state hospital?" she did it with austere confidence.

Babbitt signalled to an assistant at his right hand. Man. Severe part in dark hair. He looked down at a flexiscreen in front of him, then back at Eulalie: "There's a private one, in that district. They have all been sent there."

"But we have beneficial relations with the board?" she asked.

"Of course."

"The medical staff have access to their memory streams?"

"Yes," said Babbitt, eyes shining.

"Download a contradictory account," said Eulalie. "Have them remembering they received substantial compensation offers. Also have them recall one of the leaders—the one most easily compromised on community or political standing—giving them instructions to stay."

Babbitt leaned forward, expectant.

Back straight, outwardly confident, Eulalie continued: "Sow the seeds of doubt in the movement. This way, those with the most moral authority—those foolish enough to get injured—will be in conflict with the rest of the protestors."

A fault-finder with a patriotic pin on his lapel and no ideas of his own said: "But they will be contradicted by other witnesses, of which there are far more."

"Good," said Eulalie, face smooth. "It muddies the waters."

The fault-finder replied: "But the difference between the exo-memory and natural recollection here is too great. This is an *adjustment* bureau. These proposed changes are wholesale—it's too risky."

"We will help them remember correctly," said Eulalie. "Put large deposits in the bank accounts of the injured, back-dated, and say *look, the compensation was here all along. If you wish to reject it and keep protesting, then that is your decision.*"

Babbitt was smiling. Karla couldn't help but be reminded of Batman looking at Robin after she'd just brought him an unconscious hooker.

The fault-finder, missing the sentiments of Babbitt completely said, hands open: "The exo-memories will have to be perfect, in every detail. They'll get wide coverage in the media."

"Of course they will be perfect." Eulalie looked around the table. "That's our job, isn't it?"

"Precisely," said Babbitt. Definitively, all heads turning back to him. He pressed his forefinger into the tabletop, eyes on Eulalie. "It is precisely the job of the Bureau. Good work, Miz Chen. Now." He pitched his voice to the rest of the room. "Listen: we'll instruct the Internal Harmony Service to move the weekend, speak to major business in the district so they agree—we'll call it a productivity measure. The local university will conduct scheduled exams on those days; and any local government agencies will remain open. The Thursday Shift will handle this June Fourth Incident under your direction, Miz Chen. You will create a memory that is perfect. You will do it in one week."

Sunday 16th – Friday 22nd, 2090 // Seaweed Green - Papaya Orange

They worked eighteen-hour days for the next week. Many slept at the Bureau, in rooms lined with cots, designed for that purpose. When Karla's visitation day with Kindred loomed, she'd raised it with Eulalie; her supervisor answered, simply: "It's a June Fourth Incident." She'd said nothing else.

When Karla had gotten home that night she'd kicked a hole in the bedroom wall. Jeeves asked: "Redecorating, ma'am?" Karla had switched the butler's voice mode off for the rest of the evening.

Eulalie barely said another word to her unless it was related to the false memories they were creating. And the plan: well, it worked. The protests fizzled out after the manufactured infighting. Claim and counter claim was brought against the leadership by those hospitalised. Reliable media partners ensured the adjusted version of events received a lot of air time. The people of the restive region dragged themselves to work and to study on the re-positioned Monday, grumbling, to be sure. Babbitt got special dispensation to release the new Green Lantern film on the faux weekend that followed, restore community morale, give them something else to talk about.

Karla was slouching down the corridor towards her apartment when someone said: "Good evening, Miz Tessier-Denk. How was the talking club?"

Karla jumped. Literally. Back a step, one hand up. The lighting along the corridor was out, apparently. Just slats of moonlight streaming through the barred window down the far end. A man— the voice sounded like a man's, anyway—a few feet up from her apartment door. Hat and coat, all in shadow, Karla couldn't make out any features distinctly. Save the orange tip of the cigarette he was smoking.

Karla kept her hand up. Cigarette Man was about ten feet away. "Do I know you?"

"No," said the voice. Calm.

"You can't smoke in here, buddy." Karla was frightened, a rough edge coming into her words.

The man exhaled a slow cloud of smoke, his irises glittered in the gloom. He said: "How was your talking club?"

Karla took a deep breath. The door was halfway between her and the man. Wouldn't be able to reach it in time, if the stranger wanted to block her. Silence in the corridor, save the whine of a hydrogen generator somewhere, the scuff of her shoes on the plascrete, and the thumping of her heart in her ears.

"Who the fuck are you?"

The man smoked, Karla's on-retina pinged. The message opened without Karla telling it to: **(Name withheld) Internal Harmony Service**.

"That's who I am," he said.

Karla's fear coalesced, twisting her stomach. "I don't know what you're talking about, officer."

"But you know what a talking club is, yes?"

"Sure. I've heard the rumours."

"Then you'd know that a woman in your position shouldn't be involved with that type of deviant association."

Karla had had enough. With the week. With Eulalie. With this jackboot harassing her from the shadows. "Listen, buddy. You can innuendo random shit all you like, but I don't know what the fuck you're talking about. You got some sort of evidence, send it to the Bureau. Now"— she pointed with her suitcase—"I'm going inside, warm up some shitty food, and watch the shopping channel. You got anything else to say?"

The officer did not. Just smoked and watched as Karla went inside. She closed the door, pressed her back against it. "Jeeves, is there anyone outside?"

"No Ma'am, not that I can detect."

"So he's gone?"

"Ma'am, no-one was outside your door, at any time in the last hour. Just you."

Karla ran a shaking hand through her hair.

July – October, 2090 // Seaweed Green – Papaya Orange

Weeks passed. Karla didn't hear from the mysterious jackboot. Not directly. She'd seen him, she thought—in the rear compartment of the bus, the next aisle of the supermarket, once even in a darkened corner of the Drunken Angel. But when Karla turned and stared, or walked over to investigate, there'd be no one there. Like a ghost. Karla even went back and checked her exo-memory to make sure the first meeting actually happened.

There was nothing. Her feed showed her talking to thin air, no smoking man, no agent of the state.

Just a blank white wall.

So as the weeks passed and the sightings stopped, the tightness in Karla's stomach eased. And life got better. Good, even.

Her son visited every week; the Lego city grew—Turtle Plane attacking a Japanese military lifeboat, Punisher's Car, Deadpool getting a burger at McDonalds.

Kindred was working towards Superman's Fortress of Solitude, which was bigger even than the Bat Cave. Her son had agreed, with serious eyes, to save up all the money he could in his e-piggy bank, for a year, to put towards the set.

Karla was working towards a bigger goal, as well: a sleepover. She wasn't entitled to it, but she could certainly ask. Ambrosia would be given a difficult decision when she did. Her response had to negotiate that fine line between Officer of the Cultural Adjustment Bureau and a legally confirmed bad spouse. That one needed time, though. A period of no-fucking-up Ambrosia probably figured Karla didn't have in her.

As for Eulalie: they kept meeting for Thursday drinks. Something was happening, she could feel it. They talked about everything, uninhibited, except for the times Eulalie'd lean in and warn when a government agent was lurking at the bar, or give Karla a kick when a guerrilla marketer tried to engage them in conversation about movies or shoes. Vigilant, making sure they preserved their shame and political scores. Eulalie could always pick them; Karla was oblivious.

And it grew and Karla was right: three weeks later they slept together for the first time. After some initial nerves on Karla's part—it had been years since she'd been with anyone—it was good. Really good.

The third time they slept together, Eulalie asked her to take out her memory pin. It was a thing people did, to make sure sometime down the track a disgruntled ex didn't post a freaky fuck session up on the freewave. A mutually-assured-destruction type move that would blast the community standing of both right into the red.

So when Eulalie asked, she did, excited, imagining latex suits and amyl nitrate. But all Eulalie wanted to do was talk. For hours, everything uninhibited, until she asked: *So what are your true colours, Karla?*

She'd replied: *Oh, I don't know. It's different, now, with my son. I'd probably be a double yellow, I guess.*

Eulalie seemed disappointed by that but Karla didn't know how to respond. Not sure whether she wanted her to be better, or worse. And when Karla had asked, in turn, what her true colours were, Eulalie just turned away and said, over her shoulder: *You've got your son tomorrow. Get some sleep.*

Monday October 2nd, 2090 // Dragon Green – Seaweed Green

Taylor, first position, has the shield up, my left hand on his shoulder; behind, Yang has a hand on mine. Breathing, loud in my ears, claustrophobic in the gas mask, never quite got used to it, even after all these years. Overlaid on-retina, the infrared of the target in the room beyond the door, phasing in and out *flicker flicker, flicker flicker.* Green map, the other corner of my vision, floorplan of the Charter Nine base. Art district, converted warehouse, abandoned now. Nooks, crannies, unregistered rooms, corridors, back alleys, blindsides, too many. Eyes in the sky, hunter-killer drones so high they are invisible, fly drones buzzing through the building at knee level, yes—all that—but the terrorists are using a jamming device, nano-cam feeds fritzing, snow.

The six bio-signs of the team runs down one side of my vision. Clutters my visuals. A second squad waits via the rear entrance. A mission with too many moving parts, too many unknowns.

Doesn't matter, have to move. Stasis is death. Forward, always forward.

I focus on the door ahead, place the flat of my hand on Taylor's bicep, ease him to one side, with me. I whisper: "Yang—the Thor. Team—armour piercing."

Black figure, easing past, all spideriron black, save the dull steel hammer in his hands.

I say: "Go."

Yang heaves, the door explodes inwards under the blow.

Squeeze, Taylor moves with his black shield raised, we pass Yang.

Move, move, weapon left, trust the man behind for the right.

Meal area, long room thirty feet, dawn, orange through dirty windows, half-eaten meals, battered fridge, hate slogans graffitied on the walls. Woman, shocked, at a bowl of cereal. Young, purple bandana, wild eyes.

I bark: "Hands up." The other men are yelling, two more into the room behind me, two more holding the entrance.

One exit from the room, far end, flimsy wooden door. The men moving to cover, Taylor with me, shield up, my pistol on the woman.

The breakfast table strewn with equipment, flexiscreens, wires, flat battery.

Woman. Wild eyes calming, shouts: "Charter Nine—smash the state!" and reaches for the battery near her hand, no not a battery a—

"Grenade!" I roar, firing, first shot takes the woman's arm off at the elbow, second third into the head: *Boom Boom Boom.*

Snap-flash, slow motion, the soft orange light slanting through, bathing everything in its aura. One note, piano, a ringing E-flat, no sound but the piano eternal as the wall to my left explodes and I can see the bullets displacing the air as they pass me, pass my men, shatter a teapot on the breakfast table, puncture the fridge, slam into the wall opposite. I yell, I don't know what: the piano note smothers everything as I crouch behind Taylor, his shield jarring as three four five bullets pound it. I'm firing back into the wall, returning fire, but not enough.

Plaster spews over us, cloud, like snow. Snow falling, movement slowing, the piano note rising in intensity hurting my ears, a crack in the centre of the tactical shield, forming, spreading—how is that possible? They must be using—

BOOOOM.

Time returns.

BOOOOM.

Speeding up.

BOOOOM.

A roar, the piano gone.

A hole, a metre wide, opens up in the wall opposite. The room, the building, vibrating with the force, and again, another hole, exploding outwards, away, showering debris into the room beyond, a third hole and heat signatures, outlines, pop up on-retina; whatever was jamming my suit's sensors disrupted, warnings flash—six combatants, two I can see through the holes, others their outlines. Anderson, fourth in line, moving with the QBZ shotgun, braced against his hip, blasting. In the body armour he looks like an automaton. Erect, faceless behind the polarized visor, a black machine of death.

A man, a terrorist, dusted with white plaster, rises, shotgun in hand, I put three into his chest. The man looks at the ground, disappointed, I suppose, that his heart has been shot out of his body, and collapses.

The next terrorist, a woman, disappeared from the bellybutton up. Disintegrating, blood and matter spraying the wall behind, coating map and slogan and comrade, one of whom is trying to take cover behind a filing cabinet. Three others, screaming fundamentalist chants as they fire shotgun and autopistol.

Two Type 109s, open up my side, backing Anderson, tattooing the room opposite with their kinetic poetry, rupturing bodies with their sonatas.

bratatat

bratatat

bratatat

And then it is over.

I swallow.

I breathe.

I order everyone to check in, they check in; a quick glance at their bio-signs tells me no-one's been hit.

A drone, circling above somewhere in the warm morning light, says into my ear, metronome: *Building is clear, no heat signatures or movement, building is clear, building is clear—*

Karla pulled the slender Kandel-Yu interface from her head. "Wow, that's perfect. Shit." Dizziness overcame her for a moment and she put a hand down on the work station to steady herself. The interface, a three-inch-wide silver band designed to slot down over the eyes, clunked. "But I thought—I thought…"

"You'd just be ghost-riding?" asked Eulalie. She reached across, took the interface from her, and stood, erect, holding it evenly with both hands.

"Yeah." Karla leaned back in her comfortable chair, nestling into the head rest. "But that. That was like—like I was him."

"Sergeant Wu."

"Wu? Yeah. Him." Karla ran a hand through her hair, surprised to find it soaked with sweat. "That wasn't just exo-memory."

"No. This," Eulalie's eyes flicked down at the interface, "is what will play as Wu falls asleep, this is what he'll dream. It's not just sight and sound, like exo-memory. It's feeling, emotion, it has an element of the surreal. Real memory is an art form, Miz Tessier-Denk, which you will have to learn if you wish to prosper here."

"Is this a June Fourth?"

"Potentially. Wu confessed serious levels of confusion, even guilt, to his army psychologist. We need him to remember it correctly. We need the public record to be unimpeachable."

"How fake is it? The memory?"

She raised an eyebrow.

"Oh. So—completely fake."

Eulalie shook her head. "Not completely. That never sticks. Not with high-impact, emotional events like this, in any case. These sorts of incidents burn paths right along our neurons, forge new synaptic links. Even with the amnesia drugs the enforcement officers take afterwards."

"Oh. So?"

"So what was real?" Eulalie shrugged with her eyebrows. "The deaths are all real." She paused, looking Karla over. "The terrorists were armed, of course; we just tweaked it to ensure Wu knows he acted correctly. Self-doubt is a liability we cannot risk in our security forces."

A woman's exploding head flashed across her mind's eye. Karla breathed. "Okay."

"You will be required to view newly programmed memories via the Kandel-Yu interface. I suggest you become accustomed to it. The only way to test for authenticity is a human subject, trained in the nuances of adjustment."

Karla's lips felt dry.

"Some feel anxious, even confused, the first few times after using the Kandel-Yu. Valium is available for adjustment officers, complimentary and as required."

"Oh no, I'm fine. Just have to—"

"Take the Valium, Miz Tessier-Denk. Many here do. There is no shame in it. You need to sleep."

Karla nodded. "Thanks."

"I'm not doing you a favour, not now or at any other time. We need you at one hundred percent for the next few days as we finalise our response to this counter terrorist incident. For that you need to sleep."

With that Eulalie turned and sat down at her station.

Karla wondered, as she sometimes did, which Eulalie was the real one. But then the screaming woman retina-flash, the splatter of blood, and the smell of burnt pork—no, burnt flesh–

She gripped the arms of her work chair, tight, though she feared she might fall, and let out a long breath. Yeah. Valium might be a good place to start.

Thursday October 12th, 2090 // Seaweed Green - Papaya Orange

The ninth time they slept together, it was good, as always. They lay there in the bed afterwards, happy, comfortable. Their bodies bathed in the neon alighting from the city below, all spread out like a blanket, to the horizon. The room so silent, except faint, through the glass, the rumble of the inner-city express. Their breathing, slowing now, finding its rhythm.

Karla said: "I feel like an actor with you."

"You?"

"I'm jealous of the way actors are able to have conversations."

"I. What?"

"On screen," said Karla. "Because they have a script, they know they aren't going to be interrupted. They have time to consider their words, say what needs to be said, secure in the knowledge the other person isn't going to butt in, you know, take a pause or a hesitation as a cue to speak."

Eulalie turned on her pillow to watch her speak. She waited.

"No one's really listening to anyone anymore. It's all interruptions and agendas. There's no real conversations. No sentences, even, that aren't rushed, where each side isn't just waiting for their turn to speak. But when you're an actor, you have the script. You can pause, think, Shatner the shit out of your lines, and no arsehole is going to interrupt and tell you about their fucking home renovations as you're trying to take a breath."

Eulalie pushed a hair away from her face, still waiting.

"So: I felt like an actor with you."

"Right. So when we're together, you feel like all the cameras are on you."

"Well, no—"

"And you can weave into the conversation glory-of-you-type pauses and poses. Centre of the universe, as the universe looks on."

"No, I—"

"That sounds kinda narcissistic."

"Ah shut up."

"I bet that speech sounded better in your head."

"*Way* fucking better."

Karla turned on her pillow, smiling. She ran the tips of her fingers down Eulalie's face, over her perfect, flawless skin. Eulalie closed her eyes at her touch.

When she opened them again, the mirth was gone. "How did you get your orange rating?" Eulalie asked. "Really."

Karla laughed, quiet and short, though to herself. "Oh, I was mostly telling the truth."

"Mostly?"

"Like I said: the orange was a product of a wild, rebellious youth." She spoke softly, supine after the sex. "I was at uni. Stupid, angry all the time. I'd drink and write inflammatory posts on my Ego feed. Use phrases like *princeling kleptocrats* and *robber baron state*. I called for campus-wide protests that no-one turned up to. The usual undergraduate bullshit. Anyway, that kind of stuff always gets reported. So I was warned and in my indignation created this stupid meme comparing the president to an orangutan. I was unlucky—it lasted three whole hours on the freewave until it was finally taken down. The fuck the censors were doing that day, I don't know. So way too many people saw it, way too many. That alone pushed me five or six shades, right into deep yellow. Gold-yellow, I think."

Karla stretched her back and sighed. "I thought I was some sort of firebrand at university. My girlfriend at the time said I was just *shouty* and *self-righteous*." She laughed a little to herself again, at the memory. "Yeah."

Eulalie prompted: "and the orange?"

"Oh. I projected the orangutan meme onto the wall of the faculty building as my art instillation piece for the final exhibition of the year. Fuck I was an idiot. Drunk. Fucking high on my meaningless act of defiance. Pissed in the flower bed next to the audience, then passed out in it."

Eulalie laughed, despite herself, hand over her mouth.

"I know, I know," said Karla. "Two hundred people there. Fucking uni patrons, chardonnay set, acting all shocked over the rims of their wine glasses. Put my little pissing routine up all over their Ego feeds. So I got kicked out. Obviously. Had to work unskilled labour for the next few years until I was allowed to do a correspondence course for the rest of my credits."

"Shit. How bad did your colours run?"

"My worst?" she shrugged. "Double orange."

"Jesus Christ Karla."

"Yeah." She grunted. "Exactly. I was lucky, real fucking lucky, I didn't tip over into red."

Eulalie gave her a *yeah* that clearly had more behind it. But she didn't add anything, just waited for Karla to continue.

Karla let out a long breath, thinking back to that other lifetime. "So I did what most do these days. Posted a self-criticism on my Ego page, and then stopped talking. Friends, strangers, on the freewave, anywhere. Barely said a word, kept to myself, got kinda accustomed to solitude. Went and saw the right movie or streamed the right *tai* series from time to time, to make sure my financial activity followed the correct political line. Every six months my shame went down a shade, you know. Like I was on a diet, except with the shit that came out of my mouth, rather than went into it. Not so hard, once you train yourself." Karla brushed a wayward hair that had fallen over her eyes. "I'd gotten back to green on my shame score, had a university degree, and was working for the State when I met Ambrosia."

"Ah. What happened there?"

Karla gave a short, humourless laugh. "Ah well. I'm a fuckup from way back, you will have noticed, so I fucked that up as well. With Ambrosia it was mainly insecurity. I didn't think she'd accept me for who I was—and, well, after she was promoted as a government lawyer, and I kept treading career water, my fears came true. I was no match for her fierce efficiencies come the divorce, especially given my political hue."

Eulalie said nothing, listening, though waiting for something. Karla wasn't sure what, so she said: "Political is the hardest. Five years. Five fucking years for an increment reduction, even in government service. Seven years to get out of orange, thirty-five after that to work through yellow. Motherfuckers. Thank Christ I got that Bureau job, and…" She trailed off.

"And what?"

"And met you." She took a deep breath, as though savouring the clean air of this new life. "God. I haven't talked this much in years."

"Yeah."

"Yeah? That's it? So." She looked over at Eulalie. "Where's your life story?"

"Meh."

"Meh?"

Eulalie moved her shoulder.

"You're shrugging? You don't get off that easily."

"I think you're right," said Eulalie. She stretched, arched her back. "You talk too much. Suck my pussy."

"Huh?"

"You heard me."

"Well," Karla sighed, deflated. "Okay."

"Such enthusiasm. You suck my pussy, I'll let you do that thing you keep asking about."

Karla made a little *o* with her mouth. "Really?"

"Really."

She jumped up, standing with a salute. "Permission to muff dive captain!"

Eulalie said: "Permission granted."

She dove.

Eulalie laughed.

Saturday November 11th, 2090 // Seaweed Green – Papaya Orange

Taylor, first position, had the shield up. Sergeant Wu's hand on his shoulder, the man behind Wu had a hand on his. Wu's breathing was loud, claustrophobic in the gas mask—never quite got used to it, even after all these years.

Overlaid on-retina, the infrared of the target in the room beyond the door, phasing in and out flicker flicker, flicker flicker. *Green map, the other corner of his vision, floorplan of the Charter Nine base. Art district, converted warehouse, abandoned now. Nooks, crannies, unregistered rooms, corridors, back alleys, blindsides, too many. Eyes in the sky, hunter-killer drones so high they were invisible, fly drones buzzing through the building at knee level, yes—all that—but the terrorists were using a jamming device; nano-cam feeds fritzing, snow.*

The six bio-signs of Wu's team ran down one side of his vision. Cluttered visuals. A second squad supported via the rear entrance. Ready to start a mission with too many moving parts, too many unknowns.

Didn't matter, had to move. Stasis was death. Forward, always forward.

Wu put the flat of his hand on Taylor's bicep, easing him to one side. He whispered: "Yang—the Thor. Team—armour piercing."

A tall figure slid past, all spideriron black, save the dull steel hammer in his hands.

Wu breathed. "Go."

Yang heaved and the door exploded inwards under the blow.

Wu squeezed Taylor's shoulder; he moved forward with his black shield raised, past Yang.

Move, move, Wu's weapon pointed left, trust the man behind for the right.

Meal area, long room thirty feet, dawn, orange through dirty windows, half-eaten meals, battered fridge, slogans graffitied on the walls: 'We Obey Only the Constitution!' and 'Elections Now!' and "Ban the ban!" and 'Remember 2046!'.

Woman, shocked, sitting at a bowl of cereal. Young, purple bandana, wild eyes.

Wu barked: "Hands up." The other men yelled, demanding to know how many more terrorists were in the building. Two of the team moved in behind him; the last two held the entrance.

One exit from the room, far end, flimsy wooden door. His men moved to cover, Wu's pistol stayed on the woman.

The breakfast table was strewn with equipment, flexiscreens, wires, flat battery, rusting.

On-retina, an order popped up:

Eliminate the terrorists

Wu whispered: "She appears to be unarmed."

A red dot blipped on-retina for a few seconds before resolving itself into the words:

Eliminate the terrorists

The woman, wild eyes calming, hands above her head, said: "Tea, gentlemen?"

When Wu barked: "Light this place up!" it felt disembodied, like he was watching from a point behind his own shoulder. His first shot took the woman in the centre of the chest, second third into the forehead: Boom Boom—

Karla gasped, jack-knifing awake. Her hair damp with sweat. She blinked away the afterimage of a shattered woman's skull, and grasped for the bottle of Valium on the nightstand. She popped the lid, hands shaking, and dry-swallowed two. Afterwards she fell into a restless, empty sleep.

Sunday November 12th, 2090 // Seaweed Green – Papaya Orange

Memories submerged, the incident a half-remembered dream, but Karla knew when she exited the lift and the lights were out—just fucking knew—the smoking man would be waiting. Stomach twisting as she walked down the shadowed corridor, the dark gremlin of her paranoia gleeful at being proven right, her mind racing over whispered stories of the Internal Harmony Service. They'd ask you to come for tea, a common rumour went, and you'd never be seen again. Or if you were, it was ten years later, a completely different person. Frayed-haired, tics, barely able to remember even family.

As Karla approached, the man said: "Remember the deal, yes?"

Karla didn't ask the question she wanted to, or freeze like her legs were demanding. She walked up the door and said: "Jeeves. It's me. There's a man out here in the corridor, make sure he doesn't enter behind me."

The man said: "She shouldn't have included you in the talking club. That was selfish." And as he was speaking, Jeeves whispered in her ear: *Welcome home, Ma'am. Though I'm afraid I do not detect anyone in the corridor.*

Karla didn't hesitate, and when the door closed she pressed her back against it, eyes closed, waiting for fists to bang at the door. They did not come.

Not then, anyway.

Friday December 22nd, 2090 // Algae Green – Papaya Orange

On the twenty-first of the month Karla's shame went down a shade, which meant it was the anniversary of some stupid shit she'd done. Or not done. Or said in the wrong company. Or not said. Still, it was met with relief. A portion of that invisible weight she carried, lifted from her shoulders.

The twenty-second was early Christmas with Kindred. Even better. Presents, far too many. Spoiling her son in such a way as would come back to haunt her on future Christmas Days, no doubt. But Karla didn't care. Her Ego feed buzzed after she'd uploaded her Christmas shopping list, as was the practice—they praised her generosity; the fatuous gorgons of social media averting their gaze and declaiming instead she was a 'great mother' because of her list of purchases.

Kindred was up at the dinner table, looking at his oily fingertips, favourite noodle lunch demolished, when he asked: "What happens if your colours go red, Mummy?"

Surprised, Karla halted her repairs on the freshly broken Bat Car. "Huh?"

"Red. Mummy One said if I'm really naughty, and don't do

what I'm told, I'll be a red."

Karla took a long breath. "Don't they tell you about this at school?"

"At school today I made a pasta man out of pasta."

"Ha. Right. Well." Karla thought for a moment. "Well, if a lot of people see you being naughty, well, you can get penalised, in trouble. And the colour of very bad, the worst kind of trouble, is red. If you go red, you're kinda like Aquaman—everyone thinks you're useless, and you can't live among regular people anymore." Karla put down the Bat Car. "Strangers become cruel and mean, everywhere you go, buddy. And well, they make it so you can't see your family anymore. It's—

Karla stopped when Kindred stuck out his bottom lip, tears welling. She pulled him over to her lap; he turned and pressed his face into his mother's breasts.

"Kindred, Kindred, what is it?"

His little voice was muffled by tears and t-shirt.

"What?"

Again, muffled, all she could hear was *I did.*

Karla pulled her son away gently, so she could look him in the face. "Calm down. You're safe here. Look at me, look at me. Now what's wrong?"

Top lip smeared with snot, he whispered: "I did a red thing."

Karla briefly considered removing her memory pin. But it was too late for that. "I'm sure it wasn't so serious, Kindred. I'm sure—"

"I pooped in Jimmy's dad's shoe!"

Karla couldn't quite grasp the sentence. "You…"

"I was bursting and I thought it was the toilet but it was the cupboard and it was too late so I pooped on Jimmy's dad's big red shoes and didn't tell anyone and then two days later Jimmy was crying at school he got in so much trouble and he couldn't remember doing it but he eats so much dried fruit maybe it was him and he forgot and I never told anyone not even Mummy," and then the confession ended in more snot and tears. Karla laughed quietly and hugged her boy fiercely.

When Kindred had calmed down she looked him in the eyes. "Don't worry. You aren't going to be taken away. Mistakes happen. You're four—"

"Nearly five!"

"Nearly five, and little boys—"

"Big boy!"

"Big boys who are nearly five are allowed to make mistakes, even pooping mistakes, and I won't be angry and your other mummy—well-look, you're not going to be a red." Karla made a cutting motion with her hand. "You're not. You're a good boy."

"But I wiped my bum with a shirt."

"Kindred." Karla rubbed her forehead. "You can't be a red yet, because you're too young."

"Oh." Kindred looked relieved.

"But when you get older, and if you do something really bad. And I mean really bad, the worst thing you've ever done. Make sure you never tell anyone but me." Karla paused, running a hand through her son's hair, wishing again she'd removed her memory pin. "What I mean is, you have to be honest, Kindred. You have to be honest with everyone. But be honest with me, first. I've got this job, buddy. It's an important job. If you ever get into trouble, I can help fix the problem. Understand?"

"How do you fix it?"

"I can just fix it, like I can fix the Bat Car."

"But you haven't fixed it yet."

"Look, I will. Like I fixed the Bat Cave when you fell on it."

"But we still can't find Robin's head."

"Kindred. Buddy." Karla sighed. "Let's just play okay?"

"Yeah!" Kindred exclaimed, jumping down from his mother's lap, the roller coaster of a four-year-old's emotion back on high.

Late January, 2091 // Algae Green – Papaya Orange

For her seventh Incident, a freewave protest movement emerged to denounce the continued feminisation of low-skilled labour. Childcare workers, cleaners, hairdressers, increasingly vocal, were demanding better wages. The kind of jobs that would have been automated, if not for human quotas.

The Bureau responded by creating a furore over the latest Cat Woman film, calling for it to be banned because her costume objectified women. Media picked up the story; online it became endlessly debated. Celebrities weighed in with think pieces. The film was withdrawn by the studio after bomb threats were made to one of the cinemas showing it. The heat went out of the women's pay protests.

But Eulalie argued for more, pushing, again, for memory manipulation. She proposed that some of the women running the campaign be brought in for questioning regarding the bomb threats, for their pins to be taken for examination, and for three to be given memories of a fourth planning the threatening messages.

Most adjustment officers at the crisis meeting were against it. Even Karla thought it an unnecessary risk, given they'd already won. But Babbitt, eyes glittering, agreed.

The three women chosen were cleaners with young families and precarious finances. They were offered better-paid jobs, and placements for their children in selective public schools. The women soon came to believe the official version of events, and supplied their adjusted on-retina recording of the incident to the media.

The fourth woman disappeared.

Eulalie was promoted, though her new position title was not disclosed. The Cat Woman director issued a fulsome public apology.

Wednesday May 16th, 2091 // Algae Green – Papaya Orange

The woman, wild eyes calming, hands above her head, said: "Tea, gentlemen?"

When Wu barked: "Light this place up!" it felt disembodied, like he was watching from a point behind his own shoulder. His first shot took the woman in the centre of the chest, second third into the forehead: Boom Boom Boom. She slid, top half of her head gone, under the table.

Snap-flash, slow motion:

Soft orange light slanted through the windows, bathing everything in its aura.

One note, piano, a ringing E-flat, no sound but the piano eternal as the wall to Wu's left exploded; he could see, he could see, the bullets displace the air as they passed him, his men opening up with everything, shattering a teapot on the breakfast table, slamming into the wall opposite, wood splinters flying from the unopened door.

He yelled, wasn't sure what, the piano note smothering everything as he crouched behind Taylor, shield up. Wu put the rest of his bullets into the next room, abandoned or teeming with insurgents, he had no clue, as plaster spewed from bullet holes, like snow. Snow falling, movement slowing, the piano note rising as time stopped; then reversed, the woman sliding back up in her seat, her skull reconstructing, held together, again, by the purple bandana, and she asked him if he would like some—

BOOOOM.

Time returned.

BOOOOM.

Sped up.

BOOOOM.

The piano gone.

A hole, a metre wide, opened up in the wall opposite. The room, the building, vibrating with the force, and again, another hole, exploding outwards, away, showering debris into the room beyond, a third hole and heat signatures, outlines, popped up on-retina; whatever was jamming his suit's sensors disrupted, warnings flashing on-retina, six combatants, two he could see through the holes, others their outlines. Anderson, fourth in line, moving with the QBZ shotgun braced against his hip, blasting. In the body armour he looked like an automaton. Erect, faceless behind the polarized visor, a black machine of death.

Reload. Clack-clacked *his pistol.*

A man, a terrorist, dusted with white plaster, rose, hands in the air: Wu put three into his chest. The man looked at the ground, disappointed, Wu supposed, that his heart had been shot out of his body, and—

Karla awoke with a start. The curtains to her bedroom were open, bathing the room in the soft glow of neon and streetlight. Her mind churned, drifting away from her dreams, settling instead on the years she'd lost with Kindred. How pissing in a garden bed had been punished with the loss of her child.

Lying there, nothing moving but her eyes, awake until the dawn came.

Wednesday May 23rd, 2091 // Algae Green – Papaya Orange

On their six month oral-versary (as Eulalie called it), Karla made her signature spicy red-sauce pasta for dinner. At exorbitant expense, she got a meat permit for one meal, and added thick cut, marinated beef to the dish. Eulalie first said she was wasting the meat by serving it in pasta, second tasted the sauce-and-chunk she proffered with a spoon, and third said: "*Wow.*"

"You're damn right," Karla had replied.

Eulalie chewed and groaned. "It's like an angel came in my mouth."

Karla laughed and shook her head.

Eulalie brought two bottles of pricey Australian pinot noir. She wore a red silk cheongsam, her hair up. Elegant, refined, arms bare, neck collar, curves, pale skin glowing, an exotic transformation. When Karla opened the door, she looked her up and down and said: "Holy shit."

Eulalie gave her a mock-demure sexy smile and said: "You're damn right."

Karla found herself nervous, eager to impress, distracted by the ghost of relationship fails past. *I will tell you of the shadows of the things that have been: drunken crying and singing under her window until the police came; a thousand messages until she changed her number; the one who left you for your middle-aged fine arts supervisor; the one who looked through your undeleted browser history; the one who found you eating salsa in your underpants, watching...* Karla gritted her teeth and whispered at herself: Shut. The fuck. Up.

So it wasn't until their second bottle of wine that she'd relaxed enough to notice Eulalie was not relaxed. Staring into her food or at her glass, clutching and unclutching her white cloth napkin.

"What's wrong?" asked Karla.

"Hmm?"

"Something's wrong."

Eulalie turned her wine glass on the spot.

"Hello?"

Eulalie looked up at her, angry: "*what?*"

Karla held her hands up, surrender. "Shit. Woah. I'm just pretending to be sensitive, and listening, and concerned, all that relationship shit; you know: maybe get sex out of it later."

Eulalie shook her head and laughed, despite herself: "Dickhead." She sighed, gave her glass another half-turn, and downed it. "Alright. Take out the pin, cowboy."

Eulalie and Karla sat on the bed, clothes still on, facing each other. Eulalie Chen looked amazing, god she looked amazing in that cheongsam. Enough to make Karla sneeze. Her mind started to wander to one of her more detailed Viking-shield-maiden fantasies, until she saw the look on Eulalie's face.

Distant. She'd downed her wine quick all evening. Little bit unsteady on her feet already, eyes with just a hint of drunken glaze, and worried. Ruminating. She clutched her hands together, under her breasts, like an opera singer about to sing an aria.

Karla thought she was going to break up with her, so when Eulalie said: "My father was a red," Karla replied with a "Huh?" at first relieved it wasn't a break up, and then terrified it sounded like something far worse.

Eulalie sighed again. The river of her vitality dried up. The life glow gone. "He was a political red. He died in a protest march."

Karla touched fingertips to her forehead involuntarily, pulled them away again. "Jesus. Why? What for?"

A bitter smile passed her lips. "I don't know Karla, I don't know. I was young. Twelve. Shit. Twenty years ago." She looked up at her. "They *adjusted* me."

"Jesus. Fuck." She put the backs of her fingers to her lips. "Shit Eulalie."

"That about sums it up."

"I don't—"

"There's something here." Eulalie put a finger on her forehead. "I don't know what it is. Natural memory is so, you know, flawed." She lowered her hand slowly to the white sheets. "But this I remember: Baba was a red. They shot him."

All Karla could find was silence. She reached out and held Eulalie's hand.

She didn't look at Karla when she spoke. Just at a point in the air somewhere between them. "Mama couldn't deal with it. They downloaded an adjusted history into her exo-memory. But she couldn't let go of the real ones. I think she started some sort of women's group. Widows. Mothers. Grandmothers. They'd get together and talk about their lost ones. So they wouldn't forget. Mama wouldn't let me there, in the room, but I think they started talking about other things as well. Forbidden things."

"A talking club," Karla said, quietly, thoughts spinning back to the encounter with the smoking man.

"Mama was obsessed with memory," she continued, ignoring her. "With his memory. She started paying respects to Baba's resting place. His first one, anyway. They'd buried him in a flowerbed near a school. The soldiers that killed him dug a shallow grave, near where he'd been shot, to hide the body. Later, someone higher up decided to conceal their crime properly, so they dug him up again and took the body away, wouldn't let Mama have it back. She begged them, but they denied all knowledge. But she knew, she knew. She'd talked to someone, an old comrade of my father's, I think it was, who'd witnessed. She sat me down one day and made me remember. She said his death would lose all meaning if I couldn't recall it. Made me promise to remember, promise to repeat what had really happened to Baba, to myself, day after day. Then she, I think, then she started visiting…"

Eulalie's voice broke, and she stopped herself. From everything. Talking, crying, making a scene. Just pulled her hand away from Karla's and gripped hers together, knuckles white.

Karla said: "I got something for you." She pulled a half-full bottle of Jack out from the drawer of the nightstand, eyes lingering for a moment on the vial of Valium next to it, three-quarters finished. She left the Valium, took a slug of the bourbon, and passed the bottle to Eulalie.

Eulalie had smoothed her face, even managed to raise an eyebrow when Karla passed her the bourbon. "Next to the bed?"

Karla shrugged, Eulalie said *thanks* in a way that felt real, and took a sip from the bottle. She passed it back to Karla and continued:

"Mama was detained after they caught her at the grave. They took her away, told her she was mistaken, that her husband hadn't died there. They said he'd had a heart attack while at a peaceful march. The body cremated after going unclaimed, the ashes subsequently misplaced. They'd give her compensation for the administrative error, and a sincere apology." Eulalie shook her head. "Yeah, I remember that. Mama said they were trying to buy her silence, that I remember clearly. After that, I'm not sure what happened. Everything unravels, everything fades. Except for one thing." She looked into Karla's eyes. "They put a drone there, in that spot. Just for Baba's grave. Twenty-four hours a day, in case anyone came to pay tribute. I think that's how they caught her, it must have been. Think of the resources involved in that, Karla. The surveillance of just one middle-aged woman in mourning. How big must the system be?"

Karla couldn't answer that. She couldn't think of the point where surveillance ended and life began. "So they took her away?"

Eulalie nodded. "Yeah. I have an exo-memory of her talking with her friends, trying to convince them to take the local police chief hostage, demand that the State take responsibility for Baba's death. But that's bullshit. They put that into my head, I know they did." She blinked rapidly, though trying to clear it from her mind. "No. She would have gone back, and men with sunglasses grabbed her and put her in the back of a van. That's what *really fucking happened.*" There was an urgency as she finished the sentence. Like she was trying to convince herself of the truth.

"Jesus Eulalie. I just. I'm so sorry."

She said nothing.

"But how can you—" Karla hesitated, wondering if it was the right thing to say.

"How can I be double green?"

"Yeah."

Eulalie took in a long breath, and for a moment, Karla didn't think she was going to answer. Until she said: "I testified against my mother."

Karla stilled. "I'm sorry... you—"

"Testified against my mother." She waited, face smooth, watching Karla.

Her mind fumbled around a series of responses, each less appropriate than the last. Each a little more obtuse. In the end all she came up with was: "Ah."

Eulalie sighed again, like Karla had failed some sort of test. "Mama told me to. Begged me. She was done, anyway. I saw her in this holding camp. Normally when they're gone, they're gone; they cease to exist, but they took me to this camp, windowless vehicle, so I wouldn't know where it was. Walked me out across this field. Little girl, hands brushing the sunflowers and tall grass, convinced they were going to put a bullet in my head." She glanced at Karla. "Ever stop and think the kind of society that makes a twelve-year-old contemplate extrajudicial killing?"

Eulalie didn't wait for Karla to try to answer. "On the other side of the field was the camp. Down deep inside it I saw my mother. Huge, all white room, through a long glass partition, just Mama on one side, just me on the other. She'd greyed quickly in those last few months. She looked tired, really tired. Tired of life. Mama looked at me and said, over and over: *you know I did it, you know I wanted the police chief dead, you know your father died of a heart attack. They'll make sure you'll stay green.* Mama was clenching her hands so hard they bled, under her nails. Fuck."

Eulalie was speaking through it, through her pain, getting it all out, like she feared her momentum would fail if she paused for a moment. "I remember that. Clear as fucking day. Natural memory, in my exo-memory, that fucking confession is crystal clear. Those *cunts.* They wiped most everything else; my memories of her in those months after Dad's death are fading, confused. They took a lot of them out of my exo-memory I think, replaced others. Made me dream their lies as well—a fucking twelve-year-old girl." Now she looked at Karla, now she grabbed her hand so hard it hurt. "How can a little girl be such a threat, huh? How fragile must their power be?"

Karla asked: "Why are you telling me this?" and immediately regretted doing so.

She relaxed her hand. "Why do you think, dickhead?"

"I…"

"Because we have something, you and I, a future. And—" she swallowed, "—I can't do this alone anymore. I'm tired. I feel—I feel like my mother looked that day, in the camp. Just tired of life."

Karla took her hand back, pressed it to her forehead, and then to her chest. Didn't say anything, and for once that was just the right thing.

"I think. I think it was the first June Fourth Incident, Karla. I think it's where it all started. And… I'm going to do something about it."

Karla looked around the room on instinct. For a smoking man, sitting in the corner, watching. For a two-way mirror, because this was a test. For the glint of a fly drone, sitting on the ceiling, watching. Because this was a set up. This was the Bureau of Cultural Adjustment testing her loyalty. This was—

"*Karla,*" she said. Eulalie's voice on the edge, brittle. Every version of her gone. Her calm confidence, her anger, the soul lines of her mourning, all gone. Looking to Karla like she was looking to her for strength.

"Fuck," Karla said, running a hand through her hair. "Fuck." She hefted the bourbon and skolled, a long, deep pull. Then said, voice rough with booze: "What are you planning, Eulalie?"

Stillness fell across her, like a resignation. "It's already done."

Thursday May 24th, 2091 // Algae Green - Papaya Orange

The smoking man was waiting in the darkness again. When he said: "You and your girlfriend enjoyed the talking club, yes?" Karla reacted without thinking, the strain of the night before pushing against her eyeballs, the press of a bourbon hangover in her temples. She swung her briefcase, knocking the cigarette from the man's hand, sparks spraying orange, and used her other hand to grip the man's collar and push him into the wall behind. "Fucken stalking me. Months. Spouting this cryptic shit," she said, spittle flying at *shit*. "I don't know what the fuck you're…"

Her righteousness stumbled at the curb when she realised she was talking at a blur. Literally. The man's face had the same look as an old photo, when the subject moves their face just as the picture is being taken. It meant this man was wearing a filter. One that interacted with the nanos attached to Karla's optic nerves, altering what she was able to perceive. If this man had the authority to wear a filter, then—

The blur pressed his thumb into the back of Karla's hand and twisted her wrist. Practiced and smooth, forcing Karla to bend her knees, wincing, under the pressure.

The blur let go and stepped back, patting his pockets; Karla raised her hands, thinking for a moment the blur was going to pull a gun. But all it pulled was soft packet of cigarettes, Double Happiness brand, and propped one in its mouth. Lit it, and spoke without removing the cigarette. The cigarette bounced up and down as it spoke, plain to see, the lips behind a grey smudge.

"Oh, I know," it said, with a voice probably filtered as well. "I can detect lies, real time, with the programming in my head. I'm persuaded you don't know about the talking club Eulalie Chen runs in the Drunken Angel."

"She doesn't—" started Karla. But she stopped, thinking about that group that always sat in the booths.

"Yes," said the officer. "There it is. She is the gatekeeper. Those seats up at the bar, where you sit—that's the gate, yes? Testing your aptitude for discretion on behalf of the others."

Karla pressed her lips together.

"Yes, yes, I know," said the agent, as though Karla had just spoken out loud. "She trusts you, completely. Their talking club usually takes a year of vetting before they let anyone in. Some don't want you ever, what with your substandard political rating."

"Get the fuck out of my head."

"Just your face. Irises. Not inside, not yet."

"Talking clubs aren't illegal."

"Depends on what they talk about, yes?"

Karla was about to tell him she was leaving when the officer said: "I know, I know. It's bad, but not so bad you have to fear me. But we both know this isn't about the talking club. There's something else you have to fear me about though, isn't there?"

Karla swallowed again, took a step away.

"You and Eulalie have a sexual relationship. Pillow talk, yes?"

Karla gritted her teeth.

"Now now. Think about how far you've come. From double orange all the way to the *Cultural Adjustment Bureau*. You realise you are the only officer in the Bureau from that background, yes?"

Some perverse pride bloomed in Karla's chest, immediately withering, immediately disgusted with herself.

"There there," he said. "You *should* be proud. But there's something you need to know about yourself, Karla: you're no hero." Blur held up a hand, cigarette between his fingers, smoking curling towards the ceiling. The smoke detector above, for some reason, ignored completely his presence. "Don't even try to disagree, Miz Tessier-Denk. Even if you are not aware of it yourself, the State knows it, the Bureau knows it, and I know it right here, looking at your face. You're no hero, yes?"

The blur moved in close. It smelled of cigarettes and clove. The shifting, smudged skin made Karla nauseous just to look at it. The blur said: "And just so you don't forget it."

Karla's vision pulsed red, slowly, everything on-retina bate-abating the hue. She took an involuntary step backwards, fingers grasping in front of her face, like she could pluck the offending colour from her mind. Memories rushed back of the last time it happened. "Wait-no—" as she spoke the words her political, on-retina, turned a shade deeper orange, "—you can't—"

"Of course I can, yes. I have a well-founded suspicion you are consorting with political deviant-roaders—"

"But she's a double green."

"—Including a sexual relationship with the founder of a talking club. The case I've compiled is more than sufficient to warrant a temporary political penalty, yes?"

A number pinged on retina: **B-263-54**

The officer said: "Temporary, just temporary, I'm sure. You need to unburden yourself, yes. When you are ready to do so, here is the number, call it and you can talk to someone with intimate knowledge of your case. He will help you emerge from this setback. Call it and come in to us, Miz Tessier-Denk, before your colours slide further."

"For tea?" asked Karla.

"No," it said, earnestly. "We do not take good citizens to tea. We'll just talk, and you can go on with your life as if nothing happened, yes?"

"But what about Eulalie?"

"That is not the word or memory you should be invoking, Miz Tessier-Denk. That signifier will be washed away in the stream. The memory you should hold on to is that of a five-year-old boy, and the days you spend with him."

"He's not a memory, he's my fucking son."

The officer shook its head, blur wish-washing. "Everything is memory, save the thin edge of the present, yes? Your son is just a pattern of neurons firing inside your mind. We can fix that, as you know better than most—that can be adjusted certainly, yes?"

He put a hand on Karla's shoulder, she flinched. "Call us," he said, "soon. We need to get your colours right, your line correct." He dropped his hand and walked past her, down the corridor.

Karla didn't turn around. Just stood there, fists clenched, heart screaming.

Friday May 25th, 2091 // Algae Green - Halloween Orange

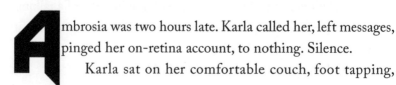mbrosia was two hours late. Karla called her, left messages, pinged her on-retina account, to nothing. Silence.

Karla sat on her comfortable couch, foot tapping,

looking out at the view over the city, not seeing it. In that space she thought over and again about the last conversation she'd had with Eulalie. After, at work the following day they'd barely spoken. She felt a distance had opened between them, neither daring to say anything of substance. The last real thing Eulalie had said to her, well, it was a fucking doozy.

Waiting, waiting, she went to the bathroom. Washing her hands, her reflection looked back, dull-eyed. She touched the glass.

"Jeeves?"

"Yes Ma'am?"

"Do you report on me to the State?"

"You know I can't possibly answer that, ma'am."

Karla felt the exhaustion in the pits of her eyes, in the ache in the palms of her hands. "No. Yeah. Jeeves, I want you to switch off your audio and visual functions, permanently, not just when Eulalie is visiting."

When it didn't answer, Karla said: "Jeeves?"

"The thing is, Miz Tessier-Denk, what with your worsening political rating and all, I'm always on now. I may be required as a witness." When Karla said nothing, Jeeves said: "You understand I find this quite unsavoury, ma'am, and I'd really rather not be in this position."

"Indubitably."

"Quite so."

"Jeeves?"

"Yes?"

"Your name is now Fuckchops."

"Ma'am?"

"I'm changing your name."

"I see."

"Fuckchops?"

"Yes."

"Nothing."

When Ambrosia finally turned up, she acted all confused when Karla asked why she was late. Little theatrical furrow of the brow, the bitch. "Oh," Ambrosia said, as though it were a perfectly explicable notion. "I was concerned after the notification regarding your political rating. Especially as no details on the penalty were provided." She waited for an explanation, arms crossed, and when Karla gave none, Ambrosia said: "As you may appreciate, your new status worried me deeply. I felt obliged to review our custody arrangements and see if there were any implications to your visitation rights. I felt it my duty as a parent."

Her notion was perfectly explicable. Karla could say nothing, do nothing, to protest. Her every utterance, expression, captured by Ambrosia on-retina, able to be used in family court.

So she pushed her fury into that tight knot in her gut and, with a straight face, said: "I understand. No-one is as concerned as me. The problem will be rectified soon."

Ambrosia smiled, sourly. "Of course. I know you take the responsibilities of your new, vital position with the State very seriously. I'm sure all the followers of your Ego feed are just as concerned by this new development. Let's hope—as you say—it is resolved one way or the other, very quickly. It's worrying for me, as a mother, to place Kindred in such uncertainty."

Karla wanted to scream: *The only thing you ever mothered was your fucking career*. Instead, she nodded and mumbled acquiescence.

All the while Kindred watched them with serious eyes. When Ambrosia closed the door, he said: "Mummy. Are you in trouble?"

Karla ruffled her son's hair. "No no no. It's nothing, buddy."

Still serious: "If you become a red, will I be able to come over?"

Knot, tightening. "Who said anything about red?"

"Mummy."

"Right. Well. That's not going to happen."

"She talks about it a lot."

"Does she now?"

"She told her new boyfriend last night you were a red dee-vee-ant."

"Did she?"

"They were very loud and they woke me up. I was hiding in the corridor listening."

"Ha. Well. You probably shouldn't do that."

"You're not going to leave me again, are you?"

Scream. Karla wanted to scream. She breathed out long and got down on one knee, held her son by his shoulders. "Kindred, I'm never going away. Never again. I promise. Do you understand?"

"Good," said Kindred, brightening. "Because we haven't built the Fortress of Solitude yet."

"Ha." She cleared her throat. "True. Come on." She picked Kindred up. "We're behind on our schedule. I believe today we are due to complete Lex Luthor's Warsuit, so he can fight Batman in the Bat Tank."

"Go Lex Luthor!" yelled Kindred, fist in the air.

As Kindred played, impersonating the voices of the various Lego characters, crushing Batman under the Warsuit, Karla's mind drifted back to a spot she'd rather it didn't go.

She'd sucked down the bourbon while Eulalie had told her, everything. Wishing nothing but the amnesiac oblivion the sudden drunk would bestow on her recall. But Eulalie said it all and Karla's mind reached out to her every word and now it all bounced around her skull, refusing to go away.

This is what Eulalie had done:

Every June Fourth Incident, where Eulalie had been the lead adjuster for the Bureau, she slipped a Trojan memory into her product. That is, every time they adjusted a set of protestors, she put additional memories into their heads centred on the date of June Four. The memories had a slow neural burn, growing gradually as the anniversary approached. Building and building until on that day, everyone infected would gravitate to the city square, angry, wanting to protest. The motivation for each personalised—corruption, nepotism, discrimination based on political colours, growing inequality—the virus would make each grievance rhyme with the experience of the individual and feed it into their dreams. It'd all add up, she said, to a call, subconscious, to insurrection. She was creating a second June Fourth, she said. She believed the mnemonic touchstone might shake the first one loose—in the chaos and confusion, minds unfettered, breaking free of their ruts, would be spurred to remember that other event, the one her father was killed in, the *real* June Fourth.

Or, she continued, even if the protests were put down, the Cultural Adjustment Bureau would be tasked with covering it up. They'd open the files on how they did it the first time—they'd have to, to check whether any individuals crossed over both Incidents, help the Bureau pinpoint those for adjustment. If nothing else, Eulalie believed she'd be able to see her father's name on the list, and know it wasn't a heart attack. Have that clarity, closure.

She'd been excited as she'd said it all, sharing it with someone for the first time. That weight of self-censorship, self-restraint on every word, every action, lifted, finally. Eulalie said even if it didn't shake loose the first event, this second June Fourth would *commemorate* the original. Even without knowing it, her father's death and the all those of the others would be honoured.

There'd been a few different strands in what she was saying, but even then Karla didn't think the logic fit together. Whether it was meant to be a commemoration, or a revolution, how one event was meant to flow into another, why any light would be shed on the first June Fourth. That happened, sometimes, with unspoken fantasies. Words never aired often hid the flaws behind them, as well. This Karla knew from bitter experience.

Sensing her hesitation, Eulalie had said: *Something this big can't be adjusted. You can't cause a whole population to forget.*

She'd said: *But they did the first time.*

Eulalie had replied: *This will be different.*

Wednesday May 30th, 2091 // Seaweed Green – Construction Cone Orange

Karla Tessier-Denk was awoken the next morning by the on-retina pulsing of political censure. She was two from political red. Her shame had gone a shade worse, as well. Probably someone had seen her political situation and trawled through her social media accounts looking for the slightest perceived fault. Found it, complained or flagged or forwarded to others. The usual. If Karla had wanted she could simply click on her community rating and see what was being said about her, across all social platforms, anonymous and otherwise. She didn't bother.

Karla had more serious matters pulling at her guts. Like a message waiting, on-retina, from the courts:

An application has been filed on behalf of Ambrosia Maddison Whitewater to Family District Court 7 for suspension of the visitation privileges of Karla Tessier-Denk in relation to their

biological son, Kindred Philip Whitewater.

Reason: political deviancy and colour deterioration.

Interim Judgement: based on the current political rating of Karla Tessier-Denk [Construction Cone Orange] visitation privileges will be suspended. The accused has one week to file an explanation and make appropriate self-criticisms.

Family District Court 7
Ministry of Family Justice
– The Peaceful Family is the Beacon Illuminating Our Work –

A second message came up on-retina. She didn't open it or accept it—just appeared uninvited. An important guest inside her head:

Your political rating is Construction Cone Orange. You have had a two-shade deviation in two days.

Under section 145.6 of legal code (Harmonious Society Act), the Internal Harmony Service now has the right to ghost ride your visual feed. This may be enacted, without subpoena or warning, for up to three hours per day at periods and times of the choosing of the state. Our surveillance of your visual feed will increase to six hours at Mango Orange, and twenty-four hours at Basketball Orange level. Your memory pin password has been locked; it may no longer be removed from your cochlear implant.

– Seek Facts from the Truth –

Friday June 1st, 2091 // Jungle Green – Mango Orange

Reload. Clack-clacked *his pistol.*

A man, dusted with white plaster, rose, hands in the air. "Don't shoot!" *he begged.*

Wu put three into his chest. The man looked at the ground, disappointed, Wu supposed, that his heart had been shot out of his body, and fell.

The next agitator, a woman, disintegrated from the bellybutton up, blood and matter spraying the wall behind, coating map and slogan and comrade; one of whom was trying to take cover behind a filing cabinet. Three others, already dead, bodies jutting awkward angles on the ground.

Two Type 109s opened up next to Wu, tattooing the room opposite with their kinetic poetry, rupturing the last body with their sonatas.

bratatat

bratatat

bratatat

And then it was over.

Wu swallowed.

He breathed.

A drone, circling above in the warm morning light, said into his ear, metronome: Building is clear, no heat signatures or movement, building is clear, building is clear—

The room opposite, now an abstract art installation. Political posters pocked with bullet holes, walls sprayed with red blood dripping, drying.

In the furthest corner, inside a silver cage hung from the ceiling, a yellow bird sang, oblivious.

Karla awoke. Emotions flat, weight on her chest. She stared at the ceiling. The Jack and pills waited on the bedside table. Bourbon and Valium, now a regular meal, reserved for the witching hour. Her mind went *tic-tic*, saying: they took your son, *tic-tic*. "No," she replied, voice loud in the empty room. "No."

Saturday (morning) June 2nd, 2091 // Parchment Yellow – Mango Orange

Coffee cup in hand, Karla walked into her cubicle. Eulalie turned in her seat as she entered. She said: "Are you okay, Miz Tessier-Denk? You look quite pale."

"I'm fine."

"Have you been drinking?"

"I said I'm fine. Just—just haven't been sleeping so well. Thank you for asking." Karla's coffee cup played a rat-a-tat on her desk as she tried to put it down.

"Karla?" she asked, from behind, tremor of tension in her voice.

She turned back to Eulalie. The woman's hands were folded in her lap, back straight. It occurred to Karla that Eulalie looked tired, as well. A stray strand of hair hung down over her forehead. She was looking at a spot just over Karla's head. The spot where her colours would be floating. Yellow-orange.

Karla cleared her throat. "I think I've come down with something."

"Oh," she said, still looking at the same spot. "I hope it's not serious."

"I think I may have caught it from you, actually, Miz Chen."

"Oh."

"Maybe you should go home and get some rest. It is irresponsible to be at work while you are contagious."

"Oh." A crease formed between Eulalie's eyebrows. "I'm very busy, Miz Tessier-Denk."

"No doubt. You must excuse me, but I have an important meeting," Karla said, turning away from her. "With the director. I need to prepare for it."

She waited for Eulalie to say something. Sipped her coffee,

synced into her computer. All the while waiting for a noise or word from behind her. She was sure Eulalie was sitting there, in the same position, hands in her lap, staring at her back. She clenched her eyes shut, willing herself not to turn around, but was about to go ahead and turn the fuck around anyway when she heard Eulalie shuffling around her desk, whispering a set of commands under her breath.

"Goodbye, Karla."

Karla turned and Eulalie was standing, her bag slung over her shoulder. "Now you mention it, I am feeling under the weather." Eulalie knew. She knew. She knew but she wasn't angry, no tears, no mouth curled in anger. Just shattered, her face fallen in on itself, her stature shrunk to a child's. That's all.

"I'm sorry."

"You shouldn't be," Eulalie whispered. "Everyone gets sick."

Eulalie walked out and Karla went to speak, but the words got mired in her fear. Went to stand, but just clenched her stomach instead.

Karla could see the elevators from where she sat. When they closed behind Eulalie, she stared fixedly at the smooth steel doors.

The office of Whittaker Babbitt Jnr was the office of a powerful man. Straight lines, hard wood, muscular leather seat cushions, fat bronze fountain pen upright in a polished wood holder; a gold-framed picture of the president. Small black moustache, paternalistic forehead, looking down with all-seeing, all-knowing eyes.

The director sat behind his imposing desk, looking down at a flexiscreen, backwash green from the readout on his face. Karla entered, and waited, uncomfortable and ignored, while Babbitt did that thing all powerful men in the movies did: put the peon in their place, struck a pose of arrogant indifference while the nobody sweated.

Karla sweated. Beads rolled down her temples. Eventually the director looked up and said: "ah, Miz Tessier-Denk", as if the motherfucker hadn't realised she was there.

Babbitt leaned back in his chair and drummed his stubby fingers on table edge, looking Karla over with eyes that gave not the slightest pretence of having a human behind them. "We were very pleased that you called. But, I forget myself—something to drink?"

Karla was about to say no on instinct, thought about the situation she was in and said: "Yes. Thanks. Whisky," instead.

Babbitt looked at a point past Karla's shoulder and said: "Kevin, make it two."

Karla started and said *oh*, turning to see Kevin-from-the-talking-club rising from a chair in the rear corner of the room. Kevin smiled his very white-toothed smile at Karla before popping open a smooth wooden panel on a nearby cabinet. The interior was laden with bottles of assured postures that suggested: Brandy, Gin, Whisky.

Kevin poured two, gave one to Karla, and walked over to Babbitt's desk, saying "sir" as he handed the director the glass.

Karla sipped and the booze was smooth. Expensive. Refined. Cuntishly good. Her eyes over the edge of the glass, taking in Babbitt and Kevin.

Babbitt answered her thoughts, indicating the man next to him with an open hand. "Kevin is with the Internal Harmony Service, and also an officer here at the Bureau."

Karla said *oh*.

Kevin nodded, still smiling inoffensively, as he lit a cigarette and then moved back to his original position behind Karla, out of her line of sight.

"Did you imagine, young lady, they sit at their desks in a nondescript building somewhere in the city, waiting to don long coats and round people up in unmarked vans?" The director smiled at the thought, comfortable in his role as Big Man in Charge. "Listen: the Service is everywhere. Every department, bureau, and agency. The police, the judiciary, the executive. Your local sports club, bar, and gym." Babbitt contemplated his whisky glass. "I did a stint in the Service myself. Helps one understand the way of the world, and the why of how things need to be done."

Kevin said, from behind: "It can really change your life," like he was talking about the S-U-X 3000.

"Oh," said Babbitt, "I nearly forgot. The Service is everywhere, including in every talking club."

Karla turned and looked over Kevin, again. The way he held his cigarette, his stillness as he settled into the corner, watching her. Strangeness, about his movements—his face showed nonchalance, his body a coiled purpose.

"You're the smoking man. From the corridor."

Kevin affected a shrug in reply. *You got me.*

She imagined nonchalantly grabbing the man's cigarette and stubbing it out on his eyeball.

Babbitt finished his whisky and placed the glass on the table carefully. "So we know you weren't actually part of it, and we know that's not why you came here today." He watched Karla, both sets of fingers drumming the table edge. "You called me last night because life has changed for you, for the better: you're sleeping more, eating healthier and drinking less, you've cut right down on your pornography consumption." She reddened, he continued: "You've even started exercising at the gym in your building, lost four kilograms, I believe." Babbitt pointed at her. "And you came here, today, because you realised some simple truths: you have an important job with excellent benefits; you have a son who now visits regularly, with whom you spend hours on end playing Lego every Friday."

Karla's mouth popped open, then closed again. It was easy to forget what the rest of the world knew. Everything Babbitt had listed was information her health insurance provider, bank, and neighbourhood watch committee all had the legal right to. Everything, except the time spent with her son, and even then Ambrosia's lawyer had permissions to access that information. Babbitt's list would be the least the Bureau would know.

Babbitt continued: "You came because you understand our mission. You also understand your interests, with perfect clarity. The beauty of this, young lady, is that your interests and those of the State imbricate, perfectly, in this room."

Karla drank the rest of her whisky, it gave good heat. She coughed a little, and asked: "You give this speech often?"

Babbitt smiled at that. Snake eyes twinkling, still without any depth. "Not since the Service, actually. My role here requires a different set of speeches."

Karla looked down at her empty glass. She still felt half-drunk from the night before. Sour hangover sweat hung in her nostrils, making her nauseous.

Babbitt said: "We thought she might open up to an orange," and Karla's eyes returned to the plump dictator in the silver vest.

"I don't..."

Babbitt waited, while Karla said nothing, brain grinding to a halt as it looked up at the immensity of the lie hanging over her. The job at the Bureau, the branch she'd been assigned to, the person she'd shared a cubicle with.

Babbitt prompted: "You're a smart young woman, of course you do. Of course you do."

Karla said: "I was…" She cleared her throat. "I was a plant."

"Yes. You were. An effective one, at that. That was always the deal with your employment, and you fulfilled your end of the bargain."

"Because—because of her family history."

"Precisely. We wanted to know what her true colours were. I never believed she was a double green."

There was a snap, then a sudden pain. She looked down to see her palm covered in blood.

"Kevin," said Babbitt, unperturbed, "get a bandage for Miz Tessier-Denk's hand would you? She seems to have broken my good crystal."

Karla stared at her hand until Kevin wrapped it with a white bandage. Conjured, as if from thin air.

"So what will you do with me…" Karla trailed off, ashamed of her first instinct.

Babbitt laughed, looking over at Kevin: "See. We chose so well." He settled his gaze back on Karla. "That's the attitude we need with us, here, as we go about our work. No. No your place with us at the Bureau of Cultural Adjustment is assured. Now." Babbitt made a little noise in the back of his throat, then struck: "We thought she would open up to you because of your colours: true, but more importantly, because you were a romantic match. According to the AI we ran through the more contingent scenarios, you would likely have been married."

The director delivered the blow with an indifference far more terrifying than any malice.

Kevin moved past the director's desk, lit a cigarette, and sat in a fat-cushioned chair to one side and behind the director, mildly curious, nothing more. Quiet in the room, as Karla's mind screamed at her. Quiet, except for an old-fashioned clock, which Karla heard for the first time, *tick-tock, tick-tock.*

Karla pressed her thumb into the centre of the bandage of on her hand. She winced. "You motherfucker."

Babbitt smiled, genuine. "Oh, you have no idea."

She set her jaw.

Kevin said: "Physical violence won't get you anywhere, yes?"

Karla breathed out, and Kevin said: "Yes, that's better."

Babbitt said: "Listen: you would never have met this woman if it wasn't for us. Be thankful for that. Be thankful, and let this episode rest, there. No wallowing in self-pity or futile rage, giving into the remorseless ego that marks even the most small and inconsequential life. You have been lucky, Miz Tessier-Denk, to have been chosen for such an important mission. Not a woman of inconsequence, anymore. You've made your mark, found the perfect moment to burn brightly. And if this does not console you, if keeping your nation safe is insufficient to crack the myopia of a peasant mind, then consider this: you've made it to the bunker, where it is safe. Congratulations. You may bring your son with you, and keep him safe, as well."

She pressed her thumb into the wound again. The bandage began to show the red. "I don't know what you're talking about, old man. But I guess you're going to tell me, now this dog has been kicked enough, I figure now's the moment you have to make some speech describing the exquisite beauty of your system of repression. Show me the size of your sack, here in your big man's office, with its leather testicle cushions and bronze phallic dick-pen." She gestured at the thick fountain pen near Babbitt's hand. "Lay it all out; because it isn't enough that I comply, I have to believe, right?"

Babbitt's smile dropped. "Like I said: you are smart. An intelligence you've largely wasted. Let me make something clear: at the end of all this, you will believe. At the end of it all I'll trust you so completely I'll make you the lead officer on June Fourth incidents in Fast Response. You will serve with distinction."

Karla didn't believe.

Babbitt drummed his fingers, *drum-drum, drum-drum.* "Listen. The world is made up of two political entities: the bunker and the camp. Not just the real camps, the ones we send the reds to, and not just the real bunkers: the ones we retreat to should the vulgar masses rise up against the rule of law. Not just the architecture of our cities—bunkers like this building and the district it resides in, where those of dubious political standing may not enter. Not easily. Districts protected by law, by drone, by truncheon, and by thirty-dollar lattes. Camps like the public housing at the edge of the city, where the other, the enemies of social harmony and economic growth may not leave.

"No—not those. The external cityscape is not enough. To truly make the world one of bunker or camp, one must control memory. We remodel the neural architecture of the human mind as bunker or camp. So the people believe harmony is worth fighting for on the one hand, or simply too powerful to confront, on the other. So the masses become comfortable with their place, in the camp: with their bread and circuses to distract them, their comic book heroes and three-dollar cheese burgers. Bunker and camp, subsumed in consciousness, intrinsic to neural architecture, so no-one, but no-one, knows either exists.

"To make this all work, young lady, we require one crucial additional ingredient: speed. A system that reinforces bunker and camp, instantaneously. We have to be faster than human thought." He opened his palms. "And so we are. Ever more powerful artificial intelligences crawl over your every purchase, every keystroke, your fitness monitor. Our speed has now moved us beyond that of human thought, to a *precognitive* capacity. So we knew, for example, that

Eulalie Chen would betray her privileged position in the bunker and that you, Karla Tessier-Denk, would be the individual that would take her to the camp. No great deed comes without sacrifice, and you have made your sacrifice, so now it is time to take your reward."

Drum-drum drum-drum. "Bunker, or camp, Karla."

"Well," said Karla. Lips dry. Head pounding. "You know the answer already, apparently."

"We do. We do. So tell me about Eulalie's plans to betray us."

Karla sighed. One hand cradled in the other. It's not that something in her was breaking. Nothing so trite. More the realization that a part of herself had fractured long ago and could never be fixed. A fracture the shape of a five-year-old boy.

"Could I get another whisky?"

For once, Babbitt said nothing. Didn't feel the need to open his fat mouth and fill the air with his authority. He just nodded, and a few seconds later Kevin had placed another drink in her hand.

She told them everything. About Eulalie's parents, her vendetta, her desire for knowledge of the first June Fourth and to commemorate it with another. Karla said it all and when she was done, her glass was empty. A little booze buzz returned, making it all feel a little distant, a little less real.

"There's more," said Kevin.

Babbitt glanced at Kevin before bringing the dead weight of his eyes back down on Karla. "Yes, Miz Tessier-Denk?"

Karla swallowed and looked down at her glass. The buzz faded.

"She's not quite sure," said Kevin. "The memories are unclear. She may have had her pin out when Eulalie confessed." He paused and then: "yes, that's it, she had her pin out. And something else—a drug to corrupt natural memory formation. Neothebaine perhaps? No. Nothing so professional. Not just alcohol, surely?" Kevin directed his next comments at Babbitt: "Unprofessional. She was drunk, that is all. I suspect there are enough residuals in her synaptic networks for her to tell us what we need to know."

Babbitt waited, motionless. Karla swallowed, unable to look at either man. Weariness fell across her shoulders like snow.

"Yeah, there's more," she sighed. "But it doesn't matter. You can't stop it happening. She's already done it."

Babbitt stilled. Kevin smoked and watched.

Karla wondered briefly about the weight of betrayal. Whether it compared to the weight of self-censorship, or of cowardice, or self-loathing. She decided it felt about the same. "Eulalie put a Trojan into the false memories the Bureau implanted in the aftermath of all the June Fourth incidents she was involved with. It's a virus—I don't know how it works." She looked at Kevin. "I don't."

"She doesn't," agreed Kevin, and then, "but there's more."

Karla gave them more: "If any of the infected protestors have gone to an Omissioner for a memory sync, the clinic will carry the virus. If anyone infected sends a memory clip to a friend, the friend will get it. Millions will have it by now. In a few days, when the real June four rolls around, all those people will be gathering in the square." Karla paused. "Eulalie's plans work at the speed of *fuck you*. Faster than a confession; faster even than those little algorithms you have scuttling over our lives, like spiders. There will be hundreds even in these offices infected by it." She pointed with her glass at Kevin. "Harmony officers, too, starting to feel aggrieved, wondering why they've stood behind a corrupt system for so long. I have it, darkening my dreams. It may even be in your head, now, Director."

The director leaned back, interlocking his fat fingers across his breast. "Ah. What a talented woman. Such a waste." He said it with genuine respect in his voice, then shrugged. "For me, it doesn't matter so much." He turned his head and tapped at the spot where his cochlear implant should be. No dull sheen of metal, just naked skull and hair. She creased her brow. She'd never met anyone unplugged before.

Karla had no time to dwell before the director said: "But we shall deal with it. Military march at the square of course. We may even have to move the weekend. We'll feed reports about a memory virus to the news, assure all that a patch is being developed. And then we will develop it: we still have two days—plenty of time should we put every tech on this one issue. Ten thousand of our finest neuro-technicians will get there, soon enough. We'll make it a compulsory download, of course. And after all of that, if we have a few who stubbornly turn out, well, we always have the camps, don't we?"

He said it all without hesitation or concern. Years of work on the part of Eulalie, resolved within seconds, dealt with in a few short commands, soon to be given.

Babbitt dead-eyed Karla again, and said: "It was good of you to tell us so quickly. Had you held out for another day the damage would have been far, far worse. Thank you, Miz Tessier-Denk."

Karla's weariness grew.

"Chin up, young lady. We will adjust your memory with a correction procedure before the end of the week."

"Huh?"

"Well, we can't have you remembering this incident. Not precisely the way it played out; not with your easy capitulation. No, that won't work at all. It would cause you all sorts of discomfort, distract you from your work."

"She'd rather forget, anyway," said Kevin.

Babbitt held up a fat finger. "She cannot forget it all. No. She will need to remember Eulalie was a double green that jeopardised social order because of a personal grievance. She needs to recall Eulalie as a one-night stand—perhaps two—that could have destroyed her custody rights with her son. Intensify the sense of betrayal. But yes, the grand and sweeping love affair of Tessier-Denk and Chen, this will need to be adjusted right out of the frame."

Kevin nodded.

"Plus we'll need your help as we patch Eulalie's little culture hack," said Babbitt, returning his attention to Karla. "You're a talented officer."

"She hopes it works," said Kevin, "that she forgets her betrayal."

"Oh, it will work, fear not, young lady. Not least because you want it to. Listen: *Past events have no objective existence, but survive only in written records and in human memories. To make sure that all written records agree with the orthodoxy of the moment is merely a mechanical act. But it is also necessary to remember that events happened in the desired manner.*' A great man said that. Your exo-memories are, of course, the written records, the mechanics of which are elementary. The harder part, the desired events, these will upload into your natural memories during your dreams. It will get to the point where you will no longer be sure what is real, and what is imagined. You'll have two histories in your natural memory, but your exo-memory feed will agree with only one. Eventually, the history that is politically superior will be the one you remember. But here's the thing, *Karla*"—and her name sounded ugly in Babbitt's mouth— "you will collude with amnesia. Listen: you will embrace it. Forgetting is a survival mechanism, yes. But it is also a hallmark of *political* aptitude. The memories of the best among us are malleable, suiting whatever is required of them at that particular moment."

"Which man?"

"Sorry?"

"Which great man said that?"

Babbitt furrowed his brow, just for a moment. "You know, I'm really not quite sure. It's what you would call a received wisdom, here at the Bureau. The correctness of it shines though, doesn't it? A burning bright light to lead us in the chaos that swirls all around."

Babbitt leaned back in his chair, pleased, it seemed, with his work on the specimen in front of him. "You have been most obliging, Miz Tessier-Denk, most obliging. So, ask me anything you wish. I know there is something there—it's sitting on the tilt of your shoulders; a question that shines in your eyes. So come: ask."

Karla's lips were dry, stuck together. She felt a pressure on her chest, like someone were kneeling on it. But she asked her question: "What happened on June Fourth?"

The boss paused, lips curling into a smile. His black, depthless eyes twinkled, and he laughed. Laughed, like Santa Claus, just before raping an elf: *ho-ho-ho-ho.*

"What?" asked Karla, anger rising.

"Oh dear."

"*What?*"

"And there I was insisting you were smart."

Kevin said: "Calm, stay calm."

Babbitt's faced eased a little on the red joviality. "Nothing," he said. "Nothing happened on June Fourth. It is the most unremarkable day of the year. It is a day where nothing has ever happened, and nothing will ever happen."

"But. Eulalie—her father. He died on June Fourth. He was shot. At the—at the original June Fourth Incident."

Babbitt laughed again, and Kevin smiled along with him. "Ah— what arrogance! Eulalie Chen's father, Li Qiang, was no political activist. He was drinking and smoking heavily with friends in a bar. No doubt he had failed to tell his wife of his plans that particular evening. February thereabouts I believe it was, 2060. He had a heart attack, was rushed to hospital by ambulance, and died en-route. You see, Karla," Babbitt leaned forward, "this is the problem with memory. So fallible, so malleable. What that young woman has conjured in her mind is quite remarkable."

She grunted. "Yeah. Right. You seemed to have all the talking points about her dad all lined up."

Babbitt ignored the comment. Karla had a feeling the director had already moved on from the conversation, now he knew he would get everything he wanted from it. He said: "She is a strong-willed woman. We need a confession from her. Sooner, rather than later is better. We caught her leaving the building just now, in something of a hurry."

Karla swallowed.

"We've asked her in for some tea and will have the problem resolved eventually. But it never looks good for a political deviant to turn up several months later on the freewave, haggard, robotically mouthing a confession. Authenticity is our business here, at the Bureau. So you will need to talk to her, help her understand the situation." Babbitt waited, fingers on the table edge in front of him, for her to answer.

"I don't—"

"Yes you do," said Babbitt, eyes boring into her. "You know exactly what you must do."

Saturday (evening), June 2nd, 2091 // Corn Yellow – Basketball Orange

They took her there in a windowless vehicle. Men with guns walked her across a field extending out to the horizon, in all directions. Nothing, no habitation visible, save a large, square white building at the crest of a gentle ridge. Karla's hands brushed the tall grass, the morning wind moved her hair.

A sign over the entrance said: **Reform Through Labour**. White foyer, receptionist behind a long white counter, her face as cold as porcelain. Clean steel elevators, no floor numbers, retina-thumbprint-voice command from one of the two officers accompanying.

Strong-jawed, both, features hidden under the black brims of their pale-green military hats. Large, polarized sunglasses covered much of their faces. At first she thought the smell of sour body odour was her own. Halfway down she realised it wasn't her, but the guards. Their forearms and faces covered in a thin sheen of sweat, rancid in the closed space of the elevator. One of them, lips parted, tilted his head in Karla's direction.

The doors opened noiselessly to a white corridor, all white, save three lines on the floor: red, orange, blue. Orange and blue eventually branched off down other white corridors; Karla rode the red down to a steel door shaped like a sphincter. Both guards grasped her on her upper arms with sweaty palms.

They emerged in a long, high-ceilinged room, and sat her down on a white bench, facing a mirror an arm's length away. The guards left, leaving behind the lingering sour of their sweat. Underneath it, the space had a faint antiseptic smell.

Mirror. Her face an older version of the person who used to look back at her in her twenties. The haggard acquiescence, the alienated paranoia, the sweat stains marring a white collar, all the same.

The mirror became transparent; her face disappeared, replaced by Eulalie's. Staring back at her, sitting on a white bench. Unlike hers, Eulalie's long bench was the first of a row of bleachers, stretching back and out to the left and right. Eulalie sat alone in the stands. Dressed in a red jumpsuit, erect posture, hands folded in her lap. Karla couldn't help but notice the deep purple bruises on her knuckles. Vivid, against the white of the room.

There was a tired gleam in her eye, pallor over her face. The pallor of decay. Like part of her had already died.

"I got this condition," said Karla. Somehow she managed to make her voice even, conversational.

It took Eulalie a second, but eventually her eyes focussed, and she said: "Yeah?"

"Rare," said Karla. "So rare it doesn't even have a name. You see, when I get stimulated, I sneeze."

Another second, and Eulalie repeated: "stimulated."

"You know." Karla gestured with her hands. "Horny."

"Oh."

"So, you know, that first couple of weeks at work, when I was sneezing all over the place, and you told me to see the doctor. Well, my only medical problem was proximity to you and a moist patch that wouldn't go away."

The gleam in Eulalie's eyes turned to a distant smile and she said: "Dickhead."

"Always."

"As pre-gulag pep talks go, Karla, this isn't up there with the most inspiring."

"Yeah, well." Karla looked down at her hands. She was mirroring Eulalie, resting them in her lap. "I was trying to think of the things I never told you about, before I came. So there'd be no lost moments between us. But I couldn't think of anything. Just the sneezing thing. And, I guess. The cowardice." Her voice wavered with the last words.

She sighed. "You're not a coward Karla. That's just what they want you to believe."

"I told them everything."

"Did you?"

"Yeah. I did. And I am. I told them about June Fourth. I could have held out, and I didn't. Just a couple more days, your plan. It could have worked."

"No." Eulalie said it simply, in a way that brooked no ambiguity. "Another lie they've seeded into your subconscious. There are always methods to get to you to talk. There are always ways to get to you and quickly. Remember the brain-mapping procedure you went through as part of your induction? Well, they could have strapped you down, plugged you into one of their machines, pinpointed the neural clusters of your most traumatic memories, and fired them over and over again, while you laid there in the chair, screaming for them to stop."

Karla felt a twinge from that day, so long ago, the despair; the pounding on the thin wooden door of her apartment. Kindred, two years old, head buried in her chest—

Eulalie's words cut through the memory: "Play that tune over and over. Pluck that nerve. A thousand times in a handful of minutes, over and over, until you're vomiting, screaming, begging for them to stop."

"Eulalie."

"You know how I know?"

"I. Well—"

Eulalie's eyes were fixed on hers. "Because I've ordered it, Karla, and I have done far, far worse. I was an Internal Harmony officer. Everyone who gets to my position goes via that route. The secondment was a test; I passed the test. One of many they set for me over my career: I excelled in them all." Whatever energy Eulalie had was leaking from her with the confession. "Because I understand how they interrogate, I've taken certain steps to make their neural techniques less effective. They would know this, which is one of the reasons they recruited you. You were my first mistake. But you were the mistake I made, knowingly. I put you at risk because I was lonely, because I wanted to feel a human emotion again. Cold, hard calculation for years on end, never slipping, never giving them an opening. I thought, I desperately hoped, I could get away with it, just once. No. No. And you are the consequence of my error. Weakness. They are using you against me as they would use Kindred against you."

"I—"

"What do you think that room you are in actually is, Karla?" she asked, indicating the bleachers on her own side. "You're not viewing me, I'm viewing you. You're in a cage, and they will do whatever they need to do to make me talk. Men, juiced up to the eyeballs on ice-9, Neothebaine, sildenafil. Hold you down on those white tiles and fuck you until I scream for it to stop."

Karla's mouth felt dry. She thought about the guards that accompanied her down, the antiseptic smell of the room. She looked around sharply.

"Karla," Eulalie said, "your guilt is a tiny thing, next to mine. The things I've done, the people I've condemned, the ruthlessness of it. I brought you into this world. If you and your son are under threat, it is because of me. Don't forget that." She turned her hands over in her lap, looking at them for a moment, before returning her dulled eyes to Karla. "And don't forget this. I would let them do it to you, if I thought it was necessary. If I had to choose between you, and the revolution, I would choose the revolution. I would let them hold you down and commit their abuses, while you screamed and begged for it to stop. I love you, Karla, I want you to know that I've fallen in love with you. But that's a small thing, in our world now, and it's not the reason I'll confess."

Karla waited. Quiet, down in the white-white holding centre. Pain forming behind her eyes; the glare of the room getting to her.

Eulalie broke the silence: "I'll confess and tell them everything because they can't stop it now."

Karla sighed. "They've got everyone working on it. The whole Bureau."

"They can't stop it because this isn't about software, or a virus." There was a strain in Eulalie's voice, the pressure of her belief on the words. "It's about the human heart. You can't deprogram the human heart."

Karla looked down, but when she looked back Eulalie hadn't noticed. The woman seemed to be looking into the glass between them, film of water over her eyes. "June Fourth exists, Karla—*it exists.* Deep down, in the subconscious of this society. All I did was call to it."

Still Karla said nothing.

"They admitted to you, didn't they," said Eulalie, "that June Fourth is real? The truth of what happened to my father." The glaze was gone now, replaced with a shining intensity.

"Well," Karla started, hands twisting in her lap. Voice steady, she said: "Yeah. Yes. Your father was a hero. They killed him for his commitment to the cause, then lied, then erased it all."

Tears rolled down Eulalie's face. Just like that. The relief breaking her, shoulders shuddering, bowed in on themselves.

Karla sat, nauseous in the stench of her lie, while the woman she loved cried. Too much a coward to say anything more, until the guards grabbed Karla with jittering hands and took her away.

Sunday June 3rd, 2091 // Jungle Green - Golden Yellow

Karla sat on the couch, looking at the Lego world she'd built with her son. Spread out, a city of superheroes. Behind it all, the Fortress of Solitude box stood, rising over it like a monolith, wrapped in a big red fucking bow. At the corner of her vision the adjustment program blinked, smiley-face icon, ready for upload.

She made the call.

Ambrosia's face appeared after the third ring, superimposed on retina, upper left.

"Oh, Karla," she said, a little flushed. "I've been meaning to contact you. Your Ego feed has been off the charts since your political turned back to yellow. I don't think I've ever heard of such a rapid improvement—I mean, normally years—"

"I want joint custody."

Ambrosia's expression didn't change. "I see. Well, according to proper legal—"

"Shut up." Her voice was flat. Drained. Karla spoke like she hadn't any strong feelings on this or any subject, because there were no strong feelings left to be had. "You will do it or I will release every fight we ever had, every time you ever screamed or swore or threatened, everything on to the freewave."

Ambrosia's face smoothed. "That will hurt you just as much as me."

"Nothing can hurt me now."

"I have this conversation on-retina, I can—"

"This conversation is not real. The only version that is real is the one I will present to the court, perfect in every detail. It will show your selfishness, the unholy pursuit of your career over your family, and your abuse of your son."

Smoothed, now to stone. "How dare you. I never laid—"

"Shut up. Bitch. You're not listening. I'm *telling* you what your history looks like, and what your future could look like. I'm not going to explain it again."

Ambrosia's face gave way. Something new entered it. If Karla had given enough of a shit to care, she would have noticed it was respect.

Ambrosia said *yes*.

Karla cut the link.

She leaned back on her very comfortable couch, not looking at the expansive view. The adjustment program blinked in the corner of her vision. Ready for download should she give the command, so when she dreamed later that night, she might dream of a new and better reality.

Karla Tessier-Denk ran a hand through her hair. She decided the weight of betrayal, cowardice, and self-loathing were all the same, more or less. They were the weight of air, they were the weight of the world.

She got up and went to the bedroom.

DARK ON A DARKLING EARTH
2193

ist turns to jade-white ice that scars and wilts the maple trees. I follow the Stomach of the White Tiger shimmering overhead in a moonless sky, taking me towards the capital on the sea. I carry a dying solar torch in one hand and the pistol in the other. My joints ache from the cold and I'm ten times the age of this sleek young weapon, my hand shaking as I try to hold it horizontal. It would be better if I knew what the buttons did, but that doesn't really matter. It's not like I'm going to be shooting anybody.

The white sand path is slender, curling its way up into Wu Mountain, a thin pale line in the darkness. I just need to walk this path, then I am home. Just this path and I see my sons and my wife again. My too young wife with her crooked mouth and crooked hair, and my too energetic sons and their scraped knees and faces pressed into my skinny thighs. Just this path, and a thousand more like it, five thousand *Li* of winds and mists and cold as the world turns to winter.

That's all.

My numb fingers lose their purchase on the torch and it clatters at my feet, turning itself off in the process. "Ah," I mutter, "your mother!"

I lean forward, preparing to groan mightily as I bend my beleaguered back, when the *snick* of a twig breaking straightens me up. I jump as a large shadow moves onto the path, and accidentally press one of the buttons on the side of the pistol. It makes a spitting sound and sparks fly at the point where the needle strikes the shadow. I jump again at the fact I managed to fire the pistol and drop it as I turn to run. My escape, unfortunately, is short-lived. I step on my robe and trip myself up, sprawling, face bump-and-sliding against the cold hard path.

The shadow stands over me and a voice comes with it, deep and angry: "Silly old son of a bitch." There is a *clack-clack* as preparation for my execution takes place.

I turn onto my back and put my hands over my face. "No! Please don't kill me—please. I am an Omissioner, an Omissioner!" If I were a prouder man, I would be embarrassed by the pleading, the begging in my tone. If I were a prouder man.

A second voice from the shadows, a woman's, lands with the steel rod of authority: "Wait."

The big shadow over me pauses, the stars above glinting on the gun barrel as he lowers it. A torch blares into my eyes and I blink rapidly into the beam. The small circle of light ranges over my body until it alights on the chest of my robes.

"Look," says the woman.

The man's shadow reaches down and grabs the front of my robe roughly, at the insignia. "You're an Omissioner?"

"Yes," I say, for the first time being pleased to admit it. "I was cut off from my—"

"We can't have this conversation here, we're too exposed," says the woman. "Bring him, corporal; we'll see what is truth and what is the lie back at camp."

He grabs me, far more roughly than required.

I am pushed and shoved for a dark and cold ten minutes up a steep thin path, the mist returning to press against us. We arrive at a campfire set in a clearing among tall trees, the tops of which I cannot see. I'm thrown down in the arc of flickering orange light. Despite the jarring in my old bones, I am glad of its warmth on this bitter night. I put my hands out to the heat of the fire and glance around the clearing.

There are bedrolls here and a silver dome tent, and I smell the tantalizing smell of cooking rice. Boots scrape behind me and I turn to see the man I shot, the corporal. He glowers above, cracking his knuckles. His uniform is a faded green, his black armoured vest worn and scratched (with a new scratch courtesy of me) and his jawline looks like standard-issue military—extra-large size. His brow is as low and thick as his voice: "Don't try anything."

A woman with a sergeant's insignia stands next to the corporal. She removes a dented black helmet to reveal hair as short as the corporal's. Her mouth looks like it hasn't laughed in a long time and she's as lean as she should be, given the way of this world. Everything about her—her posture, her way of speaking, the way her black boots gleam in the low light—speaks to a woman who suffers no fool.

A third soldier stands nearby. She's much younger—a private by the look of it—with long, ragged dark hair she wears down, an ironic smile, and a pistol she lets ride low on her hip.

I stand, gingerly, and push the mane of grey hair back from my face. "I am Omissioner Du Gongbu, formally of the Thirty-Third," I say, bowing at the sergeant. "Pleased to make your acquaintance."

She doesn't return the bow. "Thirty-Third—are we at war with you?"

I point at the faded army markings on the breast of her armoured vest. "You're from the Twelfth Special Brigade," I say, and then I lie: "We are allies, having fought the battles of Huaihua and Shaoyang together." I have no idea whether we were allies, of course, or whether either army had fought in those battles. But they are all too young here to remember who was meant to be fighting who.

The sergeant steps over to me, limping slightly, and stands a foot away, eye to eye. Up close she smells of honest sweat and rifle grease. She holds out her hand. "Let me see your Memento of Office."

Without hesitation I pull at the heavy gold chain around my neck, removing the badge from under my shirt. It glints chrome as I place it in her hand, the symbol of the paradise flycatcher, feet grasping the 智. The state of the world is such that even fools like me are given the mark of wisdom, intelligence and knowledge.

She pauses, mouth a fixed line, while she studies my claim. I've thought about throwing the Memento away a hundred times. My indecision may yet prove beneficial. The magnum-jawed corporal tries to say something but she holds up a hand, cutting him off. She stares at it for another long half-minute, before the tension eases ever-so-slightly from her shoulders.

She takes a step backwards and bows, deeper than the one I gave her. "Then it is an honour to welcome you, Omissioner. I am Sergeant Hu. This is Corporal Zhong." She points with her chin at the man I shot. His eyes still hold an undisguised desire to snap my old-man's neck. "This is Private Xu." The young woman nods at me and sits on a nearby log, resting her forearms on her knees. There's the flash of the devil in her eyes.

"This is our cook and his son, On." A man emerges from the shadows, smiling at me, open and unreserved. He wipes his hands on a dirty white cloth and his son grasps his leg, looking out at me from behind his father's thigh. The son is slim, the cook has the face of a fat man but the same lean body everyone else has here.

"Have you eaten?" asks the sergeant.

"Pleased to meet you all," I say, with a flourish of my faded red-ragged robe. "Not in three days, Sergeant Hu."

They make concerned noises, even though such a thing is quite common. The cook disappears and soon comes back to place a bowl in my hands. It is a small bowl of rice, some bamboo shoots and a few drops of fish oil. It's the best meal I've had in months; I bring the chopsticks from bowl to mouth with unseemly haste, still standing, gulping it down in a short minute. My stomach twists when the food hits it, partly with pleasure, partly in shock.

The cook passes me a bucket and scoop when I finish. I hand him the empty bowl and drink deeply of the fresh water, slurping it from the wooden scoop.

There was a time when my hunger would have brought me shame, and shamed others to see one of my rank brought so low. But those days are long gone. The cook simply nods, smiling, and takes the bucket and bowl away when I finish. The rest take their seats around the fire and look at me with that familiar air of expectancy, with that yearning that has followed me across this cold earth ever since I donned the Omissioner's robes.

I sit down on one of the blackened trunks near the fire. "Tell me sergeant, do you have wine?"

"No," grunts Corporal Zhong.

"We've been saving a bottle we found," says the cook, earning a glare from the corporal.

"What do you need it for?" asks the sergeant.

"Wine is a gift from the gods, to warm our hearts and make us speak the truth," I say. Then I lie: "The first rule when meeting an Omissioner is this: give them wine. Do this, and they will speak the truth of your memory, and do so with a warm heart."

"I don't remember that rule about the Omissioner," says Private Xu, eyes twinkling.

"Of course you don't, child. Someone as young as you remembers nothing." I say it stern enough so she blushes and drops her gaze for a moment.

The sergeant watches me, face like iron, then directs her voice at the cook. "Pour the Omissioner some wine."

The cook disappears into the shadows at the edge of the fire.

"Why did you leave the Thirty-Third?" asks the sergeant.

I lie: "We were ambushed by the Fifty-Eighth, in a pass down near Qingcheng. They fired the camp, saying we brought contaminated food and bodies from the cities."

"A purist line?" questions the sergeant. "I thought the South was dominated by eco-revisionists."

"Don't you mean eco-rightists?" someone asks.

The private pulls her memory card from her pocket—a translucent golden square glowing with its own internal luminescence—her face softly lit in its deep yellow backwash. "No—the opposition in the South are holders of the Liu-Deng line, in league with the American eco-reactionaries."

While they argue over imaginary foes, the cook gives me a bamboo cup half-filled with wine. I nod and smile up at him, hiding my frustration at the miserly portion.

"Americans?" someone says, "There's no Americans left. There's not even an America anymore."

"What role do the Rixin-Kong line holders have in all of this?" asks Corporal Zhong.

"Who are they?" asks Private Xu.

"I met them on the road when I was travelling to join the Thirty-Third," he says, looking at the sergeant, even though the private had asked the question. "They said they were comrades of ours, collecting funds for the war effort. One of them showed me a memory card listing us as allies. I helped them out as much as a could."

The sergeant shrugs: "I've never heard of them," and looks at me "Omissioner?"

I looked up from the dregs at the bottom of my cup. "Rixin-Kong? Never heard of it."

"But you're the Omissioner," says the private, with ironic politeness that apparently only I hear.

"I know." I look over at Corporal Zhong. "Tell me, what did the Rixin-Kong look like?"

He squints into the fire. "I just remember that name. I wrote it down after." He takes out his memory card, tapping his finger on the glowing golden square, looking for the entry. "I've written here they were a ragged group of soldiers, close to starvation. Only one had a gun. Six men and a woman, the woman was the one that spoke to me. She wore an armoured vest, dark blue with a silver dragon."

"They weren't Rixin-Kong line holders."

"No?" he rumbles. "What were they then?"

"Bandits."

He lowers the memory card slowly.

"There are no Rixin-Kong revolutionaries. By your description it sounds like deserters from the Guangxi campaign—the Third

Flying Squadron—convinced you they were on your side. Such occurrences are common these days. They carry around memory cards that show them as allies with just about everyone." I could have left it there. But my hip still hurt from where he had flung me onto the ground, and my wine cup was empty. "Being gullible is one thing. But gullible in a world without memory is fatal."

The corporal stands, a deep rumbling coming from somewhere in his chest. I smile up at him; now they've confirmed me as an Omissioner he can't lay a hand on me.

"Enough," says the sergeant, her voice as flat and smooth as a pond of ice. Just one word is all she needs and the corporal sits, and the smile is gone from my face. "You've had your wine," she continues, indicating my cup with her chin. "Now earn your keep. Tell us our stories and our history: tell us who we are."

I nod my head at her in an outward display of complete agreement. Inwardly I wonder how many bottles of this wine the cook has secreted away. "What would you like to hear?"

"Tell us of great events. As Omissioner, you would have dined with generals, with the poets who weave the common memories of our nation, with the princes and princesses who seek to bring unity."

I lie, partially: "Yes."

"Then tell us of the great men and women who lead this campaign. Tell us of what this war means to them," the sergeant says There is something in her eye as she says it, but I don't quite catch its meaning.

I look into the fire. I tell the truth: "The generals complain all day long and watch plays at night; they eat three full meals a day and fart, then go to sleep in warm beds. That's what the war means to them."

I expect a rebuke from the sergeant, but instead she almost-smiles—or smiles as much as a person who never smiles could—and says: "Tell us then of this place." She indicates the darkness around us with her eyes.

"This is Wu Mountain," I say, and she nods in reply. She pulls her gold-shimmering memory card from her pocket so she can record the key facts; they all do, except the corporal. It is Wu Mountain, this is true. As always, the rest I say is a lie:

"Here is where the Xia Emperor, dressed in his dragon robe and carrying a great golden axe, swept past with his mouth filled with fire, scattering the deviationist tribes of Chiang Kai-Shek.

"But I'm not going to tell you that story.

"Here is Wu Mountain, where the stone monster, whose scales move with the autumn winds, and whose feet are larger than elephants, stopped to rest on his journey east. The monster that was lured to the caves with promises of warmth and protection by the treacherous Gang of Four and their leader, the beautiful witch Jiang Qing, who drugged the tea she gave to the monster when it sat down at her table."

Private Xu narrows her dark, gleaming eyes at me when I say this. The rest look on in wonder, as all do when an Omissioner gives the gift of truth.

"But I'm not going to tell you of this.

"I'm going to tell you of Lao Zi, who tried to walk against the lines of the earth, who attempted the journey west from Wu Mountain, through the purple mists of the pass."

I speak low enough so they have to lean forward.

"Lao Zi, the great warrior of the Fourth Epoch, carried the silver crossbow of the Jiayu Pass. Lao Zi was the assassin who shot a silver bolt ten miles to strike the heart of the foul dictator Joao Ferreira the Black. Lao Zi was the master tactician who played Go against the Mongol General for two years, deliberately prolonging the game until the Mongol's superior army deserted and his campaign against Lao Zi's homelands collapsed.

"*Lao Zi walked here in the shadow of Wu Mountain. Then, as now, swallows that should have migrated swooped around his head, frightened and confused. It was here that he came across a grey turtle, old and weeping, making its way slowly east.*

"*Lao Zi stopped and said: 'What is wrong, old man?' The turtle replied: 'Lao Zi, do not head west. All roads there now lead to the city of Chang'an; all passes and all ways must run through it. That city is now a city of ghosts. The ghosts play the same games they've played for a hundred years. They play them over and again, living out the dreams of others, remembering the memories of others: lives and memories that they swap each and every day. But you will never live to see that bleak place, Lao Zi. The trail between here and there is long and harsh and even such as you, with all your talents, will perish.'*

"*Lao Zi placed his hands on his silver crossbow, and said: 'You know my name by my reputation; as do all in this land. But you don't know me, old man.'*

"*The turtle sighed and said: 'The gibbons will tell you three times the truth, and three times you will know it. But arrogant in your easy competence, you will ignore them.'*

"*Angry, Lao Zi said: 'Arrogance? It is you who are arrogant to speak to me like this, old man. Why take your word and not another? There are a thousand fools between here and Chang'an; only a fool would pay heed to even one.'*

"*The grey turtle replied: 'I know Lao Zi, because I am you. I am you, living in the Sixth Epoch, a thousand years from now. If I speak with arrogance, it is what pride still lingers from the folly of your youth. If I seem mournful, it is the knowledge of what that arrogance cost me. Turn back now or you will be forced to walk the road east for all eternity, a million Li on turtle's feet, doomed to repeat and repeat again. Turn back, Lao Zi, for my sake, for yours.'*

"*Lao Zi ignored the turtle, leaving without a word. He walked until he stood near at a deep gorge. In this place the gibbons bounced and watched him from the trees and called to him. And he found it was true, the things they said, and he wept. Three times they called to him, yet three times he failed to heed them, the only fool on the path to Chang'an.*

"*He walked to the west, until the purple mist crossed the pass. Lao Zi was consumed by it, as was foretold. When you look west, friends, think of him. And know that if the turtle is slow, it is because he knows he will never arrive at his destination.*"

They are silent after that, their faces flickering orange from the fire, all turned to me.

"West?" asks the corporal, looking over at the sergeant.

The sergeant still looks at me. "We were heading west, Omissioner. Are you saying it is a mistake? Are the purple mists... are they real?"

I give her an ambiguous raised eyebrow, the sort that suggests I know all the answers, but I am, in my wisdom, encouraging them to work it out for themselves. I am quite pleased with myself after the story. Except for the turtle-from-the-future part, which I often use in these tales, I'd made everything up on the spot. That's the thing about stories that are lyrical and vague, filled with familiar symbols and primal dreams: anyone can read anything into them. So I spin my tales while the listener weaves their own truth to each one. They let me have my wine and I let them have their fictions. This is the circularity of the dead world I now walk through, and it is enough for me.

Almost enough, anyway.

"The West was a long shot," grunts the cook.

The corporal squares his shoulders. "Where the sergeant says we go, we go."

"The cook is right. West was always a long shot," says the sergeant, and the mumbling from the others ceases. It is hard to tell in the firelight, but her eyes seem to gleam.

The private has been watching me throughout. "What the Omissioner's story tells us is this," she says, "the journey east is too long. If we head that way we live as the turtle does, on a journey that never ends."

"Um," I say, "I'm not sure—"

"South—it means we must go south," continues the private, "like I keep saying. We can't survive the creeping winter. We must head towards a warmer climate."

I want to interrupt and tell her she's wrong, but it's too late. The conversation heads where I don't want it to go and in so doing, veers away from my home. The private looks at me while the others speak, eyes twinkling. I was right; she has the devils in her. I grit my teeth. I should just have had the turtle tell them to go east: kept it simple. But no, I tried to end the story with a flourish. Old fool. So they speak of their new plans with each other over the fire while I look into my empty wine cup. I am attached to these people now—to leave this remnant unit would be called desertion. And the iron-faced sergeant woman was the sort to shoot deserters.

My wife and sons never felt further away.

I am awoken the next morning, the large face of the cook smiling over me as he shakes my shoulder. I grumble at him for doing so, groan at the cold in my bones, and curse both as I sit myself up. He puts a warm cup of tea in one hand and rice porridge in the other, and leaves me to my grumbling, still smiling. The mists have not relented with the early morning; they press in on the small clearing, drawing a veil cross the darkened forest beyond. The others have already packed their bags and are chatting to each other quietly.

The warm breakfast is a pleasure I have not had for many weeks, and I relish it. When I give the bowl back to the cook, his face reddens as he opens his mouth and then closes it again.

"Is there something you want to ask me, cook?"

"This dish," he holds up the bowl, "what's the name of it again?"

I raise an eyebrow. "Congee?"

He beams and bows deeply. "Yes, that's it—congee. Thank you, Omissioner."

The cook seems worse than average. Maybe that's why they just call him cook. He's probably forgotten his own name.

We walk most of the morning and afternoon, with a brief break for lunch. I slow them down, but not too much. In this world you can either march all day, or you can die, and I've been marching as long as I can remember. I still complain, of course. I am old, so it is my right. About the cold, my sore hip, the lack of wine. The others pay due respect to my office by not telling me to be silent; Corporal Zhong just glowers twenty shades of loathing at me. The mist is always with us, whether thirty feet away or three, pressing down on the earth and our moods. Eventually its oppressive omnipresence is enough to stop even my old-man complaints, and we are left with silence bar the scuffing of feet and a thin wind that rattles the bamboo.

We are setting up camp in the dark trees that evening when the sergeant emerges from the mist, red-faced from running. "Omissioner," she puffs, "I've found something. You need to see this."

I'm already sitting down near the fire and not planning on leaving it anytime soon. "What is it?"

Her eyes harden: "Now."

The corporal stands. "You heard the sergeant—now."

The orders in stereo only harden my desire to stay where I am, but I've decided the sergeant scares me. So I grumble and complain, but get to my feet anyway. After a twisting walk down a fading stone path we come to a large, grey door covered in moss and moisture. Water has worn down the markings on the stone, but despite its age, despite the decay, the symbol engraved on the door is plain to see. It matches the symbol on my Memento of Office—the 智.

"This is something important, isn't it?" asks the sergeant. The others have gathered behind her now, curious. Even the cook is here, his son staring up at the huge door from behind his father's apron.

I rake back the grey hair from my eyes and step over to a short stone pillar that stands next to the door. My heart thumps in my chest and suddenly my throat is dry. This can't be what I think it is. Not after all this time. The top of the pillar is angled at forty-five degrees towards me, made of a dark metal that time has made little impact on. It is completely blank, just a flat, black panel with enough shine still in it that I can see my reflection: an old man with deceptively quiet eyes and a thin white beard growing from the end of his chin.

I pull the Memento from my shirt and pass it over the touchplate. Nothing happens. For several long seconds, anyway, while the others look on in silence.

Then something does happen: the touchplate glows a soft golden hue, and satisfying *clunk-clunks*, metallic and deep, echo from inside the door. With a hiss of compressed air and a gasp from someone behind me, it opens.

I move to enter, but the sergeant pushes me to one side, signalling Zhong and Xu to go first. Zhong leads, machine gun to his shoulder, while the private pulls the pistol from her hip and shadows him down steep stone stairs. We follow. The stairs end at another door, this one cleansteel and chrome. My Memento opens this door as the last, and we follow Zhong and Xu through.

We enter another world.

The space is brightly lit, a smooth oval space with moulded

furniture in harsh whites and soft reds, the walls lined with books and viewing screens and paintings of worlds long forgotten. The lines are crisp here, real—when I reach out and touch a cushion the sensation of the soft leather against my fingertips is sensual and startling. The space is large, and interspersed among the moulded chairs are plinths, perhaps twenty, an object on each. One near me has old coins with square holes in the middle, the next, a calligraphy pen and scroll with ancient script; the one after that a bronze cauldron with intricate patterning on the side—western Zhou period, I'm sure; lacquered black wood platform shoes on another, a horn shaped jade cup on the next, pure and curled and gleaming.

It's like waking up from a long dream. Senses long blurred are now sharp, vague thoughts now linear and clear.

"What is this, Omissioner?" asks the sergeant, now at my shoulder. She speaks in the whisper of her awe.

I tell the truth, readily: "A memory shelter. I heard of these, secreted away as minds faded and wars began. I thought it a myth, passed from general to general, Omissioner to Omissioner." I nod towards the shelves and the screens. "Here is our collective consciousness, the fibres of our civilization. These books and manuscripts and artefacts embody us, and in those screens there on the walls you'll find a hundred million recordings and facts and virtual archaeologies."

Her hand touches my elbow, her fingertips sparking as they alight on the cloth of my robe. I start and turn to her. She bows deeply. The corporal and the cook and even his son do the same. The passivity of shock and wonder now settled on their faces.

The sergeant's eyes are wide, glistening. "You have saved us, Omissioner. We owe you our lives." She turns and indicates walls. "And you have given us purpose. To protect this, to learn it, to preserve it will be the duty of our lifetimes. And yours will be to teach it all."

I'm wondering how to respond to this rather lengthy proposed timeframe when the private appears at the mouth of one of three corridors that lead from the room. "Omissioner—you must see this."

Thankful of the excuse to end the conversation with the sergeant, I follow Private Xu down the short white corridor. I stop when we enter the next room. Then I fall to my knees, and clasp my hands together. Then tears roll from my eyes.

As far as my eyes can see, bottles of wine set behind glass in white-glowing cabinets. Fine Chinese reds from Xinjiang and Ningxia, and there—bold Sicilian vintages and fine French Bordeaux, and a little further along, rows of crisp Australian whites and complex, alluring New Zealand Pinot Gris. And more. So much more. A lifetime of more.

The private stands next to me, hands on hips. Her voice is filled with her ironic smile. "I guess I'd weep too, if I found my personal nirvana."

I nod, feigning agreement, as tears trickle down my face. I weep not because I have found it: I weep because I have to leave it behind.

I spend the afternoon drinking a fine Ningxia cabernet and reading a slim volume of ancient poetry. I am content.

As the evening arrives, the sergeant tells me they have found a store of food that will last for years, and the cook is preparing an extravagant meal to celebrate our first evening in the memory shelter. The sergeant and I seat ourselves at a large white table we have decided is for communal meals. Soon Private Xu saunters in, cigarette dangling from her mouth, and Corporal Zhong follows, sitting down with a large can of Laotian beer in his hand. A peace has settled on the small unit now—contentment even.

The sergeant says: "Tell us another memory of Wu Mountain."

I don't have the energy to lie after the long walk and the excitement, so I tell the truth: "I won't talk about Wu Mountain tonight. Tonight I will honour the discovery of the memory shelter with a poem by our greatest poet, Du Fu. If there's one poet you need to remember, it is him." They all reach for their memory cards.

I breathe in deeply. "This is a poem for those who have left for war, and those who wait for them at home."

In a quiet, clear voice, I remember every line to them:

"I have this feeling
You won't come back from frontier duties

But autumn is here
And I get out the laundry stone

Soon you'll feel the cold
The way I feel our separation

I clean your winter clothes
Whether I want to or not

Send them off to where you're stationed
Near the Great Wall

A woman uses all her strength
Beating the laundry with a club

Maybe if you listen hard
You'll hear it way out there."

They remain silent after I finish. Unmoving, watching me but not watching, eyes distant.

The private sits with her finger poised over her gold-glowing card. "I can't write what that is. I can't describe that."

I smile. "I know." Then I lie: "Don't worry, I'll tell it again in a week."

We eat a fine meal of Dongpo pork, soy eggs, pickled vegetables, Baozi, wontons, and hot and sour soup. There is wine and—for the first time since I join them—there is laughter. The cook sits and eats with us and his son, a smear of chocolate above his eyebrow, watches me with eyes wide as I speak. I am sated by the meal and made expansive by the wine. I tell them truth and lies about the war and where I've been and what I've seen, and they hang on every word.

But the day has been long and taken its toll. They drift away to bed—comfortable, warm bunks for more than fifty have been found down one of the corridors—and soon all that remains are the private and I, she with a packet of Double Happiness brand cigarettes, me with an Australian Pinot Noir. Such a shame, what happened to Australia—they really did make such magnificent wine.

I watch her in silence. She watches me. I drink my wine; she lights a cigarette and burns through it.

Finally she says: "Why do you want to go east, Omissioner?"

"Why do you wish to stop me?"

She shrugs. "Habit. I don't like being told what to do." She lights another cigarette, touching the tip of the last to the fresh one. "Plus I think you're lying. I think everything that comes out of your mouth is a lie."

I eye her uniform. "If you don't like taking orders, why did you join the army?"

She blows a cloud of smoke upwards. "How the fuck should I know?"

It's a good question. I sigh.

Maybe it's the wine, maybe it's the hope that there are some good devils in her, maybe it's the fact I have no allies and I'm desperate. But whatever it is, I do something foolish, I tell the truth: "My wife and two sons are there."

Xu leans forward, slender forearms on the edge of the table, cigarette trailing a slow line of smoke to the ceiling. "And the sergeant would never let you go there for that reason."

I raise my eyebrows in the sign for 'obviously,' refill the wine in my glass, and pour a fresh one for her.

"It's worse than you think, Omissioner."

I'm unhappy, and don't manage to keep it out of my voice. "Why is that, private?"

She frowns. "If we're going to drink together, we can drop the formalities. My name is Xiaofan."

I pass her the cup, then indicate for her to continue.

She leans back in her chair, sipping her wine on the way back. "I returned from guard duty one night, close to dawn. Freezing, barely able to see two feet away with the mist. This is maybe a month ago. Maybe a year, I'm not sure. Anyway, when I got back to camp I saw Sergeant Hu looking at her memory card. Everyone else was asleep, and she was crying. I was shocked. She's like a bronze statue, our sergeant. I was with her once when she was shot four times in the legs, lying in the mud in her blood and filth. I start panicking and she says to me calmly: 'Pass me a med-kit private, and then return fire on that position.' No pain on her face, no anger—like she was asking me to pass her the soya sauce."

We both smile at this.

She continues: "But there she was, crying. She'd put the card on the ground next to her and buried her face in her hands. I snuck around behind her. I shouldn't have done it. But we walk through this world like zombies, not knowing where we're going, or what we're feeling, or why we're feeling it. Dead inside or trying to be dead inside. So if someone feels something, especially the sergeant, well I want to know why. So I looked at the card. It said one thing: 'Father is east.' That's all."

After a long pause, she continues: "Hu was leading us east, into the depths of an entire continent, based on one line in a memory card. I respected her after that Omissioner, more than that, I—" She breaks off her voice and her gaze, unwilling to finish the thought.

We sit in silence after that, mutually agreed. I finish the bottle then start another, watching the cloud of smoke circle the girl's head.

Xiaofan says something.

"What?"

"I said: I'm sorry." There's no ironic smile in her voice.

I shrug and sip my wine. "Like the sergeant said: it was a long shot, Xiaofan."

She nods, and the regret in her eyes is real.

It's a long shot, but I don't care. I'm still going back to my family. And now I have an ally.

I saw something on patrol earlier. Let me show you."

The private stands near me, hands on hips. She has a way of leaning one hip to the side and resting the palm of her hand on the curve that an old man like me finds quite distracting. I'm sipping a blunt-but-satisfying Chilean red and reading poetry again.

I keep my eyes away from her hips: "Is it worth it?"

"It's worth it."

I sigh. "Let me bring my bag."

Thirty minutes later we are sitting on flat, almost dry stones at the top of a steep ridge. The mist is less pervasive today, affording us the view of a serene, dark watered lake, the edges of which are firm with white ice. In the distance the dark, jutting shapes of hills, fingers of hills, pushing themselves up into the mist or the clouds or whatever lies above us. The silence here is perfect, and draws me in.

Xiaofan snaps her lighter shut, drawing my attention to her. She drags long on the cigarette, looking at me out of the corner of her eye. "Better pour the wine then, old turtle."

I wince at the name she gives me, but she is young and doesn't know its colloquial meaning. I draw two bamboo cups and a bottle of wine from my travel bag, fill us each a cup.

She drinks deep on the wine. When she speaks, her voice is far away.

"This mist follows me everywhere. Not just out here, but in my mind as well. I can't think straight, I can't feel straight, I can't grasp anything with my thoughts. Sometimes I think this is all a dream. I worry that if I don't wake up soon I will become this dream and my reality will fade away." She looks at me. "Am I going crazy?"

I shake my head and then tell the truth: "This is a dream, dreamed by our country. It sleeps deeply now, and we are fated to walk through its slumber. Through its half-remembered places, through the longings of its history, through the world it abandoned to despair."

She sighs with frustration. "Oh Du."

"What?"

"Don't ever switch careers to counsellor."

"Were you seeking reassurance?"

"No. No, I guess not. Maybe just not the one person in this world more melancholy than I."

I smile a sad smile. "Drink your wine," I say, "so we can have another."

We're finishing our first bottle when she says: "You didn't ask about what I was going to show you."

"I assumed you'd get around to it."

She nods down the slope. "Look—down there, at the edge of the lake."

I follow her gaze, past the dark, frost-scarred trees and thin tendrils of mist. There, there it is. A boat, small and silver, tied to a stump at the edge of the lake.

I nod, slowly. My salvation: a small, lone boat, tied up.

My eyes are still on the boat as I speak. "How dear are memories, Xiaofan? It's like asking someone how important is the heart beating in their chest. I don't just hold the memories of others; I hold their identities, their sense of self and place and time. They, in turn, hold to me as tightly as if I were part of their soul. You'd think, in a world without a past, the man with memory would be king. But no, in that world, he who remembers is a slave."

"Have you run away from many groups like ours?" she asks, quietly.

"Three."

She sips her wine, her bottom lip glistening as she takes the cup away from her mouth. "Zhong will kill you, if you try to escape. He's that way inclined."

"I know." I drink deeply, watching the mist roll over the waters.

We're silent for a while until I bump her with my shoulder. "Unless he has sex: that will temper his temper."

"It's not going to happen."

"No?" I raise an eyebrow. "He is the last man on earth for you, and for the sergeant."

"Man? No. She's not that way inclined."

It takes me a few seconds. "Oh."

She blows out a cloud of smoke and cold-misted breath. "Yes: 'oh'."

"And I take it you're not that way inclined towards the sergeant?"

"No."

I shake my head. "A perfect circle of instability."

I reach for the bottle and fill my glass. Xiaofan lets me fill hers as well. This makes me happy. I am a man used to drinking alone, but it is heartening to find a kindred spirit, even for just one evening. All souls needs communion, even the old and bitter ones. These, most of all.

I sigh with contentment. The evening comes and the cold of the stone is starting to freeze the bones in my arse, but the wine and company warms my chest. "And you're not interested in Zhong either, I take it."

She rolls her eyes. "You'd have a better chance, Du Gongbu."

I smile, feeling the warmth now in my cheeks, as well. I'm an old man, but still, old men have egos too.

"Even if I was," she continues, "I'm married."

"So you're trying to get home as well?"

"No."

"No?"

Her eyes shine. "I…" The muscles in her jaw tighten and she sighs through her nose, closing her eyes. Like something unwanted has passed over her vision.

I understand her reaction. It's one I've seen a hundred times. "You don't remember where home is."

She shakes her head, jaw still tight. Afraid perhaps speaking will cause the emotion to flow out. Her lips quiver, cyanotic with the cold.

I reach out—with some hesitancy—and put my hand on her shoulder. I whisper: "Do you remember him?"

She shakes her head, clears her throat. When she speaks, her voice is thick: "I lost my memory card. I only found a replacement for it a few months ago. All I have now are snatches of images of him: standing in the kitchen, bamboo steamer in his hand or next to me in bed, asleep. I have this one memory of him, casually walking around the lounge room whistling this silly tune, while I lie on the sofa reading. Suddenly he pretends to trip over and he falls on me, making me lose the page I am on, kissing me all over my face. I remember him doing that a few times, actually."

We both smile at that.

But hers disappears quickly. "But I don't—" A tear escapes, finally, rolling down her cheek. She wipes it away angrily. "I don't even remember his fucking name."

She covers her face.

I leave my hand on her back while she sobs quietly. Overhead, stars shine bright in a clear night sky, the mist above us gone. I imagine I hear the Milky Way as it flows, and watch the Jade String inch across the sky while this girl weeps tears for a man she can't remember. There's a tightness in my chest, and I scowl at myself. I'm too old for such sentimentality.

After a time, she stops sobbing and then, after a few minutes, says with a thick voice: "Is this all there is, Omissioner?"

I pause. "Yes. This is all. Eternity is one gigantic corpse. We take our turns weeping and grieving, while great men do great things."

She lets that ride for a few seconds and then laughs, with humour and bitterness. "Wow. Thanks for cheering me up."

I rub her back and smile back at her. "There's only one medicine I can recommend." I pull a fresh bottle from my satchel. She looks up at me, eyes red, and I hold the bottle out to her, my eyebrows raised in a question mark.

"Ha," she says, pushing her hair back from her red eyes. "I think for once you've got the occasion right. Pour me some damn wine."

So we drink it all and tell each other stories as the bitter winds of the night blow down from Wu Mountain. We huddle close, letting wine and company and nostalgia warm us. She tells me splinters of what she can remember of her old life, and I tell her the parts of mine that hurt a little, but not too much, in the telling.

Too soon the mists come heavy again and the wine is gone and all we can do is walk back to the camp, and sing. It is a patriotic tune, I think, and I get more excited than an old man should and fall and hit my head. Xiaofan puts my arm over her shoulder and helps me back, while I mumble and slur and try to tell her the time I defeated the jade dragon with my wits.

She laughs. "If you told me your enemy was a jade bottle of wine I might believe you."

The next day, after my hangover abates enough, I make my agreement with Xiaofan. I make a promise to her, and it is no lie.

In the weeks that follow I teach her and the others how to use the equipment in the shelter, how to record memories and how to access them. Xiaofan enters all her memories of her husband, while she still can. The cook's boy sits on my knee while I show him how to use the programs on the screen that will, in turn, teach him to read and write. I explain to all the history of the artefacts and show the cook which wines he may use for cooking, making sure he writes it all down on his memory card.

After one month, my end of the deal is done, and I ask Xiaofan to fulfil hers.

She does. She helps me escape.

Just before dusk, during her watch, she hugs me fiercely. "Stay safe, old turtle," she says. Then she lets me leave.

The boat starts when I press the ignition button, sputtering itself into existence. I had one, brief chance to test the engine two weeks earlier. It started straight away then, as well. I smile, despite myself.

Then the engine stops, and so does my smile. I press the button again, jabbing it until my finger hurts. Nothing happens. I check the power pack: it is dead. The solar collectors must no longer function. This boat, like this world, is an illusion.

I sit in the gunwale of the boat, feet sodden, my fight as dead as the battery. The wind picks up my old white hair, holding it vertical in the breeze, like the crest of a wild crane. My hands rest on my thighs, palms open, as though in supplication.

My wife and my two sons, they are this ache in my chest. My too young wife with her crooked smile, touching my shoulder as I sit writing my poems, and my too energetic sons, waiting to throw the ball with me. They are this numbness where my soul should be. I weep the bitter tears of defeat and pray this plague of forgetting blesses me again and again, removes them from my mind. That my mind fades as this day closes: in a purple dusk, beautiful in its remnants, then gone forever.

My wife and sons are lost. An old turtle like me can't make a journey of five thousand *Li*, even if I could get this boat working. A hundred more rivers like this and a thousand more paths besides, they are too far, for this old man. My heart, I think, has always known it. My choices now are death, or to endure.

It's a shame I'm too stubborn and selfish for death.

The clouds run close to the ground now, dark on a darkling earth. I sit here, unable to feel my feet, and watch the memory of the world pass away. I smile and think: at least, at the end, there will be wine.

AFTERWORD

They say: write what you know; write what you care about; write the stories you want to read. The problem is that these can be three very different things.

A lot of the stories in *Neon Leviathan* are dark. You may have noticed. Not always what I want to read, but sometimes what I *need* to. Why this darkness? Well, I'm not much one for self-revelation, and the preceding stories should all be read as things in themselves. Suffice to say I was an aid worker for over a decade, and inevitably came into contact with pervasive corruption, and with the worst of human suffering. It is a profession with high rates of PTSD. Noir as a sensibility is one to which a former aid worker might understandably be attracted.

But I'm not interested in writing only from the dark heart of modernity. It can't rain all the time. The pain has to be leavened with humour; the social realism with the wild and hallucinogenic. Philip K Dick was a formative influence on me: he blew my mind when I was twelve. He wrote about the surreal and paranoid world just under the surface of the quotidian. That, for me, is good science fiction: speculations so strange yet grounded into the everyday that they make you to think twice about the nature of reality.

Then there is East and Southeast Asia. East Asia has, obviously, been central to such seminal science fiction noir texts as *Neuromancer*, *Blade Runner*, and *Ghost in the Shell*, fusing their near-future visions with the techno, teaming, sometimes squalid city-life of places like Hong Kong and Tokyo. Those aesthetics have certainly made their mark on my writing. Although Southeast Asia is a region where I've spent most of my adult life—whether through work or study—it is also a place I can only write about as an outsider. This is fine. Noir and cyberpunk have always been the stories of the outsiders. Nothing wrong with that sensibility.

Having said that, after three years living in the Old Quarter in Hanoi, I am in a position to make the following observations. Hanoi is a vibrant, frenetic, unapologetic city; a city always on the move, yet anchored in its rich culture. A thousand years old, yet rapidly changing as the future arrives; at the feet of its gleaming skyscrapers wait the street urchins in conical bamboo hats, selling fruit from the backs of their bicycles. A city with an underbelly, with those of a mind to look: the dive bars, the labyrinthine back alleys; the blinking neon signs of the karaoke joint-cum-brothels; the Buddhist temples sprinkled in among a raucous and fevered nightlife. Hanoi is a noir metropolis with a ringside seat to the coming Chinese century. I would certainly cite that city as an influence.

And finally, I do like a good fight scene. You may have noticed that, as well.

So the stories came from many places: from need, from want, from fear and from my failures, and from lived experience. I used it all and I gave it all.

ACKNOWLEDGEMENTS

Adrian, for taking a chance on an unknown author. Kaaron, for a true writing friendship built over working-class wine. Louise, Mongolian comrade, who reads everything. Her, and all the numerous readers I've had over the years, who have given their time to assist me in becoming less bloody terrible.

Most of all my partner, Sarah, whose support of my financially questionable decision to become a writer has been unwavering and fundamental. Thanks babe. My sons: Willem, mischievous prince and double croissant; Robert, my companion and best friend every day on the streets of Hanoi. You three: sun, stars, sky.

ABOUT THE AUTHOR

T. R. Napper is a multi-award-winning author, including the *Aurealis* for best short story. His work has appeared in annual *Year's Best* Anthologies, and he has been published in respected genre magazines in the US, the UK, Israel, Austria, Australia, Singapore, and Vietnam.

Before turning to writing, T. R. Napper was a diplomat and aid worker, having lived throughout Southeast Asia for over a decade delivering humanitarian programs. During this period, he received a commendation from the Government of Laos for his work with the poor. Napper is also a scholar of East and Southeast Asian literature; he received a creative writing doctorate for his thesis: *The Dark Century: 1946 – 2046. Noir, Cyberpunk, and Asian Modernity*.

He does not own a cat.

Lightning Source UK Ltd.
Milton Keynes UK
UKHW010634170821
388998UK00002B/491